PENGUIN FOLKLORE LIBRARY

A THORN IN THE KING'S FOOT

Advisory editor: Neil Philip

Duncan and Linda Williamson are both of Scottish and Norwegian descent, but their backgrounds have little else in common. Linda is a native of an American Midwestern capital, Madison, while Duncan is a member of the Scottish travelling people originally from Argyllshire.

They share a mutual regard for music as the primary art: studying classical keyboard performance led to a first degree at the University of Wisconsin for Linda, while fifty years of playing the Jew's harp, mouth organ and tin whistle around campfires has given Duncan a sound base for mastery of his people's oral traditions.

The couple's main interest is education, particularly how the inherent values of oral literature should be communicated for the benefit of humanity. Linda has a doctorate in Scottish Studies from Edinburgh University, while Duncan is a professional storyteller on the Scottish Arts Council's Writers in Schools scheme. Their first publication was *Fireside Tales of the Traveller Children* (1983), transcribed by Linda from Duncan's oral narration. Another in a series of 'traveller tales' on individual themes will be *Tell Me a Story for Christmas*, a collection to follow *The Broonie, Silkies and Fairies* (1985). Other lore and stories have appeared in *Tocher 33* (1980), *Scotsgate* (1981) and *Scottish Short Stories* (1984).

DUNCAN AND LINDA WILLIAMSON

A THORN IN THE KING'S FOOT

FOLKTALES OF THE SCOTTISH TRAVELLING PEOPLE

PENGUIN BOOKS

Penguin Books Ltd, Harmondsworth, Middlesex, England
Viking Penguin Inc., 40 West 23rd Street, New York, New York 10010, U.S.A.
Penguin Books Australia Ltd, Ringwood, Victoria, Australia
Penguin Books Canada Ltd, 2801 John Street, Markham, Ontario, Canada L3R 1B4
Penguin Books (N.Z.) Ltd, 182–190 Wairau Road, Auckland 10, New Zealand

First published 1987

Made and printed in Great Britain by
Richard Clay Ltd, Bungay, Suffolk
Filmset in Monophoto Baskerville

To Ben in England and Donald in America

CONTENTS

CONTENTS

PREFACE

For more than three decades the Travelling People of Scotland, an indigenous group of nomads, have been acclaimed for the proficiency of their traditional singers and storytellers.* Activities of singing and storytelling were always of supreme importance to the 'travellers', and thus one would expect to find among them individuals who excel in the art of traditional narration. Such a man is Duncan Williamson, and *A Thorn in the King's Foot* is a collection of folktales from his rich oral tradition.

Duncan has recorded literally hundreds of traditional stories during the past ten years; his repertoire of narratives is endless! Choosing a viable set for the confines of one book was not easy. For the Penguin Folklore Library we decided that one criterion of inclusion should be a story's Scottish ethos, that folk outwith Scotland should sense the spirit of this particular nation in its content. Then, in line with the aim to represent good traveller storytelling, we thought primary attention should be given those tales which the travellers themselves consider *good stories*, or in cant, *barrie mooskins*.

What makes a story good to a traveller is its power to move him, its magical force. And the technical difficulties of communicating an oral story in print boil down to re-creating its aural power on the page. The oral folktale is like the folksong: both share a fundamental appeal to the ear; both owe their life to the human organization of sounds. In print, a story from oral tradition must stimulate the ear through the eye, and touch the other senses – in the reader's imagination – if it is

* Before Hamish Henderson started fieldwork among the group in the mid-1950s, the qualitied culture of the Scottish travelling people was not duly acknowledged.

to succeed with its *proper* force. This is the aim of my dialectal text.

The only way to communicate a story from oral tradition is to suggest convincingly its linguistic substance, 'the gamut of emotions and attitudes of the people can . . . only be expressed with accuracy and poignancy through the speech of the people' (*The Scottish Arts Council*, 1984:8). Duncan Williamson's traveller speech is a mixture of both English and Scots. Highland English was the language he spoke in his early years, 1930 to 1943, at home in Argyllshire; Scots was acquired later when he began travelling and camping with his relatives in the Lowlands, the north-east and the south of Scotland. English predominates in the majority of narrations chosen for this collection, but none is exclusively English or Scots. Rather, the dialect is fluid – with both English and Scots pronunciations of words occurring within single thoughts. No absolute rule can be laid down, when a Scots or English form in the Scottish–English dialect will occur; but it can be asserted with confidence that variations in sounds of the same word within thoughts appeal more to the narrator than do exact phonetic repetitions. Rich aural variation is the hallmark of the 'living' tale, the breath of oral tradition.

Upholding the narrator's integrity, I have followed his lead and used different spellings of repeated words in a sentence when called for. These variant spellings I have generally limited to two, one English and one Scots. Frequently internal vowels and final consonants of repeated words oscillate: so that such double spellings as 'was' and 'wis', or 'looked' and 'luikit', or 'I' and 'A' are juxtaposed. Apart from the traveller cant, my Scots spellings conform to entries in *The Concise Scots Dictionary*, and this reference can be consulted for pronunciations.

In oral narration exact repetitions of words and phrases from thought to thought are frequent. Their function is important, informing the narration and reinforcing the patterns of sound. But to the eye repetitiveness can be cumbersome, spoiling the flow of the thought; so I have generally limited the quantity of exact verbal recurrences within passages to two, at the most three.

Wholly phonetic transcriptions of folktales, such as those published by university presses, are not the most effective way of communicating narratives. Ideas and structural rhythms suffer because of the reader's lack of familiarity with innovative spellings. In preparing these stories for reading I have held in check the tendency to mimic every verbal utterance. For example, many of the words beginning with 'th' –

'their', 'that', 'the' – were pronounced with an initial 'd'. But I have only adhered to the narrator's most prominent uses of 'de' and 'dher' (in the construction 'dher wur'). And students of Scots may note here that Duncan Williamson's dialect, as in the case of most travellers, belongs to no one single district; it is an amalgam of features from different Scots-speaking areas. This is not surprising when one considers his active travelling life, the lengthy period from 1943 to 1980 when he was nomadic, across the breadth of Scotland.

Behind my presentation of the text lie three concepts of the language of the traditional story. Firstly, the story of traveller tradition is originally oral. As a group, the travellers of Scotland are non-literate. Some can read and write, but this does not colour their attitude towards oral tradition – they reckon the best stories are not transmitted in print, but by the human voice. This same attitude I have adopted in writing down their tales: conventions are dispensed with if they are not in accord with a concept of the story as oral. For example, I do not use the apostrophe of omission (an eighteenth-century literary device) for truncated final consonants – 't' and 'f' ending such words as 'of', 'most' and 'kept'; 'o', 'mos' and 'kep' are orally correct.

Secondly, two distinct languages have a bearing on these traveller narrations. The bilingual aspect of the text will prove no problem for those who can suspend their preoccupation with the English language, what readers see in everyday print. Modern Scots, the language of Lowland Scotland since 1700, has its own phonetic system and rules for representation in writing. These are discussed in William Grant's *Manual of Modern Scots*. For example, the 'in' endings of Scots gerunds and participles (these sometimes ending in the older 'an(d)') should not be confused with the 'ing' terminating the same parts of speech in English.

Finally, traveller folktales are not the refined creations of a literate society, but are the religious and educational institutions of a race of primitive people who still speak a primordial language. (As a traveller's wife I have been privileged to hear this.) It would be helpful to approach these stories in the spirit of reading poetry or song – allowing for a measure of your own insight and letting the unwritten messages between lines speak foremost. The text abounds in traveller idioms and phrases with special meanings, which would lose their magic in translation. Footnotes are provided where difficulties in comprehension are expected. For example, in the few richer colloquial narrations, phrases with ellipses of verbs and prepositions are noted with English equivalents. More typical definitions of Scots words and usages are listed in the Glossary, added for the benefit of readers less familiar with seeing Scots in print.

In my Notes on Narrations are further explanations of editorial practices, the delicate steps taken from taped recordings to print. All the narratives were first recorded from Duncan Williamson for the Sound Archives of the School of Scottish Studies, Edinburgh University; their tape registration numbers appear alongside titles in the Notes. The main information supplied there, however, relates to the story as Duncan knows it, including its differences in other recorded performances by him and other versions of the same story he has heard. In a few cases I have detailed aspects of the storyteller's art, how the narrator used his voice in performing – what cannot be captured fully in a text.

In the Introduction Hamish Henderson has discussed the wider Scottish and, in some cases, world contexts of the stories. Our collection of traditional tales for Penguin readers will be best appreciated in the light of earlier and more recent publications of Scottish folktales, summarized by Dr Henderson.

I should like to thank the senior technician at the School of Scottish Studies, Fred Kent, for his time, skill and generosity with recording equipment – ensuring the accuracy of my transcriptions. To the Scottish Arts Council Duncan and I are grateful for a joint Writer's Bursary in 1986, enabling us to complete the manuscript. And now we are happy to hand over this book to an international audience of folktale lovers; it is our double wish that you all feel the great presence of wonder in *A Thorn in the King's Foot*!

Linda Williamson, B.MUS., M.MUS., PH.D.
Lizziewells, Collessie, Fife
November 1986

INTRODUCTION

In the mid nineteenth century the great Highland collector John Francis Campbell of Islay uncovered an enormous treasure of folk narrative in Gaelic-speaking Scotland, and fruitful collecting has continued there right up to our own day, particularly in the Outer Hebrides. In sharp contrast, the number of versions of folktales in Lowland Scots which had been put on record by the halfway mark of this century was surprisingly small, considering the bounding exuberance of the Scots ballad tradition. Campbell himself thought that storytelling among the Lowland country folk had largely died out by his day, and he stated, in his introduction to *Popular Tales of the West Highlands* (Vol. 1, 1860, p. xxxix) that he had searched for tales among 'the peasantry of the low country', but with no success to speak of.

Campbell knew of the existence of a manuscript collection of *Ancient Scottish Tales* written down in 1829 by the maverick Peterhead printer-antiquary Peter Buchan, but after examining these he gave it as his opinion that this was probably a collection of Gaelic folktales which had somehow found their way into the 'borderland' milieu of the north-east Lowlands.

Campbell's opinion is by no means to be set aside without careful consideration, but in the light of subsequent collecting it can be shown that he was definitely on the wrong track.

One reason for this misapprehension is probably to be located in the language in which Buchan's tales are couched. Although he claimed that the stories were 'from the recitation of the Aged Sybils in the North Countrie', one glance at the text shows that the originals have been lifted as with a crane out of the folk speech in which they must originally have been told, and revamped in a florid stilted English which is all too clearly Buchan's own. Furthermore, in the matter of nomenclature he has allowed his fertile imagination to run riot. Here is an example:

About the year 800, there lived a rich nobleman in a sequestered place of Scotland, where he wished to conceal his name, birth, and parentage, as he had fled from the hands of justice to save his life for an action he had been guilty of committing in his early years. It was supposed, and not without good show of reason, that his name was Malcolm, brother to Fingal, King of Morven. Be this as it may, it so happened that he had chosen a pious and godly woman for his consort; who, on giving birth to a daughter, soon after departed this life.

This quotation is the opening of a story called 'The Cruel Stepmother', and will be found on page 25 of the first and only published edition of Buchan's *Ancient Scottish Tales*, which was brought out by the Buchan Field Club in 1908, edited by J. A. Fairley. The story is a version of an international tale, 'The Maiden without Hands', which is listed and given a number in a voluminous compendium called *The Types of the Folktale*. This latter is an exceedingly useful work begun by the Finnish scholar Antti Aarne and subsequently greatly enlarged by Stith Thompson of Indiana University. Just as the numbers given to classical ballads by Professor F. J. Child in the last century, in his great thesaurus *English and Scottish Popular Ballads*, are a handy ready reckoner when discussing versions of these (e.g., 'Lord Randal' is no. 12), so the international folktales which have surmounted the barriers of language, geography and culture can usefully be referred to by their numbers in the Aarne–Thompson index: Buchan's tale 'The Cruel Stepmother' is AT 706.

This does not mean, of course, that the motifs in the long involved 'fairy tales' (often known by their German name of *Märchen*) will necessarily be found together in all versions of a particular story. Sometimes they are so different in sequence and coloration that it is exceedingly hard to pin down the story concerned and give it an AT number. Thus the penultimate sentence of Buchan's 'The Cruel Stepmother' ('Beatrix then relieved her father from the pain which he suffered in his foot by a thorn which stuck in it, and baffled all the medical skill of that part of the country' (*Ancient Scottish Tales*, p. 28)) provides a clue to the possibility that we are dealing here with a far-out relative of the title story of this book. However, the rejected child in Duncan Williamson's story is a hunchback boy, and not a girl, and the motif of mutilation – the daughter's hands being cut off – which usually identifies this particular story-type is completely absent.

We can state with assurance, therefore, that Buchan's fourteen tales – although lamentably wooden Anglicized 'recensions' or re-tellings, which reproduce neither the language nor the flavour of the originals – were indeed collected from Aberdeenshire country folk; and, with equal assurance, that at least ten of them had travelled to the north-east of Scotland from much further afield, and had already crossed several language barriers before being transmogrified – or crucified – linguistically by the egregious Peter Buchan. They are, in fact, easily identifiable international tales, viz. AT 300 ('The Dragon Slayer'); 303 ('The Twins or Blood Brothers'); 313 ('The Girl as Helper in the Hero's Flight'); 325 ('The Magician and his Pupil'); 326 ('The Youth who Wanted to Learn What Fear is'); 425 ('The Search for the Lost Husband'); 510 ('Cinderella'/'Cap o' Rushes'); 851 ('The Princess who Cannot Solve the Riddle'); 955 ('The Robber Bridegroom'); and, of course, 706, which we have already mentioned. One of these (303) we shall encounter again in the present volume in the guise of 'Friday and Saturday'.

It is only fair to stress, therefore, for the reasons set out above, that Peter Buchan, most denigrated and slighted of all Scots folk-collectors, deserves all due credit and gratitude for putting on record the first collection we have – and the only one till this century – of tales circulating in the Scots-speaking areas of the north-east.

When Robert Chambers brought out a second revised edition of his *Popular Rhymes of Scotland* in 1841 he introduced a new section of Fireside Nursery Stories; one of these was 'The Red Etin', a 'Scoticization' of the first tale in Buchan's collection. Chambers had been lent the manuscript of the *Tales* – almost certainly by Charles Kirkpatrick Sharpe, to whom Buchan had entrusted it – and he had understandably wished to restore something of what he presumed must have been the original language. (The same sort of service, with the same intention, has recently been performed for Buchan's *Tales* by David Purves in the pages of the Scots language magazine *Lallans*.) It is a genuine pleasure, therefore, to turn to Duncan Williamson's 'Friday and Saturday', a really splendid version of the same tale-type told in the most delectable racy Scots, which leaves both Peter Buchan and Robert Chambers far behind. Compare the concluding paragraphs of Duncan's 'wey o' t' with the following passage from Peter Buchan's 'Red Etin':

The Etin's power now being gone, an axe was taken up by the young man, with which he cut off the three heads of the monstrous Etin. His next work was to discover the king of Scotland's daughter, and to set her at liberty. The old woman showed him the place where she lay concealed. There were imprisoned along with her a great many beautiful ladies; all of whom he restored to their weeping parents, by whom he was well rewarded, and married by the king to one of the ladies who had been released from a long and dreary confinement. He also restored his brother and the former young man to life and their former shape, and married them to two of the liberated ladies; when they all lived happy, in peace and plenty. This happened through the instrumentality of a persevering and fortunate young man.

It may well be asked at this point: what happened then in the fairly recent past to change the Lowland folktale picture so dramatically? Why, in other words, have we now got such a cornucopia of marvellously told tales to offer the public? The catalyst was undoubtedly the discovery by the School of Scottish Studies of the colossal wealth of folk tradition of every conceivable kind which had remained hidden in the tents – and city ghettos – of the travelling people (or tinkers: a term they very understandably don't like because it has been used by stupid people so often as a cuss-word).*

I hope I will be forgiven if I introduce a personal note at this point. It was when I was on a ballad-hunt in the north-east as a collector for the School of Scottish Studies that I gained entrée to the world of traveller folktales. The fact that Aberdeenshire is the uncontested heartland of the Scots ballad tradition led me, in the early fifties, to concentrate my researches there, and good luck brought me – after a useful hint from a traveller salesman in Fyvie – to the city of Aberdeen itself, where in a wee house (now demolished) in Causewayend I located the late Jeannie Robertson, by general consent one of Scotland's and the world's greatest ballad singers. At first I concentrated on her rich store of song, but in the summer of 1954 – remembering Peter Buchan's *Ancient Scottish Tales*, which I had come across and annotated in the library of the Irish Folklore Commission in Dublin – it occurred to me to ask her for stories. In reply, she started to tell me her version of 'The

---

* 'Traveller' is the term members of the group use to identify themselves as distinct from outsiders. For literary reasons I prefer 'tinkler-gypsy', but this is not to say that the Scottish travellers and Romany gypsies should be understood as one and the same ethnic group – quite the contrary.

Dragon Slayer' (AT 300), and I realized that I was standing at the edge of a newly opened subterranean treasure house.

Within a few days I had recorded a number of stories from Jeannie – including a highly entertaining version of the *Schwank* (humorous tale) 'Silly Jack and the Factor' (AT 1600, 'The Fool as Murderer'), which features on one of the School's first LPs of folktales, folksongs and instrumental music, issued in 1960, and now sadly unavailable. Furthermore, as a bonus, I began to record stories from traveller visitors to Jeannie's house (which was a veritable céilidh-house* for the Gallowgate area); these included 'The King of England', another fine version of AT 303 told by Andrew Stewart, and later included in Richard M. Dorson's *Folktales Told around the World*, University of Chicago Press, 1975; and the now famous version of AT 313, 'The Green Man of Knowledge', which later was to supply the title for Alan Bruford's excellent short selection of tales from Scots oral tradition, published by Aberdeen University Press in 1982. (This includes stories from the Northern Isles, Orkney and Shetland, where the non-traveller population has retained a liking for this art form.)

In 1955 the Stewarts of Blair were discovered by Maurice Fleming, and recordings in the berryfields, and in their Rattray home Berrybank, added a rich haul to the already copious store of tinkler-gypsy folktales. Bella Higgins turned out to be a champion storyteller, her 'star turn' being 'The Humph at the Fuit o' the Glen and the Humph at the Heid o' the Glen' (AT 503, 'The Gifts of the Little People'); her younger brother Andrew – nicknamed Andra Hoochten, because of his predilection for diddling songs – supplied another story for the School's first LP, mentioned above. This was the comic changeling story 'Johnnie in the Cradle'.

By the summer of 1956, the sheer bulk of outstanding new material which was flowing into the School's archives had begun to outstrip all attempts to list and classify, let alone transcribe it; so much so that Calum Maclean asserted that same year that there was a good case for the School's research workers dropping everything else, and devoting themselves exclusively to the travellers. (By that time the Gaelic-speaking Sutherland Stewarts – a group of families whose members were still telling many of the stories (including Ossian hero tales)

---

* céilidh-house: hospitable household where topical discussions, storytelling, singing and reciting poetry took place.

collected by Campbell a hundred years earlier, plus many which he did not collect – had also been discovered, and it was plain that work among them could continue for years.) And yet the man who was in many ways to turn out possibly the most extraordinary tradition-bearer of the whole traveller tribe had not at that time emerged above the horizon: this was the present storyteller Duncan Williamson, who in 1956 was twenty-eight years of age, and therefore a youngster compared to many of the other informants.

When I say 'emerged above the horizon', I do not mean, of course, that he was not already regarded by his own people as a champion folk artist in the making, just as Jeannie Robertson had been by the Aberdeenshire travellers many years earlier. It was only that vast areas of the traveller sub-culture still lay under the waves, and that although significant catches had been netted there were broad stretches still unexplored at the end of the fifties. One of these was another 'borderland' – Argyll, heartland of the great Clan Campbell, and of their hereditary enemies the MacLeans. This Highland county, lying close on the east to the culture and language of the Central Lowlands, was an area where the travelling people had in the main lost their ancestral Gaelic. (In this they resembled the tinkler-gypsies in the Gaeltachts of the west of Ireland.) In consequence, therefore, the heritage of tales which contemporary Argyll travellers share is drawn largely from the other side of the language divide; in bulk it makes a very different impression from the *Märchengut* of the Sutherland Stewarts mentioned above, and of the other Highland travelling clans north of the Great Glen. (It must be added, though, that the experiences of Campbell of Islay in Argyll indicate a very different state of affairs in the mid-nineteenth century, for he refers to travelling tinkers called MacDonald who told stories in Gaelic.)

The language in which Duncan Williamson tells the stories collected in this book is an idiosyncratic dialect of 'traveller Scots' which retains quite a number of archaisms – e.g. 'hit' for 'it', and 'haet' for 'anything' – now obsolete in modern Scots English. It is an exceedingly powerful, colourful and flexible vehicle for narrative, and Duncan manages it with glorious magniloquent skill and flair. Some turns of phrase, and other pieces of internal evidence, confirm that several of the stories have come over from Gaelic into Scots – in all likelihood, comparatively recently – on the lips of bilingual storytellers. Indeed, Duncan learned quite a number of his stories from a Gaelic-speaking stonemason and drystone-dyker, Neil MacCallum, to whom he was apprenticed at

Auchindrain in Argyll in his adolescence. Neil told them in English, with occasional bits of Gaelic interspersed.

A good example is 'The Tailor and the Skeleton' which has been collected several times from Gaelic-speaking tradition-bearers: a version was printed in MacDougall and Calder's *Folk Tales and Fairy Lore* (1910, p. 34), where the tailor's cool reiterated rebuff to the skeleton which is taking shape before him goes as follows in Gaelic: *'Chi mi sin, agus fuaighidh mi seo'* ('I see that, and I sew this').

In 1955 another version in Scots – 'The Wee Tailor' – was collected in the Blairgowrie house of Bella Higgins, sister of Alec Stewart (the husband in the folk partnership known as the Stewarts of Blair): this was printed in 1959 in the annual *Von Prinzen, Trollen und Herrn Fro: Märchen der europäischen Völker*. In that particular version the Gaelic source of the story is explicitly acknowledged:

So he's watchin', an' out comes this hand, an' it says in Gaelic: 'Dae ye see that hand without flesh and blood on it?' 'Ah,' says the tailor, 'I see ye, but I'll sew this at the meantime.'

To clinch the matter, Duncan has testified that he always heard his Argyll informants tell the story with this version of the Gaelic sentence quoted above: *'Chi mi sin, fuaighidh mi seo,' thuirt an tàilleir* (' "I see that and I sew this," said the tailor').

The central motif of the story – the gradual coming together of a complete skeleton (or animated corpse) – is a quite widely diffused one. It appears with tremendous dramatic force in 'The Strange Visitor', one of Robert Chambers' *Popular Rhymes of Scotland* (1841, p. 64):

A wife was sitting at her reel ae night:
And aye she sat, and aye she reeled, and aye she wished for company.
In came a pair o' braid braid soles, and sat down at the fireside;
And aye she sat and aye she reeled, and aye she wished for company . . .

'The Tailor and the Skeleton' is, of course, a 'short story', compared to the long convoluted *Märchen* or wonder-tales, of which there are some splendid examples in the present collection. Encountering them, we approach the central redoubt of the Scots travellers' narrative art. Reading 'The Giant with the Golden Hair of Knowledge' – a version of AT 461, which is no. 29, 'The Devil with the Three Golden Hairs', in the *Kinder und Hausmärchen* of the Brothers Grimm – or 'Friday and Saturday' (AT 303, 'The Twins or Blood-Brothers', Grimm, nos. 60 and 85) – it is easy to visualize the blazing bonfire of the Argyll travellers' camp with enthralled listeners, adults as well as children, hanging on every word and fresh invention of the storyteller, who naturally has a whole battery of different motifs and themes which he can mould into the structure of the stories if and when he might want to diversify it, or spin it out. When an innovative storyteller has his way with one of these wondrous *Märchen*, he may combine two or three tale-types in the one narrative, so that attaching an AT number to some of the stories is like trying to spell out a complex chemical formula, when fresh ingredients are being added much of the time.

One can readily imagine a tale of this sort being gradually and artfully elongated, so that it might spill over into two or even three nights' sessions. A sense of almost limitless leisure pervades such stories, and indeed is one of the characteristic features of the travelling people's way of life: working clock-dominated prescribed hours is anathema to them, and their culture tends to shrivel if they find themselves, through force of circumstances, benighted in the urban ant-heap.

Duncan does not consider himself in the category of 'creative' storyteller I have just defined, and accordingly it is possible, with fair confidence, to attach AT numbers to most of his tales in this collection. 'Mary Rashiecoats an the Wee Black Bull' is AT 511A ('The Little Red Ox': Grimm 130, 'One-Eye, Two-Eyes, and Three-Eyes'), which is related to the Cinderella cycle, and has been found widely distributed throughout Europe, and into Asia. 'The Happy Man's Shirt' – best known, perhaps, in the guise Hans Andersen gave it, although there the joy is in the footwear – readily reveals itself as AT 844, 'The Luck-Bringing Shirt'. It might be instructive, for once, to list the folk traditions in which this tale-type has been found: Estonian, Livonian, Lithuanian, Swedish, Irish, Spanish, Catalan, German, Italian, Slovenian, Serbo-Croatian, Roumanian, Turkish and 'English–American'. Luck and happiness are everywhere, it seems, *sans chemise*, if not *sans culotte*.

'Jack and the Horse's Skin' is a very pleasing and sardonic variant of AT 1535 ('The Rich and the Poor Peasant'). It belongs to a worldwide concatenation of trickster stories which represent the *alter ego* of 'poor Jack' or 'Silly Jack', the boy of intrinsic kindness, generosity and goodness, who shares his wee collop with an unknown stranger (likely to be helpful to him because of that), and of course *has* only a wee collop – with his mother's blessing – because he is leaving her more for herself. As Campbell of Islay wrote to his kinsman, the Marquess of Lorne, son of the Duke of Argyll, dedicating *Popular Tales of the West Highlands* to him in September 1860:

You will find the creed of the people, as shewn in their stories, to be, that wisdom and courage, though weak, may overcome strength, and ignorance, and pride: that the most despised is often the most worthy; that small beginnings lead to great results.

You will find perseverance, frugality, and filial piety rewarded; pride, greed, and laziness punished. You will find much which tells of barbarous times; I hope you will meet nothing that can hurt, or should offend.

If you follow any study, even that of a popular tale, far enough, it will lead you to a closed door, beyond which you cannot pass till you have searched and found the key, and every study will lead the wisest to a fast locked door at last; but knowledge lies beyond these doors, and one key may open the way to many a store which can be reached, and may be turned to evil or to good.

It has to be remarked, however, that the character of the omnipresent 'Jack' of the Jack tales tends to change subtly according to the culture in which he is temporarily operating; in American–English tradition, although a 'good guy', he tends more to the trickster side!

My own personal favourite among all the stories is 'Death in a Nut' (AT 330B, 'The Devil in the Knapsack, Bottle, Cask'), a story whose geographical spread resembles that of 'The Happy Man's Shirt'. Here the story has deeper moral and philosophical implications than is general in folktales; the story spells out poignantly the universal tragic truth, human and animal, that there *is* veritably no life without death. It might be as well to remember, at this point, that the mental background of the 'laity' in the countryside through which the Argyll travellers moved was deeply and sombrely Calvinistic; hence, doubtless, the several references to religion in stories like 'The Sheep of Thorns' and 'The Tailor and the Skeleton'.

With 'The Twelve White Swans' we are once again in the world of marvel, where such grey-as-dust considerations do not apply. This story – and I am giving these AT numbers in every case for the benefit of readers whose interest may be sparked off by one particular story, and who may wish to follow it up – is AT 451, 'The Maiden who Seeks her Brothers', which has been found in every corner of Europe from Finland to Turkey, and has relatives as far away as India and China. 'The Ugly Queen' (AT 302, 'The Ogre's [Devil's] Heart in an Egg') can boast a similarly vast world-wide diffusion, and has turned up in the New World in numerous French, Spanish and English versions, as well as in the Creole of the West Indies. In South Africa the white farmer and his wife told – and maybe sometimes still tell – their children the same basic folktales of the human race as their black neighbours; one can claim, therefore, that the science of folklore can, properly employed, serve as a powerful humane liberating discipline.

The remaining international tale to which we can attach an AT number is also the most easily identifiable: 'Jack and the Moneylender' is AT 592 'The Dance among Thorns', which is perhaps best known as no. 110 in Grimm ('The Jew in the Brambles'). Because of the tremendous popularity of the Grimms' tales, and the many translations and retellings they have spawned, this is one case where (just possibly) print has contributed to the sustaining of the oral tradition amongst members of a group which was non-literate until quite recent generations. (The travellers told stories to people who had access to books, and sometimes heard stories from them.)

It is sad to have to relate that this is one case where folklore has been unscrupulously manipulated for political purposes; the Nazis encouraged schoolteachers to use it as a text for anti-Semitic propaganda.

The travellers themselves have all too often been the target of hostile propaganda and discrimination, and a fear of persecution (or even genocide) is reflected in the amazing burker mythology which has grown up among them in the aftermath of the Burke and Hare period of murderous body-snatching in the early nineteenth century. (William Burke was hanged in Edinburgh in 1829 for selling murdered victims to Dr Knox's anatomy school.) The travellers, being defenceless nomads whose disappearance organized society would not worry about, felt themselves natural targets for the burkers, and gradually a whole phantasmagoric scenario took shape in their minds. Until quite recently travellers would steer clear of college buildings in Aberdeen and other Scottish cities. One Aberdeenshire tinkler-gypsy, well known at one time as an accordionist, said in 1954: 'I mind when ye couldna pass the Marischal College or the King's College for the students would fairly tak a haud o' ye wi' a cleik [a hooked piece of iron] by the leg. They took ye right inside. They wanted fresh bodies.'

According to the travellers the burkers were doctors; but long before Burke and Hare the travellers called medical students 'noddies' or 'shan dodders'. In the belief of some, the burkers' coach draped in black left the college at night, manned by burkers dressed in top hats and swallow-tail coats. The coach was thought to resemble a hearse, with a zinc floor to let the blood run out. The horses' hooves were believed to be muffled with rubber pads, and the chains similarly wound round with cloth to stop them from chinking. To complete this horrific picture, bloodhounds were supposed to lope silently along beside it.

There are literally hundreds of burker stories circulating among the travellers; these invariably make the victims quite close relatives or friends. Duncan's 'The Noddies' is one single example of an enormous distinctive communal folklore. The fear of genocide has, in fact, very comprehensible historical roots, for in the sixteenth and seventeenth centuries, under Scots law, it was a capital crime to *be* a tinkler-gypsy. The famous outlaw, James Macpherson (hero of the well-known folksong 'Macpherson's Rant') was hanged in 1700 under this statute.

The travellers, being very family-minded, do not empathize readily in the real world with tramps and other 'gangrels', who are natural loners. The stories about Bartimeus, a blind beggar who solves the problems of the individuals or families he falls in with, constitute an exception to this general rule. Since it can be shown that the culture of the Scottish travellers often reflects aboriginal Celtic folkways, the possibility exists that the travellers' Bartimeus is a far-out relative of the hereditary 'breeves' or law-givers among the Celts who travelled around dispensing justice, or resolving disputes. (These, of course, were high-caste members of the *aos dana*, or learned élite – like bards, harpers, doctors, and seannachies, these last being the hereditary genealogists and storytellers.)

The original Bartimeus, incidentally, was the blind beggar healed by Jesus at Jericho: see St Mark 10:46–52.

Another biblical motif, embedded among the Bartimeus anecdotes, will be spotted immediately by readers who are at all familiar with the Old Testament. This is 'The Judgement of Solomon' (I Kings 3:16–28); it too, like several other stories from the Bible, has an AT number (926).

Stories about 'wise fools' abound in every culture, but the Scots have the distinction of choosing for the name of their archetypal 'king's fool', that of George Buchanan (1506–82), one of the most distinguished scholars in their whole history, and (according to Dr Johnson) one of the best Latin poets of his age. Buchanan taught in Scotland, France and Portugal (where he fell foul of the Inquisition), and eventually became tutor to the boy king James VI at Stirling (1570–78). Far from being this king's 'fool', he was reputed to be a stern disciplinarian. On one occasion a lady of the court came on him while he was giving the young king a vigorous flogging, and tried to intervene. Buchanan finished the job, and then said to her: 'Madam, I have whipped his arse. You may kiss it now.'

It is a curious example of the 'doon-takin'' (or deflating) tendency among the Scots that this formidable poet-pedant should have had his name borrowed and given to a fool in folktales.

The extraordinary merman story 'La Mer la Moocht' is unique in the archive of the School of Scottish Studies. Although the language in which it is told shows that it has been thoroughly assimilated into Scots traveller tradition, the possibility cannot be excluded that its ultimate origin is somewhere in a printed text. The shifting nomenclature, and the fact that one of the storytellers from whom Duncan heard it thought that it came from Greece, might point in that direction. In any event it is quite out of the ordinary on a number of counts – not least in that the physical beauty of a king from the Other World is made attractive to mortals of both sexes.

The only fairy tale known to me which remotely resembles this one is Hans Andersen's 'The Little Mermaid', but the story-line of that is quite different.

The two ballads – narratives in song – fall into place among the prose narratives with perfect naturalness. Both are magical fairy ballads, the first ('Thomas the Rhymer') made famous internationally by Sir Walter Scott in his *Minstrelsy of the Scottish Border* (Vol. II, 1802), and the second ('Tam Lin') by Robert Burns, who contributed the longest (and, by general consent, the best) version – text, plus tune – to James Johnson's *The Scots Musical Museum* (Vol. V, 1796, no. 411).

Both these ballads are now very rare, and both (in Duncan's narrations) are wonderful examples of an 'internal' collaboration of recollection and re-forming in the mind and on the lips of the singer; together with an 'external' searching for the missing parts of the narrative he did not hear until later in life, in his mid-fifties, from older traveller relations. Duncan's balladry is re-creative folk art in a quite astonishing individual manifestation. We are privileged to be in on the same process that in earlier centuries must have produced many now standard versions of the great classical ballads. Anyone wanting to look up an earlier stage in the development of Duncan's 'Tam Lin' will find it in the Addenda section in Vol. IV of Professor Bertrand H. Bronson's *The Traditional Tunes of the Child Ballads* (p. 459).

'Thomas the Rhymer' (no. 37 in Professor F. J. Child's *English and Scottish Popular Ballads*) is generally believed to have some connection with the famous thirteenth-century prophet and seer Thomas of

Ercildoun – this place-name is an older form of the modern Earlston, in Berwickshire – whose prophecies (according to Robert Chambers writing in 1870) were still, in the early nineteenth century, preserved throughout Scotland on the lips of the common people. He was known as True Thomas, because the queen of Elfland was supposed to have given him a tongue that could never lie. It should be added that Thomas is by no means the only character in Scottish history who (according to tradition) disappeared into Elfland, either for seven years or for ever; as late as 1692 the Reverend Robert Kirk, author of *The Secret Commonwealth of Elves, Fauns and Fairies*, was believed to have been claimed by the subjects of his research, and immured for all time in the fairy mound.

The 'Huntly bank' of earlier versions is on the Borders, but Duncan's version places it in the town of Huntly in Aberdeenshire; and he sets Thomas's high legendary status as prophet and seer against a truly lowly beginning – as the grandson of the local clockmaker, and little better than a village idiot. So George Buchanan is not the only one!

Duncan's version of 'Tam Lin' (Child 39) exemplifies the reality of much ballad transmission. In a really thriving ballad community, such as that of the Scottish travellers, a singer will often hear different versions of the same ballad from quite a number of other singers, with sometimes striking variations in both text and tune; if he begins to sing one, his growing version will as likely as not be 'hit' by one or more invading versions (not necessarily the ones he will eventually prefer), and this process can continue virtually for his or her lifetime. However, in most cases (probably) the singer's version will gradually gel, until it becomes pretty fixed and stable, if not immutable; finally, he will be prepared to defend it, and claim hotly that it is the 'right' traditional version. So it is, of course, for him.

The ultimate source of this particular prodigy of recreation was Duncan's grandmother Bet McColl, 'a real warrior o' a woman', but his sister-in-law Betsy was the immediate provider; the latter had learned it in childhood from Old Bet. As versions of the ballad have been recorded from traveller Johnstones, also west coast tinkler-gypsies – one of these can be heard on the Scottish Tradition LP *The Muckle Sangs* (Tangent TNGM 119/D) – one can safely assume that Duncan, in the course of his wanderings through Highland and Lowland Scotland, will have heard other versions. What is clear is that, knowing the story-line, and hearing different versions at various times, Duncan has effectively chosen the right lines and events for him out of what were merely fragmented narrations; and has now given us a quite distinctive west coast 'wey o't'.

Those familiar with Burns's version of 'Tam Lin' from *The Musical Museum* or anthologies may be puzzled to find that the hero (who has been saved from the toils of the Fairy Queen by the intrepid courage of the heroine) is called Lord William in Duncan's version. This is because the final verse is an importation from another ballad, 'The Douglas Tragedy' (Child 7), in which the names of hero and heroine are William and Margaret. Names in any case change in ballads with the protean ease of Tam Lin's transformations in the midst of the fairy throng.

Duncan Williamson was born in a tent on the shores of Loch Fyne, near the village of Furnace in Argyll, on 11 April 1928. He was one of a family of sixteen. His mother was Betsy Townsley; his father Jock Williamson, born in 1892, was a travelling basketmaker and tinsmith. Both Duncan's parents were illiterate, but his forebears on both sides were famed singers, pipers and storytellers, and had an enormous wealth of orally transmitted lore.

From the age of five until he was fourteen Duncan went to school in Furnace; then he started work as an apprentice to the stonemason and drystone-dyker Neil MacCallum (mentioned earlier), the source of many of his stories.

When he was fifteen Duncan decided – like Jack in the folktales – to 'push his fortune' out in the wide world; he left home with an older brother and travelled through Argyll, Perthshire, Angus and the Mearns; in subsequent years, with a cousin of his mother's, he roamed as far north as Inverness-shire, and as far south and east as Dumfriesshire and Fife. He worked here and there as a farm labourer and harvester; he also learned the trade of horse-dealing, and became an expert at it. However, in the summer months he would always return to his folk on Loch Fyneside.

Throughout his life he has been interested in stories and storytelling, and his peripatetic way of life ensured that he would pick up tales all over Scotland. He gradually came to realize that this meant more to him than anything else, and he became a conscious collector and champion of his people's oral culture. Although stories came first, he was soon adding ballads and songs galore to his capacious memory-holdall.

The first collector to tape-record Duncan was the left-wing poet Helen Fullerton, who in the fifties became interested in the campaign to secure a fairer deal for travellers as regards camp sites, and the other problems attendant on bourgeois society's often blinkered and bigoted attitudes towards the nomadic families. She got to know Duncan's mother and several of his brothers and sisters in 1958, when she was working in the cookhouse of a hydro-electric scheme in Argyll. At that time Betsy was living in a forester's hut in 'a beautiful piece of woodland at the back of Inveraray which was covered with bluebells in springtime'. The first Williamsons Helen recorded were Duncan's sisters Mary and Rachel; she also recorded Betsy 'cantering', i.e. singing pipes-imitation mouth music. Duncan himself she did not meet till the spring of 1967, when he came over from Fife on a visit to his mother. (Helen herself was by this time a university lecturer at Glasgow.) She recorded him speaking some of his own poems, which greatly impressed her, and various songs and ballads; furthermore, she got in touch with Geordie MacIntyre, the most active collector in the Glasgow area, and told him about Duncan. Geordie visited him in Inveraray in May 1967, and later went across to Fife to do further recording (near Star) in November of that year. Among other things he recorded five and a half verses of 'Lady Margaret', the ballad which was later to grow into the version of 'Tam Lin' in this volume. He also collected from Duncan a fragment of the classic ballad 'Hind Horn' (Child 17).

In 1966 the Traditional Music and Song Association of Scotland (TMSA), founded by Pete Shepheard, had organized the first Blairgowrie Folk Festival, a pioneering event which gave premier place to genuine traditional performers: revival singers came there as apprentices. These festivals gained strength rapidly, and each year the organizers invited ever more traditional artists like Alec, Belle, Sheila and Cathie Stewart, Jeannie Robertson, Lizzie Higgins, Jane Turriff and Stanley Robertson to perform for an international public of folk aficionados. All of these particular invited guests were travellers, and because of this – and because Blairgowrie is the centre of the soft-fruit growing industry which attracts many travellers in the summer months – members of the 'fraternity' started to attend the traditional festivals in increasing numbers. Among those turning up in 1968 was Duncan, and that is how he first became known to a wider folk public. Pete and the TMSA deserve great credit therefore, for drawing in to the Revival one of the most important of contemporary tradition-bearers.

Furthermore, thanks to him – and the TMSA – there are now dozens of young (and not so young) 'folk addicts' who earlier were unaware that there *were* any such things as Scots folktales (let alone storytellers to do them justice), but who can now tell the long wonder tales in a convincing imitation of the authentic traveller style (and, in some cases, go on to make their own stories, and develop their own personal storytelling style).

Duncan's first wife died in 1971; she had borne him seven children. In 1976 he married the American scholar Linda Headlee, the compiler and editor of the present collection. They have two children, Betsy and Thomas. For the first four years of their married life Duncan and Linda lived in a tent and shared the traditional traveller way of life. Later, as the children grew bigger, they moved into a cottage in Fife. Of recent years Duncan has carried his enthusiasm and his storytelling artistry into schools up and down the country, and most recently has been devoting himself with Linda to the preparation for publication of his staggeringly voluminous wealth of traditional lore.

There can be no question but that Duncan Williamson is one of the most enormously gifted folk artists now living. In a moving tribute to him (printed in *Tocher* 33) his friend Barbara McDermitt has this to say:

Duncan is a masterly teller of tales and ballad singer. I have heard him perform in public, captivating large audiences, and I have also heard him in the intimate setting of his candle-lit tent. It is the latter that is most memorable to me. With Betsy dozing on his lap and Linda lovingly looking after Thomas, both my ten-year-old daughter, Heather, and I have sat hours on end spellbound as Duncan has taken us into his special world of wonder and magic. Each tale is told dramatically and vividly with an intenseness and directness that draws you in and holds you riveted until the tale's end. Duncan's verbal facility is edged with a razor sharp timing, and his large powerful hands punctuate his stories with strength and subtlety. He knows how to build suspense, bring out humour and release emotions both tragic and joyful. One cannot listen placidly to Duncan's stories. This is also true of his ballads and songs. He treats them as dramatic stories set to music and sings them with true feeling.

Whether Duncan is telling a tale or sharing a ballad, he does so with such personal impact, you feel he is offering part of himself, an unforgettable gift, and as listener, you cannot help but be touched deeply by the experience.

I cannot better that description, which springs from a deep, intimate knowledge of Duncan, his personality and his art. It is cheerful news that a cassette, to be issued by Pete Shepheard's Springthyme Records, will give readers of this book an opportunity to listen at their leisure to recorded examples of Duncan's magical incantatory storytelling genius. In this traditional art, it *is* the spoken – and sung – word which ultimately 'bears the gree'.*

Hamish Henderson
School of Scottish Studies, University of Edinburgh
December 1986

* bears the gree: is victorious.

BARTIMEUS

Bartimeus was a beggar – this was well well back before the birth o Christ – an according tae the traivellers he was a wanderin beggar, but he wis a bright man an he settlit all these arguments, settled all these disputes. But he didna want tae be nothing else but this beggar, an whanever people were stuck fir something that they didna know they sent for Bartimeus and he came. The're many things that he done. An dae you know where he began? All this happened when he fell in the ditch: he began as 'the Samaritan'.

He lay there and everyone passed by, nobody wad lift him out o the ditch because he wis blind. And everyone passed him by, he asked fir help an nobody wad come. But naturally, 'Well,' he said, 'why dis people not help me? People hes too much troubles on their own mind tae help a puir beggar out o the ditch. Well,' he says, 'if I can crawl out an go on ma wey an teach these people better, then maybe the next poor creature that falls in the ditch'll get a help by my teachin,' because he experienced lyin i the ditch.

He was blind an a beggar an he traivellt on his wey. He travelled on in the village an everyone who really knew him gave him help an took him in. Because Bartimeus wis accepted wi everybody wherever he went. So one night Bartimeus came tae this village, he wis hungry as usual an he needed shelter fir the night.

Then he came to a house where the father and the sons wis argiean an fightin. The father had seven sons. Now these sons were woodcutters and so wis the father.

He knocked at the door an out comes the father: 'Oh, it's Bartimeus!

He's came tae pay hus a visit.' And oh, the blind beggar wis accepted.
'Come in, Bartimeus, come in!' an they tuik him in an gev him somethin
tae eat, somethin tae drink.

So he couldna see – just like Homer – Bartimeus says, 'What's the
problem?'

The auld father wis sittin an the seven sons wis sittin. 'Well,' he says,
'luik, this is wir problem, Bartimeus, we're all tigether here but we're
cuttin wood an selling firewood. But I've got seven sons, an these sons
thinks that we wur better separatin up an goin on their own way, doin
their own thing. I'm busy tryan tae tell them that by stayin together
they can make a better business off their life, by steyin together helpin
each other!'

So Bartimeus turned to the younger son, he said, 'Who's the youngest
o the family?' An this young one cam up, Robin wis his name. He said,
'Come up, son, an put yir hand in my hand. Dae you work with yir
brothers?'

'Yes,' he said, 'Bartimeus, A work wi ma brothers.'

'Do ye enjoy work wi yir brothers?'

'Oh,' he said, 'I enjoy work wi ma brothers, we do everything together.'

'Would you like to be separate fae yir brothers?'

'No,' he said, 'but my brothers wants tae be separated, they want to
go their own way.'

Bartimeus said, 'You go an sit down.' An he called the auldest
brother. Now he's told him the same thing . . .

But the oldes brother said, 'Look, ma faither's in this and ma brothers
is in this, I need to branch out an do my own thing.'

Bartimeus said, 'Go out to the stick shed an bring me seven sticks!'

Naturally, the son . . . everybody loved Bartimeus, so nobody wad
do anything against Bartimeus. They walked out to the stick shed and
he took seven pieces o sticks.

'Now,' he said, 'look, the're seven pieces o firewood: take one,' he
said to the oldest brother, 'an break it over yir knee!' An the boy took
one piece o firewood, he broke it over his knee – quite simple. 'Now,
give me the other six,' Bartimeus called for the other pieces o firewood.
'Now, bring me a piece o tow or a piece o string or a piece o leather,'
and Bartimeus tuik the six pieces o stick an bound them all tigether.
He said tae the auldest brother, 'Now, break them! Break the sticks
together!'

And the oldest brother tried to break them together – no way in the world could he break the sticks. 'Now,' Bartimeus said, 'there ye are: *separate youse can be broken, but tigether youse cuid never be.* So, that's the answer tae yir question: stey together and no one can break youse apart.'

An the aul father wis so happy. But Bartimeus moved on his way, he learned them their lesson.

Then he came tae this village. An if there were a court in the land, Bartimeus was always called. Court in these days wis very puir, very primitive, but if Bartimeus wis around, he wis always asked to sit in and listen tae the stories. So one day he wis on his way an he came tae this house, it was very late.

He knocked at the door an the auld wumman o the house cam out. 'Oh,' she says, 'Bartimeus,' the old woman luikit up, 'you're the very person . . . we have terrible troubles.'

'Well,' he says, 'dear, what's yir troubles?'

'Well,' she says, 'come in and see the master, an he'll tell ye.'

So Bartimeus wis led intae the hall, the great hall of the great house, and he says, 'What's the trouble?'

'Luik, we hev many many servants i this house,' says the auld man to Bartimeus, 'an we have some great silver's went a-missin. We can't accuse anybody for hit, we don't know who stole hit. Some o our precious silver's went a-missin – we don't want to blame anybody.'

'Well,' says Bartimeus, 'there's only one problem . . . you've no problem.'

And the master o the house says, 'Why, Bartimeus, hev I no problem?'

'Well,' he says, 'gather all yir servants together. Hit's no problem, gaither all yir servants tigether an put them round the table. I'll find the one who is responsible fir the theft of yir silver within minutes!'

And the master of the house said, 'Bartimeus, if you could do this, it would make me the happiest person i the world, because I trust all my servants. I know that 's someone, but A can't accuse anyone.'

So Bartimeus said, 'All right, bring me a kettle and a candle, bring me a kettle and a candle! Gather all yir servants roond.'

So all the servants came – the cook an the maid – an the master and the mistress. They all sat roun the table. Bartimeus got a kettle and a candle an he tuik the kettle.

'Now,' he says tae one o the servants, 'go out intae the shed an bring me a cockerel, bring me a cockerel!'

So they naturally went out an brought him a cockerel. In these days there were big kettles, great big kettles fir boilin the water. But dher wur no water in hit. So Bartimeus took the cockerel, he put hit in the kettle an he turned the kettle upside down. An then he went round the kettle with the candle, he made the bottom as black as he cuid get hit with the soot from the candle. 'Now,' he said, 'everyone sit around the table an turn out the light! I want everyone to put their finger on the kettle, and the minute the guilty person put his finger on the kettle the cockerel will crow! Inside the kettle the cockerel will crow!'

So they turned out the lights in the house. And everyone put their finger ond the kettle. (This is true!)

Then . . . Bartimeus said, 'The cock never crew.' Cock didn't crow, no way – inside the kettle. Bartimeus said, 'Turn on the light!' – no that he could see! 'Now,' he says to the master, 'check every finger, check every finger!' And the master checked, an every finger was black excepts one that was white. He says, '*That* is yir thief, because *he* wis afraid tae pit his finger ond the kettle – i case the cockerel wad crow!' There was one particular person who wis the man who tuik care o the gardens – his finger was white. Everyone had a black finger because they werena afraid, they had never stole nothing; but one particular person whose finger was white – he was the guilty person.

Well, he came to the town, ye see, an it wis the same thing happent. This two brothers who'd owed money tae each other, and the master who wis in the village couldna settle the argument: one said that he paid his brother his money an he swore that he paid hit, but they wouldna believe him, ye see. So the two brothers 's sittin.

He said, 'I never got any money. He owes me fifty gold pieces an he never paid it.'

An the brother says, 'I gev it tae him.' And every time he said 'gev it tae him', he put the stave in front o im, he said, 'I swear I gave him his money.' He had this auld cane stave an he pit it in front o him, said, 'I swear that I gave him his money!'

And Bartimeus is listenin to them. He heard the cane tappin between them.

Called for Bartimeus, the master says, 'We want tae settle this. I can't dae naethin aboot it: one says he got the mon, the other one says he never got it, what am A gaunna do aboot it? Beggarman, you tell them,' he said, 'you try an settle this!'

'O-ho,' he says, 'I'll settle hit!' He said, 'You say ye paid yir brother?'

'Yes,' he said, 'I paid ma brother,' an he placed the stave in front o his brother's two feet because they were sittin close tae each other.

'Oh, ye did? An,' he said, '*you* never received any money?'

'No,' he said, 'I never received ma money due me.'

'Well,' he said, 'you swear that ye gev it tae him?'

He said, 'I swear I gev it tae him.'

Bartimeus said, 'Well, give me the stick!' So he took the cane stave an he broke hit across his knee, there were fifty gold pieces inside! By placin the cane in front o his brother wi the money in it, he could swear that 'he gev it tae him' – because hit was in front o him all the time! And Bartimeus knew that hit was in the cane.

He came to the village, an everybody knew that Bartimeus was there; it wisna a very big village and they hed their disputes. But hit was this man that wis settlin the arguments, the master o the village, and the argument was that thes two women had one wean. And one woman said it was her wean an the ether woman said it was her wean. Noo the master o the village, who wis tryan em at the time, cuidna make up his mind who ownt the wean. So the best thing they cuid dae, they said, 'Ma lord, Bartimeus is in toon, he's in the village. We'll go get im. He's the only man that'll tell hus which is which!' Because he wis a great learnt man, although he cuid neither read nor write, he wis a beggar, he wis a tinker. They fetcht him in.

So he says tae them, 'What's yir trouble?'

'Well,' he says, 'this woman says that her baby,' (hit wis just a wee baby, newborn) 'at it's hers; an this woman says it *hers*. An I canna make up my mind which is which – which woman owns the baby.'

'Ha, well,' says Bartimeus, 'there's only one cure fir that; let *me* take over!'

'Oh,' he says, 'you take over, ye're welcome, I canna settle hit.'

'Well, I'll settle hit for ye,' he said, 'in minutes.' He says tae the woman, 'Is this your child?'

'Yes,' she said, 'it's my child, Beggarman, it's my child.'

He says tae the woman, 'Is it *your* child?'

She says, 'Yes, it's *my* child!'

'Well,' he said, 'both o youse lays claim tae the child.' He says tae the village master, 'Ye got a knife?'

'Yes,' he said; 'find the man a knife! What ye gaunnae do with the knife?'

He says, 'I'm gaunnae cut it through the middle an give em a half a piece.'

So this woman said, 'No, no, no! No, no! Hit's my baby, but before I see it halft,' she said, 'give it tae her, give it tae *her* – let her take hit! I don't want my baby halft through the middle.'

An Bartimeus turned roond, he said, 'Look, *that's* the mother o the baby, give hit tae *her*!'

That's the kind o stories the travelling folk tellt, but the're hundreds o them they told about Bartimeus, some longer than others. But he was supposed to be a beggar that wandered the country . . .

THE GIANT WITH THE GOLDEN HAIR OF KNOWLEDGE

Many years ago in a faraway country there wonst lived a king. The king had married late in life, he hed mairried a young princess from another country an they had a great weddin, it went on fir many days an everyone wis very happy fir the king. But time passed by, an the king be gettin up in years when he thought an wondered an worried why he wisnae gaunnae have any children. He talked it over wi his queen.

'Well,' she said. 'Ir Lordship, it would be lovely if we cuid hev a child.' So she prayed an she asked an she went tae all the wise women roond the country fir advice, how tae have a child. But a year passed by an sure enough she had a child, a little baby girl – an the king wis highly delightit when he found out. He preferred tae have a son but he wis quite pleased tae hev a little girl.

He called all the wise women that the queen hed visitit round his kingdom to come tae the christenin of his baby daughter, and they all came – twelve o them on the christenin day – they had a great banquet an a great feast.

Then lo an behold what the king had failed to remember – he hed left one old woman whom the queen hed visited out, completely forgot about er – she had never got an invitation tae the christenin of the king's baby daughter. An she was very angry. The king hed sent a coach tae pick up the aul women to bring em to the palace, but she hed tae walk. An the farther she walked the angrier she got, bi the time she reached the palace . . . she walked in, everybody wis busy feastin an dinin. An lo an behold the king an queen remembered they had forgotten about her.

But maids an footmen brought er forward, brought her in, sat er down at the table an they brought a common plate before her full of lovely things tae eat. The auld wumman luikit, and all the other auld women that the queen had visitit, the wise women o the country all were sittin wi their food on golden plates, an she had only a common plate.

She stood up an she says, 'This is disgrace, Ir Majesty – *why* these auld friends of mine have golden plates and I jist have a common plate like a puir peasant – when you know that I am the most powerful woman among them all!'

King said nothin. He knew he hed made a mistake. He said, 'You were all called here today tae give my baby daughter yir blessings, youse bein the wise women of wir country.'

An everyone stood up an they gev blessin in turn, till they cam tae her, her turn. When she says, 'No, I won't give her no blessin, but I will tell the truth: *when your daughter comes eighteen years of age, she will marry the son of a poor fisherman!* She will marry the son of a common fisherman who wis born the very same evening, the same evening ond the same night under the same star as yir daughter!' An like that she wis gone – she disappeared as quick as she cam.

Everybody wis upset. The king was worried, so was the queen. So after the banquet wis finished an all the auld women went ond their way, the king drew his queen beside him and he said, 'That auld woman is very powerful, she's the most powerful wisest woman in the whole kingdom an I wouldna like tae go against her in ony way. Prob'ly she's jist angry because we left her out of the invitation. But,' the king said tae his queen, 'just tae be on the safe side, we mus find this son of this fisherman an we must take im, destroy him so that he'll never mairry wir daughter – because I'm not havin my baby daughter marry the son of a poor fisherman!'

So he sent couriers all over the country searchin an seekin there an searchin here an seekin there, wherever they went askin about the new baby boy that wis born the same time as the princess, on the same night under the same star. But they were gone for months an days an they returned haggard and hungry, but they never found the baby that wis born on the same day as the princess.

The king said, 'It must be . . . the ol woman is too powerful tae tell any lies – we must find this boy! So, if youse can't do it, A'll jist hev to do it myself!'

So the next day the king went ond his way on horseback, dressed in common clothes. An he rode for days an he rode for weeks his ownself, till he came hungry an tired one day tae the seaside. Biside the seaside wis a little cottage, a few hens scratchin aboot, but there weren't a soul about. An he looked down the shoreside, there was a fisherman castin his net in the water an the king cuid see that he wis havin very little success. Every time he threw his net in, he pulled it in, it was empy. (Cause in these bygone days they jist cast their net off the shoreside to see if they could bring in ony fish.) So the king wis kin o curious whan he saw that the fisherman wis castin the net so many times an gettin nothin. He tied his horse tae a tree, he walkit doon.

He said tae the fisherman, 'You're not havin much luck!'

'No,' the fisherman said, 'I've had no luck for months. I've had no luck for months – five months ago was the last luck I had.'

King said, 'Five month ago? That seems a long time.'

'Well,' he said, 'the last luck I had was five month ago, an at this same spot: I cast ma net, it was full o beautiful fish. An you believe me,' he says tae the king – unknowin it was the king – 'it was a lucky night fir me in more ways an one – because whan I landed home wi as much fish as A cuid carry – sure enough, my wife had given birth tae a baby son!'

An then the king knew, this must be . . . the king calculated ind his own head – he knew that his own little daughter wis only five months old by this time. He says to the fisherman, 'I'm a traiveller on my way an I'm very hungry; if you could spare a drink or somethin tae eat I would pay you well for hit.'

An the fisherman said, 'Well, I have little tae spare, but, stranger, ye're welcome tae anything A hev.'

So the fisherman gaithert up his net, cairriet it ond his back an walkit up the shore ti they came tae the little cottage. The king tuik his horse, led it roond bi the house an tied it wonst more tae a tree, an he walked intae the little cottage. Puir humble little cottage, jist a fire, a table and a couple chairs, but sittin biside the fire wis the most beautiful young wumman this king hed ever seen, event as pretty as his own queen but she wis in rags. Ond her lap wis a bonnie wee baby boy an she wis sittin singin tae hit. She stood up, pit the baby intae an old-fashioned wooden cradle an hit just lay there kickin hits feets as happy as cuid be. An the king luikit doon, he saw the most beautiful boy he'd ever saw in his life an he thought ind his own mind, 'This must be hit.'

'We have little to spare, stranger,' says the fisherman's wife, 'but we'll give ye half o what we've got.' So she brought him some ale an some bread an cheese, she shared it with him.

An the king sat, he talked fir a long long while an he said, 'Ye hev a lovely baby boy there.'

'Yes,' she said, 'we hev a lovely baby boy.'

'How old is he?' said the king.

She says, 'Five month.'

'When was he born?' said the king.

'Five months ago,' she said.

'Was it night or daytime?' said the king.

She said, 'He wis born at night, twelve o'clock at night – midnight.'

'Oh,' said the king, 'I see. Well, you know, I'm a very rich man, and my wife and I has no children, I would love to have that baby boy. I would give ye anything ye want,' because the king had plenty money with him. His saddlebags wis full o money, he cairried em on his way. 'I wad give ye anything you want – I wad give ye as much gold that'll keep ye fir a lifetime, you can buy yirsel new nets, you can buy yirsel a boat – if ye'd only give me that baby boy. An I'll rear him up tae be my own son, when he's a grown man he'll come back an see ye.'

So the fisherman an his wife wis very sad about this; they loved their little baby son but they were so poor . . . They thought about all the wonderful things they cuid do wi all the money, and them bein young theirsels they knew they cuid mebbe get another baby, but they would never get a chance like this tae get as much money; so they finally consented tae give the king the baby. The king walkit out tae his horse tae his saddlebags, he tuik two bags of gold an he put them on the table in front o the fisherman an his wife – they had never seen as much money ind their life. The fisherman's wife wis kin o cryin an sad, but she rolled hit in a shawl, she put hit in the cradle an she gev the king the baby in the cradle.

He tuik the auld wooden cradle an the baby, placed hit ond his saddle an bade the fisherman and his wife 'goodbye', went ond his wey. 'Now,' he said tae himself, 'I have the baby an I'll make sure that this baby . . . who is born the same night wis foretold by one of my great women in my country, who is a great seer an the auldest even though the ugliest one, has always told truth . . .' He rode on fir many miles an he's wonderin how, the best way tae dispose of the baby, would he leave it in the forest tae be destroyed bi wild animals, or what would he – he cuidna hed the heart tae take a knife or a dagger an kill it . . . An as he's makin up his mind the best way tae dispose of the baby his horse wis danderin on, an sure enough he came tae a little lake surrounded by trees. The king luikit all around, there were not a soul to be seen – it wis jist a little lake in the hills an from the lake was a river floatin doon through the forest, an the king luikit all around – he never saw a single huntsman or a soul.

He says tae himself, 'This is the very place tae get rid o the baby.' So he tuik the cradle and the baby – as hard as he cuid swing – he flung hit right out inta the middle o the little lake. He felt it kind o sad, but he turned his back to the lake an he ond his horse, he made ond his wey. 'At last,' he said, 'he is gone, he'll drown in the lake.'

But as the king made his way home to his own palace, little did he know that these old people who made these cradles of solid oak made them real, hed made them good an they were water tight. An the cradle jist floatit like a little boat, round an round the lake it went an round and round the lake wi the current, an the baby's still lyin as dry as cuid be. The cradle floatit on its way down the river, over rocks, down through bankins, down little streams, down hit went, it traivellt fir over a mile and lo an behold – ind hit floatit tae a miller's dam!

This miller had a mill and he used the water comin from the river fir tae turn his mill wheel, an behind the wheel was a dam which collected the water tae give more force. An this particular day the miller wis oot with a long rake, a long pole, he's pullin leaves an bits o sticks that cam doon the river from his wheel, big wooden wheel that drove the mill. When the first thing he sees comin floatin down the dam was a cradle. The miller stood and he scratched his head, he knew hit wis a cradle an he seen there were something inside; an he rushed round, the cradle circled two or three times roond the dam an he took his long pole, he pulled the cradle out. He liftit hit up an he luikit in – there lo an behold wis the beautifulest little baby he'd ever saw in his life, a wee boy lyan as quiet an content as if hit wis jist in its mother's house.

The miller didnae know what tae do, he's thunderstruck, 'Where in the world . . .' The miller knew that this led to a lake in the hills, he knew the river because he hed followed it many times, 'but where in the world,' thought the miller, 'would this come from? Someone must have abandoned hit, mebbe a coach overturned an it fell in the river.' He rushed back tae his wife; they never hed any children o her own. They werenae very auld people, just middle-aged people.

An he said, 'Luik, wife, what I've got in the dam!'

'Oh dear,' said his wife, 'a baby! Where in the world did it come from?'

He said, 'It cam down the river from the lake an I caught hit in the dam.'

De wife liftit it oot an it start't tae giggle, she ran inta the hoose wi hit an placed de cradle bi the fire. 'Husband,' she says, 'ye better make yir way back up the river, because mebbe the're a coach overturned an the people are prob'ly hurt.'

The miller said, 'Yes, you take care o the baby an I'll du the rest.' So the miller walked up the river as far as he could, fir over nearly two miles till he cam tae the lake, an he searched roond the lake, he searched all round – he luiked fir wheel tracks – but lo an behold he never seen a soul. All he saw was the mark of a horse's feet on the ground round the lake: he saw where the horse cam in, he saw where the horse went out on the soft earth on the lake; he knew that someone then had threw the baby in. He walkit back tae his wife an he told her.

'Well,' she says, 'if someone abandoned hit, they must hae put hit ind the lake . . . it must be fir me and you, so we'll keep hit.' An keep it they did.

They kep the baby for eighteen long years, for eighteen long years they kep the baby. It grew up like their own son, a beautiful young man, handsome young man, tall an fair; an he wurkit from the day he was five years old wi his daddy in the mill, he never knew who he wis, he jist called them his 'Daddy' and his 'Mammy'.

But lo an behold after eighteen years had passed, one day the same king who wis gettin up in his years now, wis very old, hed went out with his huntsmen on a boar hunt. He'd huntit fir many many days an fir many many miles, an the king not bein as able tae keep up wi the rest o the huntsmen felt kin o tired, he stopped for a rest. An the huntsmen left him an he got lost, he got lost an never knew what way the huntsmen went.

So he traivellt on, he wandered on here and there tryan tae make his mind, find his huntsmen, when lo an behold the first thing he came tae wis a mill. He saw the mill wheel go round an he saw the miller's dam. 'At last,' he said, 'I've found some habitation, someone must know here, there must be someone lives here.' So he rode his horse up to the front o the mill, an the miller as usual was busy workin i front o the mill wheel, cleanin the leaves an sticks away from the dam to let the wheel turn round. The king slowly got off his horse, an the miller looked round. But now the king was dressed in his finery – the miller knew who it was!

The miller went down on his knees an he said, 'Ir Majesty, what can I do for ye?'

The king said, 'I'm lost. Have ye seen any of my couriers or my people or ma huntsmen?'

'No, Our Majesty,' says the miller, 'My Majesty the King, I have not seen anybody here fir days. Won't you come in an rest fir a while?' So he rushed the king inta the kitchen inta his little house, bade him sit doon bi the fire, called fir the woman to fetch the king somethin tae drink. The king was really tired and hungry and weary.

Then lo an behold in walks this young man. An he turns round, the miller says tae him, 'Go and take care of the king's horse!'

The young man bowed to the king and walked backwards out through the door. An the king looked – he'd never saw a handsomer or beautiful young man i his life. Then the young man walked back inta the house wonst more, he said, 'That is Our Majesty's horse tooken care of, Father,' an he sat doon by the fireside.

The king talked to the miller an the wife brought him somethin tae eat, somethin to drink, an the king was quite pleased.

'I'll get your horse ready whenever you feel like it,' said the young man.

An the king said, 'That is a lovely young son you've got. I've never seen one look so clever an so intelligent.'

'Well, tae tell you the truth, Ir Majesty, I cannot lie to you,' he said, 'he's not wir son.'

The king said, 'Not yir son?'

'No,' said the miller, 'he's not wir son. Ir Majesty, many people we hev deceived along the way for eighteen years, but, Our Majesty, we couldn't deceive you an tell you a lie because you are our king – he's not wir son.'

'Well, if he's not your son,' said the king, 'is he yir brother or yir relation o some kind, or yir nephew?'

'No,' said the auld miller, 'tae tell you the truth, Ir Majesty, it's a funny story – eighteen years ago I found him floatin i the dam in a cradle.'

Then the king remembert!

'And that,' said the auld man, 'is the same cradle bi the fireside – we've never partit with it – that's his cradle.'

An the king luikit an the king saw: this was the same cradle he got fae the fisherman. The king was upset in a terrible way, he didna know what to do! He knew now that the young man was alive and strong an guid-lookin, as beautiful a young man as he'd ever saw in his life. The king thought, he raked his head fir a plan, how he wis gaunna get rid o this young man he had no idea. He knew now that it was the fisherman's son he had threw i the dam eighteen years before. Then he said to the miller, 'Hes yir son ever rode on a horse?'

'No,' said the miller, 'my son has never hed the pleasure of ridin a horse.'

'Well,' said the king, 'I'm very tired an I wondered if he'd take a message fir me to the palace – tae get somebody tae bring a coach because I'm not able to ride my horse back that long long distance? I wonder if you would ask him, would he take my horse – it's quite gentle – all he's needs * tae do is sit on its back, jist guide it, as it'll take him back tae the palace, there they'll find a coach to bring me home.'

'Of course, Our Majesty,' said the miller, 'my son will do that fir you!'

He called to his son an told him, 'You must take a message to the palace. An the king shall stay here at the mill with me till you return with a coach to bring him back, because he doesn't feel too good to ride his horse. Do ye think you could manage tae ride the king's horse to the palace?'

An the king said, 'Remember now, it's a long way from here, it's prob'ly two days' journey.'

An the young man said, 'I'm sure I'll manage, Our Majesty, I've never been on a horse, but A've a good idea how to get there. I'll surely find my way.'

So the king calls for a paper and a quill an some ink; he writes her a letter, seals it an gives it to the young man, says, 'You take this to the queen! When you arrive there to the queen with hit, you'll be well rewarded.'

The young man bids his father an mother, the aul miller, 'Goodbye, goodday,' and he does the same to the king. He takes the king's horse, he rides on, an he rides an rides an rides fir many hours, he came to the forest. He'd never been this way before and lo an behold – he got lost! He got lost in the forest and he didna know in the worl what direction to take to the palace or to the big town where the palace was, but he'd worked hard that morning and he was tired. He came tae this little path, led the horse down, an sure enough in the middle o the forest he came tae a little cabin. He got off an tied up the horse. He walked to the cabin but there were not a soul to be seen – it was empty.

* he's needs – he needs

There was a fireplace, a table an some chairs i the cabin, some sheepskins and some goatskins on the floor, plenty firewood bi the fireside. So the young man went out, he took the saddle off the horse, tuik the bridle off, got the reins an tied it round the horse's neck, an tied hit tae a tree, gev the horse enough room so's it cuidna escape tae eat some grass, keep it alive. So after he saw that the horse was cared for an couldna escape, could reach as much grass at would keep it fir a few hours, the young man went in bi the fireside, kinneled up the fire; and he'd cairried a few pieces o meat an scones an things that his mother had given him to see him on his journey, he sat bi the fireside and had a meal. Then wearied and tired he gathered some o the skins, he lay down bi the fireside an fell asleep.

Now, unknown to the young man this cabin in the forest was owned by many robbers, about five or six robbers who robbed and stealed and thieft all over the country, an they always disappeared into the forest, they stayed in this cabin. And lo an behold they were all away out thiefin an stealin, then they cam back one by one; when they cam in one by one they came quietly, because they saw the horse tied up tae the tree outside an they wondered who it was ind their cabin. They came in very carefully, they all sat down round the table an they start't tae drink the wine they had stolen or bought, wherever they got it. An sure enough there bi the fireside lay this beautiful young man.

The chief o the robbers he said, 'We've got an intruder in wir cabin and I don't know how we're gaunna get rid of him. If he wakes up an finds . . . this place, then this place'll be no good for hus anymore.' So they're sittin talkin an wonderin what they're gaunna do, when the auldest one who was a family man hisself, who'd remembert way back many's a years ago that he too had sons that he'd prob'ly forgotten about an he'd wondered if they hed ever forgot about him, luikit wonst more – pulled back the sheepskins that the young man had hissel happed up wi – an he saw a letter stuck in his belt! 'A wonder,' says the auld man (he could read even suppose he wis a robber) – he pulled the letter from the young man's belt an he opened hit, as carefully as he cuid. He read hit aloud tae the rest o the robbers, some who cuidna read.

One was sayin, 'What dis hit say, what dis it say? Who is he, what dis it say? Is he a king's messenger, is he a king's son, is he a prince?'

'Not atall, not atall, not atall!' said the robber chief. 'Jist be quiet an I'll read hit to ye . . . He's "a miller's son", an you know the miller as well as me – many times we passed by his place – an he's been guid to

hus, he's never interfered an never gien away wir secrets in any way
. . . An he's on his way tae his death!'

'"Tae his death"?' said the rest o the robbers.

'Yes,' he said, 'at the present moment the king is at the mill, an this
letter says that "when this young man arrives at the palace he's got to
be put to death immediately, because *this is the one*".'

'What in the name of creation,' said the robbers, 'what would a
young man like that do to anybody to warran' his death?'

De auld one went to his bag, an he was a scholar, he'd cairried many
books and papers even suppose he was a robber; he had in his bag
some quills an some ink, because he used to leave messages fir people
along the wayside. He took the letter that the king had wroten an he
threw it in the fire. Then he wrote in a hand as good as the king:
'When this young man arrives at the palace, *he is the one* that we want.
And I want you to a-marry him immediately to my daughter the
princess. (Signed) *The King*.' Folded hit, put it back, stuck it i the
young man's belt – an the young man's still sleepin on. The robbers
sat, they had their drink an they quietly went their way inta the forest.
The young man had slept through all this, he'd never knewn a thing.

He woke up, rubbed his eyes, wondert fir a wee while where he was
an then he remembered. Got up, tidied up the rugs that he'd used, put
them back where he found them, made sure the fire wadna do any
harm (it was burned out bi this time), walked out o the door, there was
his horse standing quite contentit full o grass . . . The robbers were
gone. Put the saddle on the horse, an the bridle, climbed up o' the
horse's back an made his way down through the forest. He hit the
highway, the track gaun through the forest an he made his way on, he
rode fir miles. And sure enough at last he rode into the town where the
palace was, the king's palace.

He landit up to the king's palace, the king's castle; an these castles in
the auld days were jist made o stone, a few hamlets an houses round
aboot – they werena like the big towns ye see nowadays – there was a
few guards walkin aboot. He walked tae see the queen. They asked
him why he had come, an he said he had a message from the king, that
the king had sent a message that he must deliver to the queen immediately. And when he showed the message to the guards signed bi the
king's hand, they led him before the queen. He bowed to the queen, his
horse was tooken care of an he gave the letter to the queen.

And then the queen turned round, she smiled. She called fir all the
men an all the cooks an servants, says, 'We're gaunna have a great

banquet. The king is off on a journey, he will be returning in a few days, but I have got strict orders that this young man has got to marry his daughter! Whatever he's done for hit I don't know, but that's his orders.'

An then they all prepared fir the weddin: sure enough the young man was led an he was dressed i the finest o clothes, he met the princess, an the princess when she saw him jist loved him immediately. They became good friends, they talked an they sat an they talked an they walked, an within two days they were married. And the banquet and the dancin went on fir three days.

The king had waitit an waited an waited fir the return of the coach, but nothing turned up. But efter three days the king got tired. Now, the miller had an auld donkey an cart at he used fir takin grain to the village, an the king finally made the miller yoke the donkey i the auld cart; made him as comfortable as possible, an the miller and the king made their wey on the journey. They traivellt for two days. When they landed in the town at the palace all this great carry-on was gaun on. De king wondered what wis the trouble. The miller wantit to go home, the miller wantit tae return. People were singin, dher wur flags wavin, everybody wis happy, they were dancin i the street; de king wondert what wis happ'nin in the world! But they drove the aul donkey an cart fae the mill up to the palace, the king stepped oot an the first person he met wis the queen.

An the queen run forrit, she threw her arms round the king an welcomed him back.

He said, 'Did ye get my letter?'

'Yes,' she said, 'I've got your letter.'

'Have you done my orders,' he said, 'what I told ye to do?'

'Of course,' she said, 'Our Majesty – an come and see them!' Come an see them, don't they look handsome?'

'"Look handsome"?' said the king. 'What do ye mean?'

She says, 'Aren't they a handsome couple!' And there wis the young miller's son walkan i the garden, dressed in finery, his arm around the princess an dhey wur the most beautiful couple ye ever seen. The king was outrageous at this.

He said, 'My letter said, "*This is the young man that was born under the same star as the princess* – the son of a fisherman who was supposed to marry my daughter – which the old woman foretold eighteen years ago." An my orders was "to put him to death"!'

'Yir orders,' said the queen, 'was "to marry him immediately to the princess".'

46

'I wrote the letter,' says the king, 'I should know what I said!'

'Well, Ir Majesty, I don't know,' said the queen, 'but I've cairried yir orders to the hilt – there's nothing we can du about it now! He is mairried to the princess.'

An the king was upset! Went inta his room, he stood by himself fir hours an hours an hours, an he sat, he sat an he thought an he thought an he thought. An then at last he called the young man before him, shook hands with him – kindly an nice as if there were nothing wrong. He says, 'Young man, you hev married my daughter.'

'Yes,' said the young man, 'I've married yir daughter, an such a lovely princess she is; I'm proud tae marry yir daughter, I love her dearly.'

'Well,' he said, 'if you love her so much as that, I'm her father . . .'

'I know,' says the young man, 'ye're her father, Our Majesty the King, an I'm privileged to be married to your daughter, I'll do everything within my power tae see that I make her happy,' he said, 'an you and the queen as well. Anything ye ask of me – it shall be done.'

'Guid,' says the king, 'I'm proud of that. I'm a worried man,' said the king.

An the young fisherman, who wis very intelligent, said, 'Why should you be worried, Our Majesty, because you have everything under the sun, you've got a large kingdom an you've everything you need.'

He said, 'I don't have the knowledge of a king.'

'Of course, Your Majesty, you have "the knowledge of a king"!'

'But,' he said, 'I weary an I worry for something that I shall never have.'

'What is it?' said the young fisherman's son.

He said, 'Away, they tell me, in a faraway land miles from here is an island – A don't know if it's truth or fiction but I've never been there or none of my people's ever been there – but they tell me that ind that island there lives a giant, a great giant who is very kind and tender but who has the *golden hair of wisdom*, an anyone who possesses the hairs of his head, event three of them or four of them or just one, will have the wisdom that he has. And I would give my life, everything I own, to have three hairs of that giant's head; if you would get them fir me, I would appreciate it very much.'

'Well,' says the young man, 'if it's possible, Our Majesty, an it can be done . . . I'll do my best – when would you like me to start?'

'I would like you to start right away,' said the king. He called fir the queen an he called fir the princess, the three o them sat together an the fisherman's son sat there beside them. An the king told them the same story I'm tellin you. The princess wis very sad, she didn't want her young man to go away on a long journey. But the king said, 'It's only fir a matter of time, my daughter, he'll return an then you'll have him fir life!'

The young fisherman's son he wantit to please the king as much as possible, he said, 'I'll go, Our Majesty, I'll start off – even tomorrow morning.'

So he spent one more night wi the princess; an in the morning the king gev him the best horse in the stable, as much money as he wantit, an set him on his journey. An before he left he promised the king he would never come back, unless he could bring back the three *golden hairs of wisdom* that the king required.

Now this made the king very happy, fir he knew in his heart – he'd never wantit from the beginning for a fisherman's son to marry his daughter – he said tae himself, 'At last I've got rid of him, he's gone for ever!' He walked back tae his palace an he sat in his chamber. The princess his daughter came in, she looked very sad. An the queen came in, she sat down, she really loved the fisherman's son who was newly wed to her daughter the princess.

An the princess says, 'Daddy, my husbant he is gone on a journey – where did you send him to?'

'Oh,' he said, 'my daughter, my baby, my lovely princess, I've sent him on a journey, he's gone on to do something for me an he'll return to you, it won't be long before he comes back.' But deep in his own mind the king thought, 'He is gone for ever, because I have heard there's no one who hed ever went out to search fir the three *golden hairs* from the head of the Giant of Wisdom has ever returned!'

So the fisherman's son left the palace that morning, bade 'goodbye' tae his young wife the princess, the queen an the king, and he went on his way. An he rode an he rode an he rode an he rode fir many many's a miles, through forest an through towns an through villages fir many many miles, fir days an fir days. The king hed gev him plenty money tae carry him on his way. He's askin everyone along the way, woodsmen, foresters, ol people, young people, hev they ever heard of the Giant with the Golden Hairs of Wisdom? But lo an behold he'd never got a clue.

But he travelled fir many many miles on horseback, his horse wis weary an so was he. He cam down this track, an lo an behold over the mountain he saw a little village before him. He said to himself, 'In that village there must be something to eat,' because he was hungry an tired.

An he rode into the village, it was small, and when he rode into the first o the village he passed two-three houses an the houses seemt tae be empy. He rode on to the centre, there was about twenty-five or thirty people all gathert round in the village green. An they wis talkin tae each other, some wis raisin up their hands an they were speakin, they were talkin. When the young stranger rode up on horseback they all stopped an be quiet, never said a word.

So de fisherman's son he said, 'People, what's yir trouble?'

An one auld man with a long white beard cam up, he stood beside the young fisherman's son's horse an he pit his hand on the side of the saddle, said, 'Stranger, where hev you come from?'

The fisherman's son said, 'I've come a long long way. Could you tell me something, are there any food in the village?'

'We have food,' said the auld man, 'we hev drink, but we are sad.'

'Why are you sad?' said the fisherman's son. Everything seemed prosperous in the village, 'Why are you sad?'

'Well,' says the auld man, 'look there before ye.'

An the fisherman's son luikit – there was a tree right in the middle the green – all the people wis gathert round it. A tree an the leaves were hangin down, them all withert an the tree was dyin. The fisherman's son thought this kind o queer, he said, 'Why is the tree so important?'

An the auld man said, 'Luik, my son, you don't know, you have come from a faraway place, but this tree is so important to us. Where are you going? Where are ye bound for, stranger?'

An the young man said, 'I am going to seek three hairs from the head of the Golden-haired Giant of Knowledge.'

'Oh-dear-oh-dear,' said the auld man, 'if only you could find im an tell hus the truth!'

'What "truth"?' said the fisherman's son.

'Tell hus why our tree, our favourite tree, has never borne fruit fir many years.'

'What kind o fruit?' said the fisherman's son.

He said, 'The *fruit of heath*. This tree in our village, my son, has bore fruit fir many many years, an anyone who eats the fruit cuid live to be a hundred years old, never hev a headache, never have no trouble, never even have a hard day – but they would live fir evermore an feel well all their days! But suddenly the tree hes begun tae wither an the fruit is gone. Please, help us, stranger!'

'Well,' says the fisherman's son, 'I'm on my journey to seek the Giant with the Golden Hair of Knowledge, but if you would put me up fir the night an give me somethin to eat, I'll prob'ly tell ye – I'll prob'ly tell you on my way back when I return once more.'

So all the villagers gathered round, they made the fisherman's son welcome. They gev him a place tae stay, they gev him food. And he made a promise that when he returned he would find the truth of why their Tree of Health had never * bore any fruit.

So next morning, after a nice rest an some food an some breakfast, the young fisherman's son he rode on once more. An he rode an he rode an he rode, he travellt fir many many miles an he never cam across a village. He travelled over hill and over dale fir many's a day till he was hungry an weary an tired. At last, once more down a glen he comes, and lo an behold there once more is another village before him. He rides inta the village, and lo an behold his horse wis tired an weary an so was he. Once more when he lands in the village the little thatch cottages looks empty, the're not a soul to be seen so he rides through. And then there in a little green i the village are all the villagers, they're gaithert round a little stream that runs through the village. The young fisherman's son stops, an they saw there were a stranger among their midst. An auld woman with long grey hair walks up.

She says, 'Where hev you come from, stranger?'

He said, 'I've come a long way from here.'

'Have you any news to tell us?'

'"News,"' said the fisherman's son, 'what kind of news do you require?'

'Please help us!' she said.

'Well,' said the fisherman's son, 'it's *me* that seeks help, not you. I am hungry an I'm tired an weary – cuid you help me?'

'If I help you,' she said, 'my son, wad ye help me?'

He said, 'I'm seekin for the island of the Giant with the Golden Hair of Knowledge.'

* never – not recently

50

'Oh,' she said, 'my son, I have heard many people talkin about him, but he lives in an island far away from here. But please, please, help hus!'

'And what's yir problem?' said the fisherman's son.

'It's wir stream, my son,' she said, 'our stream – which used to run beautiful wine from our village – we enjoyed it an we drank from hit, we enjoyed it and it never seemed to end, never seemed to stop. An we all gaithert here, we had wir sing-songs an we all enjoyed wir drink by the lovely stream that flowed wine for evermore. But now hes it gone dry – no one knows what happened to our stream. Please, stranger, help us!'

An the fisherman's son said, 'If you help me, I'll help you.'

'What are you seekin, my son?' says the auld wumman.

'A'm seekin shelter, A'm seekin shelter fir the night, a place tae lie down an lay my head, because I'm weary,' said the fisherman's son; 'an I'm bound fir the place of the Giant with the Golden Hairs of Wisdom.'

So they tuik him, they gev him a place to stay an they fed him; they made him promise in his return, they wad pay him handsomely an reward im if he cuid find the secret – why their stream who run the beautiful wine through the village had now dried up.

So next morning, true tae his word, the fisherman's son got up, saddled his horse, bade 'goodbye' to the villagers an rode on his way after a nice rest. An he rode an he rode an he rode, an he traivelled an he traivelled; they hed gev him some food tae carry him on his way an he travelled fir many many miles, ti at last he rode till he came tae the open sea – they were no more land. No more land of any way * an he landed on the beach, he hed come tae Land's End. He rode around the beach for a while on horseback, jumped off his horse, led his horse luikin fir someone tae talk to. But there was nobody there, not one single soul. So he led his horse who was tired an weary around the shoreside. An lo an behold the first thing he spied was an auld man sitting in a boat, an old man with a long beard sittin in the boat.

He walked up to the auld man, 'Excuse me, sir,' he said, 'cuid you tell me, where am I?'

An the auld man said, 'My son, where have you come from?'

'I have come from many many miles . . . I've been riding for months

---

* of any way – in any direction

an days an weeks without end. I have passed through many towns, I have passed through many villages, but now I seem to be at ma end of my place, I can go no further.'

'Where are ye bound fir?' says the auld man.

'I'm bound,' says the fisherman's son, 'to seek the Giant with the Golden Hair of Knowledge.'

The auld man said, 'Luik, ye hev come tae the right place: I am the ferry-man an there in the distance is yir island. An there in tha' island lives the Giant with the Golden Hair of Knowledge – but woe be tae ye, my son – it wouldna be safe for you to go there.'

'Please,' said the boy, said the fisherman's son, 'take me there! Take me there, I want to go!'

'Your life will not be worth nothing if you go there,' says the auld man.

'I want to go, I must go,' said the fisherman's son, 'I mus go!'

'Well,' says the auld boatman, 'I row across there sometimes an back an forward, but I don't take any passengers, but I'm stuck to this boat an I jist can't get out. I mus row tae the island, an row back an row forward two times a day, because I'm stuck here an I jist can't leave this boat in any way. I don't take any passengers – no one comes here anymore. But in that island lives the Giant an if you want tae go there, my son, I will take you; but before you go ye mus make me one promise!'

'What would you want me to promise?' says the young fisherman's son.

'Promise me one thing,' he said: 'Find out fir me, why that I am stuck tae this boat an can never leave this row – that I mus row from the island back an forwards, back an forward every day, every day nonstop – because I jist can't leave this boat! An no one seems to want tae go there because it's too dangerous for them.'

'Take me,' says the fisherman's son, 'an I will find the secret fir ye when I meet the Giant with the Golden Hairs of Knowledge!'

'I will take you,' said the auld boatman, 'but ye must give me one promise.'

'I'll promise ye anything,' said the fisherman's son, 'when I find the Giant with the Golden Hair of Knowledge.'

'Ye mus tell me,' said the auld boatman, 'why I must sit here and row the boat from here to the island, row it back again day out an day in, I'm confined tae this boat for evermore, that I must never leave this boat for one minute, that I must row for eternity!'

'A will tell you,' said the fisherman's son, 'in one condition – that you row me!'

'I will take ye there,' said the auld man, 'but woe be tae ye, my son, what happens to ye – hit'll not be my fault!'

Many many hunderd miles back behind him in the palace of the king, the princess she is worried. Now her young man has been gone fir many many days, fir many many months; an the king he is happy an the king he is pleased, an the queen is worried because the queen loved her daughter, an she loved any man – if her daughter was happy so was she. The king rubbed his hands in glee after two month hed passed, the king rubbed his hands in glee after three month hed passed, the king rubbed his hands in glee after four month hed passed – no return of the fisherman's son! He said, 'He's gone fir evermore. I tried tae destroy him wonst, but the second time I have succeeded – he is gone for ever!' But the fisherman's son is not gone for ever.

He tuik his horse an he tuik this harness off it, he tuik the reins an he wrapped it around the horse's neck, he tethered it out on a nice piece of grass. He said to the auld boatman, 'You will come fir me tomorrow.'

'I'll come fir ye tomorrow,' said the old boatman.

'I will spend one night in the Giant's castle,' he said.

'You'll never spend a lifetime in the Giant's castle,' says the auld man, 'your life won't be worth nothing when you land there! But I'll take ye.'

So after he'd tuik care of his horse, de young man got in the boat an the auld man rowed him across from the end o the land to this little island that sat out in the middle of the sea. He rowed across an he rowed across an he rowed to the beach: 'There ye are, my young man,' he said, 'hit's on yir own head what happens to ye frae now on. But I'll be here tomorrow morning at the same time, an if ye miss me ye'll have tae wait till I return again.'

The fisherman's son jumped off the boat on this island an he walked up the beach. This was a funny island; dher wur trees, dher wur flowers, dher wur birds, dher wur animals, everything; an he walked farther and farther an the more he walked it got more beautiful. At lastten he walked fir about five or six hundred yards inta the middle of this little island, he came to a castle, the most beautiful old stone castle he'd ever saw. He said, 'This is where I'm bound to go.' An he walked up three stone steps tae the great oak door. He knocked hard on the door because he wasn't afraid, because he hed come tae do something fir the king – an he made sure he wis gaunnae do it – suppose it cost him his life! He knocked again and then he heard footsteps comin.

Then lo an behold the door opened, out cam a woman, a very auld woman. But she wis three times as big as the fisherman's son! She was tall and thin with long grey hair and a long flowin dress on her that swept the floor – the fisherman's son cuidna even see her feet.

The old woman was surprised when she saw the young man standing at her door, she rubbed her eyes, said, 'My son, what are you doing here?'

He said, 'Mother,' (he was very kindly this fisherman's son), 'mother, I hev come a long long way tae find you.'

'Well,' she says, 'ye found me now but peril fir you it might be!'

'Why?' said the fisherman's son. 'I've only come fir three things; please, help me!'

An the old woman never saw a human bein for many many years, all she lived there on the island with her son the Giant with the Golden Hair who was out huntin fir deers i his forest, an no one hed ever come near his place. She said, 'If my son finds you here, young man, your life won't be worth nothing.'

'Please, mother,' said de fisherman's son, 'please help me! I hev come a long long way tae find the truth.'

'What "truth" do ye want tae find?'

'I want to find three hairs of your son's head.'

She says, 'Hairs of my son's head is impossible tae get.'

'Please, mother,' he said, 'help me; I've come a long long way.'

'Well,' she says, 'come in.' So she tuik him in an she gev him somethin tae eat. 'Now, sit down an tell me yir story.'

So the story he told the auld wumman is the same story I'm tellin you, he said, 'I'm jist a fisherman's son an I married a young princess, her father sent me out tae seek three *golden hairs* from the Giant of Knowledge.'

She said, 'That is my son, and the're nothing in the world that my son doesn't know – he knows everything! He is giftit with the *golden hair of knowledge.*'

'Mother,' he said, 'if ye cuid only get me three hairs from his head to bring back tae the king, I'd be happy to live with my bride the princess fir evermore.'

And the auld wumman felt sad fir him, she says, 'My son will be home in very few minutes, he's out huntin. But what else dae ye seek?'

He said, 'I seek . . . as I rode on my way I came to a village, ind that village there is a tree an that tree bore the *fruit of life*; an all hits people were happy to eat the fruit, they lived happy ever after, no one tuik any trouble, no one tuik any disease an no one ever suffered from nothin. But now the tree is barren an grows nothing anymore – I want to know the reason why.'

'Oh,' says the auld wumman, 'I wouldn't know about that, but my son would know.'

'Then,' he said, 'I rode fir many many more miles an I came to another village; there in the village everyone was sad because they had a stream that beared pure *wine*, an everyone used to drink an enjoy the wine that ran through the stream – but now they are sad because the stream hes gone dry.'

'Nice,' says the auld woman, 'but my son would know about that better than me.'

'Then,' he said, 'at the end of the land I came tae an auld boatman who took me here, who ferried me across. An he wonders why that he should be stuck in that boat, rows it back, foremost, back an foremos from the mainland tae the island with no passengers in hit day out an day in?'

The auld wumman says, 'I don't know about that, but my son wad know.'

But she wis busy talkan tae him when they heard what was like a thunderclap, she said, 'He's comin home!' An the auld wumman wis sittin in a high chair an her dress was hangin tae the floor, 'Climb in bilow my chair, son,' she says, 'before he finds ye!'

An the fisherman's son, with the long dresses the aul women wore in these days an the high chair which she's sittin on, he climbed in bilow the chair an she pulled her aul dress over the top o him. He sat there quite content, whan who should walk in but a monstrous young giant with golden hair hangin down his back; but he never saw im, but he knew!

'Mother,' he said, 'hev you made something fir supper – I'm hungry!'

'Yes,' she said, 'my son, I've something fir supper for you, I've roastit . . .' An he hed a deer on his back, he threw the deer doon on the floor. 'Yes,' she said, 'son, I made ye supper.'

'What . . . any trouble or anything happen while I been gone?' He says. 'Things seems queer around this place . . . hev you hed any visitors while I was gone?'

'No, my son,' she said, 'no visitors. Only the aul boatman who hes been –'

'Oh,' he said, 'him; he'll keep on his rowin as long as . . . he'll go on rowin his wey till the end of time.'

She brought forth a haunch of deer, roasted haunch o deer roond the fire an she placed hit before him, he ate it up. Then she brought a big flagon o wine. She said, 'My son, you know you been gone fir a long time.'

'Yes, Mother,' he said, 'I had a long hunt today, but I might be luckier tomorrow.' An he sat by the fire after drinkin three or four gallons o wine.

She says, 'My son, you look tired and weary, come beside yir mother,' because this auld woman loved this son like nothing in the world, an she tuik him beside her. He sat on the floor and she sat on a high stool. His head on'y cam tae her knee, he placed his head on, an bein him huntin all day an after a feast and a drink o wine, he fell sound asleep on his mother's knee. She begin tae run her fingers through his golden hair, which wis long an beautiful. An then she wapped one of the golden hairs round her finger, an she pulled it. An the Giant wakened up!

He said, 'Mother, what hae ye been doin, you been pullin my hair!'

'Oh, my son, I'm sorry tae wake ye up, but I had a terrible dream.'

'Mother,' he says, 'what was yir dream?'

'I dreamt, my son,' she says, 'a long way from here in the mainland far from our island there is a village, an in that village there is a tree an that tree bore beautiful fruit, the *fruit of health*, and all these people loved that fruit of health, they enjoyed it. But now they are so sad because their tree is withering an dying.'

'Ho, my mother,' he said, 'if they only knew! If they only knew: there's a wicked wicked wicked wizard hed cast a spell on that tree an put a padlock an chain round the roots; if they only knew – jist tae dig up the root o the tree an break the padlock – their tree would blossom for evermore. Please, let me sleep, Mother!' he said, an he placed his head on his mother's knee once more.

Now the aul wumman hes one hair on her finger. She waitit till the Giant fell asleep once more. She wrapped another hair roond her finger an she pulled another hair from his head.

The Giant woke up, 'Mother!' he said, 'what are ye pullin my hair fir?'

'Oh, my son,' she said, 'while you were asleep I had another dream: I dreamt there's another village many miles from the first one; an through that village there runs a beautiful stream o beautiful sweet wine, an now the stream hes stopped the villagers are so upset – there's no more wine fir them an they're so sad! They would give anything in the world if their stream would run wine once more.'

'Ha,' says the Giant, 'it's quite simple! If they only know: under the steppin stone in the well there is a frog an in that frog's throat is a crust o bread thrown by a child in the well, stuck in the frog's throat. If they dig up the steppin stone that leads to the stream an takes the crust from the frog's throat – then their stream will run again for ever. But they'll never know an no one's gaun tae tell them!'

De wee laddie's sittin in bilow the aul wumman's dress an he's hearin everything.

The Giant stretched his feet out again bi the heat o the fire an he laid his head upon his mother's lap once more, then he fell asleep. When the aul wumman gaithert another hair roond her finger once more, an she pulled – he woke up: 'Mother,' he says, 'stop pullin my hair!'

'Oh, my son,' she says, 'I hed another wonderful dream.'

'Mother,' he said, 'ye've hed better dreams an me! What's your problem this time?'

'Well,' she said, 'son, I had another dream an I think I won't dream anymore tonight. But tell me: why is hit that the auld boatman who rows across from our island tae the mainland back an forward, back an forward, although suppose he never takes you or takes me, he mus be confined tae that boat all his life an never can get a-free from hit?'

'Ha-ha-ha,' said the Giant, 'I know, but he'll never know!'

'But what's the problem,' said the aul wumman, 'why hes he got tae do this?'

'Well,' said the Giant, 'it's quite simple: there's no problem if he only knew, but he'll never know by me; if only he would give a shot o the rows to the first person who comes in the boat, an give *them* a shot an let *them* row. When the boat leaves the beach – not in my island but on the mainland – an jump out, then the person who takes the oars will take his place, will be confined for evermore tae row back and forward ti the end of eternity!' And the Giant fell asleep once more.

Whan the Giant wis aleep, the wumman beckoned tae the wee fisherman's son – the Giant wis aleep – 'Now,' she said, she tuik the three *golden hairs* from her finger – 'take them carefully, luik after them an bring them back to the king. But remember – did ye hear what I told ye?'

'I know,' said the son, 'I heard every word.' The fisherman's son rolled the hairs up in his hand, put them in his purse around his waist an he quietly stole away from the castle of the sleepin Giant with the Golden Hairs of Knowledge – fir he know he hed done what he hed set out to do.

He walked for many miles till he came to the beach, bi the time he reached the beach it wis daylight. There lo an behold wis the auld boatman waitan on the beach fir im, the auld boatman said, 'Tell me, my son, hev you found the secret fir me, why I row this boat back and forward from side to side fir eternity?'

An the young man said, 'Luik, aul boatman, after ye take me tae the mainland I'll tell ye!'

'Jump in, then,' says the auld man, an the young fisherman's son jumpit in the boat. The auld man rowed back to the mainland an he jumped out. 'Now,' said the boatman, 'tell me why I'm confined tae this for evermore!'

An the fisherman's son said, 'The Giant of Golden Knowledge says: "You are confined fir only one reason – the first person who comes here to ask you to row them across to the island, tell em you're tired an give em a shot o the oars – when it leaves the beach on this side, jump out an you'll be free for evermore! An the person who takes the oars will be confined tae the boat fir the rest o their life."'

'Guid,' says the aul boatman, 'guid.'

He bade the aul boatman 'farewell', goes back tae his horse and his horse hed ett all the grass around where hit wis tied to, but it was still there. He takes the saddle, saddles his horse, puts the bridle on it, jumps on his horse's back an rides back, because the aul wumman hed gev him a good meal in the Giant's palace, he rides back. Lo an behold when he landed in the same village he hed come to, the second village, there wis the people once more gathered round the stream. And they're all moanin an they're very upset, why this stream was dry.

Up comes the aul wumman wonst more wi the long grey hair, 'Welcome back, stranger,' she said, 'did ye find your quest?'

'I have found my quest, mother,' he said.

'Please,' she said, 'tell hus an we'll make you rich, we'll give ye a donkey with as much gold as you can carry, if ye will only tell us why wir stream doesn't run *wine* anymore!'

An the young man said, 'I have been with the Giant of Golden Hair of Knowledge an he says: "Under yir steppin stone there is a frog, an in that frog's throat there is a crust o bread thrown by a careless child an he cannae swalla hit; but you must retrieve the frog an take the piece o bread from his throat – wonst ye retrieve the bread yir stream will run again!"'

The auld wumman talked to some o the men, within seconds they liftit the flagstone, an there lo an behold wis the frog. Sure enough they tuik the frog, they relieved the frog of a crust o bread in his throat and within seconds the steam was runnin most wine once more.* An everybody i the village ran into hit, they were divin into it, they were sprinklin it on their faces, they were drinkin hit, they were playin – de kids were swimmin in it – de most beautiful *wine* of all! An the auld wumman said, 'Stop, we must help our young stranger who hes found the secret.' She called once more fir the donkey, load't it with two bags of gold, she gev it tae the young stranger the fisherman's son tae go on his way.

He tuik the donkey behind his horse wi two bags o gold, he rode on an rode on fir many days an many days an many days. At last he came tae the first village, and lo an behold when he landed, sure enough there wis the people gaithert round the green once more. They're weepan, they're a-crying an the tree wis gettin withert, the leaves are fellin off an it looked in a horrible state.

When he rode up the old man with the long white beard cam, he said, 'Welcome back, stranger, where have you been?'

He said, 'I have been to the island of the Giant with the Golden Hair of Knowledge.'

'Have you found our secret, stranger?' said the auld man.

'Yes,' he said, 'old man, I have. '

'Why our tree doesn't nourish de most beautiful *fruit?*'

Said the young fisherman's son, '"Take a spade an dig under the tree an you will find a chain an padlock around the root of yir tree. Break the padlock of the chain – then once more yir tree will blossom in life with *fruit of health!*"'

No sooner said an done, three men ran with spades, they dug up under the tree and lo an behold there was the truth: under the tree wis a chain an a padlock; they broke the chain, threw the chain away, covered the roots up once more. And lo an behold de amazin thing happened – the tree wis blossomt in minutes – it wis hangin with fruit! An the people were runnin, the children were runnin,

---

* most wine once more – more wine than ever before

they're pickin it off an they're eatin em. They're happy an they're clappin their hands.

An then the old man said, 'Stop!' an they all stopped. 'We thank our friend, the young stranger who hes come here tae found the secret of our tree, we mus reward him handsomely.' An then once more they called fir another donkey, hit wis given two large bags of gold. Once more the fisherman's son went on his way with two donkeys laden with four bags of gold.

He travelled on an he made his way back, all the way he hed come, till at last after many days' travel he landed back in the palace. An there was the queen an there were the princess to welcome him home. His donkeys wis tooken care of, his horse was tooken care of, the four bags of gold were cairried up an placed before the king. An the fisherman's son walked up, from his purse he tuik out de three *golden hairs of knowledge*.

'You are back,' said the king.

'I am back,' said the fisherman's son, 'an I done yir quest: there is yir three *golden hairs*,' an he put them in the king's hand.

'Where in the world did you find em?' said the king.

'I found them at Land's End,' said the fisherman's son, 'an after the Land's End there's an island, there lives in that island the Giant with the Golden Hair of Knowledge.'

'But,' said the king, 'there's only three hairs – that will only give me a little knowledge – it won't give me all the Giant knows!'

'Well,' said the fisherman's son, 'if ye want anymore knowledge ye'll hev to go and find it yirself, because I cam home to spend the rest o my life with my wife the princess.'

'Well,' says the king, 'you have deserved hit. But *I* myself will go, I will find the Giant with the Golden Hair of Knowledge through your directions.'

'Go,' said the young fisherman's son, 'you are welcome,' an he told the king where tae go.

Princess wis happy to see her young man back an she cuddled him and kissed him, an so was the queen. Now he hed plenty gold.

The next day the king said he would go on his way, and himself, he wis not content with three *golden hairs*, he wantit many many more. So he choose his best horse an he tuik as much gold at would carry him on his way. He left the queen an he left the young fisherman's son and the princess to take care of the kingdom till he cam home, an he rode on his way.

The king rode fir many many miles, he rode through the first village, he never saw the tree of fruit; he rode through the second village, he never saw the stream of beautiful wine; an he rode ti the End of the Land, all he saw wis an auld man in a boat. He looked out an there wis the island, 'That,' says the king, 'is the place I want tae go to!' An he says to the auld man, 'I leave my horse here if you will take me across there.'

'Willingly,' says the auld boatman, 'I'll take ye across. But,' he said, 'I been rowin fir many many days an I'm tired; would ye do me one favour?'

'I'll do anything,' said the king who was an aged man bi this time, but wis still fit an strong.

'I been rowin all day,' said the auld man; 'please, take a little shot of the oars an row hus across tae the island!'

'Sure enough!' said the king an he spat on his hands. He jumped up in the front o the boat an he tuik the oars in his hands. When the minute he tuik the oars in his hands, the auld boatman jumped out an walked away, left the king. An the king wis left there fir evermore, he rowed back and he rowed forward an he rowed back an he rowed forward, but he could never never never get his hands away from the oars or he cuid never leave the boat.

The young fisherman's son had his young queen, he became king after the queen hed died, an him and his princess lived happy in their palace, they had many children. But the king still rowed on from time to time an of course, as the story says, *he's still rowin yet!* An that is the end o my story!

MARY RASHIECOATS AN THE WEE BLACK BULL

L ittle Mary's father and mother wis out goin to the village with a
pony and trap when there came a terrible storm. The pony got
frightened in the thunder, hit ran away, boltit, and little Mary's
father and mother was killed in the accident. She was left all alone – no
one tae take care o her. Then after her mother an father's services had
finished, they were buried, lo an behold one old woman came forward
an she says, 'I am Mary's grandmother an I want to take care of the
child.' So everyone wis happy. People in the village thought that puir
Mary, after her mother and father wis killed, didna have any friends or
no one to take care o her, but up turned the old grandmother. So little
Mary went to live with her an this 's where my story begins.

After a spell of time and many tears, Mary had cried because she
missed her mother and father very much, she finally settled down with
her grandmother i a little cottage beside of a large forest. Her grandmother wis a nice an kindly old soul an she loved Mary dearly; she
kept some hens an some ducks and mostly geese, a lot o geese. Granny
used tae every month go to the market and sell some of the male geese
which she had brought and reared up, an kep the female geese tae
produce more. So Mary really became to love her grandmother after
she forgot about her daddy and mammy, she stayed with her grandmother for many many months. Now she begint tae feel she wis at
home at last, she'd found someone who really did love her. But her
grandmother was very puir even though she owned some geese and
some ducks an some hens, because whatever she got, the few pennies

she got at the market, she used to buy food fir herself and food fir little Mary that she took care of. But one evening Grandmother wis sittin knittin by the fireside.

Mary came in by the fire an sat beside her, said, 'Granny, you know it's all right fir you tae sit knittin here, but it's not very fun fir me.'

And then Granny said, 'Why, Mary, why?'

'Well,' she says, 'I dinna hev any friends to speak to, I can't play with the hens or with the geese or the ducks that you have an I feel very lonely.'

'But,' she says, 'Mary, you have me!'

'But, Granny,' she said, 'some days ye're knittin an some days ye're ironin an some days ye're wurkin and I need someone tae speak to, someone tae love an someone t' take care of.'

'Well,' she says, 'Mary, prob'ly I might get ye a dog or a cat.'

'No, Granny,' she said, 'I don't like dogs and I don't like cats.'

'Well then, Mary,' she says, 'would ye like tae come with your granny to the market tomorrow?' De old woman felt very sad of her wee granddaughter, it was her only son's daughter an she wantit t' do everything in the world to please her an make her feel at home.

'Oh yes, Grandmother,' she says, 'I would love to go with you to the market tomorrow.'

'Well,' she said, 'Mary, if you want tae go wi me, you must go to bed bright and early an make sure that you're up to help me tomorrow, cause I've got seven geese an we're gaunna walk em to the market you and I. We'll sell them, we'll get some money an then everything'll be okay, an you'll see some people there.'

'Oh, Granny,' she says, 'I would love tae go . . .' cause she had never been with her granny to the market before.

Now in this market I'm gaunna tell you about in my story, all people came from around the country and they sold all their animals, some sold sheep an some sold goats, some sold calves an some sold hens an some sold ducks. And they all met in the market in the village wonst a month. Mary's grandmother used tae always makit sure that she took somethin tae sell at market, an when she sold something it kep her goin in money till she had something else to sell. But Mary never knew very much about this, this was a new experience to Mary.

So, she was so excited that night when she went to bed she could barely sleep, she wis going to the village tomorrow and her grandmother had promised that she would buy her something in the market that would make her happy. True to her word, next morning Mary got down from her bed an she walkit down. Granny wis up. They had little tae eat – they were very poor – some goat's milk and some porridge.

An Grandmother said, 'Now, Mary, you promised you would help me.'

An Mary said, 'Yes, Grandmother . . .'

So her and her granny gathert seven o the fattest geese that they could find in the yard, Granny tuik a stick an Mary tuik a stick an both o them drove the geese, walkit em to the market. Mary was runnin in front an keepin them out o gates, Granny was comin behind an drivin the geese – they hedna far to go, mebbe about two miles. When they landed i the market, the man they heard who was auctioneer knew Mary's grandmother very well, an he saw the fat geese comin in, he helpit and put them in a pen. Once the geese wis penned in the market, they would be sold as seven fat geese. Grandmother tuik Mary an she bought her a wee bit o lunch.

'Now,' she said, 'Mary, we'll come an see the things gettin sold.'

The' were goats, there were sheep, there were cows, there were bulls, there were calves, all gettin sold in the dozen, hens an ducks an geese gettin sold. When you hev somethin tae sell you must wait yir turn. So, the auctioneer sat up there an he sold the things: he sold cattle an he sold sheep and ponies, he sold goats an he sold donkeys, he sold everything till it came tae Mary's grandmother's geese an he sold them. He sold everything at wis in the market. But lo and behold one thing he didna sell was a wee black bull calve, a wee black bull calve – nobody seemed tae want hit. Auctioneer tried to sell it an nobody want't it.

Everybody wis finished, they bought everything they needed, they sellt everything they needed, they went their way. And lo an behold the wee bull calve wis left on his own ind a pen. And Mary after walkit round an seen all the animals she cam up beside the wee bull calve, she put er arms roond its neck an said, 'You poor little creature, you've never been sold. Everybody his left you, but,' she says, 'I love you, you're so nice,' an she pettit the wee bull calve, a wee black calve.

Grandmother was up by the auctioneer gettin paid for her geese, she cam down an she searched fir Mary, she couldna find her. And she went round all the ring, all the pens searchin. Then she found Mary, Mary wis sittin beside the wee calve with her airms roond its neck.

She says, 'Come on, Mary, it's time tae go home, I've sold ma geese an everything at's in market's closin down fir the night. We must go home.'

'But Granny,' she said, 'Granny, how about the wee calve here – hit's never been sold – the're no one to take care o't.'

'Mary,' she says, 'I don't know who owns hit.'

'Granny,' she said, 'please, Granny, buy hit fir me!'

Granny says, 'What in the world would you do, Mary?'

She says, 'It'll be company to me, I'll take it home with me and I can look after hit, I can talk tae hit an I can feed it grass. It's a pet I want; don't want a dog, I don't want a cat. Granny, buy me this wee calve, please!'

'Well,' says Grandmother, 'I hev got some money fir ma geese today, I'll go and see the auctioneer an see what he says about hit.' So aul Granny, tae keep Mary happy, she walkit up tae the auctioneer an said, 'You've sold everything in the market today?'

An the auctioneer said, 'Yes, I've sold everything apart from one wee calve, a bull calve, nobody seems tae want hit.'

'Well,' she said, 'would you sell it tae me?'

And the auctioneer knew the old grandmother, he says, 'Granny, what will you du wi a bull calve? It'll grow inta a bull, hit'll prob'ly get ye inta trouble when it grows up tae be a big bull, it'll no be a calve for long.'

She said, 'Would you sell it to me? My wee granddaughter hes made friends with hit an she wants it, she won't have nothing else. A've offered her a dog, A've offered her a cat an she disna hev no time fir hens or geese.'

'Well,' the auctioneer said, 'hit's not worth very much, it's only just a wee black calve. I don't know where it cam from, it came in among some cattle today, some farmer brought it from the forest an he said it wisna his. Nobody seems to own it, nobody seems to know who owns hit . . . Why, if you want hit, I'll not sell it tae ye, I'll give it tae ye because the market's closin. Take it with you if you feel fit!'

'Thank you!' says the old granny. 'You sure you don't want some money for hit?'

'No,' says the auctioneer, 'I don't want nae money fir hit, because the're not an animal left becepts hit in the market – take it with ye if it's any good to ye. But bring hit back when it gets big an I'll sell it for ye!'

The old grandmother toddled doon, she was very old, she toddled doon tae Mary, Mary wis sittin with her arms round the wee calve an it was lickin her hand. It wis jist a wee black calve about seven or eight weeks old an its eyes wis shinin sae bright as stars. Mary had her arms round its neck.

Her grandmother says tae her, 'Mary, we hev tae go home.'

'Granny,' she says, 'we can't go home. Not tonight we can't go home an leave this little creature itself, because it's no one to take care of hit.'

She says, 'Mary, *you* can take care of hit!'

'Oh, Grandmother,' she says, 'did you git hit fir me? Did you buy it fir me?'

'Yes,' she says, 'Mary, it's yours, from now on it's yours. You have hit, you keep it an I hope it'll be good to you, an take care of hit – because it's your friend an I got it for ye.'

Lo an behold they opened the gate, Mary and her old grandmother walkit oot an the wee black bull calve followed them. It followed Mary as if i' had known her for many many months. So Grandmother got a few messages in her way at she needed to buy, they walkit home to their little house near the forest an the calve walkit wi them, behind them. And Mary jist loved it from the heart – every step she was takin she wis lookin back tae see wis it still there – but hit walkit on behind her, its nose behind her all the way!

She says, 'Grandmother, I love this like nothing else – I don't want dogs, I don't want cats, I don't want nothing.' Now Mary wisna very old, she wis about twelve, a handsome young lassie with long hair, beautiful young girl. So they walkit home tae their little house beside the forest, as Mary was so excited, dher wur nothing in the world at meant anything to her but this calve. 'Granny,' she said, 'we'll find some place fir hit tae sleep?'

'Oh Mary,' she said, 'you'll find it some place tae sleep – we'll put it in one o the sheds at's empy now, the ducks are gone an the geese is gone, we'll put it in the shed that the geese used to be in.' So, no way in the world . . . before Mary got a bite tae eat that night, she took it inta one o the sheds whaur the geese slept, she made a bed fir hit o beautiful hay, she brought hit a pail o water an she put it – she never tied it – she put it in the shed. And after she had tuik care of hit, she walkit in tae her grandmother, they had a little lunch together an her grandmother called her beside her, said, 'Mary, come here an I want to talk tae ye. Sit on my knee, Mary,' an Mary sat on her grandmother's knee. 'Now,' she said, 'you must understand, ye're growin to be a big girl and you've got something tae take care of.'

'Oh, Granny,' she says, 'I love hit so dearly, I love my calve so dearly. Granny, I'll look after hit, it'll not be any trouble tae you in any way. I'll look after it, I'll take care of hit, I'll feed it and it'll not give ye any trouble. But please, please, Granny, please, please, would you give me a promise?'

And Granny says, 'Yes, I'll give you a promise.'

'Granny, please, will ye never sell it?'

'Oh well, Mary,' she said, 'if you love it so much as that, I'll not sell it.'

But anyway, they begint tae settle down an times pass by an months pass by, an Mary took care o her calve an Granny tuik care o the hens, tuik care o her ducks. And Mary loved her calf – she went walkan with it, she took it everywhere she went. But Mary walkin with her calve an feedin it an takin care of hit, her clothes begint tae get kind o withert, kin o tackery an torn. One day she cam in.

Granny says, 'Where have you been, Mary?'

'Oh,' she says, 'A was out in the forest walkin with ma calve.'

'Mary,' she says, 'ye're in a terrible state. Yir coat is torn an it's ragged. Ye know I'm very poor an I canna buy ye a coat or anything.'

'Granny,' she says, 'well, patch it fir me!'

'No,' she says, 'the're too many patches on it already, I can't pit another patch in hit.'

'Well, Granny,' she says, 'make me a coat, knit me a coat!'

'Mary,' she says, 'I canna knit ye a coat, A dinna hev enough thread. But I'll tell ye what tae do, Mary, my aul grandmother a long time ago wis very clever an she taught me many things. If you will gae out inta the moor, in the rushie moor, an cut me some rashes, I'll make ye a coat.'

'Oh Granny,' she says, 'ye couldna make me a coat from rashes!'

She says, 'Mary, I'll make ye a coat like the auld people used tae do a long time ago. If you make up yir mind to cut me some rashes like the rashes I want, I'll make ye a coat!'

Well, Mary wis very pleased. 'Granny, I can cut ye rashes.' And beside where they stayed wis a rashie moor where all the rushes, we call them 'rashes', they grew very high, five foot high. And people long ago used tae split the rushes up, they wove them, they could make cloth fae them like they do wi the flax. So Mary made up her mind that she wis gaunna have a coat. She went inta the back o the shed, she got an old sickle that wis used by er grandfather who had died many years before, and she went out on the moor, she cut the rashes, bunches and bunches and bunches o rashes. And the calve cam with her.

The calve was noddin, pushin her wi his head an he's noddin with her, he played an he jumpit an he cockit his tail roond his back an he runned round the field. Mary wis still cuttin the rashes. The calve was always with her, but it was gettin bigger an bigger as the days went by.

Mary gathered bundle an bundle an bundle an bundle o rashes, she brought them back. And her granny sat, she split them down, she took the hearts off an she weaved them, she sut an she weaved em day after day, day after day. And lo an behold she made Mary a coat – the most beautiful green coat that you ever seen in yir life! Nobody in the village had a coat like this, because it was made from rashes.

When Granny was finished wi the coat she said, 'There ye are, Mary, there's yir coat!' An Mary tried it on – Mary loved this coat like nothing in the world – she put it on an it jist fittit her, made from rashes.

So she used to walk tae the village; Granny smoked a pipe an she used tae go fir tobacca an some things fir her. And when all the people in the village seen Mary comin, they saw her wi this strange coat on her made from rashes, even the children used tae call her 'Mary Rashiecoats'. But Mary visitit the village many many times an the people in the shops used tae call 'Mary Rashiecoats', not when she was there, but they said, 'Oh, here comes Mary Rashie-coats again wi her wee black bull.' Whaurever she went the black bull went wi her, an the bull got bigger and bigger an bigger as the days went on.

Now many months had passed by, a year had passed by, two year had passed by, an Mary Rashiecoats still had her coat an Mary Rashiecoats still had her black bull. Mary and her bull enjoyed life together like nobody in the worl did. An Granny still sent her to the village an the bull went with her. Now the bull wis gettin so big that sometimes when Mary got tired, she used t' jump on the bull's back and the bull would walk with her on his back – no bridle, no saddle, nothing – this wis Mary's pet fae the world.* And the people i the village always said when she came, 'Here comes Mary Rashiecoats and her black bull,' everyone knew Mary Rashiecoats.

But life with ol Granny became very hard, because she had no money and her hens didn't lay, her ducks didn't lay an the geese didn't lay, things begint tae get badder an worse an worse fir aul Granny. And she wantit tae take care o Mary . . . It came market day once more.

An one night Granny called her, 'Mary, I want tae talk to ye.'

'What is it, Granny,' she said, 'what's the trouble?' Now bit this time

* pet fae the world – the best pet in the world

Mary had grown inta a beautiful young woman an the bull had grown inta a beautiful young bull.

She says, 'Mary, tomorrow's market day an I hev very little to sell. Ma geese hev not grown, A hev no hens tae sell, I've not nothing. An Mary, A'm very sad tae say this to you . . . but we need money very badly.'

'Well, Grandmother,' she says, 'what can I do?'

'Mary, A'm sorry,' she says, 'tae ask you, but I was wonderin if we cuid sell the bull in the market an get some money fir me an you?'

'Oh no, Granny, Granny, Granny,' she says, 'no way in the worl! Suppose we starve tae death, Granny, I cannae sell ma bull.'

She said, 'Mary, luik, he's gettin too big now an I canna see that we need him anymore. Ye've had im fir –'

'I've had him now, Granny,' she said, 'fir two years an he's my pet an my love an I love him an we have great times together – Granny, I could never part with him in my life!'

'But Mary,' she says, 'I'm your grandmother and I'm gettin auld. I cannae supply food an clothes fir ye anymore, I had tae make ye a coat from rashes an we need the money. Wouldn't it be nice if we sold the bull an we got some money, because someone'll take –'

Mary says, 'Someone'll take him, they'll kill him an use him for food, they'll kill him! No way I'm gaunna sell ma bull!'

And Grandmother said, 'Look, Mary, tomorrow we must sell the bull, there's no other way!'

Mary was very upset at this. She jist walked upstairs an went to bed, never seen said 'good night' tae her grandmother, went to bed but she couldna sleep, no way in this world, no way cuid she sleep. Her grandmother went to bed, an she waitit an she waited an she waited till she thought er grandmother wis asleep. Then lo an behold the moon cam oot, the moon was shining clearly. Mary quietly slipped down the stairs, as quietly as a mouse, and walkit out tae the shed where she kep the bull; she put her arms round the bull's neck an it rubbed its head against her. She said, 'Little friend, Granny wants to sell you fir money, but I'll never sell you, no way, little bull, I'll never sell you,' an the bull rubbed his head against her. She says, 'Me and you, we're gaunna run away – where they will never find hus – we'll go inta the forest, I'll take care o you an you can take care o me – we'll run away into the forest!'

So the moon was shining and Grandmother was asleep, Mary quietly opened the shed an then she walked away, the bull went with her. Off they went inta the forest an they traivellt an they traivellt an they traivellt fir many many hours.

When old Grandmother wakened up in the mornin she called fir Mary, Mary wis gone. She walked down an she called round the place, round the shed, but Mary wis gone. An she walked inta the little goose shed where Mary kep the bull, de bull wis gone. Grandmother was upset and she wondert what happened, but Mary an the bull wis gone. But the aul grandmother worried, she went back in, she made hersel a cup o tea an she wis upset. She searcht, she called an she shoutit an she tried her best to find em – she looked round all the fields and all the moors – thought they were out fir a walk or something, but no way – Mary an the bull wis gone. So now we'll leave aul Grandmother fir a little while an we travel with Mary and the bull.

Wee Mary Rashiecoats and her bull tried tae get as far away as possible in case Grandmother wad get in touch with her. And they travelled on, they traivellt on an they traivellt on, the moon came up an the moon came down, the next mornin the sun came up an the sun went down, and they travelled on an they travellt on an they traivellt on, and Mary led her little bull as far as they cuid go tae get as far away from her grandmother as possible – in case Grandmother would sell her little bull!

But as usual when people travels, Mary got tiret an Mary got hungry. She was so hungry and so tired, she came tae a large tree at the end of the forest, she pit her back tae the tree and she sat down so exhausted she couldna go another step; so hungry, so tired, so exhaustit efter travellin so many many miles she couldn't go another step!

When the bull cam up, it put its head right beside Mary an it spoke tae her an hit said, 'Mary –'

Mary just . . . she said, 'You can speak to me!'

And the bull said, 'Yes, Mary, I can speak tae you. I didn't want tae speak to you before but I want tae speak to you now. You have run away with me, ye hev saved my life. Your grandmother got me, ye took care o me an now it's up to me to take care of you! What would it at * you would like?'

'Oh,' Mary says, 'little bull, if you really can talk to me an do any wonderful thing – I'm hungry an I'm tired – I'm hungry, I need something to eat!'

---

* what would it at – what is it that

'Luik in my ear!' says the bull. An Mary luikit in the ear an there in the bull's ear wis a wee bit o cloth.

'Pull it out!' said the bull. An Mary pulled the wee bit cloth oot.

'Put it on the ground!' says de bull. An Mary put it on the ground. And lo an behold when the cloth wis spread on the ground, there wis the most beautiful things in the worl tae eat at Mary could ask fir! There were sweetmeats, there were food, dher wur everything that Mary could ask for – fruit, vegetables, meat, everything. An the bull jist stude there with his head noddin.

An Mary said, 'Is this fir me?'

An the bull said, 'Eat to your heart's content, Mary!' It shook its head there, hit never said another word.

So Mary sat an she ett an she ett, she ett fruit an she ett vegetables, she ett meat ti she wis so full that she couldna go another bite. She wondered to herself, 'Why is this shui' happen tae me? Is this my bull?'

An the bull said, 'Are you finished, Mary?'

An she says, 'Yes, I've had a lovely session, I've had everything I need tae eat.'

'Well,' he said, 'throw the crumbs on the ground an put the cloth back in my ear!' An Mary threw the crumbs on the ground, she finished an put the cloth back in the ear.

'Now,' says the bull, 'put yir arm round my neck an we'll go on wir way!' So Mary put her arm round the bull's neck an they walked on an they walked on an they walked on, fir hours and hours an hours, till at last they came to the end o the forest, there were no more forest! There wis a open plain an grass growin as high as the bull's feet, Mary an the bull made their way through it. When lo an behold they came to a cliff-face, a great clift an there was no passage to pass by – they couldna get by no way in the world.

And Mary said, 'We can't walk through the rocks – we've got tae go this way.'

An the bull says, 'Not, Mary, we'll go *this* way: follae me!' An Mary followed the bull. He said, 'If ye're feart, hold on tae my tail.' An they came tae a narra passage in the rocks, Mary grippit the bull's tail, an the bull went on an on an Mary's haudin on tae his tail – when they pass through a narra passage – and lo an behold whan they came tae the end o the passage there was a great valley, a great valley! And the bull stopped.

An Mary said to the bull, 'Why you stoppin?'

And the bull turned round, he says tae Mary, 'Luik, Mary Rashie-

coats, you mus remember, Mary: listen to what I tell you an do whit
A say – don't have no fear! But anything ever happens, don't hev no
fear, just listen tae me and do whit A tell ye!'

An Mary walkit up, she pit her hand roond the bull's neck an they
walked forward. But they hedna walkit more than two yards, when lo
an behold – *right* before them was the greates biggest ugliest-luikin
hunchback they ever saw in their life – he's standing there right before
them!

An he said, 'Where are youse going? *Why* hev you come here? *Why*
hev you entert my valley? No one is allowed inta my place!'

Mary wis terrified an the bull whispered quietly to her, 'Fear no
fear, Mary, have no fear!'

An the ugly hunchback said, 'Oh-h, such a beautiful calve! It'll jist
make such a wonderful supper fir me.' An he came over an said, '*Come*
with me, both o youse, because I been at hunting today and I hev not
found any deer or found nothing! But now I found a wonderful calve
that'll give me such a wonderful supper. Come with me!' an he catcht
the calve by the ear an he pulled hit. An Mary hanged on to the calve's
neck. He pulled it bi the ear an he led it in through the valley up to a
great castle among heavy rocks, bild among rocks, he pulled the calve bi
the ear.

An the calve went naturally, hit never done nothing, it jist went –
pulled by the ear by this great hunchback who was big and large and
ugly. He half pulled the calve, half forced it, an poor Mary she's
hinging on, she's wonderin what's gaunna happen but she doesn't
know, an she believed that the calve had told her 'tae have no fear'.
Then, up they cam tae this large castle in the cliff, wonderful castle
bild on the rocks! An the ugly big hunchback pulled them intae a large
room. On the floor wis a great big fire and a great pot boilan. The ugly
hunchback pulled an he shoved them in this room.

An he turned round to Mary, 'Now,' he said, '*you*, wumman, you
must make me somethin tae eat, because I been hunting today and I'm
starved from hunger, I need somethin to eat! And I've got myself ae
fattit calve that needs tae be *roastit* an *boiled* an made me fir somethin
tae eat. But I'm tired an A'm hungry. And *wumman*,' he said, 'if you
don't make me somethin tae eat, you shall die!'

Puir Mary, she wis upset, she wis trembling in her shoes. But she
knew that the calve had told her to be calm. The bull calve never said
a word, an poor Mary Rashiecoats she stood there.

And then the great hunchback said, 'Aer is my bed an there is my

fire! There is my *pot* an there is a knife ond the table! And I am tired
and weary, I am going to sleep. You'll kill that calve an put it in the
pot an make me somethin tae eat.' The great hunchback stretcht oot in
his bed, he was the uglies' hunchback you ever saw – hump on his back
and plooks on his face an long fingernails an curled toes – he wis the
mos uglies' hunchback ye ever saw! But he owned all this great castle.
An he's lyin in bed because he wis tired, and Mary an the puir calve is
standing there in the great hall with a great fire burnin, the great pots
by the fireside.

When lo an behold, the calve spoke tae Mary, 'Mary, don't be
afraid, little one. He'll be asleep fir five minutes an ten minutes an
fifteen minutes, but now and again his voice will speak tae you. But
listen: when his voice speaks to *you*, hit won't be talkin to you – hit'll be
talkin to *me* – but we'll be gone! Take the knife on the table and cut my
ear!'

'Oh,' Mary says, 'no way can A cut your ear.'

'Please,' said the calve, 'cut my ear, cut my ear. Go on, Mary, cut
behind my ear!'

'Why,' says Mary, 'should I cut yir ear?'

He says, 'Cut ma ear an get three drops o blood from my ear!'

So Mary took the knife, shakin an tremblin an worried, an wondert
what she'd do wi her wee calve.

He says, 'Cut ma ear, Mary, don't be afraid – it won't hurt me in
any way – an take three drops of blood from my ear. Put them beside
the fire, an then me an you shall escape.'

So Mary tuik the knife an she cut the calve's ear, behind his ear. An
she tuik three drops o blood an she put them – one drop there, one
drop there . . . ond her chair by the fireside.

The calve said tae Mary, 'Mary, search roond the kitchen an see if
ye can find some salt, a wee bit o salt.' And Mary run around the
kitchen, and lo an behold there was a bag o salt. She tuik a handful o
salt an the calve said, 'Get two handfuls o salt an find a wee bag, put it
in the bag!' So she take two handfuls o salt, put it in the bag an he says,
'Mary, *hang* on to that an don't let it go – fir the peril o yir life – don't
let it go!' said the calve.

Mary done what the calve told her, cause whitever the calve hed
told her seemt tae work out all the way an she believed in it.

'Now,' said the calve, 'climb on ma back,' an Mary climbed on the
calve's back. 'Put yir arms roond ma neck, Mary, an we shall be gone!'

So Mary put her arms around its neck, an the calve went out through the door an wis gone. And it went 'perump, pitterohn, pitterohn, pitterohn, pitterohn, pitterohn' runnin an runnin, rinnin an rinnin as fast he cuid go.

'Haud on, hold on, Mary,' he said. 'An it disna matter whitever happens, don't let go o my neck!' So wee Mary Rashiecoats didna ken whit tae do – she's haudin on to the calve's neck and de calve's rinnin on an runnin on an runnin on tae try tae get away from the ugly hunchback.

But back in the castle the wicked ogre hes wakent up, an he called fir food, '*Is it ready yet, wumman*, or I'll eat you alive! I'll eat you the way ye are!'

An the first drop o blood said, 'Not yet,' (the blood from the calve's ear).

The ogre stretcht back, he fell back, then he lay again, lay fir a few minutes . . . An Mary and the calve's rinnin on an runnin on an rinnin on! An the ogre said, 'Is hit not ready yet, I'm gettin hungry – I'm dyin fir somethin tae eat – hev ye roastit that calve fir me yet, wumman!'

And the second spot o blood said, 'Not yet, it's not ready yet but will soon be.'

And the ogre laid back wonst more. And then Mary and this calve run on an run on an run on once more! When lo an behold the ogre wakent up wonst again an he said, '*Wumman*, it must be ready now!'

An the third spot o blood said, 'Yes, it's ready, come an get it!'

And the ogre got up, he rubbed his eyes an he walkit tae the pot – it's empy. An he seen,* 'They have deceived me,' he said, 'they have deceived me, the're nothing in the pot!' An he pit his hands in, there were nothing in the pot. 'Where is ma calve an where is that wumman?' An wi his vision he looked out and he seen them in the distance: the black calve an Mary Rashiecoats on its back – they're rinnin on an rinnin on. 'Oh,' he says, 'they may run, but I'll get them before the night is out!' An the ogre set off as fast as he cuid, he's runnin as fast as he cuid.

An Mary an the wee black bull, they're goin an goin an goin an they're rinnin fast, whan they come to a lake – there was no more land – hit was only a lake. And the bull said tae Mary, 'Hold on, Mary, hold on, don't be afraid! Hold on tae my neck!' an Mary held on tae his neck.

* seen – realized

An the bull – inta the water – he swam an he swam an he swam. An Mary luikit back – she saw this evil ogre comin – he's comin paddlin as fast as he cuid be. An he's 'fw-woooph, fwi-i-iphf' soukin the water as he's comin. As fast as he souks, the faster they go; the more he souks, the closer they're gettin tae im. An the bull said, 'Mary, throw in the salt, throw in the salt!' An Mary tuik the bag o salt, she cowpit it in the water. And lo an behold when the minute she pit the salt in the water, there came a iceberg o salt, a mountain, a mountain o salt!

An the ogre came an he 'whoooo-opf' – soukin – an he's spittin an he's 'whooochk' – soukin – an he's spittin all the salt oot, because he couldnae take the salt, couldnae take the salt! An he ran an he ran, an he's soukin the salt an he's spittin the salt. Bi the time he spits the salt, Mary and the bull is getting farther and farther away . . . An he's spittin the salt and he's soukin the salt – try an get efter them.

And then lo an behold, they came tae the end o the water, Mary and the black bull comes tae the land once more. And when they came tae the land, it was a long narra valley – clifts an high sides – as high as the clifts cuid be.

But after he spat oot the water the ogre still made his way, the evil ogre made his way as fast as he cuid efter them. After he spat all the salt from his mouth he managed to scramble oot o the lake, an he's crawled ond his hands an knees, he spat the last mouthfu oot, said, 'I'll get them before the day is out!' An he's came through the valley.

An the bull says to Mary, 'Hang on, Mary, hang on, it's not much further now!' They rode through this narra clift, high precipice on each side, narra clift fir as far as the eye cuid see! An then de ogre's comin as fast as he cuid, hurryin as fast as he cuid!

He said, 'I'll get them before the night is out!'

They reached the middle o the valley, this high cliftin valley an Mary said tae the bull, 'We're not gaunna make it, the ogre's gaunna get hus!'

'Don't worry, Mary,' said the bull. He turnt roun an he said, 'Don't worry, Mary, luik i my ear, ma other ear, an see whit ye see!'

An Mary luikit in his ear an she pickit oot a pea, a wee green pea.

He says, '*Throw* it behind ye, throw it behind you, Mary.' An Mary tuik the wee green pea, she threw it behind – in the passage that they passed through – an the're whan the pea hit the land, there were a magnificent explosion! The whole valley seemed tae explode in fire an flame an the rocks came tumbling down bihind them. An the bull stoppit.

An he said, 'Now, Mary, this is hit. You don't need tae worry anymore, this is hit!'

'Tell me,' said Mary, 'tell me, little bull, what's gaun on?'

'Mary,' he said, 'don't worry, we must turn an go back.'

'Go back?' she said. 'No way am I gaunna go back!'

'We'll go back noo, Mary,' he said. 'Get aff my back an lead me back!'

Mary got aff his back and when she led him back, there was the ogre buried to the neck in boulders and rocks an only his head showin, his ugly head. An Mary and the bull walkit up, the bull stoppit beside the ogre an he said, 'Luik, Ogre, this is the final end fir you. Ye know what ye've done tae me!'

An the ogre said, 'Please, please, *set me free, set* me free!'

An the bull said, 'You set me free *first* before I set you free! You set me free!'

An the ogre said, 'All right, I'll set you free if you set me free.'

'No,' said the bull, 'I'll not! Till you set me free – *you* set *me* free first,' said the bull.

An the ogre spoke some words from his mouth. And lo an behold, after the ogre spoke this words . . . there was a great change . . . The bull wis gone fir evermore. An there stude the mos young handsomest man you ever saw in yir life! He stude there before Mary, an Mary wis upset – she didna know whit tae say – de most handsomes young man in the world you ever saw stood there dressed in green and a sword by his side.

'Now,' said the ogre, 'I've set you free – set me free!'

'I'll set you free,' said the young man, an he tuik his sword, he whipped the head of' the ogre! The ogre's head fell over an roll down in among the rocks.

Mary hid her eyes, she says, 'What's happened?'

An the young man pit his arms roond Mary an he says, 'Luik, Mary, little Mary Rashiecoats, it's a story I hev tae tell you: I was the prentice to that ogre an he had magical powers. Ye see, he reared me up an taught me all these wonderful things, but all these things were evil, I didna want none of his evilness anymore. An I tried tae escape, he turned me into a calve an sent me to the market tae get slaughtert, so that I could never indulge in his powers an tell anyone. But you, Mary, have saved me from disaster.' He put his arms roond Mary an he said, 'Mary, the ogre's castle is mine because it was mine before – hit'll be mine again – an you must come wi me an be my wife fir evermore!'

'But,' she says, 'what about puir Grandmother?'

'Don't worry about Grandmother, Mary,' he said, '*we'll* find her, an we'll bring her here with us. And she'll live here happy ever after,' and so they did! And that is the end o my story.

THE BOY AND THE BLACKSMITH

Many years ago there lived an aul blacksmith, and he had this wee smiddie bi the side o this wee village. He wis gettin up in years; he wis a good blacksmith when he was young, but he wis getting up in years. But one thing this blacksmith had was an auld naggin woman who wadna give him peace, and the only consolation he cuid get was tae escape tae the comfort o the smiddie an enjoy hissel in peace an quietness. Even though she was as bad, narkin and aggravatin him, she always brung him in his cup o tea every day at the same time. But times wis very hard fir im an he was very idle, he hedna got much work to dae one day.

'Ah but,' he says, 'well, ye never know who might come in – I'll build up the fire.'

So he bild up the fire, he blowed up the smiddie fire an he sat doon. Well, he sat by the fire fir a wee while, he's gazin intae the fire when a knock cam tae the door. An the auld man got up.

'Ah,' he said, 'prob'ly this is somebody fir me; but whoever they are, they dinnae hae nae horses cause I never heard nae horses' feet on the road.'

But he opened the smiddie door an in cam this boy, this young man, the finest-luikin young man he'd ever saw in his life – fair hair, blue eyes – an he wis dressed in green. An he had a woman on his back.

'Good mornin,' said the blacksmith tae the young man.

'Good mornin,' he said.

He said, 'What can A do fir ye?'

He said, 'Are you the village blacksmith?'

He said, 'I am – well, what's left o me.'

78

'You wouldna mind,' he said, 'if you would let me hev a shot of yir smiddie fire fir a few minutes?'

'Oh no,' the man said, 'I'm no wurkin very hard the day. If ye can – come in and help yirsel!' The old man thought he wis gaunnae use the fire, mebbe fir a heat or something.

So the young man cam in, an he took this bundle off his back, left it doon o' the floor. An the old man luikit, he wis amazed what he saw: it was a young woman – but she was the most ugliest-luikin woman he hed ever seen in his life – er legs wis backside-foremost, an her head was backside-foremost, back tae front! And her eyes wis closed – she wis as still-l-l as whit cuid be.

Noo the young man turned roond tae the blacksmith an he said, 'Luik, old man, you sit doon there and let me hev yir fire. An luik, pay no attention tae me – what I'm gaunna do – whatever ye see, don't let it bother ye!'

The aul blacksmith said, 'Fair enough, son!'

So the young man rakit up the fire an he catcht the young woman, he put her right on the top o the fire. And he covered her up wi the blazin coals. He went tae the bellows, an he blowed an he blowed an he blowed an he blowed an he blowed an he blowed! An he *blowed* her till he burnt her tae a cinder! Dher wur nothing left, nothing but er bones. Then he gaithert all the bones and he put them the top o the anvil; he says tae the auld man, 'You got a hammer on ye?'

The old man went o'er an he gied him one o thon raisin hammers, two-sided hammer. An he tuik the bones, he tappit the bones inta dust – till he got a wee heap on the top of the anvil – every single bone, he tapped it in dust. An the auld man 's sittin watchin him! He wis mesmerized, he didna ken what wis gaun on.

The young man never paid attention to the auld blacksmith, not one bit. Then, when he hed every single bone made intae dust, gathert all in a heap, he sput intae it, sput intae the dust. An he rumbled it wi his hands an he stude back fae it. Then the amazines thing ye ever seen happent . . . the dust begint tae swell an begint tae rise – an it rose up on the top o the anvil – it tuik into this form. An it tuik into the form o the bonniest young wumman ye hed ever seen in yir life! The beautifules young wumman ye'd ever seen in yir life an she steppit aff the anvil. The young man smiled at her, she pit her airms roond the young man's neck an she kissed him, she wis laughin and cheery. And the auld man never seen the likes o this afore in his life.

The young man pit his hand in his pocket, tuik oot seven gold sovereigns an he says tae the auld man, 'Here, you take that fir the shot o yir fire.' And he tuik the young lassie's airm. But before he walked oot the door he turnt tae the auld man, said, 'Luik, remember something: *never you do what ye see another person doin!*' And away he goes, closed the door.

But the aul blacksmith, he sut an he sut, an he sit fir a lang while. He put the seven gold sovereigns in his pocket. Then he heard the door openin and in comes this aul cratur o a woman.

'Are ye there, John?' she said.

'Ay,' he said, 'Margaret, I'm here.'

'Well,' she says, 'I brought ye a cup o tea. Hev you no got any wurk tae do instead o sittin there in yir chair? Are there nothing in the world you cuid find, cuid ye no get a job to do? You been sittin there noo fir the last two hours and ye've done nothing yet! How're we gaunna live? How're we gaunna survive? Here's yir tea!'

Auld John took the cup o tea up an he drunk hit. An he luiks at her, he thinks, 'I've spent a long time wi her, an she's jist about past hit. Wouldna A be better if I hed somebody young,' he said, 'tae have aroond the place instead o luikin at that auld wumman the rest o ma life?' So he drinks the tea as fast as he cuid. He had made up his mind – an afore you could say 'Jack Robinson' – he snappit the aul woman!

She says, 'Let me go! What are ye doin, aul man?'

He says, 'Come here – I want ye!'

He catches her an he bundles her – intae the fire wi her. And he haps her up. She's tryan tae get oot an he's haudin her doon wi a piece o iron. He's pumpin wi one hand an holdin her doon wi the other hand. An he pumpit an he pumpit, he blew an he pumpit an he blew. And her shrieks – you cuidha heard her oot o the smiddie – but fainter an fainter got her shrieks, ti he finally *burned* her tae an ash! Dher wur nothing left o her. The last wee bits o clothes belangin tae her, he put them in wi the tongs on the top o the fire . . . He burned her tae an ash! He's cleart back the ashes – an there wis the bones o her auld legs an her hands an her heid an her skull lyin i this – the way he placed her in the fire. He says, 'That's better!'

Gathert all the bones he cuid gather an he put them the top o the anvil, he choppit em, he rakit em up and he choppit em. And the wee bits that he cuid see that were hard, he choppit em again and rakit em, gathert them up in a nice wee heap. He got her a-all ground intae a fine dust! Fine powder. There's a good heap on the top o the anvil.

Then he stude back, says, 'This is the part I like the best.' So he sput in it an he rakit it wi his hands. . . . Nothing happent. He sput again intae hit – nothing – he tried hit fir about five or six times, but nothing happent.

So he sut an he scart't his heid. 'Well,' he said, 'that's hit. I cannae dae –' and then he remembered whit the wee laddie tellt him. 'Now,' he said, 'she's gone now.' And he felt kin o sad, ye ken, she wis gone. 'What am I gaunnae dae? I'm a murderer noo, whit am I gaunnae dae?'

So he finally rakit all her bits o bones intae an auld tin aff the anvil. He dug a hole in among the coal dross, he pit the tin in an he covert hit up. He went inta the hoose, he collectit his wee bits o belongings that he cuid get – what he thought he wad need – his razor an his things that he needit an his spare claes. He packit a wee bag, locked the smiddie door, lockit the wee hoose an off he goes – never tae show his face back the* smiddie again – i case somebody would find oot whit he'd dune.

So, he traivellt on an he traivellt on, here and there an he's gettin wee bits o jobs here an wee bits o jobs there, but this wis always botherin his mind. He traivellt on an he traivellt on. Noo he's been on the road fir about a year, but things begint tae get bad wi him. His claes begin tae get torn, his boots begin tae get worn, he cuidna get a penny nowhere. But he landed in this toon.

An he's walkin intae the toon, when he cam to an old man sittin ond a summer seat wi a white beard. So he sat doon beside him, he asked the auld man fir a match tae light his pipe. (There were nothing ind his pipe – just dross!) So he got tae crack wi the auld man.

The man said, 'Ye'll be gan doon tae the village tae the gala, tae the fair!'

He said, 'Are there a fair on i the toon?'

'Oh, there's a fair here every year,' he said, 'a great fair gaun on i the toon. They're comin from all over tae try their luck at the fair. What's yir trade?' the auld man said tae him.

He said, 'I'm a blacksmith.'

'Oh well,' he said, 'you shuid do well there. The're plenty jobs fir blacksmiths, they're needin plenty wurk. But, isn't it sad – hit'll no be the same fair as hit wis last year.'

'How's that?' said the auld smith.

* back the – back at the

'Well, ye ken, it's the king's daughter,' he said. 'The poor lassie she's paralysed, an she's the only daughter belonging tae the king. He adored her tae his heart, brother. She cannae walk – somethin cam ower her, she cannae walk an she's in a terrible state – er puir legs is twisted, her head is turned backside-foremost. An the king would give anythin i the worl if somebody cuid dae something for her! But they sent fir quacks an doctors all over the worl, but naebody can dae nothing for her. But,' he said, 'seein yir a blacksmith, could ye help me?' (He had this wee box of tools, ye see.) 'I have a wee job fir ye.'

The old smith says, 'Right!'

Go roond: an it wis a skillet the auld man hed, he said, 'Cuid ye mend that tae me?'

'Ay,' he said.

Tuik him roond the hoose an he gi'n him somethin tae eat. The auld smith mended the skillet, and he gien him two shillins. This was the first two shillins he had fir a long long while.

So the auld blacksmith made his wey doon tae the toon an the first place he cam tae wis a inn. He luikit, folk were gan oot an in an the fair wis goin – oh, it was a great gala day! 'Well,' he says, 'I canna help hit, fair here or fair there I mus go in here!' So he went in. An drink i these days wis very very cheap, bi the time he drunk his two shillins he wis well-on!

Then he cam oot an he walkit doon the street. Och, what a place he cam tae! But then he thocht tae his ainsel, 'I'm silly, I'm moich – me, a learned blacksmith – I cuid be well aff!' He says tae this man, 'Whaur aboots is the king's palace?'

What'd the man say, 'Up i the hill,' he said, 'that big place up i the hill – that's the palace. Up that drive, follow the drive!'

So wi the drink in his heid, he walked up tae the palace, an he wants tae see the king. The first he met wis a guard, king's guards.

The guard says, 'Where are ye goin aul man?'

He said, 'I want to see the king.'

An the guard said, 'What di ye want tae see the king fir?'

'I come,' he said, 'tae cure the king's daughter.'

'O-oh,' the guard said, 'jist a minute! If you come tae cure the king's daughter . . . where dae ye come fae? Are ye a doctor?'

'No, I'm not a doctor,' he said; 'I'm a blacksmith, an I come tae cure the king's daughter.'

Immediately he wis rushed intae the king's parlour an pit before the king and the queen. The auld blacksmith went down on the floor o' his knees an he tellt the king, 'I can cure yir daughter, Ir Majesty.'

'Well,' the king said, 'if you can cure my daughter, I'll make ye the richest man . . . ye a blacksmith?'

'Ay,' he said, 'I'm a blacksmith.'

'Well,' he said, 'I'll give ye a blacksmith's shop an everything ye require, and all the trade! I'll see that nobody else goes nowhere, excepts they comes to you – if you'd cure my lassie. Make her well is all I require! But,' he said, 'God help ye if anything waurse happens tae her!'

The aul smith said, 'Have you got a blacksmith shop?'

'Oh,' he said, 'they've got a blacksmith shop here; in fact, we've one fir wir own palace wurk an ye'll not be disturbed.'

'Well,' he said, 'hev ye plenty smiddie coal?'

'Come,' the king said, 'I'll show ye myself, I'll take ye myself tae the smiddie.' He went down, an all the smiths were at work in the palace smiddie. He said, 'Out, out, out, everyone out!' Locked the back door. He says, 'There – anvil, fire, everything tae yir heart's content.'

The auld smith kinneled up the fire, pumped it up – blowed it ti it wis goin! He says tae the king, 'Bring yir daughter doon here an I don't want disturbed! I don't want disturbed.'

O-oh, jist within minutes the young lassie wis cairried doon o' the stretcher an placed i the smiddie. The auld man says, 'Now, everybody out!' Closed the door. An the young lassie's lyin, legs twistit, head backside-foremost – the identical tae the young wumman that he had seen in the smiddie a long time ago! Smith said, 'If he can dae it, so can I!'

So he kinnelt up the fire an he placed her ond the fire. He blowed, and he pumpit an he blowed an he blowed, an he blowed an he blowed an he blowed an he blowed. And he *burnt* her ti there were no a thing left. (Noo, he had tellt the king tae come back in two hoors. 'Two hoors,' he tellt the king, 'yir daughter'll be as well as cuid be.')

So, efter he collectit all the bones oot the fire, he put them on the top o the anvil. He got the hammer and he choppit an he choppit, he grint them all doon and he gathered them all up, put them on the top o the anvil. An he sput in it. He waitit. He mixed hit again. An he sput an he waitit. But he sput an he waitit, he sput an he waitit, he sput an he waitit. But no, there was no answer, nothing wad happent.

Then he heard a knock at the door. He says, 'That's them comin fir me. Ach well – it's death fir me an the're nothin I can dae aboot hit.'

He opened the door, and in cam the young laddie, brother! In walked the young laddie an he looked at the blacksmith.

'Didn't I tell you,' he said, 'a long time ago, *not tae dae whit ye see another body daein!*' And he drew his hand, he hut the blacksmith a welt the side o the heid and knockit him scatterin across the floor! 'Now,' he says, 'sit there an don't move!'

Young laddie gaithert the ashes that wis scattert the top o the anvil in his hands, an he sput in them. Then he mixt them up, an he waitit . . . A thing like reek cam oot o the anvil aff o the bones, a thing like reek cam oot. Then the thing took a form . . . the mos beautiful lassie ye ever seen – the king's daughter back – laughin and smilin like the're nothing happened!

And he said, 'You sit, don't move! Don't you move one move! Sit an wait till we're gone before you open that door!' He walked over an he pit his hand inta his pocket, 'But, I'm no gaun tae lea ye bare-handed –' he says, 'haud yir hand!' tae the aul blacksmith. 'Noo, remember again: *never never dae whit ye see another body daein!*' 'Nother seven gold sovereigns in the aul blacksmith's hand. 'Noo,' he says, remember, never let hit happen again as long as ye live! And don't open that door till we're gone.'

Jist like that the young laddie an lassie walkit oot. An then there were a clappin o hands an the music startit, and everything died away. De aul blacksmith sut an he sut and he sut . . .

Then he heard a knock at the door. He got up and he opened the door, in cam his aul wumman.

She said, 'Are ye there, John?'

'Aye,' he said, 'God bless ma soul an –'

She said, 'Dae ye never think o doin any kin o wurk atall, do ye sit an sleep all day? Nae wonder we're puir.' She said, 'Here's yir wee cup o tea – drink hit up – I see a man comin alang the road wi a horse, an you better get the fire kindled up!'

'Thank you, Maggie,' he said, 'thank God, Maggie, thank you, my doll, my darlin, thank you!' An he pit his airms roon her, he kisst her.

She says, 'Ach ye go, John, what dae ye think yir daein? It's no like you ataa! Were ye asleep, were ye dreamin?'

'Mebbe,' he said, 'A wis dreamin, Maggie, mebbe A wisna. A better kinnel the fire up.' He luikit doon: here's a man comin doon the road wi a pair o Clydesdale horses.

Tuik the horses into the smiddie, man pit the horses in the smiddie, he said, 'John, A want a set o shoes.'

'Well,' he says, 'wait a minute, A hev tae go intae the hoose fir some nails. A keep em i the hoose.'

Man says, 'I'll jist light ma pipe bi the smiddie fire ti ye come back.'

Aul Jock went roond the hoose. He says to the aul woman . . .

She says, 'Ye've nae tobacca.'

He says, 'A want ma pipe an my tobacca.'

She says, 'We need tobacca – it's finished an ye'll hev tae wait till we get money – when ye get them horses shod. Ye ken we've got nae money fir tobacca.'

Shoves his hand i his pocket, he said, 'We've nae money hev we?' Hand i his pocket, brother – seven gold sovereigns in his pocket – he says, 'Here, Maggie.'

She says, 'The name o God, where you got that?'

He said, 'I made that while you thocht I wis sleepin.' An that's the last o ma story. So ye can believe that – if hit's true or a lie!

THE HAPPY MAN'S SHIRT

Many many years ago there once lived a king in this large kingdom an he had a lovely queen an two lovely daughters. He had everything that he required under the sun: he had soldiers who hed fought for him, wisemen in his kingdom whom he loved, a beautiful queen who loved him dearly, the most beautiful horses for many many kingdoms around . . . But still he was very very sad. Even when his little princesses used to come and throw their arms roond their daddy's neck an cuddle im, kiss him, an his queen used to come and sit doon beside him, he still felt very sad. Nothing in the world seemed tae make him happy. When his troops rode out an fought a battle, won, came home an told him they had won another great battle against invadin armies, the king was still as sad as ever. An bi the king bein sad, all the people in the country were – everyone wis sad. An the king was just a young king – everyone wondered why he was so sad.

Then one day the queen said, 'We can't jist go on like this fir evermore. We must help our king tae try an get rid of his sadness, make him happy once more. So she called the wisest man in the court, she said, 'I want you to make the king happy.'

'Oh,' the wises man said, 'I've heard the stories an I've saw the king, but there's little I can do fir him.'

'There must be something,' said the queen, 'you could do. You are the wisest man in the whole kingdom, the most knowledgeable and the most understanding – there mus be something you cuid do to make him happy.'

'Well, Ir Majesty,' said the Wiseman, 'there's only one thing'll make yir king happy: he must find a happy man, a *real* happy man, and he must wear that happy man's shirt!'

'Well,' sayd the queen, 'it's not a very hard thing to ask, there must be plenty happy men in the kingdom.'

So the very next day she called the king before her, she said, 'Our Majesty, I love you, you are my husband and you are the king. But we are very sad fir you, because you are so sad an down-heartit – you make everyone in the kingdom sad!'

An the king said, 'My dear, I'm just natural . . . it's jist how A feel. If there were something A cuid do to make me happy, then I would do it to please everyone. But it's jist how I am an I can't help it.'

'There is one solution, my lord,' she says, 'if you will do it for me.'

The king loved his queen very much an there's nothing in the world he wadna do for his queen, he said, 'What must I do to make me happy? Everything seems natural to me –'

'But you're so gloomy,' says the queen, 'you don't smile, you're never happy and you make everyone sad jist by luikin at you!'

'Well,' says the king, 'tell me what I must do.'

An the queen said, 'You must find a happy man's shirt, wear his shirt and then you'll be happy, an the whole kingdom will be . . . everyone'll be happy.'

'Well, bring to me a happy man,' said the king, 'an I'll wear his shirt. Bring him to me an I'll try it just to please you.'

So the next morning the queen sent couriers all over the kingdom lookin for a happy man. But lo an behold, they came draggling back on horseback, they came draggling back on foot, no one could find a happy man – everyone was sad – because the king was! An then the king waitit an the king waitit an the king waitit, but no one ever turned up, he got sadder and sadder. An then the queen could stand it no longer, she called fir the Wiseman once more. Right before the king and the queen came the Wiseman.

'Tell Ir Majesty the King,' said de queen, 'what you told me to make him happy.'

'I told you, Your Majesty, I told you,' he said, 'that the only thing tae make him happy is a happy man's shirt!'

'But,' she says, 'we've searched the whole kingdom an we can't find a happy man's shirt fir the king. Our couriers an wir soldiers have rode the kingdom over an there doesn't seem to be a happy man in the whole kingdom.

'All because the king is unhappy,' said the Wiseman.

'Everyone has searched.'

'Not,' said the Wiseman, 'everyone hes not searched.'

'Are there someone who hes not searched?' said the queen.

'Yes,' said the Wiseman, 'the king himself has not searched fir a happy man's shirt! An I believe that *he* is the only one that can really find a happy man's shirt.'

So the king was willin, just tae keep the queen happy an keep the whole country happy, he would set out the next morning to find a happy man an bring back a happy man's shirt. An true to his word, even though the king was sad, he took little possessions with him, all the clothes that he stude in, on his back, an he walked away from the palace. He walkit on his way – without a penny, without food, without nothing – he swore he would not come back till he would find a happy man an get a happy man's shirt. Well, everyone at the palace lined up to see the king on his way, they askit him tae take a horse with him, they askit him to take guards with him.

'No,' says the king, 'I shall take nothing. I shall go as I am and I won't return until I find a happy man – I can get his shirt!'

So naturally, everybody bade 'farewell' to the king. An the king was gone, the king travelled on an the king traivellt fir days, he found little jobs here an he begged little bits o food along the way. An the farther he went into the wilderness . . . he'd travellt fir many many miles, he wis gone for months, he never returnt. An the queen got worried about this.

She called ten of her great soldiers together, she says to the captain 'Luik, I can't stand it anymore without* the king bein gone: you must set out an bring him back – happy or unhappy – I would rather have him here unhappy than not have him atall. So go,' she told the soldiers, 'and find the king! Bring him back tae me even suppose he never finds a happy man's shirt.' So the very next mornin away rode ten of the king's soldiers an the captain, they rode out in their search fir the king.

Now de king he is travelling far and travelled wide, an the more he's traivellt his boots gets worn, his coat gets worn, he gets dusty an he gets ragged, an he's travelled fir many many months. He's askin everybody along the way that he came to – farmers, crofters, woodcutters, shepherds – are they happy?

And everyone says, 'No, we're not happy, we are very sad.'

An the king said tae himself, 'Are there not a happy man in this

* without – with

country of mine, are there not a happy person in the land? Am I – is everyone like me – mebbe it's my problem, mebbe I'm the cause of hit! Where in the world am I going to find a happy man?'

Till one day, he came walkin over this hill an down he comes to a little brook. Sittin by the side of the brook with a fire was a beggarman, with a long coat an a long beard, an he's sittin by the fire. He's got a little can an he's holdin it with a stick on the fire, he's singin tae himself an he's boilan himself some tea on the fire.

The king walks doon, the king says, 'Hello!'

The beggarman looks up, he sees this man standin before him dressed in clothes that wonst were beautiful but now were ragged and torn, boots that wonst were beautiful but now were worn through . . . 'Ha-ha!' says the tramp, 'good morning!' says the beggarman, 'good morning!'

'Good morning,' says the king, 'I see you're busy havin yir breakfast.'

'I am,' says the beggarman, 'it's little I have fir breakfast, but we must make it do! It's all we hev,' and he smiled an he laughed at the king.

An when he smiled and laughed at the king, it gladdened the king's heart. The king said, 'Tell me something, who are you?'

An the man said, 'I am a beggarman. Some people call me a "tramp", some people call me a "tink", but I don't care what they call me, as long as they don't call me "down". I'm always on my way, travelling all over the country an seein many things, seein many sights, havin a little to eat – when A haven't got it, I can sleep without it.'

'Done!' says the king, 'you mus be a real happy man.'

'"Happy man"!' said the beggarman. 'Of course I'm happy! I'm the happiest man in the world.'

The king got down an he sat beside him, now the king became interestit. De beggarman took the little can off the fire; he had a little tin mug an he halft it in two – he said to the king – 'Would you like somethin to drink?' An the king accepted it – whitever he had in his can – black tea without sugar or milk.

And the beggarman drunk it up, he smacked his lips an said, 'Isn't that wonderful!' And he smiled at the king.

The king tastit it, it wis bitter an strong, it tasted horrible. An the king drank hit down, he smiled back. An this was the first time the king hed ever smiled fir years. The king felt good about this.

An the beggarman rubbed his hands together, he said, 'You know, it's wonderful tae be alive on a beautiful day like this, even though ye've only got some tea and nothing to eat.'

The king was amazed, he at last had met the most happies man he had ever met fir years. 'Tell me something,' says the king, 'why is it you're so happy?'

'Well, tae tell ye the truth,' said the man, 'why shuid I not be happy? Because I have nothing fir anyone to steal, I have nothing to give anyone, I hev nothing fir anyone to take off me an A never hurt anyone, that's why I'm happy. I don't owe a penny – no one cuid steal hit from me – A cannae give nobody a penny. All I have is the clothes on my back and the boots on ma feet, I travel on the worl an I try tae spread a little happiness as I go along my way.'

The king said, 'Luik, dae you know who I am?'

'No,' said the man, 'ye're jist like me – a beggar.'

'No,' said the king, 'I am not a beggar, I am the king!'

'You are the king!' said the beggarman. An he startit, 'Ha-ha-ha-haaaa, ha-ha!' and he clappit his hands, he went down on his knees, an he laught an he laught an he laught ti the tears run down his cheeks.

And when the king saw the beggarman laughin, the king startit tae laugh at the actions o the beggarman, an the king laught and the king laught ti the tears luik down the king's cheeks. There was the king an the beggarman down on their knees in front of each other in front o the fire, laughin to each other ti the tears run down their cheeks, when who rode over the hill but ten soldiers on horseback an the captain o the guards!

The captain and ten of his troop pulled their horses to a stop. For there before them they saw: the king in rags beside a beggarman, both them on their knees beside the little fire laughin fit tae kill each other with a wee drum of tea between them, and the tears were streamin down their cheeks. The beggarman wis laughin because the king hed said he's the king. An they're laughin an they're laughin an they're laughin tae each other. The captain o the guards had never . . . he recognized the king . . . but he'd never saw the king so happy in his life. They rode down, they all jumped off an surroundit the beggarman. An when the beggarman saw, all surrounded by the soldiers, he stude up an so did the king. All the soldiers bowed, 'Ir Majesty,' they said, 'at last we have found you, we have found you, Ir Majesty.'

And the beggarman was amazed, the beggarman went doon on his knees in front o the king, 'I'm sorry, Ma Majesty, I am sorry, My King. I apologize for performin in bifore you.'

'Performin before me?' said the king. 'I really am the king, you know!'

'I'm sorry,' says the beggarman, 'I insultit you an upset –'

'Insultit me an upset me?' said the king. 'You've made me the happies man in this world! I hev never laughed so much in all my life an I hev never met a happier man. Pray tell me, would ye do me one favour?'

The beggarman went doon on his knees, he held up his two hands as if he wis about to pray an he said tae the king, 'Ir Majesty, anything you ask of me – what I have I stand in, is my rags – but anything that you want from me, I will do it fir you, My King.'

The king said, 'Luik, I've been searchin fir a happy man fir many many months – you're the only one I've ever met – an A'll never be *real* happy till I can wear a happy man's shirt! Please,' said de king, 'give me yir shirt!'

And then the beggarman startit tae laugh again, 'Ha-ha-ha-haaaaa, ha-haaa,' said the beggar an the beggar laughed an the beggar laughed ti the tears run down his cheeks. An the king startit tae laugh all over again, an all the troopers joint, the troopers startit tae laugh. Fir close on ten minutes everyone laughed, till the beggarman couldn't stand any longer.

Then the king said, 'Please tell me, what's so funny?'

An the beggarman bared his coat, he said, 'Ir Majesty, you ask me fir something I don't possess, I don't even have a shirt!'

The king walked over, he put his arms roond the beggarman an he called fir a horse, an he says, 'Beggarman, you'll never want for another shirt – as long as you live.' He demanded two o the troopers to go on one horse, him and the beggarman got on the other horse an they rode back to the palace before the queen. When the king entered the palace everyone wis happy to see the king returned. An the king walked in his rags with the beggarman by the hand into the queen's chamber. The queen heard the gigglin, the laughin comin down the corridor.

'Oh,' she said, 'Ir Majesty – returned – he's come home!'

And this was the king and the beggarman, both were in rags. The king was still laughin, he couldna speak to the queen an he wis sayin, 'An I met him – ha-ha, ha-ha, ha-haaa-haaa, an I met him an he sat there . . .' The king laught an he laught an he laught, till he finally realized he was back home in his own palace an he told the queen the story: 'I set out to find a happy man an wear a happy man's shirt. And the mos happies man A ever met in my life didn't even have a shirt! But,' he said, 'he'll have many many shirts – all the shirts that he cuid ever wear – an he will stay with me in this palace, be my companion fir the rest o my days.'

And so the beggar did – steyed wi the king the rest o his days. And every night when the king sat at the table tae take his dinner, the beggarman had tae turn his back to the king when he got his food, because they cuidna look at each other – when they luikit at each other both o them wad burst out laughin – an then the meal would be destroyed. That made the queen very happy, an that is the end o my story!

GEORGE BUCHANAN THE KING'S FOOL

Noo, tae let ye understand afore the story starts, George Buchanan wis only a simple laddie that stayed with his faither an mother in this wee croft. An he'd never dune nothing, but everybody treatit him as a fool. But he wisna foolish, he wis too fly! So he actit the fool because he wis that fly, ye see.

But one day he was on the road, he wis only aboot fifteen or sixteen at the time an he sees this knight come a-ridin on this horse. But he didna ken hit wis a king, he thought it wis a knight. (This is away back when the king used tae travel roond his subjects unknown tae see what like the folk really was, way back in the ninth an tenth century a king wad dress hissel as a knight an set sail through the country tae see how the people wis gettin treatit. They didna ken who he was, but he wis their king aa the time.)

Anyway, he set sail an he's ridin on, he comes tae this wee fairm at the roadside. Ah, it wis jist a wee stane buildin o hoose, an this laddie wi his bare feet, a laddie aboot sixteen he's standin i the middle o the road. King stops his horse, 'Let me pass by,' he said, 'ye want me to run ye doon?'

He said, 'You cuidna run me down, knight, you cuidna run me down.'

He said, 'Why no could I run ye down?'

He said, 'Before ye cuid run me doon, ye hev tae come aff yir horse t' run me doon – *you* cuidna run me doon on horseback. You'll no run me down, yir *horse* wad run me doon – no you!'

'Very good,' says the king, 'very good, very good! What's yir name?'

He says, 'My name is George Buchanan.'

'Where dae ye come fae?'

He says, 'Doon fae that croft doon there.'

The king cracks a guid while tae im, says, 'What is yir faither daein?'

'Well,' he said, 'tae tell ye the truth, knight, my faither's *makin bad worse.*'

'God bless me,' sayd the king, '"he's makin bad worse" – that's terrible. An wha is yir sister daein?'

He said, 'My sister's *greetin fir the fun she had last year.*'

'Well, by God,' said the king, 'ye'll have tae tell me . . . ye're a better man an me, I dinna ken wha you ken . . . What *is* yir faither daein?'

'Well, I'll tell ye what my faither's daein,' he said. 'Luik, hit's rainin.'

'Ay,' says the king, 'hit's rainin.'

'Well, my faither cut a wee taste hay last week,' he said, 'an it's wat, he's shakin it oot tae dry an it's rainin: he's "makin bad worse".'

'Aye,' says the king, 'that's fair enough. But what's yir sister daein – hoo cuid she be "greetin fir the fun she had last year"?'

He said, 'My sister's haein a wean – she's "greetin fir de fun she had last year"!'

'Well, by God,' says the king, 'I never heard the like o that. But I'll tell ye something . . . what's yir name?'

He said, 'George Buchanan.'

'Well, I tell ye, George,' he said, 'I'm gan doon tae the ale-hoose doon the toon there, an I want you . . . ye're suppose tae be clever.'

'Well,' says George, 'I'm as clever as what ye cuid be.'

'I want you to meet me tomorrow,' he says, 'George, *luikin at me no luikin at me.*'

'Hmm,' George says, 'that's funny.'

'An,' he says, '*ridin an no ridin.*'

'Oh,' says George.

'An *claes an nae claes,*' says the king, 'an I'll be waitin on ye. If you do that fir me,' he says, 'you'll be my man fir evermore!'

'Well,' says George Buchanan, 'ye pit me tae a task noo,' he says tae the knight. (He didna ken hit wis the king!)

Anyway, away goes the knight, the king, ridin into the toon. Noo, in the toon was a wee ale-hoose, ye see.

George goes back, he meets his faither an he tells his faither. Faither said, 'Hoo're ye gaunna dae that?'

'Well,' he said, 'I dinna ken . . .'

His faither had a wee bit net, herrin net ower the stack fir catchin fish. George stripped hissel nakit and he wapped hissel wi the wee bit net, a bit fish net. He got his faither's goat bi the halter an away he goes the next mornin right tae the ale-hoose where the king wis stayin, one fit on the ground, the other fit on the goat's back. He wappit hissel in the net an he's luikin at the king side-on as he's comin tae the ale-hoose. The king wis waitan on him comin. An he wis luikin at him an no luikin at him, George's luikin side-on, he wis dressed an no dressed an he wis ridin an no ridin.

'Well,' says the king, 'I never seen that before. That's true: ye're dressed an no dressed, ye've claes an nae claes,' (a bit o net, see) 'an his fit on the goat's back but his ither fit wis on the ground. Well, George, ye've won yir point,' he said. 'Fae now on, ye'll be my man.' So that's the first beginnin why George Buchanan the King's Fool met up wi the king. The king turned roon an tellt George, 'I am the king!'

An George bowed doon, he met the king, 'Well, Ir Majesty, I'm sorry,' he said, 'I'm sorry fir the things I've dune.'

'No, George,' he said, 'ye mightna be sorry. Fae now on you'll be my man.' An fra then on he wis known as George Buchanan the King's Fool.

So, the next day George set out wi the king – because the king thought the world o im. Onyway, on rodes George an the king an they were good mates efter this. They rode tae this toon, an the king thought he wad play a trick on George, ye see! They cam tae this ale-hoose, oh, they both wis dyin wi hunger . . . They're on their rounds roond the country, see!

'You hold the horses, George, an see that they get a guid thing tae bite, see they get something guid tae eat,' he says, 'an I'll send ye oot some dinner.' In goes the king tae the cook-house, ye see. He says tae the cook, 'Have ye got a bone, a bare bare bone?'

'Well,' said the cook, 'we're after makin * some soup, the're bound tae be a lot o bare bones lyin around.'

'Well,' he said, 'pit one on a plate an give it out tae my man holdin the horses out on the street.'

Away they go, an the cook pickit the barest bone – there werena as much flesh on hit at wad hae feed a robin – on a bare plate, out tae George. George is haudin the horses, ye see. Noo de king hed warned George afore he went inta the ale-hoose, 'George, see that ma horse gets plenty tae eat! An I'll send ye oot somethin tae eat.' Out comes

* we're after makin – we've just made

the maid wi this bone on the plate, she said, 'The king sent this out fir yir dinner.'

George luikit – bare bone, not nothing ond it, jist white-washt. 'Guid enough,' says George, 'okay.' George took the bane, never said a word. Oot in front o the ale-house wis a lovely park, lovely grass tae that, tae the horses' fetlocks. George goes an tied his own horse among the beautiful * grass that he cuid get. He taks the king's horse an he ties it bi hits mooth tae a rock, tae a big stane. He's got his teeth close tae the stane as he cuid get an he tied hit securely.

De king set on, oh, the king hed a beautiful lunch, ye ken, roast chicken an everything, ken! Out he comes. George's horse is eatin the beautiful grass. 'Well, George,' he said, 'did you enjoy your dinner?'

'Ay,' he said, 'King, I enjoyed my dinner, it wis beautiful.'

He said, 'I see yir horse is enjoyin itsel; what about my horse, George?'

'Oh,' he said, 'yir horse is gettin luikit efter.'

'Ye enjoy your dinner?'

He said, 'I enjoyed my dinner same as yir horse is enjoyin hits dinner, Ir Majesty.'

'But, George,' he said, 'my horse is eatin tied tae a rock!'

'Well,' he said, 'Ir Majesty, my dinner wis a bone: *the nearer the bone the sweeter the meat, the nearer the rock the sweeter the grass!'*

An the king pit his hand the top o George's back, he gien im a clap, he clapped George on the back, says, 'Come on, George, I'll get ye somethin guid tae eat!' An he tuik George in, he gien him the best tightener in the worl, see? Anyway, that was hit – got each other.

So, away he goes wi him the next day. They rode on, further on ti they came tae another toon. An the king did this this time: he tied the horses up – a good feed – an he inta the best hotel he cuid get, the king got the best dinner fir him an George he cuid.

'You know, George,' he said, 'we'll have a good supper tonight in the town an me and you'll heve everything in the world.' He tuik im up an he ordered the best room fir George an the best room fir hissel. An up goes the king tae this room, he calls fir George.

'Well,' says George, 'what is hit, Our Majesty?'

'Well, George,' he said, 'I've had a good supper.'

'Yes,' he said, 'Ir Majesty, ye've had a guid supper; ye've a guid bed?'

He said, 'Yes, A've a guid bed an A hev everything I need. But –'

* beautiful – best

'But,' he says, 'what do ye want from me?'

'George,' he said, 'A want ye tae do one thing fir me: George, I cuid do with a lovely *piece o chicken*.'

He said, 'Ir Majesty, ye no get nae supper?'

'Aye, George, I got a lovely supper,' he said, 'aye, A got a lovely supper. But that's no what A want – I want a *piece o chicken*.'

'Oh, I see,' says George, 'ye want "a piece o chicken". I'll get ye "a piece o chicken", Yir Majesty.'

Away goes George down the street. De first thing he meets wis an aul wumman in the street, ye ken, one o these aul down-an-out wummen. He says tae the aul wumman, oh, she's aboot eichty years of age, ken, he says, 'Ye want tae earn a sovereign?'

'Ay, laddie,' she says, 'A cuid dae* earnin a sovereign.'

He says, 'Ye'll no need tae dae anything fir hit; ye've on'y jist got tae mak an appearance an that's aa: my king is luikin fir "a chicken".'

'Ah, but,' she said, 'laddie, I'm nae chicken.'

'But,' he says, 'that's no matter, I dinna want a chicken; you jist come wi me up the stairs tae the king's –'

'Oh,' she said, 'laddie, I cuidna go tae the king's . . . ye'll get me banisht, ye'll get me jailt if I go . . .'

'My king,' he says, 'rode inta de toon tonight . . .' he tellt the auld wumman, see! 'An he thinks I dinna ken what he wants. He's hed a guid supper an he haen a guid drink, ye see, an he's lyin i his bed, he asked me tae gae an get him *a chicken*. An I'm no gaunnae get him nae chicken; but *you* come wi me up tae his room, mak an appearance an I'll gie ye a gold sovereign!' Noo, a gold sovereign 's an awfae money in these times.

'All right,' she says, 'if that's aa ye want, laddie, I'll go wi ye.'

Right, away goes George Buchanan an he takes the aul mort wi him – oh, an aul mort about seventy an her nose touchin her chin! An the king's lyin back in his bed, aw, lying back in his bed after a guid feed an his belly full, ken, jist . . . a young mort he's luikin fir, ken!

George knocks o' the door – 'bump, bump, bump.'

'Come in, come in, come in!' says the king.

'It's me,' says George.

'Oh, it's you,' he says, 'George. Oh yes, did ye do what I told you, George? Did ye get me a lovely *piece o chicken*?'

* cuid dae – could do with

'Yes,' said George, 'I'm here.'

'Did ye get me my *chicken*, George?'

'No, no, Yir Majesty,' he said, 'I cuidna get ye a chicken, but I got ye a fine *auld hen!*'

'Get that out o here,' he said, 'George! Get her out o here – I never asked fir an "auld hen", it's a "young chicken" I want!'

'Well,' he says, 'Ir Majesty, I cuidna get ye a chicken, I thought the next thing best wis an auld hen.'

'I don't want no "aul hen",' says the king, an then it dawnt on the king that George kent what he wis wantin, ye see!

But anyway, they steyed there fir a couple o days. The king says tae George, 'You're ey hangin aboot here, George. Ye no go oot among the young folk an enjoy yirsel, George?'

'Ach,' he says tae the king, 'nae enjoyment fir me knockin aboot these young folk.'

'Well,' he said, 'away down an enjoy yirself. Don't bother me, George, away an enjoy yirsel i the town; we're only here fir a short time.'

Away goes George oot through the toon. The end o the toon wis a brig, a brig crossin the burn. George walkit ower the brig, but on the top o the brig he meets a drunk man. In these days every man carried his sword.

He says tae George, 'Where are ye goin?'

George said, 'I'm gaun over the brig.'

'No,' says the man, 'ye're no gaun over this brig the night!'

'Ah, but,' says George, 'I'm gaun ower the brig, I'm gaun fir a walk.'

'Oh,' he says, 'ye're no passin me!'

George says, 'I'm gan over de bridge!'

'No,' says the man, 'you're no gaun over de bridge.' He was a knight tae! An he drew his sword, he said, 'Past me you must go if ye want tae go oer the brig.'

'Well,' said George, 'there's only one thing fir hit,' George he drew his sword an the two o them fought. An George whippit – he whippit the man's heid – an the heid fell ower the brig, head clean fae the shoulders, see? Noo, cuttin a body's heid aff in these days wis an awfae offence; hit was murder, tae intend tae be hangt in these days. George wis in an awfa state, ye see, the man's body's lyin noo nae heid, top the brig.* George didna ken what tae dae. 'The're only one cure,' he said. Back tae the king he goes.

* lyin noo nae heid, top the brig – lying headless on the bridge

'Bump, bump' – knock o' the door.

'What is hit noo?' says the king.

'It's me,' says George.

'George,' he said, 'didn't I tell ye tae go an enjoy yirsel?'

'Well,' he said, 'Majesty, I enjoyed mysel. But I want tae come fir forgiveness.'

'George,' he says, 'what do you want forgiveness for?'

He says, 'Majesty, can I speak tae ye a minute?'

'Right, George,' he said, 'come in. Ye know I'm busy, I'm nearly asleep.'

'Cannae help ye,' says George, 'if ye're asleep or no, ye must speak tae me!'

In comes George Buchanan tae the king, the king's lyin in his bed. King o the whole country, he cuid dae onything for ye. 'What is it now, George?' he said.

He said, 'Ir Majesty, I'm sorry tae disturb ye, but you tellt me tae go doon the toon fir a walk.'

'Right,' says the king, 'I tellt ye "go tae the toon".'

'An,' he says, 'A wis enjoyin masel, and the end o the toon I cam tae a brig.'

'Yes,' says the king, 'true enough, the're a brig end o the toon.'

'An,' he says, 'I walkit over de bridge.'

'Right,' says the king, 'true enough. George, what ye worryin aboot?'

'Nothing, Ir Majesty, A'm no worryin aboot nothing. But on the top o the brig I met a knight.'

'Well,' sayd the king, 'guid enough.'

'An,' he says, 'the knight wadna let me cross the brig.'

'Guid,' says the king, 'an whit di' ye dae aboot it?'

He said, 'He drew his sword.'

'Well,' said the king, 'whit di' you dae?'

'Well,' he said, 'Ir Majesty, I drew my sword tae, an we hed a fight.'

'Well,' said the king . . . king get excited noo, ye ken! 'Did yese hae a guid fight?'

'Yes.'

'I'm glad ye enjoyed yirsel!'

'Oh, A enjoyed masel,' he said, 'Ir Majesty.'

'But,' he said, 'what did ye dae ye want me tae pardon ye fir?'

'Well,' he said, 'A *knockit his hat over the brig.*'

'Tut, tut,' said the king, 'that's nothing – what dae ye –'

He said, 'I want ye to pardon me fir *knockin his hat over the bridge.*'

'Of course, George,' he said, 'ye're pardoned, ye're pardoned as pardoned cuid be!'

'Well, Ir Majesty,' he said, 'his head wis in the hat!'

Well, the wonst he pardoned him fir knockin his hat oer the brig, he cuidna dae naethin aboot hit. Well, him and George got on after that like wildfire, they were the best friends in the worl an George remaint wi the king ti the rest o his days. An there's millions o stories tellt about George Buchanan the King's Fool . . .

JACK AND THE HORSE'S SKIN

Wonst upon a time there lived this fairmer an he had two sons. He'd married late in life and his first son he thocht the worl o, he wadna let him du nothin, he treatit im like the lamb o God, see? But two-three year hed passed an he had another son. When this son wis born his wife deid at childbirth. An he wis so heart-broken at lossin his wife, he blamed the son the young laddie fir the cause o it, and he hatit this laddie that he'd never hated nothin in life before! He said, 'I'll look efter ye an take care o ye, but ye'll never get nothing aff me. A'll see that ye survive, but that's aa ye'll ever get. You'll work for everything you get in this place, everything you get – ye'll work fir! And whan I dee you'll never get one penny.' He never tellt this tae the laddie, but this is his promise he made.

But onyway, the two boys growed up together. An the auldest brother never needed tae dae a haet, jist walkit about the fairm shootin here an shootin there enjoyin hissel. But the youngest brother, he hed tae dae everything aboot the fairm, he done every single thing! An finally the fairmer dee'd, see! An he left in his will that the youngest brother wasn't tae get one single ha'penny, 'Give him nothing,' he said, 'give him nothing. Give him the old cotter's hoose at the fit o the road, let him stay in hit fir the rest o his days, an fae that day on give him nothing!' Noo, the young brother's name wis Jack, an puir Jack wis turned oot wantin a ha'penny an the other brother got everything he wantit, the hale farm – cattle, everything under the sun. An he said, 'Remember, dinna even treat him guid; if ye see him on the road,' the auld father used tae tell him, 'dinna even speak tae him.'

But anyway, Jack got doon tae this wee hoose the fit o the roadend – free – that's aa he got, a free hoose fir the rest o his days. No work, nothin, an his brother wadna give him daylight. His brother used tae drive wi a carriage and pair by an he'd mairried this gran bene mort. But this wumman the auldest brother mairried she wis the miserablest wumman in de worl, see!

But Jack mairried this wee lassie i the toon, an wi gettin a wee job here an a wee job there, fiddlin here an fiddlin there, he managed tae raise up one wee lassie he had, reart her up ti she wis aboot six or seven year auld. But oh, things begint tae go bad wi im. But the lassie he mairriet wis the nicest young lassie in the worl, ken, an she agreed everything wi im, ken! She said, 'Ye cuidna help hit – he wis one o these misfortunes o life and cuidna help hit.'

So one day things wis so very bad wi im he says tae her, 'Luik, we hevna even a bite for the wean the morn an I've nae mair wurk, A cannae get a job. Why is it my brother, ma ain brother,' he said in his heid, 'up in that big fairm got everything he needs, an I hev nothing – not even as much as half a slice o bread fir the wean tae go tae the school the morn? An the wee cratur's in rags, an they drive aboot wi a fancy carriage and pair – everything they need – an I workit fir aa that fir them! He owes me an awfae lot, he owes me an aafa lot! I'm gaun up the morn an tell im I want a job.'

Up he goes, rings the bell o' the door, big fancy bell. An his wife comes oot, 'Well,' she says, 'what is hit you want?'

He said, 'I want to see ma brother. Tell him I'm here.'

The brother comes oot tae him, he said, 'What is hit, what d' ye want, Jack?'

'Look, tae tell ye the God's truth what A want,' he said, 'I want a job! No, I'm no wantin nothin aff ye, A'll wurk fir what ye can give me. Ye ken A'm a better worker than you – I workit fir aa you've got. If hit werena fir me, ye wadna hev half what ye got. Hit wasn't ma fault my mother deid – I never killt her.'

'You know what my father said before he died,' he said, 'that you were tae get nothing aff me.'

Jack said, 'I dinnae want nothing aff you, I jist want paid fir what I dae.'

'Well,' he said, 'seein as yir ma brother, I'll give ye so much if ye plough that field doon fir me doon there next t' the village, an make a guid job o it.'

'Well,' Jack said, 'gie me the money noo, I'm needin meat fir ma wean.'

He said, 'I'll give ye two gold sovereigns tae ploo that field. Noo I want a guid job.'

Jack says, 'I'll make a guid job tae ye aa right.'

'Otherwise,' he says, 'it'll be worse fir ye.'

Jack goes back doon, he gives his wife the two gold sovereigns, ye see. He said, 'Go doon tae the shop an get some messages fir the wean an buy whatever . . .' Gold sovereigns then – you could buy an awful lot o stuff. The wumman went doon.

But the next day wis Sunday. Jack said, 'I cannae help . . . Sunday or no, I'm gaun oot an ploo that field tae him.' So he walks up an he gets this two beautiful horses belongin tae his brother, yokes them intae this ploo. Down he goes tae the field an he starts – early in the mornin before his brother wis up. And it wisna a very big field, mebbe about five acre, he's plooin up an he's plooin doon, he's plooin up, he's plooin doon, ye see! But who cam doon but his brother an his wife: hit wis such a beautiful day tha' they thought they wad walk tae church, an they walkit past the field. Jack wis in the field – 'Gee up my horses,' he wis sayin, 'Gee up, my horses!' – turnin at the fit o the field!

An the other folk wis passin by forbyes, an they luikit roond, they seen Jack an they seen the brother passin by. Oh, he wis insultit, brother dear: his brother wis plooin o' a Sunday an cryin his horses *hese* horses – whan it wisna his horses ataa!

Jack finisht the field the evenin, goes back up; his brother met him a' the door, he said, 'If I'd hae kent you were gaunna dae that the day, you would never get nothin fae me! Man, ye're a dirty man, a dirty rascal – that would ploo that field o' a Sunday! No only that, ye insultit me, made a fool o me wi aa my beautiful neighbours walkin tae the church: you called my horses yours, ye said "Gee up my horses!" The people thinks hits yir horses. But ye'll never du that o' me again. The on'y kind o horse you've got is that thing doon there that ye hev there fir years – nothin but a heap o skin and bone.' (An Jack hed an auld horse but hit wis that puir that Jack cuidna even work hit.) 'But,' he says, 'ye'll no have hit nae mair. Efter tomorra ye'll no hev hit: tomorra I'm comin doon an I'm gaunna finish hit, I'm finishin it off!' So Jack cuidna dae nothin aboot hit, ye see.

But true tae his word, the rich brother cam doon next mornin, a gun in his oxter. He walkit inta the square an Jack's auld horse was tied luikin ower the fence. Bang – in the broo – shot. An he walkit roon tae Jack, 'Noo,' he said, 'let that be a lesson tae ye, an never show yir face about my place again! Noo ye've nothin – what ye deserve.' An away he goes back wi the gun in his oxter.

When he lands back in his hoose his wife hed his supper made, she said, 'Whit wis all the cairry-on aboot?'

He said, 'Hit wis that brother o mine, that trash brother o mine, he made a fool o me. Tae get ma own back, A went down an I shot his auld horse, finisht hit. Now he'd got nothin, he'll hev tae move out sooner or later!'

Puir Jack, he's lef noo wi this aul object o horse lyin deid in the garden in the square, his wee gruf. 'Ach well, puir aul creatur,' he said, 'the're no much A can do aboot hit.' So he sut an he skinned hit, he took the skin aff, ken, he buried hit. 'I'll prob'ly gang an sell the skin tae somebody, I might get two-three shillins fir the skin.' He scrapes some o the fat aff hit, rolls the skin in bilow his oxter an away he goes. He wanners here, wander there, tryan tae get the price o tea tae his wean for hit. Wanners here, wanners here and there . . . but in these days skins wis worth money. But naebody wad buy the skin fae him, not a body wad buy the skin fae him. He wannered fir aa day fir miles, an he crossed this pad.

'Ach well,' he said, 'I cannae get hit sellt, I better mak my wey hame.' An he seen a wee light away in the top o this muir. 'There's one hoose – where the're light the're life,' he said. 'An afore I gae hame the night, A hev tae get this skin sellt.' He walkit up an he cam tae this wee croft.

Noo, wi the wey he cam across the moor, he cam intae the back o the croft, ye see, an he's luikin fir the door but he cuidna get the front door. An he keekit through the windae, he seen this fire an an auld man an an auld wumman sittin in front o the fire. See, the window wis open – wee Jack 's keekin through the windae, his skin bilow his oxter!

De auld man says tae the auld wumman, 'Bring me a drink, auld wumman, bring me a drink!' The auld dotent wumman she went tae the press, she tuik oot this full big flagon o whisky, ye see, she fillt this glass tae the auld man an she gien it tae him. He sut an he drunk hit. He was well-on this auld man, see? 'That's better,' he said. 'Noo put hit back. Don't you take any!'

'Well,' she says, 'I'm away tae my bed.'

'Well, go to yir bed,' he said tae her, 'but bring me my box o money before ye go, ti I get hit coontit jist in case ye stole any.'

De aul wumman went up the stair an she cam back doon wi a tin box, she left it doon in front o him. Hit was full o gold sovereigns, the auld man liftit them up an he luikit a' em, 'Oh, he says, 'I think they're all there. Now, auld wumman, cairry hit back up an put hit back where ye got hit!'

Jack's luikin through the window, sees aa this, ye see. Skin bilow his oxter, he walks roond tae the front o the hoose an he goes tae the door, he knocks – 'chop-chop' o' the door.

The auld man shouts tae her, 'Hey, auld wumman, come down a minute, there's somebody knocking at the door this time o night, there's somebody knockin at the door. Go an see who hit is!'

De aul wumman cam oot tae the door an this wis Jack, the skin bilow his oxter. She said, 'Who is hit?'

He said, 'Hit's only me, a puir salesman on the road luikin fir shelter, or mebbe I could sell ye a skin fir yir floor, a nice skin fir yir carpet?'

'No,' the aul wumman says, 'we dinna need any skins, we've got all we need.'

An he's sittin a' the fire well-on wi the drink, ye see, he said, 'Who's there, who's at the door? Who ye talkin tae, wumman? Whoever hit is, bring him in here ti I see im!' The auld wumman had tae dae whit the aul man tellt her.

She says, 'Ye better come in.' So she tuik Jack intae the kitchen.

An the aul man says tae Jack, 'Who are you?'

Jack said, 'I'm only a salesman, I'm sellin horses' skins fir the kitchen floor.'

The auld man said, 'We dinna need skins. What are we gaunna du wi a skin fir the floor, we've got carpets.'

'Ay, but,' Jack said, 'ye're a fuil if ye dinna buy this yin.'

The man said, 'What's different wi this one than any one?'

He said, 'Auld man, this is a magic skin, an this skin knows every single thing in the world – you've only got tae ask hit, it'll tell ye.'

'Hah, be on wi ye,' he said, 'hit knows nothing! Tell me,' he said, 'what does hit know? Let me hear hit tellin somethin, an I'll buy hit fae ye.' He's well-on wi drink!

Noo the auld wumman's floor wis bare boards, she never even hed a carpet o' the floor. An the wat green skin – Jack spread hit oot on the floor, ken – he gien hit a rub wi his fit, skin wi his fit. An the green fat on the skin 'squeakit' – ken, the way a skin squeakit o' the floor! 'Du ye hear that?' Jack said.

The man said, 'I heard hit, but what did hit say?'

'Hit said that you hev got a bottle o whisky in that cupboard an ye had a good drink, an ye never offered yir guest one sip!'

'True enough,' the auld man said, 'ye're right. Did hit say –'

'At's what hit said,' says Jack.

'Well,' he said, 'hit's no wrong. Bring that bottle oot here!' Brung the bottle oot again, another glass. He says, 'Gie one fir ma visitor,' the aul man said. 'Now let's hear if hit kens onything else!'

Jack got the full glass o whisky – oh, in guid mood noo – full glass, waterglass full. Spread hit on the floor again. The auld wumman's sittin o' one side, the aul man's sittin o' the other side. Jack pit his fit tae the skin again, gi'n hit a 'squeak'.

'Jack,' he said, 'what did hit say this time?'

Jack said, 'Hit said that you hev a box o sovereigns up bilow yir bed – gold pieces – an every night i the week you go to coont them but tiday the're two a-missin.' (Jack only said that, brother, he didn't even ken!)

The auld man said, 'What?'

He said, 'The're two o yir sovereigns a-missin.'

He said, 'Wumman, go up there an get my box an bring hit doon!' The auld wumman wis two minutes up the stair an she brung the box doon. The aul man cowpit hit out on the floor, and he sut an he put them all back one bi one, one bi one, one bi one, one . . . he cam tae the last one – he says, 'Ye're right, the're two a-missin. Aul wumman, what di' ye do wi em?'

She says, 'A hed tae pay the van man tiday, A gien him two sovereigns fir bringin the messages. We needit hit.'

'I told you,' he said, 'to ask my permission when you go to my box tae take oot any sovereigns. But, that's no the problem. Young man, are ye gaunna hev another drink?' an him an Jack sit an finishes the bottle. 'Noo,' he said, 'I'm gaunnae buy yir skin, I'm gaunnae buy yir skin!'

'Well,' Jack said, 'I don't think ye've enough money tae buy my skin.'

'Well,' he said, 'I'll tell ye what A'll dae wi ye, I'll give ye half o my box o sovereigns fir yir skin!'

Jack says, 'Right, hit's a deal!'

An he said, 'Hit'll learn me everything I know, they'll no cheat me when I go to the market. Everything that goes on in the village I'll ken what happens, an I'll hev great fun when ma cronies comes in tae see me, hit'll tell me all what they're sayin aboot me an all these things.'

Jack gets half o the box o sovereigns, oh, mebbe aboot fifty sovereigns, see! Packs them all in his pockets an bids the aul man an the aul wumman 'good night' and away he goes. Hurries hame as fast as he cuid tae his wee hoose, late bi the time he gets in. His wife an the wee baby's in bed, went tae bed withoot any supper.

So the next mornin he got up, he gien her a couple o sovereigns, said, 'Luik, run doon to the shop an get some breakfast fir the wean. An she's no gaun tae school the day, dinnae pit her tae school – I hev a wee job fir her.' Efter they hed some breakfast she says, 'Come here,' to the wee lassie. 'Ye ken the road up tae yir uncle's fairm?'

'Yes, Daddy,' she says, 'I ken the road up tae ma uncle's fairm.'

'Well,' he says, 'you go up an ask him, tell him at ye want a shot o his gold weighs fir weighan the gold. Say yir daddy wants a lane o the gold weigh fir weighin the gold.'

The wee lassie went away, ye see, up she goes, knocks at the door. And the rich brother's wife comes oot, she says, 'What is hit you want, whit du you want here? You're no allowed up t' this place.'

She said, 'I'm only up tae ask if my daddy could have a shot o the gold weighs fir weighin the gold, he wants to weigh some gold pieces.' (Because tae let ye understand, in the aulden days the sovereigns didna hae nicks on them. People used tae scrape them, scrape some gold dust aff em, see? An they kep this gold dust on the paper, ye scraped some aff till ye hed a big heap o gold dust an you could sell that, an you could still sell the sovereign. So then the government inventit weighs that people cuid weigh the gold, so the sovereign hed a certain weight. An then when they done away wi that, they put nicks on hit so's you cuidna scrape hit. But this is the day before that happened.)

So she gives the wee lassie the weighs – an before she gives hit tae her, she rubs hit wi fat, cooking fat, one side wi cookin fat an the other side wi cookin fat where they hed tae place the sovereigns tae weigh. She gives it to the wee lassie, she sends it doon. When hit comes doon, Jack looks an he sees the fat on the weighs. He goes tae the box an takes a gold sovereign, he sticks it intae the fat an he sticks another one o' the other side, see? An hit goes back up, he says, 'Take that back tae yir auntie, tell her ye thank her very much fir the lane o hit.' So the wee lassie gaes back up an she gives hit back tae her auntie.

She luiks in the fat and here wis two gold sovereigns stickin i the fat, she picks em oot. She wis aafa miserable, ye ken, this rich brother's wife, an when her man cam in she flew at him. 'Look, she said, 'he's supposed tae be puir an ye killed his horse, he's miserable livin doon there in that wee cottage without a job, an he can weigh gold; an we wi a big fairm can only survive day tae day! An he's supposed tae be puir. We canna weigh any gold, hit takes us bare than busy * tae keep this place runnin wi all this cattle an stuff.'

* bare than busy – all we can manage

So the brother says, 'Well, there mus be somethin funny gaun on. I think A better change ma attitude towards him an get *in* wi him, see what happent.' See!

So next mornin he walks doon, ah, an he's very pleasant to Jack, ken! 'Good mornin!' he said, 'good mornin, Jack.'

'Good mornin,' he said.

'A come,' he said, 'I think hit's about time me and you stoppit arguin. After all, we're brothers, I think we should bury the hatchet. What is hit between brothers anyway . . . My faither he hed no right tae accuse you o . . . my mother's fault. If ye need onything, come up tae the farm fir hit, an if ye need a day's work or that. Bi the wey,' he said, 'ma wife tells me ye had a shot o the weighs the day, the gold weighs.'

'Ach,' Jack said, 'I wis only weighan a puckle sovereigns.'

He said, 'Sovereigns?'

'Ay,' Jack says, 'gold sovereigns.'

He said, 'Whaur di' ye get them?'

'"Get them,"' says Jack, 'aye, an get plenty mair – bings o them! The best thing you ever done fir me,' he said, 'wis tae kill thon horse. I should hae done hit years ago. I sellt hits skin in the first hoose in the village fir five hundred gold sovereigns, an I've plenty money.' Noo five hundred gold sovereigns in these days wis a lot o money. Noo Jack's brother's two horses were only worth about thirty sovereigns a piece, see?

He said, 'Du ye think my . . . if I sellt my two horses, would I get –'

'Ho,' Jack said, 'ye'll get a lot more than that fir them, they're worth a lot more an that, these big horses you've got.'

'Brother,' he says, 'all right, thank you very much!' Up he goes, brother dear, gets the gun – 'bang, bang' – shot his two horses. Skint em, skint the two o them, rolled the two skins up, down through the street shoutin, 'Horse skins fir sale, horse's skin fir sale, who'll buy a good horse's skin, cheap at five hundred a piece!'

The folk's stanit him, they flung stanes at im, chased him oot o the village, chasit him fir his life oot the village! Naebody's wantin a horse's skin fir five hundred sovereigns. He hawked the whole fearin day ti his feet wis inta the blood * – not a penny did he get – nothing. He cam back, two horses skint, the two horses deid – he's lef wi the two skins. Tellt his wife.

* his feet wis inta the blood – he was completely exhausted

She said, 'He made a fuil o ye, he made a fuil o ye! He never sellt nae skin. Wherever he got the gold . . .'

An he wis so angry an so tired an so fed-up, an his feet inta the blood, he says, 'He'll never make a fuil o me again. Tomorra mornin I'm finishin his days aff.'

True tae his word, next mornin he gaes doon an he gets puir Jack, he gives Jack the biggest beatin in the worl that he ever got in his life – kickit him, weltit him aa through the stockyard – an went inta the shed, got a bag an he pit Jack in the bag, tied hit wi a string. 'Noo,' he says, 'ye'll never never play a dirty trick on me again, you're goin where ye'll never come back!'

Noo, fae where Jack steyed, they hed aboot half a mile walk tae the sea, tae the shoreside. On the road to the shoreside ye hed tae pass by the church an when ye pass by the church, oot the end o the village ye cam to the sea an then a big deep clift. This 's where he wis takkin Jack, tae fling him over the clift. But afore ye went tae the church there wis a wee hotel, a wee pub. So he got Jack in the bag, he put Jack on his back an away he goes, on he goes wi Jack on his back. But he traivellt ond a half a mile an hit wis a beautiful day, hit was warm, he cam tae the wee hotel. He thocht the best thing he'd dae is gae an hae a drink before he flung Jack over the clift intae the sea. So he leaves Jack at the door o the pub, he goes in tae hev two–three glasses o whisky an he's standin at the bar crackin. And puir Jack he's sittin in the bag.

But anyway, the brother's havin a drink in the pub when along comes . . . in these days the ministers always kep two–three cattle. An who's comin along the road but the minister, he hed five o the finest cattle, he was gaun tae pit them in a wee field on the other side o the manse. Ond his road past he had tae pass the pub. Jack heard the patter o the feet, he kent fine who hit was an he's in de bag tied wi string!

Jack said, 'I'm gaun to heaven, oh thank the Lord Almighty, I'm goin to heaven! Thank the God Almighty I'm goin to heaven at last, at last ma prayers hae been answered, I'm goin tae heaven!'

The aul minister cam along and he stoppit langside the bag, he said, 'Who's there?'

'Oh,' Jack said, 'hit's me, Our Reverend, hit's finally my prayers hae been answered: I'm goin to heaven, heaven is my place an thank the Lord, I'll be with him before long.'

The minister said, 'Ye mean tae tell me, you're gaun tae heaven?'

'Yes,' he said, 'goin tae heaven, this is the way I'm goin tae heaven.'

'Well,' the minister said, 'I would like tae go tae heaven, I would love tae go to heaven!'

'Oh,' Jack said, 'I'm sorry, there's nae room in here fir the two o hus.'

'Well,' said the minister, 'cuid you no change yir mind an let *me* go, an you cuid go some other time?'

'Well,' Jack said, 'What is hit worth tae ye, if you want tae go tae heaven?'

'Well,' the minister said, 'if you let me take yir place as you, I'll give ye five beautiful cattle – if ye let me swap places wi ye an put me i the bag – let me go tae heaven!'

Jack said, 'Lowse the bag.'

The minister lowsed the bag, Jack cam oot. Jack tuik the aul minister, put im i the bag, tied the string back up an away he goes, drove the five beautiful black cattle back tae his wee hoose, see?

The brother he got oot o the pub efter havin two-three good drinks on him, oot he comes, 'Ha-ha,' he said, ye're still sittin there yet, are ye? But you'll no sit fir very long.' He gets the bag on his back, flings hit ond an off he goes. He walks on ti he comes tae the deep clifts, an the sea wis about sixty feet deep. An swing roond his heid – wonst, twice, three times – out in the deep he flung the bag suppost to be his brother, in the deep – down he goes. 'That's you finisht,' he said, 'ye'll never bother me again!'

But anyway, he walks hame. On the road back he hed tae walk past Jack's wee croft, wee hoose. When he comes intae Jack's square, here 's Jack standin leanin ower the fence, a smile on his face watchin these five beautiful cattle – sleek like black moles, sleek and fat – belangt tae the minister! The brother stops, he luiks, scratcht his heid, he said, 'Hit's no you is hit?'

'Aye,' he said, 'hit's me aa right.'

'But,' he said, 'hoo did ye get back so quick? An that's no yir cattle is hit?'

The brother said, 'Hit's my cattle an there's plenty plenty mair where they come frae. But if I hedna been so sore wi the beatin ye gie me, I cuidhae take a dozen back wi me.'

Brother he said, 'Jack, I'm sorry. I'm sorry, brother, I'm really sorry fir bein so bad tae ye. What happent?'

'Well,' he said, 'I'll tell ye what happened: you pit me i the bag an ye cairried me tae the pub.'

'Aye,' he said.

'An you went in, ye had a good drink.'

'Aye,' he said, 'Jack, ye're tellin the truth, I hed a good drink.'

'An,' he said, 'you cam oot an you flung me ower the clift inta the sea.'

'Aye,' he says, 'I did that.'

'Well,' he said, 'I nae sooner hit the water ti up cam an auld man wi a spear ind his hand – Old Father Neptune – an he asked me What am I daein here? An I tellt him you flung me in the sea. An he said he wasna ready fir me yet. He asked me what am I daein here, "a young man like you?" he said. "Are ye no happy on earth where ye live?" An I tellt him I wisna happy because I hed nothin tae live on, an he said he wad give me onythin I wantit. He said, "You want diamonds, gold, jewels, I'll give it tae ye – lang as ye can be happy where ye are." So I asked him, tellt im tae give me five black cattle. An he said he gien me the five black cattle. He gien me these . . .'

'Oh, brother,' he said, 'ye should hae asked fir better an that. Luik, would ye dae somethin fir me, wad ye pit me i the bag? An, brother, I'll get plenty that'll dae me an you fir the rest o wir life!'

'Ah, no,' says Jack. 'Luik, you been bad tae me, you never treatit me like a brother nae way – why should I treat you anything else noo? A've got my five cattle, I'll sell them an I'll never need . . .'

'But,' he said, 'I'll never get a chance like this again. Luik, A'll tell ye what I'll dae wi you: I'll write it doon in black and white, I'll gie ye half o my fairm an half o the animals and half o everything A hev – if ye pit me i the bag and fling me ower the sea!'

'Well,' says Jack, 'seein yir my brother, A wad like tae help ye.'

He said, 'Brother, I'll bring a hundert cattle back! A'll never be bad tae ye again, A'll mak hit ma promise – I'll never be bad tae ye again.'

'All right,' says Jack.

Jack goes inta the wee shed, brother, an this whit he taks oot – a coorse corn bag, ken one of them barley bags, coorse yin – so there'd be nae escape. 'An, but,' he says, 'luik, I cannae cairry ye, ye're too heavy.'

'I'm no wantin you tae cairry me, I'll *walk* tae the clift. An ye can pit me in the bag at the clift, fling me ower fae there. An we'll hae a guid drink afore we go.'

Fair enough,' said Jack, 'let's go noo!' Jack went in, he got a bit tarry rape oot o the barn an this bag bilow his oxter. They walkit back tae the pub an they had a good drink. An Jack said, 'I think hit's about time to go, before the Auld Man gets sleepy.'

So they walkit tae the clift. The bad brother cleembs inta the bag. Jack said, 'Wait a minute, brother, get two-three stanes at the bottom – you'll go doon quick – you can meet him all the quicker.' Pit two-three stanes in the bottom so's he'd gang doon the quicker, he tied it with a string securely an flung him ower the clift. Down he goes to the bottom, never wis seen again.

Jack walkit back, waited all that day, waited aa the next day, waitit fir a week. Brother never returned back. An up he goes tae his sister-in-law, he shows her: black and white, he said, 'Luik, ma brother is fed up wi you an he's run away, gaen away tae a distant land, he's no comin back; but he feelt sorry an he left me half o the fairm.'

'Well,' she says, 'hit's nae use to me, it's nae use to me withoot him. Ye can have the lot o the fairm, I'll keep the money.'

Jack says, 'You keep the money an I'll get the fairm.' So Jack got the fairm, she kep the money an she cleared oot. Fae that day on ti this day Jack never wantit fir another thing. An that's the last o my story!

DEATH IN A NUT

Jack lived with his mother in a little cottage by the shoreside, an his mother kept some ducks an some hens. Jack cuid barely remember his father because his father had died long before he wis born. An they had a small kin o croft, Jack cut a little hay fir his mother's goats. When dher wur no hay tae collect, he spent most of his time along the shoreside as a beach-comber collecting everything that cam in bi the tide, whatever it wad be – any auld drums, any auld cans, pieces of driftwood, something that wis flung off a boat – Jack collectit all these things an brought them in, put them biside his mother's cottage an said, 'Some day they might come in useful.' But the mos thing that Jack ever collected fir his mother was firewood. An Jack wis very happy, he wis jist a young man, his early teens, and he dearly loved his mother. He used tae some days take duck eggs tae the village (his mother wis famed fir er duck eggs) an hen eggs to the village forbyes, they helped them survive, and his mother wad take in a little sewin fir the local people in the village; Jack and his mother lived quite happy. Till one particular day, it wis around about the wintertime, about the month o January, this time o the year now.

Jack used tae always get up early in the mornin an make a cup o tea, he always gev his mother a cup o tea in bed every mornin. An one particular mornin he rose early because he want't tae catch the in-comin tide tae see what it wad bring in fir him. He brought a cup o tea into his mother in her own little bed in a little room, it wis only a two-room little cottage they had.

He says, 'Mother, I've brought you a cup o tea.'

She says, 'Son, I don't want any tea.'

'Mother,' he says, 'why? What's wrong, are you not feelin –'

She says, 'Son, I'm not feelin very well this morning, I'm not feelin very well. I don't think I cuid even drink a cup o tea if ye gev it to me.'

'Oh, Mother,' he says, 'try an take a wee sip,' an he leaned over the bed, held the cup to his mother's mooth an tried to get her . . .

She took two–three sips, 'That's enough, laddie,' she says, 'I don't feel very well.'

He says, 'What's wrong with you, Mother? Are you in pain or somethin?'

'Well, so an no so, Jack, I dinnae ken what's wrong wi me,' she says. 'I'm an ill woman, Jack, an ye're a young man an I cannae go on for ever.'

'But, Mother,' he says, 'you cannae dee an leave me masel! What am I gaunnae dae? I've nae freends, nae naebody in this worl but you, Mother! Ye cannae dee an lea me!'

'Well,' she says, 'Jack, I think I'm no long fir this worl. In fact, I think he'll be comin fir me some o these days . . . soon.'

'Wha, Mother, ye talking about "comin fir me"?'

She says, 'Jack, ye ken wha he is, Jack. Between me an you, we dinna share nae secrets – I'm an auld woman an I'm gaunna dee – Death's gaunna come fir me, Jack, I can see it in ma mind.'

'Oh, Mother, no, Mother,' he says, an he held her hand.

'But,' she says, 'never mind, laddie, ye'll manage to take care o yirsel. Yir mother hes saved a few shillins fir ye an I'm sure some day ye'll meet a nice wee wife when I'm gone, ye'll prob'ly get on in the world.'

'No, Mother,' he says, 'I cuidna get on withoot you.'

She says, 'Laddie, leave me an I'll try an get a wee sleep.'

Bi this time it was daylight as the sun begint tae get up, an Jack walkit up along the shoreway jist in the grey-dark in the mornin, gettin clear. It must hae been about half-past eight-nine o'clock, (in the wintertime it took a long while tae get clear in the mornins) when the tide was comin in. Jack walked along the shoreway an lo an behold, the first thing he seen comin a-walkin the shoreway was an auld man with a long grey beard, skinny legs and a ragged coat o'er his back an a scythe on his back. His two eyes were sunk inta his heid, sunk back intae his skull, an he wis the most uglies'-luikin creature that Jack ever seen in his life. But he had on his back a *brand new scythe* an hit was shinin in the light fae the mornin.

Noo, his mother hed always tellt Jack what like Deith luikit an Jack says tae his ainsel, 'That's Deith come fir my auld mother! He's come tae take on'y thing that I love awa fae me, but,' he said, 'he's no gettin awa wi it! He's no gettin away wi hit!' So Jack steps oot aff the shoreside, an up he comes an meets this Auld Man – bare feet, lang ragged coat, lang ragged beard, high cheek bones an his eyes sunk back in his heid, two front teeth sticking out like that – and a shinin scythe on his back, the morning sun wis glitterin on the blade – ready to cut the people's throats an take them away to the Land o Death.

Jack steps up, says, 'Good morning, Auld Man.'

'Oh,' he said, 'good morning, young man! Tell me, is it far tae the next cottage?'

Jack said, 'Ma mother lives i the next cottage just along the shoreway a little bit.'

'Oh,' he says, 'that's her I want to visit.'

'Not this mornin,' says Jack, 'ye're not gaunna visit her! I know who you are – you're Death – an you've come tae take my aul mother, kill her an tak her awa an lea me masel.'

'Well,' Death says, 'it's natural. Yir mother, ye know, she's an auld wumman an she's reacht a certain age, I'll no be doin her any harm, I'll be jist do her a guid turn – she's sufferin in pain.'

'You're no takin my aul mither!' says Jack. And he ran forward, he snappit the scythe aff the Aul Man's back an he walkit tae a big stane, he smashed the scythe against a stane.

An the Auld Man got angrier an angrier an angrier an ugly-luikin, 'My young man,' he says, 'you've done that – but that's not the end!'

'Well,' Jack says, 'it's the end fir you!' An Jack dived o top o him, Jack got a haud o him an Jack pickit a bit stick up the shoreside, he beat him an he weltit him an he weltit him an he beat him an he weltit him. He fought wi Death an Death wis as strong as what Jack was, but finally Jack conquered him! An Jack beat im with a bit stick, and lo an behold the funny thing happened: the more Jack beat him the wee-er he got, an Jack beat him an Jack beat him an Jack beat him – no blood cam fae him or nothing – Jack beat him wi the stick till he got barely the size o that! An Jack catcht im in his hand, 'Now,' he said, 'I got ye! Ye'll no get my aul mither!'

Noo Jack thought in his ainsel, 'What in the worl am I gaunna do wi him? A hev him here, I canna let him go, A beat him, I broke his scythe an I conquered him. But what in the world am I gaunna do wi him? I canna hide him bilow a stane because he'll creep oot an he'll come back tae his normal size again.' An Jack walkit along the shore an he luikit – comin in by the tide was a big hazelnut, that size! But the

funny thing about this hazelnut, a squirrel had dug a hole in the nut
cause squirrels always dig holes in the nuts – they have sharp teeth –
an he eats the kernel oot inside an leas the empty case. An Jack pickit
up the hazelnut, he luikit, says, 'The very thing!' An Jack crushed
Death in through the wee hole – inta the nut! An squeezed him in heid
first, an his wee feet, put him in there, shoved him in. An he walkit
aboot, he got a wee plug o stick and he plugged the hole fae the
outside. 'Now,' he says, 'Death, you'll never get ma mither.' An he
catcht him in his hand, he threw im oot inta the tide! An the heavy
waves wis 'whoosh-an-whoosh-an-whoosh-an, whoosh-an-whoosh-in' in
an back an forward. An Jack watched the wee nut, hit went a-sailin,
floatin an back an forward away wi the tide. 'That's hit!' says Jack,
'that's the end o Death. He'll never bother my mother again, or naebody
else forbyes my mither.'

Jack got two–three sticks under his arm an he walkit back. Whan he
landed back he seen the reek wis comin fae the chimney, he says, 'My
mother must be up, she must be feelin a wee bit better.' Lo an behold
he walks in the hoose, there wis his auld mother up, her sleeves rolled
up, her face full o flooer, her apron on an she's busy makin scones.

He said, 'How ye feelin, Mother?'

She says, 'Jack, I'm feelin great, I never felt better in ma life!
Laddie, I dinna ken what happened to me, but I wis lyin there fir a
minute in pain an torture, and all in a minute I felt like someone hed
come an rumbled all the pains an tuik everything oot o my body, an
made me . . . I feel like a lassie again, Jack! I made some scones fir yir
breakfast.'

Jack never mentioned to his mother aboot Deith, never said a word.
His mother fasselt roon the table, she's pit up her hair . . . Jack never
seen his mother in better health in her life! Jack sit doon bi the fire, his
mother made some scones. He had a wee bit scone, he says, 'Mother, is
that all you've got tae eat?'

'Well,' she says, 'Jack, the're no much, jist a wee puckle flooer an I
thocht I'd mak ye a wee scone fir yir breakfast. Go on oot tae the
hen house an get a couple eggs, I'll mak ye a couple eggs alang wi yir
scone an that'll fill ye up, laddie.'

Jack walks oot to the hen hoose as usual, wee shed beside his mother's
hoose. Oh, every nest is full o eggs, hens' eggs, duck eggs, the nests is all
full. Jack picks up four o the big beautiful broon eggs oot o the nest,
gaes back in an 'Here, Mother, the're fowr,' he said, 'two tae you, two
to me.'

De aul wumman says, 'I'll no be a minute, Jack.' It was a open fire they had. The wumman pulled the sway oot, put the fryin pan on, pit a wee bit fat i the pan. She waitit an she waitit an she watcht, but the wee bit fat wadna melt. She poked the fire with the poker but the wee bit fat wadna melt. 'Jack,' she says, 'fire's no kindlin very guid, laddie, it'll no even melt that wee bit fat.'

'Well, pit some mair sticks on, Mother,' he said, 'pit some mair wee bits o sticks on.' Jack pit the best o sticks on, but na! The wee bit o fat sut in the middle o the pan, but it wouldna melt, he says, 'Mother, never mind, pit the egg in an gie it a rummle roon, it'll dae me the way it is. Jis pit it in the pan.'

Aul mother tried – 'crack' – na. She hut the egg again – na. An s'pose she cuid hae take a fifty-pun hammer an hut the egg, *that egg would not break!* She says, 'Jack, I cannae break these eggs.'

'An, Mother,' he said, 'I thought ye said ye were feelin weel an feelin guid, an you cannae break an egg! Gie me the egg, I'll break hit!' Jack tuik the egg, went in his big hand, ye ken, Jack big young laddie, catcht the egg one hand – 'clank' on the side o the pan – na! Ye're as well tae hit a stane on the side o the pan, *the egg would not break* in no way in this worl! 'Ah, Mother,' he says, 'I dinna ken what's wrong, I dinna ken whit's wrong, Mother, wi these eggs, I don't know. Prob'ly they're no richt eggs, I better go an get another two.'

He walkit oot to the shed again, he brung in two duck eggs. But he tried the same – na, they wadna break, the eggs jist would not break in any way in the worl. 'Mother,' he says, 'pit them in a taste o water an bring them a-boil!'

She says, 'That's right, Jack, I never thocht about that.' The aul wumman got a wee pan an the fire wis goin well bi this time of bonnie shore sticks. She pit the pan on an within seconds the water wis boilan, she poppit the two eggs in. An it bubbled an bubbled an bubbled an bubbled an bubbled, an bubbled, she said, 'They're ready noo, Jack.' She tuik them oot – 'crack' – na. As suppose they hed hae tried fir months, they cuidna crack that two eggs.

'Ah, Mother,' he says, 'the're something wrong. Mither, the're something wrong, the're enchantment upon us, that eggs'll no cook. We're gaunna dee wi hunger.'

'Never mind, Jack,' she says, 'eat yir wee bit scone. I'll mak ye a wee drop soup, I'll mak ye a wee pot o soup. Go oot tae the gairden, Jack, an get me a wee taste o vegetables, leeks an a few carrots.'

Noo Jack had a guid garden, he passes all his time makkin a guid garden tae his mother. Ot he goes, he pulls two carrots, a leek, bit parsley an a neep an he brings it tae his mother. Aul wumman washes the pots, pits some water in, pits it on the fire. But she goes tae the table with the knife, but na – every time she touches the carrot, the knife jist skates aff hit. She toucht the leek – it skates aff it an aa. The auld wumman tried her best, an Jack tried his best – there's no way in the world – Jack said, 'That knife's blunt, Mother.'

An Jack had a wee bit o shairpen stane he'd fand in the shoreside, he took the stane an he shairpit the knife, but no way in the world wad hit ever look at the carrots or the neep or the wee bit parsley tae mak a wee pot o soup. She says, 'Jack, the're somethin wrang wi my vegetables, Jack, they must be frozen solid.'

'But,' he said, 'Mother, the're been nae frost tae freeze them! Hoo in the world can this happen?'

'Well,' she says, 'Jack, luik, ye ken I've an awfa cockerels this year, we have an awfa cockerels an we'll no need them aa, Jack. Wad ye gae oot to the shed an pull a cockerel's neck, and A'll pit it in the pot, boil hit for wir supper?'

'Ay,' says Jack. Noo the aul wumman kep a lot o hens. Jack went oot an all i the shed dher wur dozens o them sittin i a raa, cockerels o all description. Jack luikit ti he seen a big fat cockerel sittin on a perch, he put his hand up, catcht hit an he feel'd it, it wis fat. 'Oh,' he says, 'Mother'll be pleased wi this yin.' Jack pullt the neck – na! Pulled again – *no way*. He pullt it, he shakit it, he swung it roond his heid three–five times. He tuik a stick an he battert it i the heid, there's no way – he cuidna touch the cockerel in any way! He pit it bilow his oxter an he walks inta his mother.

She said, 'Ye get a cockerel, Jack?'

'Oh, Mother,' he said, 'I got a cockerel aa right, I got a cockerel. But, Mother, you may care!' *

She says, 'What do you mean, laddie?'

'You may care,' he says, 'I cannae kill hit.'

'Ah, Jack,' she says, 'ye cannae kill a cockerel! I ken, ye killt dozens tae me afore, the hens an ducks an aa.'

'Mother,' he said, 'I cannae kill this one – it'll no dee!'

She says, 'Gie me it ower here, gie me it over here!' An the auld woman had a wee hatchet fir splittin sticks, she kep it by the fire. She

---

* you may care – there's nothing you can do about it

says, 'Gie it tae me, Jack, I'll show ye the way tae kill it rictht!' She pit it doon the top o the block an she hut it wi the hatchet, chop its heid aff. She hut it with the hatchet seventeen times, but no – every time the heid jumpit aff – heid jumpit back on! 'Na, Jack,' she says, 'it's nae good. There's something wrang here, the're something terrible gaun a-wrong. Nethin seems tae be richt aboot the place. Here – go out to my purse, laddie, run up tae the village to the butcher! I'm savin this fir a rainy day,' an she tuik a half-croon oot o her purse. 'Jack, gae up tae the butcher an get a wee bit o meat fae the butcher, I'll mak ye a wee bite when ye come back.'

Noo, it wisna far fae the wee hoose to the village, about a quarter o mile Jack hed tae walk. When Jack walkit up the village, all the people were gaithert in the middle o the town square. They're all bletherin an they're chattin and they're bletherin an they're chattin, speakin tae each other. One was sayin, 'A've sprayed ma garden an it's overrun wi caterpillars! An I've tried tae spray hit, it's no good.'

The butcher wis oot wi his apron, he said, 'Three times I tried tae kill a bullock this mornin an three times I killed it, three times it jumpit back on its feet. I don't know what's wrong. The villagers run out o meat! I got a quota o hens in this mornin, ducks, an every time I pull their necks their heads jumps back on. There's somethin terrible is happenin!'

Jack went up to the butcher's, he says, 'Gie me a wee bit o meat fir ma mother.'

He says, 'Laddie, the're no a bit o meat in the shop. Dae ye no ken what I'm tryi' tae tell the people in the village: I've tried ma best this mornin to kill a young bullock tae supply the village an I cannae kill hit!'

'Well,' Jack said, 'the same thing happen to me – I tried tae boil an egg an I cannae boil an egg, I tried tae kill a cockerel –'

'I tried tae kill ten cockerels,' says the butcher, 'but *they'll no dee!*'

'Oh dear-dear,' says Jack, 'we must be in some kin o trouble. Is hit happenin tae other places forbyes this?'

'Well, I jist hed word,' says the butcher, 'the next village up two mile awa an the same thing's happened tae them. Folk cannae even eat an apple – when they sink their teeth inta it, it'll no even bite. They cannae cook a vegetable, they cannae boil water, they cannae dae nothin! The hale worl's gaunna come tae a standstill, the're something gaen terrible wrong – *nothing seems to die anymore.*'

An then Jack thought in his head, he said, 'It's my fault, I'm the cause o't.' He walkit back an he tellt his mother the same story I'm tellin you. He says, 'Mother, there's nae butcher meat fir ye.'

She says, 'Why, laddie, why no?'

He says, 'Luik, the butcher cannae kill nae beef, because hit'll no dee.'

'But Jack,' she says, 'why no – it'll no dee? What's wrang with the country, what's wrang with the world?'

He says, 'Mother, it's all my fault!'

'Your fault,' she says, 'Jack?'

'Ay, Mither, it's my fault,' he says. 'Listen, Mother: this morning when you were no feeling very well, I walkit along the shore tae gather some sticks fir the fire an I met Death comin tae tak ye awa. An I took his scythe fae him an I broke his scythe, I gi'n him a beatin, Mither, an I put him in a nut! An I flung him in the tide an I plugged the nut so's he canna get oot, Mither. An God knows where he is noo. He's floatin in the sea, Mother, firever an ever an ever, an nothing'll dee – the worl is overrun with caterpillars an worms an everything – Mither, the're nothing can dee! But Mither, I wad rather die with starvation than loss you.'

'Jack, Jack, Jack, laddie,' she says, 'dae ye no ken what ye've done? Ye've destroyed the only thing that keeps the world alive.'

'What do you mean, Mother, "keeps the world alive"? Luik, if I hedna killed him, I hedna hae beat im, Mother, an pit him in that nut – you'd be dead bi this time!'

'I wad be dead, Jack,' she says, 'probably, but the other people would be gettin food, an the worl'd be gaun on – the way it shuid be – only fir you, laddie!'

'But, Mother,' he says, 'what am I gaunna dae?'

She says, 'Jack, there's only thing ye can dae ... ye're a beach-comber like yir faither afore ye –'

'Aye, Mother,' he says, 'I'm a beach-comber.'

'Well, Jack,' she says, 'there's only thing I can say: ye better gae an get im back an set him free! Because if ye dinnae, ye're gaunna put the whole worl tae a standstill. *Bithout Death there is no life* ... fir nobody.'

'But, Mother,' he says, 'if I set him free, he's gaunna come fir you.'

'Well, Jack, if he comes fir me,' she said, 'I'll be happy, and go inta another world an be peaceful! But you'll be alive an so will the rest o the world.'

'But Mother,' he says, 'I cuidna live bithoot ye.'

'But,' she says, 'Jack, if ye dinnae set him free, *both* o hus'll suffer, an

I cannae stand tae see you suffer fir the want o something to eat: because the're nothing in the world will die unless you set him free, because you cannae eat nothing until it's dead.'

Jack thought in his mind fir a wee while. 'Aa right, Mother,' he says, 'if that's the way it shuid be, that's the way it shuid be. Prob'ly I wis wrong.'

'Of course, Jack,' she says, 'you were wrong.'

'But,' he says, 'Mother, I only done it fir yir sake.'

'Well,' she says, 'Jack, fir *my* sake, wad ye search fir that hazelnut an set him free?'

So the next mornin true tae his word, Jack walks the tide an walks the tide fir miles an miles an miles, day out an day in fir three days an fir three days more. He hedna nothin tae eat, he only hed a drink water. They cuidna cook anything, they cuidna eat any eggs, they couldna fry nothing in the pan if they had it, they cuidna make any soup, they cuidna get nothin. The caterpillars an the worms crawled out o the garden in thousands, an they ett every single vegetable that Jack had. An the're nothing in the world – Jack went out an tried to teem hot water on them but it wis nae good. When he teemed hot water on them it just wis the same as he never poored nothing – no way. At last Jack said, 'I must go an find that nut!' So he walkit an he walkit, an he walkit day an he walkit night mair miles than he ever walked before, but no way cuid Jack fin' this nut! Till Jack was completely exhaustit an fed up an completely sick, an he cuidna walk another mile. He sat doon bi the shoreside right in front o his mother's hoose to rest, an wonderit, he pit his hand on his jaw an he said tae his ainsel, 'What have I done? I've ruint the world, I've destroyed the world. People disna know,' he said, 'what Death has so good, at Death is such a guid person. I wis wrong tae beat him an put him in a nut.'

An he's luikin all over – an lo and behold he luikit doon – there at his feet he seen a wee nut, an a wee bit o stick stickin oot hit. He liftit hit up in his hand, an Jack wis happy, happier an he'd ever been in his life before! And he pulled the plug an a wee head poppit oot. Jack held im in his two hands and Death spoke tae him, 'Now, Jack,' he said, 'are ye happy?'

'No,' Jack said, 'I'm no happy.'

He said, 'You thought if you beat me an conquered me an killed me – because I'm jist Death – that that wad be the end, everything be all right. Well, Jack, ma laddie, ye've got a lot to learn, Jack. Without me,' he said, 'there's no life.'

An Jack tuik him oot.

'But,' he says, 'Jack, thank you fir settin me free,' an jist like that, after Jack opent the nut, he cam oot an like that, he cam full strength again an stude before Jack – the same Auld Man with the long ragged coat an the sunken eyes an the two teeth in the front an the bare feet. He says, 'Jack, ye broke my scythe.'

Jack said, 'I'll tell ye somethin, while I wis searchin fir you ma mother made me mend it. An I have it in the hoose fir ye, come wi me!' An Jack led him up to the hoose. Lo an behold sure enough, sittin on the front o the porch wis the scythe that Jack broke. Jack had tuik it an he'd mend't it, he sortit it an made it as guid as ever.

Death cam to the door an he ran his hand doon the face o the scythe, he sput on his thumb and he run it up the face o the scythe, an he says tae Jack, 'I see you've sharpened it, Jack, and ye made a good job o it. Well, I hev some people to see in the village, Jack. But remember, I'll come back fir yir mother someday, but seein you been guid to me I'll make it a wee while!' An Death walkit away.

Jack an his mother lived happy till his mother wis about a hundred years of age! An then one day Death cam back tae take his aul mother away, but Jack never saw him. But Jack was happy fir he knew *there is no life bithout Death*. An that is the end o my story.

THE HENWIFE AN AUL FATHER TIME

The old woman she wis tired as she struggled from the sea with her bundle of driftwood on her back, for she had carried driftwood from the shoreside fir many many days buildin up a large quantity tae see er through the winter. She wis an auld henwoman and she lived very close to the sea. The days were very short, it wis the middle o winter, but the aul woman had lost track of time because she never got very many visitors. She wis jist an auld woman who lived by herself, all she had wis takin her eggs inta the village day by day when she had enough to sell tae keep her alive – she had ducks an hens – and the ducks went ond the shoreside but always cam home and laid within their little shed bi the side o er little cottage. And she trusted they would no lay nowhere else.

She hed cairried three bundles, bild them up, put them up to dry, this wis the only kin o fuel that she used durin the winter, she had a large fire an depended on the driftwood. She went back fir the fourth load, tied a rope round hit, put hit on her back an cairried it up from the beach. When lo an behold she landed up the door o the cottage, there stood before her wis an auld man with a long white beard an a long coat and sandals ond his feet. Now the auld wumman had never got many visits in her life an she wis surprised tae see the stranger standin before er, he wis an auld man! An she cuid see by the way he stood stoopit an bendit he wis very very auld. She placed the bundle o sticks on her back in a heap, then turned round an said, 'Hello, stranger!'

He said, 'Hello!'

She says, 'What can I do fir you?'

'Well,' he said, 'I have come a long long way an I'm weary an tired. I wonder if you cuid give me a drink.'

'A drink,' she says, 'I've got plenty of, if ye jist hold on a moment till I lay down thes sticks – I'll give ye a drink.' The auld woman wis very glad tae see someone tae talk to. She took off the rope that she had round her sticks, piled them up so they would dry, criss-crossed tae let the wind in between them. And the aul stranger stude watchin er. He waitit patiently by her side till she hed finished her work, an then she said, 'Come with me, old man.' He looked older an her – she wis very auld bi herself – but he luikit old with his long grey beard an his long coat. But the most amazines thing she ever saw in her life was that he had sandals ond his feet, she hed never saw an auld man walkin with sandals before. So after she'd packed her sticks up to dry, she welcomed him inta er little cottage. Took in a few sticks, the fire wis very low but she soon kinneled the fire up, put some more sticks on, the dryes ones she cuid pick, an placed the auld man by the chair.* She said, 'What wad ye like tae drink?'

'Anything, my dear,' he said, 'would suit me.'

Sae she walked in . . . and this auld woman had made some wine durin the summer months, with her many elderberry bushes along the beachside she always made wine when the elderberry wis ripe. An she'd always hed two–three bottles of wine, so she took a bottle with a glass an she gev the aul man a drink. He sat bi the fire an she sat down in a chair across fra im. An he sat there with his aul ragged coat an his long grey beard an his sandals ond his feet. The auld wumman wis amazed an wondered ind her own mind, 'Where in the world did this auld man come from?' She thought, 'Prob'ly he'll tell me a story an tell me something about his life.'

The old man sat an he drunk the wine, he said, 'That is very good, did ye make it yirself?'

'Yes,' she said, 'I made it mysel.'

'Well,' he said, 'it's very gude. Di' ye made it from the berries of the elderberry?'

She said, 'Yes, I made it from berries of the elderberry. A pick the berries along the hedgerow an I make it with my own elderberry.'

'Well,' he said, 'it is very gude.'

They sat there an talked fir a few moments. But there wis a clock on

* placed the auld man by the chair – showed him the chair

the wall that the aul wumman hed got from her grandmother which we call a wag-at-the-wa clock, it wis 'tick-tick-tick-ticking' pas' the minutes. And every moment the auld man wis luikin up, watchin the clock an watchin the minutes passin by. The auld wumman wis very curious why the aul man wis watchin the time so much, she said, 'Stranger, are ye in a hurry to go somewhere? I see that ye're keep watchin the clock.'

'Well,' he says, 'I must keep my eyes ond the time because my time is very short, I soon hev tae be ond my wey.'

'Well,' she said, 'hev you far to go?'

He said, 'Far tae go I hev, but hit'll take me a long time tae get there because I don't travel very fast.'

An the aul wumman wis very curious about this, she said, 'Well, would you hev somethin to eat?'

'Well,' he said, 'I have never had much to eat fir a long time, but if you've a little tae spare before A go on my wey, it wad be very kinly accepted.'

So the aul wumman went into the back of her little kitchen an she brought back a piece o cheese an a piece o bread and a hard-boiled egg, that she hed boiled that morning from her own hens. She placed hit forward on the table an the auld man sat there, he ate hit very slowly. He turned round to the auld wumman, she watched him an he drank his wine, she watched him. An she cuid *see* . . . there were a queer thing happening by him, but he kep watchin the clock . . . Because his eyes begint tae change, gone wis the auld look from his face an his eyes began tae seem bluer! They were not watery like the eyes of an auld man, they were straight an blue-luikin like the eyes of a young man. An this upset the aul wumman. An as she sat there watchin im havin his little bite tae eat she luikit doon tae his feet, she cuid see his toes wis stickin out from the sandals. But the nails of his toes wis not auld an yellae like the toes o an auld man; the nails of his toes wis fresh like the toes of a baby. She never saw his legs because they were covered up by his coat. An the auld wumman thought this was queer because she hed never come in contact with a person like this before. De aul wumman never knew what time it was; she knew the time by the clock, but she never knew what time it was o the year.

So they sat there an they talked, she put more sticks ond the fire an asked him would he like more wine? But then naturally, he would like more wine. She saw that on the side of his face the beard begint tae disappear, bi the sides of his face. And he sat an talked for a few moments, his cheeks begint tae come clean an tidy round aboot where the hair was. An the auld wumman thought tae herself, 'What is happenin? This man seems tae dissolve before me an become a new person! What kin o person can he be?' So she wis curious an she wantit tae understand. She said, 'Would you like something more to drink?'

'Well,' he said, 'I really enjoyed that to drink.'

An she walkit in to get him another glass o the elderberry wine, it took her about five minutes tae get the wine. But when she cam back his beard hed seem tae be gone an dher wur jist a wee stubble ond his chin! And his beautiful blue eyes were shining straight over. An his hair, who was grey an long, begint tae get short an begint tae change hits colour! An the auld wumman said tae herself, 'What in the world . . . how can a person that hes come tae visit me this time of night . . .' An de auld wumman didna have one idea what kin o person hit was. But the auld man sat there. But now she cuid see hit wis an auld man ind one wey, but hit wis a young man in another way. An she luikit down at his feet once more, she saw his toes were like the toes of children. 'Oh dear-oh dear-oh,' said the auld wumman, 'what is happenin – I want tae see this happenin but I don't believe hit!'

But the old man is busy watchin the clock an she wis wonderin why he wis always watchin the time passin by. After he had his meal they sat and talkit about many things, he'd asked her about er hens an asked er about everything, asked her about er life, how she spent the life on the beach, how she enjoyed the last year an wis the last year gude to her, he said, 'Did last year treat you kindly?'

'Oh,' she said, 'well, I've had a wonderful year, my hens wis layin an there nothing wis wrong wi me an I wisna feelin ill. But hit only makes me aulder when another year comes.' (Ye see what she said, *'Hit only makes me aulder!'*) An she's luikin forward tae next year comin an what would happen. They talked for many hours. Then the auld wumman could see that there were somethin strange about this person that sat before her, so she turned round, said, 'Stranger, would you tell me the truth?'

He said, 'What is hit you want tae know?'

'Well,' she said, 'luik, you've been in my home now fir over eight hours an we've talked many things. An I've seen a wonderful change come over you.'

An the young auld man smiled, he said, 'Auld wumman, it's the same thing happening all over the world at this present moment, because everyone is welcomin the change gunnae happen within the next quarter-hour tae come. So A don't know why you should be worried about hit.'

She says, 'I'm really worriet because I can see the change – when ye cam inta me you've hed a beard and now yir beard is gone. You had the appearance of an auld man and now you don't look an auld man tae me, you look like a young man. Does the wine I give ye hev made ye drop these years, or mebbe the egg I gev ye made ye drop these years?'

An he stood up – as straight as straight cuid be – he luikit at the clock an he said, 'No, hit's not you, hit's not you, my auld wumman . . . I thank ye fir yir kindness but A must be on my way. It is *time* that hes caught up with me!'

She said, '"Time?" But there's plenty time.'

He said, 'There might be plenty time fir you, but there's not much time fir me,' an he stood up an his beard wis gone. His cheeks were as red an rosy as the face of a child, an his eyes wis blue as the blue of a newborn baby. As he stude at straight, an his feet ind the sandals wis like the feet of a newborn boy. He stood there before her an he held out his hand, an his fingernails wis like fingernails of a child. He said, 'Luik, aul wumman, I hev come tae visit you because I respect your life an A respect the things that ye hev done. But unknown to you . . . ye don't even know what time it is, do you?'

She said, 'No, I don't know what time it is.' An she looked at the clock, hit wis quarter tae twelve in the clock. He hed been with her for eight hours talkin an bletherin.

He said, 'A must be on my way.'

'But,' she says, 'before ye go, please tell me something because I am so upset – tae see an auld man comin inta my house an a young man walkin away.'

He said, 'In fifteen minutes hit'll be twelve o'clock, an then my time really begins: I have a long way tae go and a long long year to spend an many many places tae travel.'

She says, 'Who are you, stranger?'

He says, 'I am Father Time. An you be privileged, because hit's not many people I be visitit,' an he turned round, he says tae the auld wumman, 'dae ye know what time hit is?'

She said, 'Hit's five minutes tae twelve.'

'But dae you know what day hit is?'

She said, 'No, I don't.'

He said, 'Hit's almost twelve o'clock – an hit's the beginning of a New Year.'

She says, '"New Year!" I thought it was weeks away. I prepared fir hit but I never knew hit would come so soon. Wad ye do me one favour?'

He says, 'What cuid A do for you before I go?'

'Would you drink one glass of wine from me?'

He said, 'I'm sorry . . . because the clock'll soon be strikin twelve,' and like that the young man wis gone! And that is the end o my story!

THE COMING OF THE UNICORN

Many many years ago, long long before your time an mine when this country wis very young, there wonst lived a king. But this particular king was a great huntsman an he lived with his wife ind this great castle. An the only thing that this king really loved to do was hunt, he huntit small animals, he huntit big animals, an i these bygone days the land wis overrun with animals fir tae hunt. He had his huntsmen and he had a beautiful wife, he hed a beautiful palace, he hed a beautiful kingdom an he was very happy. An he got pleasure from hunting. But the king only huntit to supply food fir his own castle an fir the villages around his kingdom. He used tae collect all his huntsmen an go on hunts, mebbe three–four times a year tae give his people enough food tae supply them ti the next hunt.

But one particular day this king gathered all his huntsmen together, said 'goodbye' to the womenfolk because they'd be gone fir a couple days or mebbe more, to bring back all these animals they would salt fir the winter; bade 'goodbye' tae his queen as usual an tuik all his huntsmen, they rode out. An they rode fir many days in the forest, because in these bygone days it was mostly all forest, there werena many townships or little villages along the way. The land was very desolate but wis overrun with animals of all descriptions.

Then the huntsmen always made sure that the king should get the best shot, anything at would come up before them. So lo an behold what should stop before the king . . . it was all bows and arras in these days an swords . . . An who should the' corner i one corner but a bear, a great brown bear. The huntsmen drew back an let the king have the first shot, because it was a big bear an they knew it cairried a lot o weight, it would be a lot o food fir the villagers. The king, who was a great archer, put his bow an arrow to his shoulder an he fired, he fired an arrow an he hut the bear, the arrow stuck in the bear's chest. An the bear stood up straight when the blood start't tae fall from hits chest, hit put its paw to hits chest where the arrae hed entered, it held it there fir a few minutes. An the king was amazed: hit stood straight there an it tuik hits paw – it luikit at the blood on hits paw – an it looked at the king. And then it cowpled over, fell down dead. An the king was so sad at seein this, he was so sad.

He told his huntsmen, 'Pick hit up and carry it back. We will hunt no more today.' They carried the bear back to the palace, an the king said to his huntsmen, 'Take hit and divide it among the villagers, but bring me its skin.'

So naturally the huntsmen dividit the bear up, passt it around to all the people in the village an they brought the skin to the king. An the king gave orders fir the skin to be dried, the skin wis dried through time an brought into the palace and put upon the floor.

But every time the king luikit at the skin, he got sadder and sadder and sadder. An the sadder he got the less he thought about huntin. Now the next hunt wis comin up an the king didna want to go, he was so sad tae see this he didna want tae go hunt nae more. He went inta his chamber and he felt so sad. The bugle was sounding fir the next hunt, they called on their king, but lo an behold the king wouldn't go. And from that day on to the next months an the next months follaein an the next months follaein, the king never joined in – no more did the king join the hunt. His charger wis waitin, his beautiful horses were in the stable, his bows and arras were sharpent fir everything for him, but the king never went. The huntsmen huntit, but they couldnae coax their king ind any wey. The king was down-heartit an broken and sad. The queen was upset, she was so troubled.

'Why,' she said, 'what happened to Ir Majesty the King, what's the trouble?'

The huntsmen told her, 'He hes the bearskin.'

She says, 'Prob'ly if we take the bearskin away – its prob'ly that's at's upsettin him.'

She removed the bearskin from the floor of the palace but it made no difference. The king had his meals, he had his lunch but he hed seemingly lost all interest in life in any way. He talked tae the queen, he talked tae everybody, but he jist felt so upset that there's nothing in the worl seemed tae excite him anymore, efter him bein a great hunter an a great huntsman nobody could excite him anymore. Now the queen stood it fir a few months but she couldna stand it any longer. She cuid see her king was jist fadin away, he jist want't tae sit in his parlour an be by hisself. He wis a great sportsman an a great swordsman an he jist seemed tae lost all interest in life for evermore! He didna want tae dae nothing, he didna want tae do nothing in the worl! The queen was very upset by this.

So one day she could stand it no more, she called the three palace magicians together, told them the story I'm tellin you. 'Look,' she said, 'you must do something for the king. He doesna cuddle me, he doesn't make love tae me, he just sits there, he has his meals, he is completely lost! He's only a livin dead person. You must do something to excite him to bring him back to his own wey – an make him a king once more! An his people are worried, he hes never put in an appearance before his people. He disna join the huntsmen, he disna do nothing, he jist sits there like a statue. He takes his meals . . . He disna even speak to me! He is lost, he's in another world! What has happened to our king?'

So the three wisemen, the magicians of the palace got their heads together an said, 'We know his trouble – it was the bear – the sadness of seein the blood fae the bear that made him so sad, he disna want to hunt anymore. But if we could between hus construct something that would excite him an make him be a king again, then everything'd be all right.' So the three court magicians put their heads together. 'Well,' they said, 'what cuid we do to excite him?'

One said, 'We need tae construct something to raise Our Majesty's attention. What cuid we do?' They were very wise these men, very clever an they worked in magic in the king's court.

One said, 'If we could construct an animal, a special animal that . . . who would be swifter than the wind, fiercer than the lion an fiercer than a boar at everyone was afraid of, an we'd beg the king to help hus; then mebbe we cuid bring im back from his doldrums an make him a king once more.'

So the three magicians put their heads together an one said, 'Well, I could use ma power tae give it the body of a pony who will ride an fly swifter an the wind.'

And the second one said, 'I could give it the fierceness an the tusk of a boar.'

An the third one said, 'I could give it the power and the tail of a lion.'

So they put their heads together once more an said, 'What hev we constructed between hus? We hev a horse that flies swifter than the wind, we have the tusk of a boar and the tail of a lion. Well, there's no problem: we'll give it the tail of a lion, we'll give it the tusk of a boar and we'll give it the body of a pony and we'll set hit free. And we'll tell the king that there's a magic animal in his kingdom that no huntsmen cuid ever catch – but we'll send hit before the huntsmen.' So lo an behold the three magicians constructed an animal between them: they gev it the beautiful slender body of the swiftest pony that ever rode ond the earth, they gev it the tusk of a boar – but instead o putting it on its mouth they put it on his forehead – they gev hit the determination of a lion an the power of the lion – but instead o givin hit the lion's body they put the lion's tail ond it. And what did they say 'we're gaunnae call hit?'

'Well,' one said, 'we universt between hus* to construct hit ... We'll call it a "unicorn".' And there lo an behold became the birth of the unicorn, the most beautiful, the most wonderful, the most swiftes and the most fiercest animal of all. These three wisemen set hit free tae roam the kingdom – tae interrupt every huntsman that ever went ond their way.

So naturally these huntsmen who had got tired of waitin fir the king an tired waitin fir food, knew that the're no way they could coax the king tae go with them anymore, went on the hunt without the king! An they hunted. But whenever they went tae hunt, up jumpit before them was this beautiful animal – white as white cuid be – a beautiful pony, the tail of a lion an the tusk of a boar straight from its forehead. An hit ran before them an they huntit it an they searched for hit. But hit wis fiercest an it attacked dem, it threuw them off their horses, but no wey in the worl cuid they hurt hit, no wey in the worl cuid they catch hit. So after many days huntin it, fir weeks an months they finally rode back to the palace beraggled an tired, with not one single thing because the interest t' catch this animal.

When one o the auld court magicians walkit out an he said tae them, 'What is yir problem, men? Why hev you come home from the hunt so empty-handit?'

An they said, 'We have come home empty-handed because we cuid not catch nothin, because a animal that we hev never saw in wir life – with a horn in hits forehead, with the swiftness of a pony, with the

---

* universt between hus – got together

fierceness of a lion an the tail of a lion – hes came before us at every turn, an we tried tae fight hit but it was impossible.'

'We must tell the king,' said the court magician, 'we must tell the king about this animal! Mebbe hit will get him out of his doldrums.'

So they walkit up, they told the king an they begged, 'Master, Master, Master, deares Huntsman, dearest King, Our Majesty, we hev failed in wir hunt an the people in the village are dyin with hunger because we've no food fir them.'

'Why,' said the king, 'yese are huntsmen aren't ye? Hevna I taught yese tae hunt?'

'But, Majesty,' they said, 'hit's a animal . . . this bein, this thing that we've never saw in wir lives – the swiftness of a pony an the horn on its head of a boar an the tail of a lion – who's as swift an so completely swift that drives before hus, that we jist can't catch hit.'

'Dher never wur such a thing,' said the king, 'not in my kingdom!'

'Yes, Our Majesty,' they said, 'there is such a thing. He interrupts hus an he interferes with our hunt, an every minute he disappears an then he's gone, we jist can't go on with the hunt an wir people are dyin with hunger. You mus help hus!'

But then said the king, 'Is hit true? Tell me, please, is there something that I've never seen in my kingdom?'

'Yes, Our Majesty,' he said, 'the're something you've never seen. This animal is bewitched!'

An at that the king woked up, he rubbed his eyes an the thought of the bear wis gone fra him fir evermore. He said, 'If there's something that interrupts my people and interrupts my huntsmen, then I mus find the truth!' So the king calls fir his horse, fir his steed, he calls fir his bows an he calls fir his arras, he blows the bugle and he calls fir his huntsmen, 'Ride with me,' he says, 'tae the forest an show me this wonderful animal that upsets yese all! Hit won't upset me,' and the king was back again once more! And the people are happy, an they blow their bugles, everyone gathert in the court tae see the king off wonst more after a year! An they rode out on the great hunt, 'Lead me,' says the king, 'tae where you saw this animal last!'

So they led him tae the forest and the aul wisemen were sure that hit wis there. An *there* before him stude this magnificent animal – taller than any horse the king hed ever rode, with a horn on hits forehead and the tail of a lion, an the swiftness o the wind – an the king said, 'Leave hit to me!' It stood there an luikit at them, the king said, 'Leave hit tae me!' An the king had a great charger, he rode after hit, and he rode for many many miles an he rode for many many miles, an the farther the king rode the farther hit went. An the faster the king rode the faster hit went – till hit disappeared in the distance an then the king wis lost. Hit wis gone. Sadly and tiredly he returned tae the sound of his trumpets of his huntsmen. But the king had never ever got close enough tae fire an arra at hit! Fir days an weeks an months to pass by the king huntit an the king searcht, the king searcht fir this beautiful animal, but it always disappeared in the distance; hit always rose before him but he could never catch hit. The king searched and the king became so obsessed wi this animal – he became his ownself again. Gone wis the thought of everything, he only had one thing in his mind – that he must catch this animal. He called his great wisemen together, he called his court together, he called everybody, his huntsmen together tried tae explain what kind o animal at wis roamin his kingdom.

'Master,' said one of the great court magicians, 'it is a *unicorn!*'

'"A unicorn"?' said the king, 'how many unicorns are there on my land?'

And they said, 'Only one, Our Master, an hit's up to you tae catch hit.'

But the king wastit his time, he searched fir weeks an he searcht fir months, an he tuik his huntsmen an the people were dying fir food. But the king could never ever catch the unicorn. And then when the king became so sad and broken-heartit, he called his great men together, says, 'Luik, this is a magic animal. *I'll* never catch hit in a million years.' He called his masons before him an he called the court sculpturers before im, he said, 'Look, I know in my heart that I am a great huntsman. And I have searcht fir many months an A've done something that A should never hev done, I deprived all my people of food because we depend on the hunt. I have not killed a deer or killed a wolf or killed anything for months. But,' he says, 'youse huntsmen, go out and hunt fir food fir the villagers and spread hit among the people while I talk to my sculpturers and my masons.' He said tae these people, 'I *know* that I can never catch the animal they call a "unicorn". But there's nothing in the world I cuid love more than jist t' hev a statue of him at my door where I cuid walk an see him.'

An they asked him, 'Master, we don't know what you want.'

'Well,' he said, 'I'll tell you what hit's like and I want you tae make hit for me.' So he explained to the sculpturers an the masons, 'Hit was like a pony with a tail of a lion and a horn on his forehead and the swiftness o the wind.'

So they carved him out of some stone, they carved from stone two things like the king hed told them tae be, an they put them straight in front of the king's castle. So that every mornin when the king walkit down, there stood before him was the thing that he huntit for many many months which he had never captured – the unicorn. An the king loved tae walk down, put his hand on his statues, two of them, one on each side of the door of his palace – put his hand on his statues that stude there before him – like a beautiful pony with a horn on his forehead and the tail of a lion, an he walked around them. And when all these people went on a hunt, he went with them. But he had his *unicorn*. From that day on he huntit with his friends and distributit all the food that he ever found – deers, bears, foxes, wolfs – he huntit the lot. But from that day, the day that the sculpturers built the uncorns in front of his door, he never saw his *unicorn* again.

But when the king passed on, fir many many years still remained what the sculpturers hed made in front of his palace – and that's where your unicorn came from the day. That is a true story and that is also the end o my tale!

FRIDAY AND SATURDAY

Many years ago there lived an old fisherman and his wife, an they were very very poor. He wasn't a sea fisherman, he fisht i the river, it was a large river passed by his small house where he stayed. And in these days there were no restriction against fishin the river, catchin as many fish and selling it to anyone who want't to buy hit, and this auld man hed spent his entire life fishing – sometimes he hed good days an sometimes he hed bad days. But he hed never hed any children an his wife hed always longed for children, because when the auld man wis away fishin she wis left by herself. But he wisna an auld man, mebbe in his thirties or forties.

But lo an behold one morning she says tae him, 'Husband, you know we don't hev very much this morning fir breakfast, an I've little tae give ye.'

'Well,' he said, 'whatever ye hev tae offer will be much acceptable.' So she baked him a small oatmeal cake an she gev him whatever she had fir breakfast. He said, 'I must do something today, I must! I must catch some today.'

She says, 'Please don't stay away too long, cause ye know A'm lonely. I am lonely stayin here bi myself all the time,' because the house that they lived in wis many miles from the nearest neighbour, hit wis beside a forest an a large river passin by an many many waterfalls. The aul man hed fished fir salmon an fish, an what they cuidna eat he took to the village many miles away an sold.

But he'd had bad luck within the last two-three days, an things went from bad to worse. So he made up his mind this morning that he wad go an make sure that he would get something before he'd come home. So he'd sat, an he'd fished from pool to pool, but no luck. Then lo an behold he caught a fish, one little fish. An this wis the funnies fish he'd ever saw in his life – jist like a goldfish – it had large fins and a large mouth, an a large head and a small tail, but hit was a good wee bit fish an that wis all he got that day. So he said, 'Ye don't look very good, I've never saw the likes o you before, an I'm sure ye'll jist taste as good as the rest.' So he tuik hit home to his wife, an she met him at the door.

'Husband,' she says, 'you know, ye been away a long time.'

'Oh well,' he said, 'A been fishin a long time.'

She said, 'Div ye any luck?'

He shook his head.

'Hit's not that,' she sayd, 'if A hed someone tae keep me in company, jist a *baby* or a child or something tae pass the time away, I wouldna mind how long you stayed away.' An the fish begint tae flap hits tail.

He says, 'That's all A've got.'

She said, 'Did you not kill hit?'

He said, 'A've killed hit,' an hits tail wis goin like that – flappin in the basket.

She says, 'That's a queer fish you've caught, husband, I've never saw one like that before.'

'Well, I caught it in the river,' he said, 'hit's jist a fish. I've never caught one like that before, but it's just good enough tae eat.'

So he tuik it intae the kitchen, they hed very little tae eat, he tuik hit an he cleaned it, an he cut aff the head an he cut aff the tail. Now he had a little hound bitch, she wis whimperin wi the hunger because she hedna hed any food. He threw the dog the head an he threw the dog the tail an the dog gobblit it up. After he'd cut aff the head an tail there werena very much left. And after he cooked hit himself he said tae the woman, 'Well, the're not much fir the two o hus. I think,' he said, 'I been away all day an A hed a bannock this mornin from you, the best thing I can do – eat it yirsel!' An the wumman ett the fish hersel.

So the next mornin the puir auld man had no breakfast, an he went away back to the river again, he had a good day. He caught five or six beautiful salmon in the river, tuik them home, cookit one fir their meals an took the rest to the village an sold them. Everyone wantit tae buy his salmon an he got some money! This went on every day fir the next three months. He never had a bad day, he wis always gettin fish an he wis always sellin them, he always hed plenty t' eat. But he wis sittin one night efter he hed fed himself an he luikit, his wee bitch, his wee whippit bitch seemed to be gettin awfae fat. To his wife he said, 'She seems to be gettin very fat.'

She says, 'So am I, so am I, gettin fat too. A've wonderful news fir ye, A'm gaunnae have a baby.'

He said, 'What!'

She says, 'I'm goin to have a baby.'

'Oh,' the fisherman said, 'that's wonderful news, great, great wonderful news!' He wis over the moon. And he said, 'Bi the looks o *her* lyin there, she's like you too.'

But the auld woman said, 'There's not been a dog about the place an she's never left home.'

'Well,' the auld man said, 'she looks as if she's gaunnae hev pups.'

The auld man went about his fishin business an he'd never hed a bad day from then on. Things began tae go from worse to better, ever day seemed tae be better fir im since ever he caught this funny-luikin fish, goldfish in the river. But lo an behold he came back one day six weeks later, an there was his bitch – wi *two* beautiful wee pups, two beautiful wee pups. An he jist loved em! Two dogs they were an he jist loved em. 'An,' he said, 'when they grow up they'll jist do my baby.'

And lo an behold another six month passed, an his wife gev birth tae two beautiful boys, two beautiful little boys, wonderful little boys. But it wis late at night when they were born, one wis born at twelve o'clock an the other wis born at one o'clock i the mornin. So in these days the women cuid dae their own thing, you know, they needed no doctors or no nurses in these bygone days. An after the woman hed fixed up the babies an lay in bed, an the auld man made her a drink an fed her, she got up two days later. And they sat an discussed things, what they were gaunna do. They were jist over the moon – they hed two wonderful boys an two wonderful pups. An the old man said, 'That's one for each o them when they grow up, an the pups'll grow up wi them tigether. But,' he said, 'what we gaunna call them?'

'Well,' she says, 'husband, you know one wis born in late at night and one wis born in early in the mornin.'

He said, 'What night wis he born on? Let me scratch ma head now, oh, that was last Friday.'

She said, 'Yes, hit was Friday, one wis born last Friday night an the other one came the morning later.'

'Well,' he says, 'there's nae problem: we'll call them "Friday" and "Saturday".' And there was named the two boys Friday and Saturday. An the boys grew up an the pups grew up, the two boys became grown up tae young laddies, and they loved their two dogs! Now the auld man still carried on wi his fishin.

So one day while the boys is busy playin at home wi their dogs – this time they were about ten year old – the old man went tae his fishin once more. He had tae pass through the forest, ond his way he used tae stop beside the shade o a tree an light his pipe, an look – at the foot o the tree lyin was a sparra hawk – hit was dead. And the auld man cuid see that hit was a female hawk, he said tae himself, 'She must hae fell from a branch up there.' An he luikit up an he saw the wee nest, he heard, 'Kyoch-kyoch, kyoch-kyoch, kyo-kyoch, kyo-kyoch.' He said, 'There must be babies up there in that nest.' So the're plenty branches, the man climbed up from branch to branch, an sure enough ind the nest was two sparra hawks – an he knew in his own mind – that was their mother at wis dead at the foot o the tree.

'Now,' he said, 'if I leave them there they'll die wi hunger.' But instead o gaun to fish, he tuik the two wee sparra hawks oot the nest an back he goes to the house.

He builds a wee box for em an the wee boys cam up tae im. They were good young boys and their pups wis grown up tae dogs, great big hound dogs. The boys loved their dogs, and he loved his boys an so did the mother. 'Now,' said the father, 'a wonderful thing happent today, I found these two hawks.'

'Oh, Daddy, Daddy, give them tae hus, we'll take care o them!'

So he said, 'Luik, boys, yese take one each, have one each an rear hit up an take care o hit, hit'll be a guid pet fir yese. Ye can go huntin wi them when they grow up an teach them all ye can.' Now the boys tuik the two hawks, they brought them up to full-grown hawks an these hawks became as tame as cuid ever be, and each hawk knew its own master, it wouldna go to the other one. These hawks were great hunters.

But the auld man an his wife had an auld pony that they used tae take tae market wi his fish in his cart. So the next mornin he went out to the stable tae yoke his auld pony up, an he saw she wis lyan down ond her side. 'Funny,' says the aul man, 'she's never been sick before. She looks very sick,' so he called his wife; an his wife cam round to the stable, the shed where they had the auld horse lyan. An the auld white horse is lyan groanin an gruntin on the floor, heavin an pantin. And the aul fisherman said tae his wife, 'I think she's goin to die. We can't afford tae buy another.'

An his wife said, 'She's not gaun tae die – she's in foal!'

'I the name o the worl,' says the auld man, 'hit's impossible. She cannae be in foal . . . What's happenin in this place? First you, then my bitch an noo ma horse – what's happenin in this place? An we're miles away from everybody excepts all the people i the village, what's happenin here?'

'Well,' the aul woman said tae him, 'I don't know. I've got two lovely sons an I love my children, an they have two lovely dogs an their hawks,' she says, 'I hope we get a wee foal.'

The words wis no sooner out of the auld woman's mouth – out popped one wee foal, a snow-white foal – an out popped another foal – black as coal, a pure black foal, twin foals. An the auld man an the auld woman wis over the moon! They never believed that this could really happen to them. They called the two boys tae come in, tae keep their dogs back. The auld mare got up tae her feet an there wis the two beautiful wee foals, a black one an a white one – both males, stallions.

Friday said, 'I want the black one.'

An Saturday said, 'I'll take the white one.'

An the two foals jist stood up in about an hour's time an the boys jist couldna leave them alone. The' loved these foals like nothing on this earth. An life went on and on and on in the place, an the auld man fished all the days an his auld mare became well again. He's tuik his fish to the village an things begint tae improve fir them, nothing ever seemed to go wrong anymore.

But years passed by an the boys grew up. Each one had a horse, each one had a dog an each one hed a hawk. An they used tae go off huntin in the forest and they always brought back plenty fir their mother an father. But now as the years passed by they became about twenty years old, and the father wis gettin old an so wis the mother. An one son turned round one night and he told his father, 'Father, you know the're not much for hus here in this place with you, but ma mother here an you and ma brother. The're not much fir hus tae do. You've tuik care o hus, ye've luikit after hus, but we must go an seek wir own fortune an find a job an go somewhere.'

Father said, 'Who's gaunna take care o yir horse an yir hawk an yir hound when you go?'

'Ho,' says Firday, 'whaurever I go, ma horse an my hound an ma hawk goes with me!'

His brother tried, he said, 'Well, why don't you stay? I'll miss you if ye're gaunna go.'

He said, 'Luik, A mus go inta the world, hit's no use jist stayin here, I must go into the world and seek ma fortune in other places.'

So the next mornin Friday packed the little pieces o belongins that he owned, tied em tae his saddle, called on his dog, took his hawk in his hand, bade 'farewell' tae his mother and father, an promised he'd come back in a year and a day – that he'd come back rich. Now we'll leave the auld man and the auld woman and Saturday fir a wee while and we'll follae Friday as he travels on his journey.

So Friday set off, a handsome young man wi his black horse and his hound at his foot and his hawk by his hand. An he rode on an he rode on an he came tae villages, he spent his time, he huntit an he done all these things along the way until he came tae a large town, got in touch with all the people in the town, stabled his horse, talked to many people. Everybody in this village seemed sad somehow, oh, everybody wis hangin their head an nobody wis happy. And Friday said, 'Why is* everybody seem sad in this village? What's wrong with the place?'

Then one auld man he talked to wi a long white beard said, 'Well, you wad be sad too . . . You know, up there on the hill is the palace of the king. An the king and his wife the queen has lost their only child, who completely disappeared. One moment she walked i the gardens, the next moment she wis gone, she wis only sixteen years of age an she's never been seen since. The king and the queen are broken-heartit an that's why everybody's sad. The king has offered a large reward, he's sent couriers all over the world an nobody seems tae know what happened to her, she jist completely disappeared off the face of the earth. An there be no happiness and no nothing in this town until we find what happened to the princess.'

'Sad story,' says Friday, 'sad sad story. But the're not much I can do.' So he rode through the village an went on his way. But he's always thinkin about this . . . 'What cuid hev happened to this young wumman?' he said.

He rode on an rode on fir many miles till he came to a large forest an he rode through the forest, an it got dark! An he came tae a little house i the middle the forest an he said tae himself, 'Well, no sense a spendin an evening out in the open when ye can find shelter.' There wis a light in the house. An he went tae the house, he jumped off his horse, bade his dog 'be quiet', leit his hawk sittin in the saddle – which never flew

* is – does

away, kep by his side. Went tae the door an he knocks on the door. No answer; he knocked again.

And then a voice answered him, 'Who's there?'

'Hit's me,' said Friday, 'a traveller seekin shelter fir the night.'

'Well, I can give ye shelter,' said the voice of a woman through the door, 'but I'm not opening my door to you tonight.'

'Why not?' said Friday.

She says, 'A can see-e ye have some evil creatures with you.'

Friday said, 'They're just my horse an ma hound an ma hawk.'

'Well,' she said, 'if ye want tae hev shelter fir the night, an come in an make yirsel at home – tie them up!'

Friday said, 'I don't have anything tae tie them with! I'll leave them wander.'

'No, don't leave them wander,' she said. 'I'll pass you something through de keyhole, an tie them up!' And in this house lived a witch! A wicked witch who hatit everybody ind this earth, an she pulled one of the long strands of her hair, she passed hit through the keyhole. An she said, 'Can ye see the rope A'm passin ye through the keyhole?'

An Friday said, 'Yes, I see hit.'

'Well,' she said, 'tie up yir horse an tie up yir hound an tie up yir hawk! And then you can hev shelter fir the night.'

Puir Friday, not givin a thought, pulled the hair through the keyhole like a rope an went and tied up his horse, tied up his hound an tied the legs of his hawk. An then the door opened, he walked in an the door closed behind him. An wonst he entered i the house he met the most evilest-luikin auld wumman ye ever saw in yir life! Her teeth wis stuck out, her hair wis hangin in spirls doon her back an she wis in rags. An there was a burning fire and on the fire was a large pot, an a black cat wis sittin spittin – 'ppit, pffit, pffit' – beside the fireside. An all round the fireside was heaps of stones.

She says, 'You have come at last an I've waited long for ye!' an she sprang upon him. She took her long fingernails roond his neck an she held on an her and Friday startit tae fight. An they fought an they fought an they rolled an at, but she got the better o Friday, she got o top o Friday an she held him down bi the neck.

And Friday hed only breath to say, *'Ma horse, my hound an ma hawk, please help me!'*

An the auld wumman said, *'Haud on, hair, haud on, hair!'* An the hair held on tae the hawk and the hound and the horse, an wouldna let them go in any way. Till she beat Friday intae unconscious. Then she took a wand from the side o the fire an she said, 'You're another one tae ma collection!' and lo an behold Friday became another stone by the fireside.

Now many many miles away Saturday was with his mother an his father back ind their little home in the forest. An he huntit with his dog and his hawk an his hound. But he had a longin, because a year an a day had passed an his brother hed never returned, he wis very sad an very worried. And one day he just couldn't stand hit any longer, he said tae his mother an father, 'Mother an Father, A doubt * ma brother Friday's not comin back. God knows what happened tae him. I'll hev tae go an find what happened to him. A'll search the whole world over, but, Mother, I'll come back, whenever I find my brother I'll come back.'

'Well,' the auld man said, 'the best of luck, son, tae ye. Search as far as ye can, an try an find the truth what happened tae yir brother because I think something terrible has befallen him.'

So the next mornin Saturday tuik his white horse and his hound an his hawk, an he went on his way. And lo an behold, he traivellt the same road at his brother hed traivelled before and he found word of his brother all the way. Until he came tae this town where every people was sad, an he stayed in the same place, done the same things his brother had. And lo an behold he'd talked tae the same auld man, the auld man told him the same story. An he asked about his brother.

'Oh yes,' he said, 'hit's a long time ago, though, nearly a year ago, ae young man with the same as † yirself, only his horse wis of a different colour, passed by here an travellt on his way.'

Saturday said, 'Well, I mus journey on, auld man,' and he bade the aul man 'farewell'. He travelled on the same journey an lo an behold he came to the same forest, an he came tae the same house, it was a late evenin as usual. An he wis seekin shelter fir the night, came off his horse, knockit at the door.

An the voice answered him, 'An what to you want?'

'I'm jist a stranger on the road seekin shelter.'

'Well, A'll give ye shelter,' said the voice, 'but I can't open my door.'

'Why can't ye open the door?' said Saturday.

'I'm afraid of these evil animals you hev with ye. I'll open the door tae ye, if ye tie them up.'

* A doubt – I fear
† with the same as – like

Saturday says, 'I hev nothin tae tie them up with.'

She says, 'A'll pass ye a rope through the keyhole.' An the evil witch passed another hair from her head through the keyhole, fed it through the keyhole.

Now, Saturday thought there were something queer about this an he said, 'There's nobody gaunnae make me tie up my horse, my hound an ma hawk fir nobody. I'm tyin it up for nobody!' So he pou'd the knife from his belt, an as she wis passin the hair through the keyhole he cut hit in bits, dropped hit behind the door! An shoutit, 'There now!' he said, 'I've tied them up.' An the door opent an closed, when he was in.

When he cam intae the house there wis the evil witch once more, with the long straggly hair an the ugly teeth an the long nails an she says, 'You hev come, seekin what ye'll never find!' An she dived o' top o him, an the two o them start't tae fight. An they fought an they fought an they fought, but the witch she wis more powerful an she got o' top o Saturday, she held him down.

An he shoutit fir *his horse, his hound and his hawk tae come tae help him!*

An she shoutit, *'Hold on, hair, hold on, hair!'*

An the hair said, 'A cannae hold on, I'm lyin cut at the back o the doorway.'

An just like that the door burst open – the horse hed kickit the door open – in cam the hound an in cam the hawk. And the hawk wis stickin tae her hair an pickin her head, scratchin her head with the claws. An the hound wis bittin her legs an the horse wis kickin her. Between the four o them the' beat the witch. An the witch held up her hand in surrender.

'Now,' says Saturday, 'you are beat!'

'Yes,' says the witch, 'A'm beat. What is it you want?'

He said, 'I want you t' tell me – have ye seen my brother?'

She said, *'Don't* touch me anymore, an I'll give ye back yir brother!'

He said, 'You hev ma brother?'

'Yes,' she said, 'I have yir brother. He's the faraway stone in the fireplace. Take that stick,' says the witch, 'an touch the stone.'

'Watch her, hound,' said Saturday, *'watch her! Watch her,'* he says tae the hawk. 'If she makes a move, attack her again!' An the witch wis terrified o this. An the horse stude over her inside the little house. Saturday picked up the queer-luikin stick, an he toucht the faraway stone. And lo an behold there rose his brother once more.

An his brother caresst him, said, 'There's the evil one, give me her stick an I'll finish her fir good!'

'No,' says the witch, 'please, no, don't touch me wi the stick!'

So de two brothers shook hands with each other, glad tae see each other. Saturday said, 'If you were in a stone, what dis all the other stones represent?' An he touched all the stones along the fireplace, an there became lords and ladies and knights all along the fireplace – rose inta the house – till the house wis full! An the witch she wis sittin cowerin in the corner. An Saturday still held the stick in his hand, 'Now,' he said tae her, 'you made all these people suffer an all their people suffer before them. But *you* are going where they were!' He walked over an he toucht her, and lo and behold she turned inta a stone, he put her by the fireplace.

And all these young noblemen and all these young ladies – among them wis the princess . . . Friday an Saturday went out o the house an they all rode back tae the town an had a great celebration. An the king wis delightit tae get his daughter back, he offered him all the treasures and all the money in the town.

An Saturday said, 'No, I don't want nae treasures an I don't want nothing.'

'What do you want?' says the king.

He said, 'I want tae marry yir daughter.'

An the king said, 'You deserve hit!'

Saturday and the princess wis married. His brother Friday married one o the young ladies an they were very happy. An one year later four carriages with horses, dogs and hawks drew up into the forest beside the auld man, the auld fisherman.

The auld man an the auld wumman stood an they luikit, 'Wumman,' he says, 'there's a large procession comin down the road towards wir house.'

She says, 'Don't worry, I can see a hound, a hawk and a horse – wir sons hes come back once more.' An that is the end o my story.

THE SHEEP OF THORNS

A long long time ago away back in Argyllshire there wonst lived two brothers, and they had a large sheep farm between them. The young brother wis evil an A mean evil, he never went tae church, he workit hard but he never went tae church an he didna believe in God; an he didna believe in ghosts, he didna believe in spirits an he didna believe in nothing! An he used to walk home at night drunk, every weekend back from the town, all de way back to the farm where they stayed in the hill, big sheep farm. An his aulder brother wad be sittin waitin on him when he cam back every night. His older brother had never had a drink in his life, an he wis very gentle an very kind, he used to sit and read the Bible tae himself tae pass the time away. An he read the Bible, believed and teacht everything he learned aff the Bible, he wouldna hurt an animal, he wouldna hurt a bird, wouldna hurt nothin.

Now, on this farm they had many many sheep, it was all sheep they had, hundreds o sheep, an the older brother wis very kind and very guid to his animals. But the younges brother wis cruel. He would kick them if they didna go his way; he would kick the dogs if they werena doin the right thing. An whan it came the clippin time . . . every time a sheep grew a wee bit wool he wad clip it aff – even after he'd clippit them before!

An his aulder brother would say tae him, 'Luik, you know the winter's comin in an these animals needs their wee bit fleece tae keep them warm! Hit's okay, brother, takin their wool off in the summertime because they're hot an they dinna need hit, but in the wintertime, brother, they need their wee bit wool to keep them warm.'

'Och, they're only animals,' he said, 'we need the wool, we need the money!' An he wad go out every day round his sheep with his scissors in his bag on his back an his two dogs. An if he called to the dog, an the dog didna do whit he said, hit the dog a kick and knock hit scatterin. If a wee sheep wouldna stand tae get clippit, he would hit it a kick and jab it wi the shears! He wis bad and he wis evil! And if he ever seen a sheep that had a wee taste wool too long, he would chase hit till he cornered hit, cowp an clip hit. This upset his older brother very very much.

An his aulder brother used tae tell him, 'Luik, brother, I don't like what ye're doin.'

'What am I doin any harm?' he said, 'I'm only collectin wool to make money fir hus.'

'But,' he said, 'hit's not that; you ill-treat the animals an ye ill-treat the dogs,' and he stairved the dogs half o the time. 'An ye clip the wool aff the wee sheepies tae keep them warm in the wintertime. Brother, you can't go on like this – an another thing – ye never go tae church!'

'*Don't mention church to me*,' he said, 'i no way. I don't . . . you keep yir church, hit's not my church, it's your church!'

An his brother would jist shake his heid. He knew fine that someday his evilness were gaunnae catch up with him. So this is where my story begins.

So one day he said to his older brother, 'I think I'll go away out to the hill today an gather up some sheep, see if they're gettin any, their fleece is gettin any longer – mebbe have another bag o wool before the winter comes in.'

'Brother,' he said, 'they need their wool tae keep them warm!'

'Ach, you take care o yir Bible,' he said, 'an take care o yir rest o yir things an leave me to my business. They're as much o my sheep as they are yours!' So away he goes wi his two dogs. Whistles the dogs tae him an the wee dogs cowert, they cam wi their wee tails between their legs because they were terrified o im. An away he goes.

Now, they had a large farm and they had a large hill – fir many many miles – an the sheep were scattered, spread far and wide across the hill. So he tuik a bottle o milk with him, he took a bit o piece in his bag, an away he goes wi his two dogs an his scissors inta the hill. And he travels among the heather fir hour after hour, whistlin to the dogs, gathering round all his sheep, checkin them all tae see that they had any wool. He wisna worried if they hed sore feet, they were hurt or anything, he wisna worried if the're anything wrong wi them – he wantit tae see, could he clip some mair wool off em – to make more

147

money for more drink at the weekend fir hisself! But lo an behold, he hed travelled a good bit oot the hill * when down comes the mist! He had seen misty nights on the hill before, but never a night like this! The mist came down, he cuid barely see his finger in front o him. An the two dogs cam in behind him with their tails between their legs.

'What's wrong with you,' he said, 'what's the trouble? Go away out there an bring . . .' Dogs wadna move, the dogs whimpert behind his heels. 'What's wrong with youse animals?' he said, an he hit them a kick. The dogs jist ran roon in circles, cam back in aroon his heels again, their tails between their legs, they were whimperin to theirselves. 'What's wrong with youse,' he said, 'what's troublin ye youse animals?'

Then lo an behold the mist kin o liftit a wee bit, an standin before him wis a sheep, the biggest sheep he'd ever seen among his whole flock, an its *wool* was trailin on the grund! An he said, 'I cannae believe hit, I *can't* believe hit, that you escaped so long wi a fleece like that!' An he wis thinkin about how many pound in his own mind . . . 'Oh, must be twenty–thirty pound o wool on yir back an I'll get you an I'll clip you!' Whistled the dogs – dogs were gone. The dogs hed jist completely disappeared, dogs were gone. He whistled an he called o' the dogs an the sheep still stude; an he cuid see its eyes shinin, its eyes wis blazin! 'I'll get you,' he said, 's'pose it takes me all night I'll get you!'

He runs after the sheep, but the sheep disna run very fast – jis keps a wee bit in front o him. But the harder he goes – it always kep a wee bit in front o him. And he follaed hit, an he followed hit an he follaed, round de hill an round de hill an round de hill. He followed hit fir hours. But he's still gettin no closer tae hit. He wis exhausted, his feet were sore. But he swore in his mind he wis gaunnae catch hit bifore the night wis out. Then he went over the hill an the mist cam doon this hill . . . An he landit in a strange place what he'd never seen bifore in his life. An he cuid see the sheep jist in front o him, an he start't tae go through – this – instead o fog it wis brambles an thorns! An he's tearin his way through the brambles an through the thorns, an they're cuttin his hands an they're scratchin his face an they're tearin his claes, but he's determint he's gaunnae catch this sheep. An the sheep wis jist passin through them as if it wis jist gan through cotton.

---

* oot the hill – out on the hill

He's in such a state noo, it's an obsession wi him – he must get this sheep. An he follaed hit further an he follaed hit further an further . . . It led him through bogs ti there – he's soakin. It led him through swamps, it led him through thorns, through woods an through bankins till he was completely exhausted, till he wis down on his hands and knees. His face was cut, his clothes were torn in rags, his hands wis full o thorns an he still hed the shears in his hand, an venom in his heart – he wis gaunna get this sheep. Till he cuidna go another step, an he shook the shears at hit – '*I'll get you*, e'en suppose it's the last thing I ever do in my life I'll get you!'

An like that the mist rose. An he luikit all roon, the sky wis clear. De moor wis bare, there were not a thing in sight – the sheep wis gone! He looked farther, when he seen two–three sheep pickin the tops o the heather an their wee coats wis – they're shiverin wi the cauld – he'd clippit all the wool aff them. He sat fir a long long while. He finally stude up an he's got ond his feet, an he kin o staggert an stottert an made his wey back tae the fairm. Whan he landed back his brother wis sittin at the table readin the Bible, an he strachlit in, flung hissel doon in ae chair.

An his brother said, 'In the name of *God*, what happened to ye?'

'"*God!*"' he said, 'don't mention that word to me.' He says, 'That *damn sheep!*'

'What "sheep",' he said, 'brother?'

'One,' he said, 'that escaped hus, with the finest coat that ever we seen – its wool as thick as ma hand – an it's trailin on the grund.'

'Brother,' he said, 'we clippit all the sheep this year. I mysel was out in the hill, an I collectit every single sheep in wir own boundaries an we never left none.'

'Yes,' he said, 'there is one we misst! An he's got the best coat on im at you cuid ever see. An I'll get im, I'll get im tomorrow – may it be the las thing I ever do – I'll get him! *May it be the last thing I ever do.*' He went to the cupboard, took oot a bottle o whisky an filled hissel a glass. An his brother sat readin the Bible. He hed somethin tae eat and he sat there, he mumbled tae his ainsel all night after he drank this bottle o whisky.

De old brother said 'goodnight', went away tae his bed. He said, 'The're something terrible, something terrible's gaunna come over that young man.'

So true enough, he spent a restless night: when he went to sleep, back comes the sheep in his mind's eye again – hits eyes is blazin and hits coat's trailin on the ground – de mos beautiful wool . . . And the closer he's gettin tae hit the bigger hit's gettin, an the more wool at's on hit! An he's got up in his bed an he shout't 'I'll get ye, if it's the las thing I ever do!'

And his brother who wis in the next room to him hears him. He said, 'The're something wrong wi my brother, I'd better go in.' An he gets up an pits on his claes an he walks in, opens the door, and his brother's lyin in bed o' the breadth o his back in a mass o sweat.

An he's shakin his two hands, he says, 'I'll get you, I'll get ye s'pose the last thing I ever do!'

The aulder brother went ower an he shakit him up, he said, 'What's wrong, Dougald, what's wrong with ye?'

He wakened up, 'That sheep,' he said, 'that sheep, that sheep!'

He says, 'Forget about the sheep, ye had a bad dream.' He sat an crackit to him a wee while an then he went back tae his bed. An then the younger brother fell asleep.

But true tae his word he wis up early in the mornin, had his breakfast, changed his claes, changed his boots. He turned round to his brother, said, 'Eh, by the way, brother, di' these damn dogs come back last night; they left me on the hill.'

He said, 'They cam back last night, early last night after you left, an I wondered what wis the problem wi them, but A tuik down some food to them. The poor critters 's in a bad state – were ye beatin em?'

'No,' he says, 'I never beat them, they left me.'

'Well,' he said, 'they were in a bad state but I finally got them calmed down an A fed them. But I think if I wis you, I wad leave them.'

'Owch, "leave them",' he said, 'take them, they're no good to me anyway, I'll manage mysel!'

Soon as he had his breakfast away he goes again, the bag on his back wonst more to the hill. An that's all he had in his mind wis one thought – 'I'll get that sheep today – I'll clip that sheep, an I'll clip it so close hit'll never grow another coat like the one hit's got on hits back right noo!' He went all roun the hill, travelled all roun the hill, checkit all the sheep that he cuid see. He saw one or two wi a wee bit coat an he catcht em an cowpit em, clippit the wee bits o wool aff them an left them cold an trembly fir the want o wool, an the winter was comin in.

Then lo an behold – sure enough he cam ower the hill wonst more – down comes the mist wonst more! This time *thicker* an *blacker* comes the mist! An then he luikit through the mist an there it stude wonst more –

this time it was bigger – hits coat was longer, an hit wis trailin in the heather. 'Oh dear-oh dear-oh dear,' he says, 'whan I get my hands on you, I'm gaunnae give you a coat – I'm gaunnae give you a coat whan I get my hands on you! An suppose I chase you to the end of eternity, *suppose you are the devil* I'll get you the night!' And he set off after hit. And away it walks. And he follaes hit an he follaes hit through the mist an through the fog. But if it led him a merry chase before, it led him a ten-times worse merry chase this time – through thorns an brambles an bushes an bogs and heather an glens firever an ever – till at last, it took him inta a corner, the face of an auld clift. No escape.

'Haa,' he says, 'I got ye now, ye'll never climb that rock-face an ye're no gettin past me!' Right at the face of the rock it led him in through a narrow passage an hit stude with its head doon in the front o the rock. And he walkit up tae it, he ran foward an he made snap at hit! But when he made 'snap' at hit, instead o his hands gan intae soft wool, his hands went intae brambles – thick heavy bramble bushes – on this sheep's back! He catcht it bi the horns an hits horns wis red hot, an his hands wis scalded within seconds. But he wouldn't let go! He held on and he wrastlit, an he wrastlit with hit an he wrastlit with hit for nearly half an hour. But every time he got hit on its back, hit got him on his back. An it stood on him an hit wrestled with him, hit tore his claes, hit tore his face, it did everything in the worl ti he wis completely exhausted – ti he cuidna go another step – till there were not a stitch o clothes left on him or not a hale bit on his hands or a hale bit skin on his face which wis torn with brambles! An his hands wur burnt, he cuid barely close them. An then there were a *flash o light* an it was gone.

He stude there dumbfoondit fir a long long while, didna know what was wrong. An the mist cleared. An he luikit roun – the clift face wis gone . . . He wis standing o' top o the wee knowe above his brother's fairm. An he luikit doon, he seen the smoke comin oot o the chimney. He walkit, half-walkit and half-crawled doon tae his brother's farm. Cam in through the door; whan his brother sittin in the chair readin the Bible he cuid barely recognize him in such a sorry state.

He says, 'Brother, in the name of God, what happened tae ye?'

He said, 'That sheep. *That sheep*,' he said.

'What "sheep", brother?' he said.

He said, '*The Sheep of Thorns!*'

He says, 'Brother, what's wrong, what's gone wrong with ye? The're no "sheep o –"'

'Oh yes,' he said, 'the're a *Sheep of Thorns*, and it tore my hands, an hit's *burnt* my hands with hits *blazin horns*. And it tore my clothes an it tore my face an it destroyed my life – I'll never be the same again! Please, brother,' he says, 'take me to ma bed.'

His brother got him a wet rag, cleaned his face, pickit oot some o the thorns oot his face, doctored his hands an put him to bed an gev him a drink o whisky. An fir four days he lay there in a coma, moanin an twistin an turnin – fir four days his brother tended im. And then one day his brother went in once more, an he wis sitting up in bed; 'How are you feelin, brother?' he said.

'Well, I'm not feelin too bad now,' he says, 'at least ma mind's at peace.'

He says, 'Brother, tell me the truth, what happened?'

He said, 'I'll tell ye what happened,' he said, 'I'd been chasin *the devil* fir two days. Fir two days, brother, I'd been chasin *the devil*; but I'll never chase *him* again. Brother, wad ye do one thing fir me?'

He said, 'Ay, what wad ye A really do? What is hit you want?'

He says, 'Go and read me a wee story from the Bible!' And fir another two days his brother sat there with him an tended him and read the Bible tae him, read him the stories from the Bible! An fae that day on, when he came tae his feet he wis a changed man. Never more did he ever take another drink, never more did he ever hurt his dogs, never more did he ever touch a sheep again, unless their wool was ready to be cut! He wis a changed man completely. And these two brothers livit happy fir the rest o their life.

An the auld brother when he used to sit an read the Bible, an he wad look at his brother sittin by the fire there – also readin the Bible – wad turn roond and he'd say tae hissel, '*Thank God fir the Sheep of Thorns!*' An that's the last o my story.

THE TAILOR AND THE SKELETON

Many many years ago away back in Argyllshire there lived two brothers. An they were very good tailors, they had a wee small shop in this wee village – the aulder brother and the younger brother. But the younger had never walkit in his life, since ever he wis a baby. His older brother used to carry him aboot when he wis a wee toy laddie wherever he went any place; event when he went oot in a boat fishin he took his brother with im, he loved his brother dearly from his life. He taught his brother to be a tailor, an even though he wis cripple he becam as good a tailor as his brother. And the two o them hed this wee shop between them, they were famed fir their claes all through the country.

But even though he wis a cripple he grew up. And ond a Saturday evenin efter all the work wis done, the brother used to take an auld-fashioned wheel chair an pit his brother on, hurl him doon the street to the wee ale-hoose, hurl him in the door and pit him to the table. He would sit there and he would have his wee glass o beer or his wee dram o whisky, he'd listen to all the cracks an stories an tales that went roon the place. But the cripple brother never went to church in his life, but the oldest brother used to go every Sunday. An there's one thing – they talkit about everything in the worl to each other – but one thing they never talked aboot, they never talked aboot religion.

So that night there was a crowd of fishermen in the pub, the wee inn, they're drinkin an havin a sing-song. The two tailors they're sittin roond the table an they're talkin to some o their friends. So it was a big table, in two–three minutes' time, och, the table is surrounded – a bing o other folk sit doon t' the table – havin a drink and a talk. So the night wis gaun on, the drink wis flowin fine, when the subject got up about ghosts an spirits. Noo, when the young tailor always went wi his brother to the pub he didna drink very much, but he always tuik a wee bit stuff wi him that he needed to sew and he always covered it ower his lap, because he cuidna walk wi his legs. An to pass the time, if he hed nothing tae crack aboot or nothin to dae, he would always carry on with his bit sewin – mebbe making a waiskit fir somebody or mebbe makin a pair o hose fir somebody or doin something. So anyhow, the subject got roond about ghosts.

An this man said, 'Luik, yese is all talkin about ghosts here tonight in this little pub, an youse all hed a guid drink. But A'll tell ye something, I bet any man five gold sovereigns in this inn tonight, at he wouldna spend a night in that auld graveyard up there fir one night. They wouldna spend one night in that ol' graveyard fir five gold sovereigns because that graveyard definitely is hauntit!'

And aa the men said, 'The're nae such a thing as haunts!'

And the oldes brother said, 'Oh yes, of course the're such a things as ghosts, the're ghosts all right. You cannae believe in God without believin i ghosts. The' are ghosts – I wouldn't spend the time in the graveyard – I wouldna spend the night i the graveyard!'

Bi this time the barman cam roon, he says, 'I bet ye the're no a man in the hotel would spend a night in the graveyard, never mind you! An,' he says, 'you're offerin em five gold sovereigns . . .' the barman leaned his airms ower the bar, said, 'I'll tell ye what A'll do wi ye, the whole lot o youse –' an a hush went o'er, everybody stoppit when the barman spoke, everybody stoppit – he says, 'I'll double hit, I'll add another five gold sovereigns tae hit, fir any man that'll spend a night in the graveyard!'

The crippled tailor in the wheelchair left doon his needles an his bit cloth in his lap, he says, 'Is that so? Are ye willin to pay hit forehand or afterhand?'

'Well,' he said, 'I'll pay it onyway ye like, fir the man that'll spend the night –'

'I'll spend the night in the graveyart!' he says. 'I'm no religious an never was. An I dinna believe in ghosts an never wull, or I dinna believe in God an never wull. An I'll spend the night in the graveyard, my brother'll leave me there. If yese dinna believe me, come an see when he pits me there!'

Oh, this wis a great baet! Oh, the hale pub was in a boil noo, pub was in a boil! They were takin sidebaets, that wis gaunna happen tae him. So sure enough, that was a Friday night; they made it Saturday night – he would take his brother tae the graveyart at eleven o'clock.

He would come doon after he'd pit his brother in the graveyart, which wisna far fae the village, leave him in the wheel chair an he would come doon to the pub, sit ind the pub till one o'clock in the mornin. And then five o them would walk up wi the tailor an bring the brother back – then he'd win his baet!

Right, sure enough Saturday cam. Up they take im; he took a hose wi im, a bit stockin an some threid an some needles. An they tuik him up to the graveyard. Away at the very back wis a big stone, great big granite stone.

He says, 'Pit me beside that stane, it'll shelter me wi the wind. I'll sit here, an I'll still be sittin here at one o'clock when ye come back fir me in the mornin.'

Five o them wis there tae prove hit, and his auld brother the tailor, he says, 'Will you be all right, brother?'

'I'll be all right,' he says, 'don't worry about me. I dinna believe in nae ghosts or spirits or nothing like that. I'll be here, I'll sit an I'll finish ma hose aff, cause I've got an order fir a pair o hose fir tomorrow fir a man who's comin to collect them.'

He sat an the moon cam up – bright as cuid be – you cuid see tae gather peens an needles aff the grund, the moon wis that bright, but one o these nights wi a beautiful bright moon. An the big tombstones wis all in the graveyard, an the graveyard 's surrounded by a wuid. An he sits, he hears the aul clock chimin twelve o'clock in the village, sits sewin away bi the light o the moon . . . Whand all in a minute he luiks, beside the big stone the grun' comes up as if hit wis a mole hokin the ground. An the grund cracks, like that. An out comes a heid – bare skull – nothing but the two holes an the big teeth. An then a neck – bare bones. Then the shoulders. An he's sittin watchin, like that, sittin watchin. And he feelt his hair risin on his heid, he never felt fright before ind his life, an a cold shiver go up his back. Noo the're nothing in the world he cuid dae, because he couldna walk. An he's sittin on the chair, an his two hands 's sittin on the wheel chair, like that. And he's watchin – up it comes ti it stood full six feet right in front o him – a skeleton about six feet tall, an not a pickin o flesh on its body, but its bare bones. It liftit hits hand, like that. An it opened hits fingers.

He said, 'Dae ye see that hand, tailor?'

Tailor said, 'I see yir hand. I see hit, but I sew this.' An he's missin stitches, ye ken, he's shakin. But he's still no feart.

He said, 'Dae ye see that leg, tailor? There's no flesh or blood there – only bone.'

Tailor says, 'I see that, but I'll sew this.'

Then he lifts his ither hand, he said, 'Dae ye see that hand, tailor?'

He said, 'I see that hand, but I sew this.'

'Well,' he says, 'you hev this!' And the skeleton swung his hand at the tailor tae hit him a welt aff the chair. But the tailor duckit, an the hand went ower the top o his heid an hut the big granite stane an *crackit* it right through the middle! It fell in bits.

The tailor got such a fricht that the tailor stude up, straight up, the first time in his life, an left the wheel chair. And he never waitit or luikit back – he set sail as fast as he cuid go. He hed never run in his life, he stumbled an fell fir two-three steps till he got his balance, an then he's off! And he run an he run an he run, till he landit back at the door o the wee inn. He cam in through the door – breathless and white as a ghost – whiter than the ghost he'd seen i the graveyard. An everybody husht, stoppit whan he cam in.

An his brother the auld tailor said, 'In the name of God an creation, what happened?'

He says, 'Give me a drink!' They gien him a drink an he drunk hit up. He stude as straight as his brother.

'But, brother,' he said, 'what happened to ye? Ye can walk!'

'Ay, I can walk,' he says, 'I can walk noo; but if I hedna been able tae walk I wadna be here tonight!'

He said, 'Tell hus what happened!'

'Well,' he says, 'he cam up oot o the grund, an he made a welt at me wi his hand an he misst me! He hut the big granite stane an he made hit go in half! An I duckit, an wi the fricht I got I fell oot o my chair. But I didna wait tae see what else happened. But noo, *thank God*, I can –'

'What did you say?' said his brother.

He said, '*Thank God I can walk!*'

And fae that day on . . . the tailor collectit his baet, they went back to the graveyard, the stone wis broken in two, the grund wis back to normal . . . the tailor cuid walk. An fae that day to the day the tailor died an auld man, that tailor never misst another day in church in his life! An that's the last o my story.

THE NODDIES

This one I'm gaunnae tell ye the night is a 'burker story' that passed among the travelling folk fir many many years. The travellers called them 'burkers', but they were known to the local folk tae, as 'body snatchers'. So when the burkers couldna get nae graves t' dig or nae new-buried bodies to hoke up to sell for research, they turned their eyes on the traivellers. Because those folk were nomads and wanderers – nobody kep i touch wi them – they wadna be missed sae easy as the local people.

A long time ago there was this traveller family, a man an woman an they had about eight or nine wee weans, all wee steps an stairs, ye ken, the wumman had about a wean every year an they were aa only about a year older an each other. They traivellt all through the country, aa specially through Argyllshire. An this story was actually tellt bi the man hissel – I'll tell it in his words.

'Me an her an the weans, we cam doon this glen, the back Hielands o Argyllshire, and it was late end o the year.* I put my tent up at the side o this wee burn, an where A was campit there folk wis cuttin the wood, there was plenty sticks. So within minutes the weans gathered big heaps o sticks and I pit on a big fire, and she made a drop tea an a bit meat fir the weans. We're aa sittin roond the fire an I wis crackin an tellin stories to the weans. When a coach passed by an there were two men, they're sittin up in the front, an there were lights inside the coach, there were two men sittin inside. An they had long, them tile hats on their heids an black coats on. And you cuid hardly hear the

* late end o the year – the autumn, October month

horses' feet bicause there were rubber pads on tae keep the noise o the shoes doon.

'She turnt roon, she says tae me, "Luik, Johnny, I baet ye a pound that coach'll be back for hus the night – that's *the burkers' coach*!"

'"Ah, wumman, that's only yir father's cracks. A traivellt all the days o my life an I never ever got a fright wi burkers bifore." The man wisna feart – big strong man. But sure enough, about half an hour later the coach passed by back again.

'"I tellt ye," the wumman said, "it wad come back."

'"We'll jist wait," he said, "a wee while." An sure enough, about another twenty minutes back comes the coach again.

'She said tae the man, "Johnny, I'm tellin ye somethin, that coach is fir evil the night – it means some o hus is gaunnae be burkit! They seen us here, an ten tae one we go t' wir bed, some o the weans will be snappit awa durin the night an we'll never see them again!"

'"Well . . ." he said.

'She says, "The best thing we can dae is pit oot the fire, an I'll gather two-three blankets an we'll gather the weans together. We'll go away up through the wood inta that plantin, that young wuid up there, we'll bed oot in the wood fir the night an they'll never find us in there."

'"Well," he says, "if that'll keep ye happy, we'll dae that."

'Noo the wee weans is sitting an they're tired, the're some lying in the tent an some lyin at the fireside sleepin. An the wumman gathert them aa up, she gaithert the bits o blankets up an they put the fire oot. The wumman took two-three weans bi the hand an yin in her oxters, an the man took two-three an yin on his back; they went away up through the wood away inta a young plantin, like young Christmas trees, thick plantin where naebody'd ever find them. An amang the pine needles the wumman spread out er blankets. They cuid see the road through the wuid frae where they were high up, they cuid still see the auld road. An they seen the coach comin doon again wi the lights on, cause the coaches had candles, lamps on them in these days. An the man never went tae sleep, the man stude, he's keekin through the trees. And the woman's gaitherin aa the weans roon aboot her, see, happin em up to keep them warm fir the night. This auld man seen the coach stoppin at the camp, an hit stude at the camp fir a guid lang while.

'She said, "I tellt ye noo."

'He said, "Bing ti ye deek this,* come here ti ye deek this, bing!"

* bing ti ye deek this – come and see this

'She left aa the wee weans lyin doon tigether. The coach wis stoppit right at their tent, it was there fir about half an hoor an it went away. The man waitit an waited an waited fir a wee while, an it wis breakin o daylicht. The wumman luikit roon, she says, "Johnny, we forgot yin o the weans! Yin o my wee laddies is lyin in the tent sleepin – I forgot tae get him."

'"Oh, wumman," he says, "no, tell me no! Well, that's hit away, that's hit away noo then. I'll hev tae run doon, killt – burkers or no burkers – an get my wean!"

'She says, "Ye mightnae go noo, it's too late."

'"Wumman, dear," he said, "ye cuidha got aa the w –"

'She said, "I've got so many o them, I dinna ken . . . I left yin o them in the camp sleepin."

'De man left an tuik the wumman bi the hand, he left the wee weans lying sleepin in the bush happit wi blankets in among the wee trees, an the two o them run doon to the camp. The wumman 's greetin an tearin her hair. Bi the time they got doon it was breakin daylicht, an the man flung up the door o the tent, the flap o the tent an luikit in – the're the wee laddie sittin in the tent cross-legged, like that, sittin on a blanket – an about twenty pounds worth o money, half-sovereigns and gold sovereigns sittin atween his legs. An he wis sittin wi the money, playin wi the money, a wee laddie about three year aul.

'"God bless hus," says the man, "they-the-the-they left ye!"

'"Aye," she said, "they left him; fir only ae reason they left him, when they couldna get the big body, some o the men wadna touch a bairn! An God bless hus, it's only fir that's sake – there been a mairriet man wi a family o his ain in that group o four men, in them four burkers – or wir wean wad hae been awa."

'They snappit the wee wean, they gaithert aa the money, dher wur about half a dozen o gold half-sovereigns. The man took the wee laddie bi the hand an they went back up tae the wood. They sut ti daylight, ti it got richt clear. An the man cam doon, pulled doon his tent, packit his wee barrow, what he had fir carryin his tent, an they made their way away fae that place.'

An the man said, 'Ti the day I went to my grave, that is the God's truth, an we never went back tae that place again! An that wis away at the back Hielands o Argyllshire, an you believe me that wean was lucky!'

An that's a true story, a real true burker story. They kent it was puir folk an they gien it money. Yin o the men in the coach must hae been a

married man wi a family o his ain, an he had persuaded the other three
not to touch a wean, an they gien him bout a half-sovereign a piece
when they went awa. That wis away up by Oban, away back in the
early eighteen-hundreds.

Noo my mother tellt me, her faither tellt her a wee crack lang time ago,
it's another burker story. (My mother wis good at burkers' cracks tae!)

She said, 'This man an wumman they never had nae weans, but the
wumman kept two wee dogs, she liked two wee terriers. An this aul
couple o folk they traivellt aa through Argyllshire and aa through
Perthshire wi a wee handcairt. I cuid jist remember them when I was a
wee lassie like a dream,' my mother tellt me, 'oh, I can remember the
two auld folk! So, I wis jist a wee lassie about five year aul. My faither
an ma brother Sandy an ma mither were campit at the shore at the
graveyard, near Minnard, an that wis a regular camp fir the traivellers.
We were sittin yin day when in comes the auld man an woman with
their barrow, they cam in, they pit their tent beside my faither's. But
we seen them bings o times bifore that, but the aul wumman didna hae
nae dogs wi her this time. So the auld man pit up his tent biside my
faither's tent, and the auld man cam doon tae crack to the fire. An the
aul wumman cam doon tae crack to my mother. So we were wee toy
weans, we aa gaithered roon aboot an we were listenin tae the cracks,
the auld folk's tales.

'An it was my mother, God rest her, she said, "An what's, Josie,
happened to yir wee dogs that ye had?"

'"Oh wheesht," she says, "Belloch, dinna speak! Dinna speak, Belloch, about my dogs. It wis lucky it wis the dogs, no hus!"

'She says, "What du ye mean?"

'"Well," she says, "luik, me an him wis awa in Perthshire last year
efter we seen ye here last winter. An we were campit i this camp, me an
him we're lyin in wir bed an we heard the coach passin. An it stopped.
An the men in the coach crackit at the camp fir a wee while, we heard
them mumblin an crackin in the coach. So I gien him a dug wi my
elbow and said tae him, "Sandy, that's the *noddies' coach*!"

'"I ken, wumman," he said, "I heard it stoppin."

'Away goes the coach, she says, "They'll be back again."

'Noo this auld wumman liked her two wee dogs an she always kept
them in the tent at the back, she tied them up at the back o the tent at
night-time.

'The aul man says tae his wife, "Luik, aul wumman, roll up a couple blankets and me an you'll bing into the wuid, we'll hide in the wuid ti daylicht!"

'An he said, "The coach cam back again, it passed by the camp, then hit went away on, I seen the lights turnin. So me an her snappit two-three blankets an we run oot through the side o the tent an inta the wuid, hid in the wuid. An we sut there, we seen the coach stoppin at the camp an it wis stoppit there fir a guid lang while. We waited ti daylight, ti God sent daylight!" (Because they wouldna touch ye in daylight, ye see.) An he said, "Me an her went back to the camp. The door o the tent wis flung up – the two wee dogs were away – gone."

'An she says, "Belle, as low as my mother, ye're no gaunna believe what I'm gaunna tell ye, Alec had a big can that we used to mak aa wir meat in . . ." (They called hit a "dooduch", a kettle pot, the auld man made it hissel. They boiled soup in it an they made tatties in hit, they cookit in the one big can an they used it fir carryin water tae.) An the auld wumman went ower, and she's roart an shoutit fir her two wee dogs roond aboot the camp – they were gone. She says, "The noddies tuik em awa, the burkers, the burkers tuik ma wee dogs awa, I'll never see my wee dogs again!" She says, "I'll go an mak ye a wee moothfu o tea."

'An the auld wumman went ower to the big can tae lift the water – de two wee dogs wis cut in bits an pit inta the can – that's the God's honest truth! De wee dogs wis killt, cut through the middle in bits an pit inta their can among their water. An the coach wis gone. An that's the God's honest truth: they couldna get them; wi the spite an aggravation because they couldna get the auld man and wumman, they killt the two wee dogs an cut them up an flung them in the can. They said, "They can eat *that* when they come back – their two wee dogs." She says, "That's what happened to my wee dogs, Belle, and that's the God's honest truth, an that happened oot away above Aberfeldy with the burkers' coach."'

BOY AN THE KNIGHT

In the West Coast of Scotland is Loch Awe, an in that loch is a castle – ruins now, jist ruins – the walls are there but nothing else. The castle is called 'Woe be tae ye', what I was told, and no one as far as I know hes ever known where it really began. But durin the rainy season i Argyll the castle is surrounded by water, but when it comes a dry summer the loch dries up an ye can walk to the casstel across the beach – which 's only a fresh-water loch – it sits on about half a acre of land. And there's such beautiful grass roun the island.

So a long lang time ago there lived an ol widow an her son, they had a little croft on the mainland on Loch Aweside. She'd only one son, her husband hed died many years ago an left her the one son. But she had some goats an some sheep an some cattle, an they had a wonderful life together. But her son was jist about ten years auld, an he had so many goats they had no food fir them.

So one day she said, 'Son, take the goats out to find some food fir them.'

'Mammy,' he says, 'why don't I take them down to the island!'

She said, 'Son, you can't get tae the island today; the water is not low enough tae get across to the island.'

He says, 'Mammy, A think after a dry spell, I think we cuid get across.'

So the young boy he takes about five or six goats an they all follae him because they knew im as a baby. An the water then was only about two inches deep because it'd been a dry summer, he walks across on to the little island in the middle of Loch Awe. The castle is surrounded by all these beautiful grasses an daisies an things, he thought it would be a wonderful place to take his goats an gie them a guid feed. An his mother had decided that he could go.

So wonst he led the goats across the goats spread out an they're eatin, eatin as fast as possible this beautiful green grass, because on their little croft they hed ett all the grass down. So the young boy he walks round the castle, he's luikin up at the walls an he's wonderin in his own mind what kin o people hed lived i this a long time ago, long before his time? An he walks roond the walls, dher wur stairs gaun up, the stairs were half broken, there wis no roof on the castle an some stairs had fallen in, there were big boulders an rocks.

And then there was a small chamber that led into another room. While his goats wis busy feedin he would walk around the castle, an he walked in through this passage to a chamber of the castle – even though the roof wis gone there wis a big broad square – which might in the olden days hae been a dinin room fir the casstel. An lo an behold he walked in . . . There lyin on the floor was a suit of armour! An the boy wondered, he says, 'I've never been here before, but – a suit of armour lyin on the floor of the castle? I must tell ma mammy about this when I go back.' It wis only a common suit of armour as far as he was concerned . . .

He was a knight dressed in armour! And round his waist was a belt an in the belt was a sword.

The boy walked all around the place – so far as he wis concerned, it wis jist a suit o armour. An he luikit, he saw the sword an he thought tae himsel . . . his mother hed told him many wonderful stories about knights at he heard all the time, an he thought tae hisself, 'How in the world could anybody handle a sword like that?'

So he walked over naturally, an he pulled the sword a wee bit out o the sheath by the knight's side, an he pulled it about five inches – then the head of the knight cam up! An the boy stoppit, he stude there, boy never gev it a thought. He pulled the sword up another bit, to see how long the sword was – an lo and behold the knight sat up like this – his legs are stretched out an he sat up, he hold straight up!

An he spoke to the boy, he said, 'Pull it out!'

The boy stood back.

The sword was half-drawn from the sheath at his side, he says, 'Pull it out, boy; pull it out, boy!'

An the boy stood there, he was amazed!

He said, 'Pull the sword, boy! Pull it out!'

Boy said . . . he wis terrified – he wouldna pull it out.

'Pull it out,' he said, 'an I'll make ye the riches man in the worl!'

The boy wis terrified, ye see – cuidna go back doon!

'A'll give ye everything you require,' said the knight, an he wis sittin on his end. 'I'll give ye everything ye want!' said the knight.

An the boy wis so afraid that the knight wis gaunnae do him harm, he took the sword and he *pushed* it back into the sheath, pushed it back into the sheath, like that. An like that the knight fell back – like that. An the boy looked around . . . There was nothing. Gone was the knight an gone was everything. An the boy was so terrified, he collected his goats an hurried back to his mother on Loch Aweside.

He told his mother the same story as I'm tellin you, and his mother turned round, she said, 'Luik –'

'Mother,' he said, 'what would hev happened if I'd hae pulled the sword out?'

She says, 'Son, I'm glad you put the sword back, because hit's a long long legend I will want to tell you. Because a long time ago, as far as my great-grandfather an my grandfather tellt me, there lived a knight in that castle across there, and he stole away a young wumman tae be his bride, he took her to that castle. An he hung his sword on the wall, an her brothers came to take her back – they surrounded him an killed him – they never gave him a chance to get his hand on his sword. An they killed him because he couldna reach his sword. But if he'd hae reached his sword he cuid hev defended hissel. Son,' she said, 'if you had hae pulled that sword out, you'd prob'ly dune something an set his soul to peace, let his soul go in peace. But, son, please fir my sake, *never go back to that castle again!*'

An neither the boy ever did. An that castle is called 'Woe be tae ye', it means *no one enter* in Gaelic. An that is a true story.

JACK AND THE WATER FAE THE WORLD'S END

Jack wonst lived with his mother in this wee cottage. He workit on a peat moss cuttin peats fir his mother, he used tae sell them through the village.

So one day his mother says tae him, 'Jack, son, ye might gae doon tae yir auld auntie an tak her doon a wee puckle o thae peats. I heard she wisna keepin very weel.'

So Jack yokit his aul horse an cairt, away he goes wi a cairt o peats doon tae his auld auntie's. He cowpit em aff an his auntie tuik him in, gi'n him something tae eat. He steyed a while wi his auntie an he came back up. But when he cam back up, he found his mother lyin on the floor o the hoose. He shouted tae her, done everything he cuid, but no – she wis jist as if she wis in a coma – he cuidna do nothin. So he carried her up an he pit her to bed. He maks his way back right doon tae his auntie's.

An his auntie wis surprised to see him, she says, 'Jack, what's wrang wi you, laddie, ye're back so quick, you were here a minute ago?'

'Well, Auntie,' he said, 'it's ma mither.'

She said, 'What's wrang wi yir mother?'

He said, 'She's lyin in a coma in the hoose an I got her lyin o' the floor when A went up. I canna make heid or tail o her, I dinna ken what's wrang wi her. Ye better come up, Auntie!'

So the auntie bustlit up * her coat, an up she comes wi Jack inta the hoose. She sees her sister lyin, Jack's mother lyin i the bed. 'Ah ha, Jack,' she says, 'laddie, A ken, I kent this wis gaunna happen sometime.'

---

* bustlit up – threw on

Jack's aul mother wis lying jist as if she wis deid, no movement, nothin, jist breathin an nothing else.

'What's wrang, Auntie?' Jack wis in an awfae state fir his mither, he says, 'what's wrang wi her?'

'Well, Jack, tae tell ye the truth, it wis a curse that wis put on hus when we were young,' she says. 'An ma aulder sister she had tae clear oot, she had tae flee fir her life tae the World's End because she got blamed o bein a witch! An some day the curse wis gaunna faa on some o hus – noo it's happent tae yir mither!'

'Auntie,' he said, 'the're nothing I can dae?'

'Ah,' she says, 'Jack, the're something ye can dae! But it'll tak ye a lang lang while tae dae hit.'

He said, 'What can I dae, tell me what I can dae, gang tae some o them doctors or scribes or whitever ye call them or quacks ti I get some help fir her?'

'Jack,' she said, 'ye mightna go an get any help fir her, the're nothing ye can dae fir help fir her. Hit's a curse at's been pit on hus when we were young. Ye'll have tae go an find yir auntie at the World's End, and she'll tell ye whaur tae find the Water fae the World's End that cures everything.'

'But whaur'll I gang, Auntie,' he says, 'tae the World's End?'

She says, 'Ye'll jist have tae keep gaun on till ye come tae the End o the Worl, an find yir auntie.'

'But,' he says, 'hoo'll I ken ma auntie?'

'Well, you'll ken yir auntie,' she says, 'cause yir auntie's got two things that naebody else in the world hes got.'

'God bless me,' says Jack, 'what's that?'

She said, 'A whistlin cock an a crowin hen, an when you come to them ye'll ken ye're no far fae yir auntie's!'

'Well,' he says, 'I dinna ken what to dae.'

She says, 'There's only one thing ye can dae: the morrow when you see daylight, Jack, you may pack up an tak whit ye need wi ye, an set sail, because hit's the only cure yir mother's gaunna get. You get in touch wi yir auntie an tell her the hale story that I'm tellin you. She'll tell ye whaur tae get the Water fae the World's End tae cure yir mother. In the meantime, I'll lock up ma hoose an I'll come up, I'll take care o yir mother ti whatever time ye come back, if ye ever come back! But if ye dinna come back, Jack, yir mother'll never come oot o't.'

'Well,' he says, 'Auntie, the best thing A can dae, if ye mak me up a wee bit o meat tomorrow I'll set sail soon as A see daylight. I'll go on ma wey an I'll keep going, an I'll no *be* back ti I get the thing t' cure my aul mother!'

'Guid enough, laddie,' she says.

So that night Jack went away up, seen his mother, went tae his bed. But he wis up jist at the cock crow in the morning, packit two-three bits o things together, flung it in a bundle on his back an set sail. An he traivelled on, on an on an on through woods an glens an fields an places, takin short cuts through moors an that ti he came to this great lang narrow road leadin tae this toon. He traivellt in tae the first o the toon but he never seen a sowl, every place he cam to wis waste, there weren't a sowl to be seen! Ti at last he cam tae this auld man sittin on a saet, he wis cripplit wi sticks, two staves.

'Guid day, aul man,' he says.

'Guid day, laddie,' he says. 'Are ye on yir wey tae the toon?'

So Jack says tae him, 'Aul man, can ye tell me something, whaur is aa the folk in the village? I cam through there a minute ago an I canna see a sowl.'

'They're all away,' he says, 'tae the king's palace tae see the coronation o the wee king.'

'Oh,' said Jack, 'is that whaur the folk is today?'

'Ay, everybody's away there,' he says, 'an prob'ly ye'll be gaun tae.'

'No me,' says Jack.

'Well,' he says, 'whaur are you gaun?'

He says, 'I'm goin to the World's End.'

'Oh, laddie,' he said, 'the World's End! I wadna like tae be in yir boots, it must be a lang lang place away. But I canna help ye, I never been oot o this place in my life before. I was never awa fae here i my life, so ye better gang in an find oot fae somebody better than me hoo ye're gaunna get tae the World's End. But if ye gae intae the toon, this is the coronation o the wee king tiday an everybody's there – prob'ly somebody there'll help ye.'

'Well,' Jack said, 'if I get naething else, I'll get mysel a bite o meat onyway.'

So in Jack goes, but he travels inta the toon an Jack walks in through this gate. There wis hundreds o folk, all kinds, young folk an auld folk an they're all gaithert roon this big high platform. Ond the top o this platform stood this wee man, he wis only aboot three feet high – this is the wee king – an he wis gettin crowned that day out among the crowd oot in the courtyard, all the folk were gaithert roon. Now Jack comes walkin up right up past, an the wee king's standin on this platform. An Jack being big – he wis, oh, about six foot, tall an straight an fair curly-heided, ken, a guid-luikin young man he was – the wee king eyed him, see? Jack's tryin tae crush his wey through the folk when the wee king luikit roon, he seen him.

An he tuik one look at Jack, he says tae the guards, 'Bring me that man!' Before you cuid say 'Jack Robinson', two big guards ran doon an catcht Jack in each arm, tuik him afore the king. 'Who are you,' says the king, 'an where do ye come fae? Are you belong tae my country?'

'Well, no,' says Jack, 'I dinna belong tae yir country or yir town. I been on the road fir a month.'

An he said, 'Where are ye making tae, where are ye going tae an where hev ye come fae?'

So Jack tellt him the story, he said, 'I'm going tae luik fir the Water fae the World's End tae help ma aul mother.'

'Oh?' said the king. The king got interestit in this, ye see, an he said, 'What will the Water fae the World's End dae?'

Jack said, 'Hit's supposed tae cure everything.'

'Oh, will it cure everything,' says the wee king, 'aye? Well, I'll tell ye the truth, whoever ye be, you come up here wi me!' An he tell'd the guards, 'Clear all these folk away! I want this man in wi me.'

So Jack says, 'Our Majesty, I never done nae hairm. I'm on'y stoppit in the toon on ma journey fir tae luik fir a bite o meat.'

'You'll get plenty meat,' says the king. 'You come wi me to my palace!' So the wee king ordered Jack tae come up to the palace, tuik him inta the chamber an he says tae Jack, 'Ye hungry?'

'Ay,' said Jack, 'I'm hungry. That's what I cam in here fir.'

'Well,' he said, 'sit doon there an tell me yir story.'

Jack tellt him the story I'm tellin you about his aul mother.

King sat fir a lang lang while an he said, 'Dae ye think ye'll get there? Cuid I gie ye ony help?'

'No,' said Jack, 'I doot you cuidna gie me nae help.'

So the king called fir his prime minister tae come in, he says, 'Get this man everything he wants an get me a suit o claes, the same kind o claes that Jack's got.' He said tae Jack, 'I'm gaun wi ye.'

'Oh no,' says Jack, 'ye cannae go wi me, Our Majesty!'

He said, 'No more "Majesty", don't call me no "Majesty"; only call me "Wee King". I'm gaun wi ye tae the Water at the World's End!'

'But,' Jack says, 'what do ye want tae go wi me fir?'

'Well,' he says, 'I'll tell ye, my faither wis a big man an ma mother wis big an all my generation o my royal family wis all big folk. But *me*, the're a curse on me, I'm only three fit high! An I want tae be big an strong like you, I want tae go wi ye tae the World's End tae get water tae help me grow – mak me big an strong like you!'

'But,' Jack says, 'Our Majesty, you might get the water – it might no dae ye any guid.'

'Well,' he says, 'I can try.'

'Luik,' says Jack, 'I'm gaun on my way, an I'm no wantin tae take ye wi me tae be nae haudback tae me, because I hev a lang road to go.'

'Oh,' says the king, 'I'll be no haudback tae ye, Jack. You call me "Wee King" an I'll call you "Jack" an I'll go wi ye! An I'll do my share. I'll leave ma country in charge tae my prime minister ti A come back.'

'Well,' says Jack, 'hit's up tae yirsel if you want to go wi me, but I'll hev tae be on my way in the mornin.'

'Fair enough,' says the wee king, 'then I'll come wi ye. An I think we shall get there.' So he sent fir one o the auldest men in the country tae come up. And the auld man gien de wee king and Jack all the directions they had tae go, tellt them which wey tae take tae set sail fir the World's End. So he asked Jack is he wantin horses?

Jack said, 'No, I don't want any horses but we dinna want any horses or nothing. My feet's guid enough fir me, I might be goin places where I canna take a horse.'

'Well,' says the wee king, 'I'm gaun wi ye.'

'Luik, I canna carry ye an A dinna want ye tae be a haudback tae me!'

'I'll no be nae haudback tae ye,' the wee king says, 'but I'm gauna wi ye tae the World's End!'

So the next morning Jack and the wee king set sail and away they go. They traivellt on an they traivellt on, they traivellt on, they traivellt on an on an on an, oh, the wee king helpit aa his way. He wis the best in the world at helpin at night an helpin in the mornin, an whanever onything wis needit he wad get hit. But they traivellt on, on the road fir about a month ti it cam late one night. They cam inta this forest an they were lost, they cuidna see whaur they were gaun tae.

'We'll hev tae grope wir way through this wuid some way,' Jack said tae the wee king. 'If we cuid even get a tree fir shelter itsel tae sit the back o ti mornin, ti we see whaur we're gaun.'

The wee king said, 'Luik, you follow me, I'm wee-er an you an I can creep in bilow the branches, I'll mebbe find ye a wey oot o this forest.' But onyway, they're thrashin their way through the forest here an there, when all in a minute what did they see shinin through but a wee licht! 'Ha,' says the wee king, 'Jack, I see a licht!'

'Ye're mad,' says Jack, 'ye'll never see a licht in the middle o this wuid.'

'Ay, the're a licht,' he said. 'You follow me, Jack, an I'll mak ma way tae the licht.'

So Jack follaed the wee king, the king made his wey in bilow this big branches o the trees an they cam inta this clearin. In the middle o the clearin wis a wee hut, an a licht in the windae an smoke comin fae the chimney. The wee king went up, 'knock, knock' at the door. No answer. 'Knock-knock' again . . . hears a rumble inside the hoose.

Door disna open, but this voice shouts through, 'Who's there an what dae ye want on my property this time o night?'

'It's Our Majesty,' says the wee king, 'the king o the country!'

An this voice answers back, 'I'm the king o the country, I'm the king o this property an be on yir way, don't disturb me!'

De wee king steps back an he hits the door a kick, says, 'Open the door bifore A get Jack tae break it doon!'

An the next thing opened the door wis a wee toy man wi a hump on his back, big hump on his back, an a lang face an a lang white beard. 'What dae yese want and what are ye disturbin folk at this time o night fir?'

He said, 'We want help an shelter.'

He says, 'Who are you?'

An the wee king says, 'I'm the wee king o the country; this is Jack ma mate.'

'An where are yese bound fir?'

He said, 'We're bound fir the World's End.'

'Ha-ha, well, if ye're bound fir the World's End, yese better go on yir way,' says the hunchback.

'We're not gaun on wir wey,' says the king, 'till we get shelter.' So de wee king an the hunchback start tae argue.

Jack says, 'Come on now, at's enough o this now, we're no wantin nae . . . we're gaunna get shelter or we're no gaunna get shelter – whit are we gaunna dae about it? Two o youse be quiet an let's settle this thing atween hus.'

So they explaint their story to the wee hunchback, an the wee hunchback got interestit, he tuik them in. He gien them a guid feed, he kinnelt a guid fire tae them an gien them whatever they wantit.

So Jack stude, he tellt the wee hunchback the story, 'An the wee king bein so wee, because he's wee-er than onybody else in hese family, wants tae go wi me tae get the Water at the World's End tae see if it'll help him tae!'

'Hmmm,' the hunchback wis quiet, he never said very much. So he gied them a guid bed doon bi the fire an kep a big fire gaun to them all night. But in the mornin he packit up bundles o meat to them, says, 'Jack, I want to ask you something.'

'No,' says Jack, 'afore ye ask me noo, I'm no wantin tae hear no more o't – ye're no gaun wi me!'

'Well, Jack, luik,' he says, 'my mother an faither wis well-off people an they owned all this estate. An when I wis born they were ashamed o me because I wis a hunchback an sae ugly an misformt, they built me this hut in the middle o the forest, they gien me this. I never seen a sowl since an I live here mysel, I cannae gae aboot naebody i this state – I'm that twistit – I'm a hunchback like this an it's the weariest place in the world. Jack, will ye take me wi ye? An I'll be a help tae ye alang the road, I ken the road fir a lang lang bit.'

'Well,' says Jack, 'I dinna like takin too many folk wi me, because you there an the wee king ye'll jist haud me back. But onyway, if you'll no be a burden to me, A suppose the're no be nae hairm takkin ye – if *he's* gaun, ye're as well tae gang tae!'

'Okay,' said the wee hunchback, 'I'll help oot the best way A can, I'll no be nae burden to ye, Jack, you tak me wi ye!' So he gied them a guid bed, he gi'n them a guid breakfast an the next morning out steps the wee hunchback, he says, 'I'll lead the way fir the next hundert mile, I been alang this road fir a lang lang while. But I'll tell ye one thing, when ye go oot o the boundaries o this kingdom ye'll hev tae watch, fir the next county ye come tae is the county of the wicked queen – an I'm tellin ye, she is wickit!'

So anyway, Jack an the wee king an the hunchback pushes on, they travel on, they travel on here an they travel on, they travel on an on an on. But as true tae his word the wee hunchback helpit all he cuid, they never wantit fir nothing, he kent all the roads an everything ti they cam tae this ither county. An they cam tae this village. They had nae meat or nothing left, they hed money but no meat.

'Well,' Jack says, 'wickit queen or no wickit queen, I'll hev tae gae into the toon an see what we can buy.' But noo Jack bein so big and the hunchback bein wee an the wee king bein wee, they were three o the oddest three folk ye ever seen in yir life! They marcht inta the toon, in they cam, an the first body they met wis the captain o the queen's guards. He tuik one luik at them an he sent fir half a dozen troops, ordered them up to the palace. Out comes the queen. Oh, she wis wickit this woman!

She says, 'Take em tae the dungeons or take off their heads or hang em! They're strangers in wir country, we didn't send fir them, we don't need them here! Right away!'

'Wait!' says Jack. 'Wait, wait, wait, wait, wait,' says Jack, 'you're goin about it the wrong way!'

'Don't speak back to me,' says the queen, 'the're nobody allowed to speak back to me!' Oh, she wis wickit!

Jack says, 'Luik, Ir Majesty, we're only puir strangers on the road an we're bound fir a faraway country from yours. We wad never hae stoppit in your town only we're short o food, we hed no food – we cam in here tae luik fir some.'

She said, 'Hev youse money to buy hit? Are youse vagabonds?'

'No,' says Jack, 'we're no vagabonds.'

'Well,' she says, 'come up with me!' She ordered the three o them up, tuik them inta her chamber in the palace, sent fir all her ministers an held her coort right i front o the three o them right away. 'So now,' she says, 'say yir piece!'

Jack tellt her the same story, an the wee king tellt her his bit an the hunchback tellt her his bit.

'Well, very guid,' she says. But noo she kin o calmt doon this queen when she heard this, ye see. 'An,' she says, 'if I give yese food an give yese a shelter fir the night, yese'll promise faithfully tae be on yir way in the morning?'

'We will,' says Jack, 'Our Majesty,' an he thanked her very much.

She tellt the captain o the guards tae give them a place to stay fir the night, gie them plenty to eat an gie them plenty o food wi them in the mornin.

Jack says tae the wee hunchback, 'I thought you said, Hunchback, that that wis a wicked queen.'

'Well,' says the hunchback, 'as far as I've heard, she's the wickedest queen in the world. There's nothing can live with her, everybody in the country hates her. She's bad since she wis born, she punisht her puir aul mother tae her death an she punisht her puir aul faither the same – she's a pure devil.'

Jack says, 'She seems to be reasonable enough tae hus.'

'Ay, Jack, but wait! Wait, Jack,' says the hunchback, 'there's something ahind that – she's no daein that fir nae guid – you'll find oot soon enough, maybe afore mornin.'

But she gien them a place to lie, but they hedna gaen an bedded doon after supper fir nae mair than an hoor, whan they heard the roll-rattle comin to the door. The door wis swung open an in cam two guards, he says, 'Which o youse is Jack?'

Jack stood up, said, 'Me.'

'Well,' he said, 'ye're wantit.'

'What ye wantin me fir,' Jack says, 'I never done nae hairm?'

He said, 'You're gaunna mak an appearance in front o the queen!'

Right, two guards marcht him up inta the queen's chamber. Queen's sittin, she dismissed the two guards. 'Come ower here, sit doon, Jack,' she said, 'tell me your story again.'

Jack tellt her the story again back frae the beginnin.

'Oh,' she said, 'dae ye think ye'll succeed – what ye're gaunna dae?'

'Ay,' he says, 'well I mean tae try . . . my puir auld mither.'

She says, 'You must think a lot o yir mother.'

'Ay,' he says, 'I dae.'

'Well,' she says, 'Jack, I'm gaunna tell ye my story: I wis born wickit an I been wicked all ma days, an I've made ma people hate me, ma name been feared an hatit i the whole county o my hale shire. An I want tae be likit, I want folk to like me, no hate me.'

'Well,' Jack says, 'the only wey if ye want folk tae like ye is stop being wickit, ye get the name o the "Wickit Queen".'

'Well,' she says, 'some folk cry me that. Jack, there's one thing I want tae ask ye –'

'No,' says Jack, 'if ye're gaunna ask me what . . . "no" before ye ask hit!'

'Well,' she says, 'ye ken whit A can dae, Jack, I can put ye to the dungeons, A can hev ye hangit, I can have you beheaded!'

'Well,' he says, '*that* wadna get ye nae place, that wadna help ye nane.'

She says, 'I want tae go wi ye tae the World's End. I'll dae ma pairt.'

'Well, luik,' says Jack, 'fir my sake an my two companions's sake, I'll take ye. But tae me, fae then on, noo ye're no more a queen than what I am a king. Ye'll dae what ye're tellt, ye'll be no hindrance or no haudback, an ye're no more a queen!'

'Fair enough,' says the queen, 'you treat me like that an I'll treat you de same.'

'Right,' he says, 'the morrow mornin, when the cock crows in the mornin, be ready fir the road!'

'I'll be ready,' she says, 'Jack, I'll be ready.'

Right, back Jack goes tae where he was, the guards opened the door fir im an in he goes. First man that cam to him wis the wee king, 'Hoo di' ye get on, Jack,' he said, 'what's happenin, what's gaunna come o hus?'

'What's gaunna come o hus?' says the hunchback.

'Devil a haet's* gaunna come o hus,' says Jack.

'What did she say tae ye, are we gaunna get awa i the mornin?'

'Ay,' says Jack, 'we're gettin awa. But ye ken what's –'

'I ken,' says the hunchback, 'I kent that – dinna tell hus she's gaun tae!'

'Ay,' says Jack, 'she's gaun tae.'

'Oh well,' says the hunchback, 'I suppose she's got as much right to be wi ye as me.'

'Or me,' says the wee king. 'Well, if hit's got to be, it's got to be.'

'But,' he said, 'anyway, let's get some sleep, we've got a lang wey tae go in the mornin.'

So the next mornin, true tae her word, de queen wis dressed in the roughest claes she cuid find about the palace, an wis waitin wi a bundle ond her back fir Jack an the hunchback and the wee king. She met them, said 'guid mornin' to them. So the four o them set sail, ond they go. They traivellt on an traivellt on an traivellt on an on an on an on fir months, but they're still headin the same direction, when they cam to this great forest.

De queen said, 'I'll tell ye something, Jack, we hevna far tae go noo ti we come tae the giant's country. They tell me he's bad. An ye canna pass through his country, an we hev tae pass through by his place tae get whaur we're gaun, tae get to the End o the Land. You've got tae get his permission.'

'Well,' says Jack, 'there's only one thing we can dae is gang an ask his permission!'

She says, 'If he lets ye by, fair enough; but if he disna let ye by, ye'll hev tae turn back because the're nae ither way ye can go.'

---

* Devil a haet's – not a thing's

'Oh well,' said Jack, 'we'll hev tae talk him inta hit some way.'

So they traivellt on an on an on ti they cam to this forest, an right through the forest wis a path, at the end o the path wis a big clift. On the clift wis a archway an right on the archway wis a palace, the giant's castle an this two monster gates, an two big guards at the gates. Jack, the queen, the hunchback an the wee king walkit up. Guards stoppit them; 'What do you want,' he says, 'an where are youse bound fir?'

He said, 'We're bound fir Land's End, the End o the Worl.'

'Well,' he said, 'ye'll hev tae wait t' see what wir master says, tae see if ye get by.' So they had tae stand at the gates, an away goes one o the guards, up he goes up this big steps to the giant's castle. He knocks at the door an the giant comes oot. 'Master,' he said, 'the're some strange people at the gate an they want through.'

'What do they want here?' says the giant. An he wis shakin, ken! 'What do they want here?' He only keeked his heid oot through the door a wee bit the giant, he wis a big giant tae.

He said, 'They want to get through your country tae get to the World's End.'

'Bring em up,' said the giant, 'an let me see them first!'

The guard says to them, 'Ye can come up.' Fetcht them up the steps up to the front door o this big castle. An the giant keekit oot, he seen the wee king an he backit fae the wee king, ken, he backit fae the wee king!

'Keep him away fae me,' he said, 'keep him away fae me! Don't let him come near me.'

'God bless me,' says Jack, 'he'll no touch ye!'

An he says, 'Im there, that hunchback, dinna let him come near me!'

'Are you the master o this country?' said Jack.

'Ay,' said the giant, 'I'm the master. But I'm afraid o these wee men you've got with ye.'

Jack says, 'Wait a minute, these wee men'll no touch ye.'

'Ye promise me they'll no touch me,' said the giant, 'I'll let ye in!'

'Right,' says Jack.

So the giant tuik the four o them in, but he's ey eyein this wee king, an he's ey eyein the wee hunchback. If they cam roon that way, he wad aye gang *that* way. So he sat doon i this big chair in this big room an he says tae Jack, 'Now, tell me yir story.'

An Jack tellt him the story, the wee king tellt him his story, the hunchback tellt the giant his story an the wicked queen done the same.

'We're all bound fir the World's End tae get the Water at the World's End tae help hus. But maist of all hit's fir Jack's aul mother that's lyin at death's door.'

'Well,' said the giant, 'I'll tell ye, it's a long long way from here, but I ken the wey. An A'm the on'y one that can tak ye tae the End o the Worl. But, Jack, I'll pit ye up fir the night an I'll take ye there – an one thing ye've got tae do fir me –'

'Now wait,' says Jack, 'wait one minute, we're no makkin nae promises!'

'The only way ye'll ever get,' he said, 'if ye take me wi ye!'

'But tell me this,' says Jack, 'what is wrong wi you?'

'Well,' says the giant, 'tae tell ye the truth, I'm feart, I'm a giant an the least thing frichens me. An I've got seven brothers, they're aa giants an they're spread through the worl, they're great men. They meet every seven year, I'm afraid tae meet them because I'm that feart – even the size o them frichens me. I want tae go wi ye to the World's End an get some o the Water fae the World's End tae help me! An I'll do ma bit alang wi ye if ye take me wi ye.'

'Well,' says de wee king, 'there's gaunna be a puckle o hus noo. But A suppose ye've as much right to be there as onybody else, as me or the hunchback or the queen.'

'Ye can come wi hus,' says Jack, providin that ye let me take the lead an dae whit yir tellt! What I tell ye tae dae, ye'll dae hit.'

'Oh,' said the giant, 'I'll no interfere. I'll dae aa the heavy work, if the're onything to be done. Luik, if we meet any bandits or robbers on the way, mind, I'll run – I canna fight nane – I'm feart.'

'Never mind about the bandits or robbers,' says Jack. 'You jist come alang an dae yir pairt tae help hus on wir way an everything'll be all right.'

'But I'll tell yese,' said the giant, 'I'm big an I'm strong, I'll carry all the packs an I'll carry all the meat fir the lot o youse.'

'Fair enough,' says Jack, 'that'll be a guid help.'

So the next mornin the giant packed this great load of beef on his back an everything they needit fir to take them on their journey, an they set sail through this forest. The next thing they cam to was this desert o sand, they're sinkin in the sand an the giant's helpin them all the best way he can. An they traivellt on, they traivellt on an traivellt on an on fir months; ti at last they reacht the End o the Land, no more land! They cam tae the beach, this big beach.

Jack said, 'The're bound to be some shelter alang this beach o some kind fir tae pass the night awa.' Around this corner they cam tae this big cave an it was full o driftwood that wis washed in wi the big heavy tides, great big rotten trees. Jack says, 'This place'll do fir the night, we'll stay here till we see what's gaunna happen.'

So they went in this big cave an the giant broke this great big trees ower his knee, he kinnelt this big monster fire, an they roastit all this beef an stuff the giant was carryin with him, they had a great feed. They all made their bed right doon i this cave, all but Jack. Jack says tae hissel, 'This is Land's End; an if my aul auntie's right, at my aul auntie supposed to be a witch stays . . . she cannae stay nae farther than here. She mus be about someplace here somewhere. So when I get them sleepin I'll take a walk, I'll go one direction an I'll go another direction, and every night that we stay in the cave I'll go a bit farther every night.'

So Jack waitit till he got the rest o them sleepin an the moon wis shinin durin the night, out he goes. He goes fir about two mile in one direction . . . Nothing but rocks an beaches an heather, nothing. The next night he goes the ither direction, and he goes fir about two mile . . . Na, nothing. An he's jist gaunna turn an come back, whan he hears the bonniest whistlin in the worl comin, carried in the wind. 'I wonder what that cuid be,' said Jack. An then he hears the crowin, like a cock crowin. He said, 'The're bound to be life about here some place! Upon my word, if my aul auntie wis right, my aul auntie's no far fae here – that's the whistlin cock I hear!'

On he goes, travels further on, about half a mile on an he comes tae this bonnie wee path, all done with shells an stanes aff the shore. He follows hit up, he comes to this wee hoose inta the face o a clift. An the' wur a light burnin in the windae. An he knocks at the door.

This wumman says tae him, '*Who* is there at this time o night – in the name of God in Heaven where do you come from?'

Jack says, 'Hit's me, from a faraway land A cam, Auntie, fir yir help.'

She says, 'I'm nobody's auntie.' An she hed this monster cat, near as big as a sheep sittin in her door, an hit wis spittin at Jack.

Jack says, 'Auntie, let me in! I'm yir sister's son.'

'Are ye?' she said.

He said, 'I cam fir yir help.'

She says, 'What kin o help can I gie ye?'

Jack says, 'Let me in an I'll tell ye. I'm no fir nae hairm * – ye're my auntie, I'm yir nephew.'

* I'm no fir nae hairm – I won't harm you

The aul wumman tuik im in the door an she roared tae the cat, she tied hit up wi this big belt. An hit was sittin spittin at Jack an its een kinnelin i its heid! But onyway, they'd jist sut doon when all this whistlin an crowin startit again.

Jack said, 'What is that?'

'Well, Jack,' she said, 'that is a whistlin cock – the only one in the worl at can whistle – an at's my crowin hen on the top o the roof there, tells me when anybody is in the district. I ken when the're onybody about, that's the warnins I've got. An I kent you were here two days ago.'

Well, Jack tellt her the story ... 'Oh aye,' she says, 'well, I'll tell ye the rest o it. I wis bannt away when I wis young, an me bein a witch, I took off an I said I would never stop till I landit where there never wis another sowl to seen for evermore. An this is where I landit an here I stay.'

'But, Auntie,' he says, 'that's no the thing I want; I want you to help my mother.'

'Oh,' she said, 'laddie, wait a minute, I ken whit ye're after; you're after the Water a' the World's End.'

'Aye,' he said, 'Auntie, I'm efter the Water a' the World's End.'

'But,' she says, 'Jack, you'll never get it.'

'What do you mean, Auntie, I'll never get hit?' He says, 'The're bound to be some way o gettin it.'

'Na, na,' she says, 'the're nae way o gettin hit. Tae get to the Water at the World's End, you cuid never get there.'

'Hoo can I no get there, Auntie,' he said, 'the're bound to be a wey fir tae get there somewey?'

'*Hit's a tunnel*,' she said, 'an it's on'y three feet, it goes in fir half a mile – Jack, ye're far too big, you'll never get there.'

'Ah, but,' he says, 'mebbe I've got some wey o gettin there ...' An he up an tells her the story about the wee king, the hunchback, the giant and the wicked queen.

'Well,' she said, 'I'll tell ye wha' tae dae, bring them here tomorrow, de lot o them tae this room, bring them all wi ye. I'll tell ye hoo tae get the Water at the World's End.'

'Fair enough,' says Jack. So he sut wi his auntie an he crackit tae her fir a lang while, she made him some supper. An away he goes back the road he cam. In he comes to the big cave an they're all lyin sound, sleepin. Jack pits mair sticks on the fire, he lies doon, never says a word to them.

So the first yin gets up in the mornin wis the wee hunchback, got up an kindled the fire. An then the queen got up, and then the wee king, he says to Jack, 'I heard you gaun oot last night. It was a lang while bifore ye cam back, did ye find oot onything?'

'Ay,' said Jack, 'I found oot something, I fand ma auntie's hoose.'

'Die ye?' said the giant.

'Aye,' says Jack, 'we've all got tae go to ma auntie's hoose today an she's gaunnae tell hus what to dae.'

'Well thank God fir that,' said the giant, 'that'll be a help onyway.' So they packit up their gear an away they set sail. But the giant was in the lead, an he's jist comin up the first path when the cock start't tae whistle an the hen gi'n a crow – the giant's back fir his life, back the road he cam! 'No,' he says, 'Jack, I cuidna go up there.'

'Oh,' Jack says, 'that's naethin, wait ti ye go up tae the hoose an ye'll see worse an that. Man, dinna be feart, that's on'y a cock an a hen, that'll no do ye nae hairm, that's on'y ma auntie's whistlin cock an hen.'

So up they come tae the hoose an this big cat's sittin. Oh, the giant luik't at the cat an the giant wis terrified, he cuidna gae near this cat, see! So the auld wumman opened the door an tuik them all in, put them all sittin doon o' the floor. 'Noo,' she said, 'yese are aa here, so I want tae hear yir stories back ower again.' So de queen tellt her her story an the hunchback tellt the aul wumman his and the wee king done the same an the giant done the same. She luikit at the giant a long long while, 'I heard o you,' she said, 'an I heard o yir brothers. They're great great men, but I believe but I dinna ken if the Water fae the World's End'll help you or no. Onyway, it's no the help o the Water at the World's End – it's hoo ye gaunna get hit –hit's in a tunnel only three feet high, and it gaes in fir half a mile.'

'But I'll get hit!' says the wee king. 'I'm no nae mair than three feet high.'

The aul wumman luiks at him, 'Ay,' she says, 'I believe you'll get hit. But I'll tell ye . . .' she walks away to the shelf, she takes doon two wee leather bottles (like wee snuff bottles fir haudin gun powder) an she says, 'ye'll take them an ye'll fill these two bottles. *But,*' she said, '*I'm tellin ye one thing, I'll gie ye a torch: you'll go in ti the end o the tunnel, ye'll come to three steps an you'll turn roond an ye'll go doon the three steps backward; but fir the peril o yir life, if ye faa inta the well ye'll never be seen again –that'll be the end o ye. An you'll dip these two bottles in, ye'll fill them full o water an*

you'll come back up the three steps the same way ye went doon, back the ways.
Noo, dae ye remember that?' she says tae the wee king.

'I will,' says the wee king, 'I'll dae that.'

So she says, 'Come on then, come wi me.' She tuik em tae the facet o
a clift, no far fae her hoose wis the face o a clift. 'Noo in there,' she
said, 'the're a wee tunnel an you'll gae in that tunnel, you'll travel in
there fir half a mile till ye come tae the steps an ye'll see the wee
pool; an doon that three steps . . .' So the wee king went away wi the
torch in his hand, lichtit it tae him an away he goes in through the
tunnel.

'Well,' says the aul wumman, 'it'll be a while before he comes back,
if he ever comes back. Let's go back tae the hoose.' So they go back to
the hoose. They sat doon, an the giant's ey eyein this cat, ye ken! He's
terrified an wadna go aboot this cat fir the world. The aul wumman
made them somethin to eat.

Now, in goes the wee king efter they left him, he goes right on to the
end o the wee tunnel. He comes to the three steps an he's haudin his
torch in his hand, he gaes doon the three steps – back the ways – an he
wis jist gaunna step aff the last step when he hears the water a' his
back. He dooks in the two bottles an fills them. He turns roond, reversin
up when the torch went oot! Black oot hit went! An he steppit up
canny, back the way as he cuid, ti he got to the last step an he got his
way back oot o the tunnel.

So they were sittin in the hoose waitin fir the wee king comin back.
They must hae sat fir aboot four hours when in comes the wee king.
They're all surprised tae see him gain he cam back. Jack wis the first
runnin over, heard him comin, he opened the door an tuik him in. An
he hed the two wee bottles – full of water.

'Noo,' says the auld wumman, 'ye're back!'

'Aye,' says the wee king.

'How'd ye get on?'

'Well,' says the king, 'I near never made hit. I wis jist at the last step
when my torch went oot.'

'I thocht that,' says the auld wumman, 'I wis coontin the time you
been awa – you been awa a lang lang while. But anyway, ye got what
ye went fir. Noo, the worse bit only comes, Jack, an it's up tae you.
You're the only yin that can dae onything fir them.'

'How me?' says Jack.

He said, 'Didn't the king get the water, Auntie?'

'Ay, but,' she says, 'getting the water's nae use. Ye've a lot tae dae efter that, Jack, when ye get the water!' An then the cock startit tae whistle the top o the hoose, an the giant start't tae shiver wi the fricht, see! '*Now,*' she says, '*Jack, I'm gaunnae tell ye what to dae: yese'll aa sit in a row there, right roon the table; an, Jack, stand ower there next t' the table an ye'll dook yir finger in the water, you'll walk with one dreep o water tae each person in turn, an you'll place hit on their tongue. But if hit droops before you reach them, that's their chances gone firever – the second yin'll be nae use!*'

'Well,' says Jack, 'that is a task richt enough.'

'*Noo,*' she says, '*bifore ye dae that, I want yese to state yir tasks – what yese really want – because what ye say is the thing you'll get an nothin else.*' She says, 'First, Jack, yin bottle's fir you tae tak back tae yir auld mother. An you'll gie her a wee drink o that when ye go back. An the second bottle is for your freends. But be careful, Jack, hoo ye use hit because I'm only tellin ye, they'll never get a second chance!'

So Jack said, 'Well, we better start. Noo,' says Jack to the wee king, 'you were the first yin to come alang wi me, an you are the first yin I'm gaunna help. What do you really want?'

'Well,' he said, 'Jack, you ken what I want: there's only one thing in the world I want, Jack, an I hope you'll be able tae help me, an I'll mak ye rich fir the rest of yir days.'

'I'm no wantin nae riches fae ye,' says Jack, 'I'm only wantin tae help ye.'

'Well,' he says, 'I want to be like you, Jack. That's all I want – big an strong like you – that's what I cam fir an that's what I want, nothing else!'

'Well,' says Jack, 'that shall be!' an he dook'd his finger inta the water inta the wee bottle, he liftit his finger oot an there's one wee dreep stickin tae his finger. An the auld wumman turnt the licht doon low as she cuid, an Jack tuik it canny as he cuid go, canny as he cuid go like that, an he walkit ower, he walkit ower canny – the dreep's jist about faain aff – he pit it the top o the wee king's tongue. An the minute he pit it the top o the wee king's tongue, the wee king shut his mooth an swallowt the dreep – like that – an he fell on the floor, he twistit an turnt on the floor fir about ten minutes. An whan he rase up the greatest change i the world tuik over him – he wis the size o Jack an tall an strong – as handsome as cuid be! 'Well,' said Jack, 'at least that proved one thing, you'll no need to worry nae mair!'

'No,' says the wee king, 'but that's what I wantit!'

'Noo,' says Jack, 'you've got what you wantit. We'll hev tae wait an see what's gaunna happen to the hunchback.'

So the poor wee hunchback he's sittin no sayin a word, ye ken! He said, 'Jack, it's up to you. If you dae that fir me as what you've done fir the king, ye'll never want fir nothing.'

Jack said, 'I'm no wantin nothin, all I want's tae help ye. You've helpit me alang the road, and I wad never hae been here on'y for youse.' An he dookit his finger inta the water an he walked across, he done the same thing to the wee hunchback. An the wee hunchback closed his mooth – the same thing happened to the wee hunchback – an two minutes efter he tuik the wee drop water he wis straight as my finger an not a hunch nor a twist aboot im! He jumpit roon the floor an danced wi glee an clappit his hands, he wis that happy!

'Jack, Jack,' he said, 'that's a great thing you've done fir me.'

Noo, the giant wis sittin an the queen – Jack says to the queen, 'Noo it's your turn – what do you really want?'

'Jack,' she says, 'you ken what I want, I want tae be guid. At's all I want, I dinna want tae do nothing in this world; I want tae be guid an be guid-thocht o'.'

'Well,' says Jack, 'here goes.' He dookit his finger in the bottle wonst more an walkit ower as canny as he cuid, he pit the dreep on the queen's tongue. Queen swallowt the wee dreep . . . Greatest change in the world cam over her, she never luikit the same person i the worl. She wis as *kind* as cuid be, she ran ower an put her airms roon the auld wumman's neck an cuddled her! 'Well,' says Jack, 'that goes tae prove one thing, the water really works. I hope hit does the same fir my auld mither.'

The giant's sittin rubbin his hands an he's luikin at this cat, ken! 'Jack,' says the giant, 'remember me!'

'*I'll* remember you, I'll remember you,' said Jack to the giant. 'You'll get hit, you'll get what you want, nothing else.'

He said, 'I want to be brave like my seven big brothers, an no even feart o a leaf aff a tree when it faas. I'm sittin here, Jack, an that cat hes got me terrified to deith, I'm even feart o that cat an I'm feart o that wild beast, she's got o top o the hoose.'

'Well,' Jack says, 'here goes,' an he dooks his finger inta the wee drop water, he walks across. He placed hit canny as he cuid be in case it wad faa, an he pit hit on the giant's tongue. The giant swallowed the wee dreep o water, an the greatest change in the world cam over the giant . . .

The giant gi'n hissel a streetch an he said tae Jack, 'I feel a different man already, Jack, I wish I had somebody I cuid fight! Real giants tae fight!'

'Never mind fightin real giants,' he said, 'you've gotten what ye wantit. Now we'll hev tae be on wir wey.'

'Na, na,' says the auld auntie, 'ye're firgettin somethin, Jack, ye're firgettin me! Ye no think that I've been here lang enough, that the're a curse upon me, an mebbe you, Jack, 'll be able tae help me? And I'll manage tae gae back an see my puir auld sisters.'

'Well,' says Jack, 'Auntie, ye'll get what you want an nothin else, as you said yirsel.'

'Jack,' she said, 'hit's up tae you to try an help me the best way ye can!'

'Well,' says Jack, 'here goes.' And he dookit his finger inta the wee bottle, he walkit across tae his auntie . . . An jist as he's comin tae his auntie's tongue the lamp went oot, the drip fell aff Jack's finger!

'That's hit,' said the auld wumman, 'that's hit – the curse is still on me – the're nae chance fir me, Jack, so I'll hev tae bide here fir the rest o my days. But when ye go back, mind an tell ma puir aul sisters that I'm aa right. An mebbe sometime in the future I'll see them, but I don't think so.' So the auld wumman lichtit up the lamp, she says, 'That's hit, the're nae mair tae be done. We had wir chance, the're nae mair tae be done, Jack, dinna think it wis yir fault, it wisna yir fault.'

'But hoo wis it, Auntie,' he said, 'I cuid manage to dae so much fir the rest o them an no fir you?'

'Laddie,' she said, 'hit wis oot o yir hands.'

Anyway, the aul wumman wis quite pleased; the're nothing they cuid do about hit. Jack got his wee bottle in his pocket. They stayed wi the auld wumman that night, the auld wumman gi'n them somethin to eat. The next mornin they set on their journey, back they go the way they cam. They landed back in the giant's castle. The giant wantit them up, tuik them up to the castle, gev them as much as they cuid eat an made them as merry all as cuid be, an offered Jack all the money he cuid tak wi him.

Jack said, 'Luik, I dinna want no money, I want nothing.'

They landed back at the wickit queen's place. But na, when she landed back at her palace, she says, 'I want yese to come in fir a wee while before youse go on yir journey.' She brung them inta the palace an made them merry, oh, they feastit fir three days in the queen's palace. An the folk all gaithert roond to see the great change that hed come ower the queen. But the next day they hed tae part. But as they were partin the queen called all her heid yins together, she tellt them, 'Luik after my kingdom till I come back because I'll be gone fir a while,' an she clickit her arm inta the wee king's airm, walkit away wi him an Jack. So on they go, the wee king (he wisna the 'wee king' nae mair) an the queen an the hunchback, back the road they cam till they cam tae the hunchback's wee hut in the forest.

An the hunchback tuik them in an he made them merry as cuid be, offert Jack money an offert him everything. He said, 'Jack, this great forest an all this land belangs tae me, but I'll no need tae bide inta hit nae longer. I'll go wi youse an gae back tae my ain place where I cam fae.' So he set fire to the hunchback's hut an burnt it to the grund, the hunchback went away back tae his ain country, tae his ain folk where he left the first place.

Noo, Jack an the king an the queen, back they cam to the wee king's country, the wee king's toon where he left. An the folk wis waitan on him comin. Oh, they were glad that he landed back an he wis a big king noo, he hed a wife wi him an everything! An they made merry-makin fir three days. He wantit Jack tae bide, he offert him all the money in the worl, offert him horses to carry him back tae his mother – but no – Jack wadna tak it.

'Well, Jack, luik,' he says, 'if ye ever in yir life, if you ever feel at ye ever think ye'll come back this way, you come back to me an you'll never want fir nothing!' An the queen kisst him an the wee king shakit hands wi him, bade him 'goodbye'.

An away Jack goes; the king an queen hed got mairriet an they lived happy in their palace. But Jack set his road back, back he cam – all the way back tae his auld mother's hoose. An when he landit in the hoose wi his wee bottle in his pocket, his auld auntie wis sittin in her auld rockin chair bi the fire. It wis a year an a day since the day he left! An she's sittin rockin at the firesisde, he opened the door an cam in.

His aul auntie luikit at him an she rubbed her een, 'Jack, Jack,' she says, 'you're back!'

'Aye,' he says, 'I'm back.'

She says, 'Hoo di' ye get on? Did ye fin' yir auntie?'

'A fand ma auntie, Auntie,' he said, 'A fand her, an I seen her whistlin cock an crowin hen. An I got the Water fae the World's End – hoo is my aul mither?'

She says, 'Yir aul mother is the same way sin the day you left. She never moved a muscle, but I tuik guid care o her.'

An he sut doon, he tellt her the same story as I'm tellin you. He gaes ower to his auld mother an he opened her mooth, he gien her a wee drink o the water oot o the bottle, an the auld wumman swallaed hit.

She sut up in the bed an she rubbed her een, 'Laddie, laddie, laddie,' she says, 'are ye back! You werena a while awa – did ye gie yir aul auntie the wee puckle peats?' She thocht he wis only a wee while awa! An the auld wumman got up, she says to her auld sister, 'Did ye come back wi Jack? He wis awa doon giein ye some peats.'

'Ay,' she says, 'he brung me doon the peats. I cam back up tae see hoo you're gettin on.'

'Oh, I'm gettin on,' says the auld wumman, 'I'm gettin on all right. I must hae fell asleep fir a wee while there.'

So Jack tuik his auld auntie doon wi' another load o peats! An his auld mother an him lived in their wee hoose fir the rest o their days, an that's the last o ma wee story!

THE TWELVE WHITE SWANS

Many years ago long before your time an mine, in a faraway country there lived a king and a queen. The king had married very young because his father had died an left him the kingdom when he was only a teenager. And they wisht fir a family, sure enough a family the' did have. But every time the king would go inta his queen an see her in her chambers where the baby 's born, he wad say, 'What is it this time?'

She wad say, 'Another son.' The next time another baby wis born he would go in . . . 'Another son.'

Not that the king didna like his sons, but he wished from his heart that some day one o them could be a little girl. An this worried him terribly, he said, 'Am I not capable of havin a daughter? I must have a daughter some way!'

An lo an behold time was not good to him: years passed by, the king grew old, he had twelve sons an there wis only a year, mebbe two year between them, twelve beautiful sons. All the sons ran about the palace, huntin, shootin an fishin, an the king loved his sons a lot. But he always hed one longin in his heart, if he cuid only have a little daughter that he could take on his knee an love an tell stories to. Bicause once the sons grew up they didna have much time for him, he wis only 'their auld father'.

Then lo an behold his wife 's guanna have another baby, an the king said, 'It *must* be a daughter this time! An if it is a daughter, she will be the greatest thing that ever come inta my life. I'll do everything within my power to see that she has the most wonderful things in her life. An I'll tell you one thing, if hit's a girl I'm not havin these boys runnin about her, these sons o mine – I'm not havin them – they'll have to go an find their own way i the world!'

186

And lo an behold it did happen, the king walked inta the room the next mornin – there wis the queen an there in the queen's bosom, presented to her by the nurses and women who took care o her, wis the most beautiful little girl the king hed ever saw in his life – long golden ringlets hangin down her neck! An the king jist went crazy!

An the queen said, 'At last, my deares husband, my king, we have –'

'What I longed fir an what I want,' he said. The king jist loved her, just cuidna take his eyes off her, after havin so many many boys.

But naturally time has a way o passin, and when she wis about three year auld the king jist wouldna let her out of his sight. Sons meant nothing tae him anymore. Till one day when she was about five years old the king said to the queen, 'Luik, these boys runnin about are a trouble to my little girl. We hev to get rid of them. I know they're my sons . . . Get rid o them, put them away an let them go an be knights, send them off to somewhere else, get em out o my sight! Bicause I'm needin my little girl, an I jist love this girl like nothing under the earth.'

Now the queen was very sad cause she was the mother of all the sons plus the girl, she said, 'Please, don't send –'

He says, 'They must go! I'm not havin boys runnin around, young men runnin about when my young daughter is here.' An he jist tuik her everywhere he went.

Then one day the queen thought she hatit tae see her sons goin away bicause the queen loved all her family, she made up her mind she'll go an see her auld friend who was her fairy godmother, who had brought her to the world, the old henwoman who lived i a little cottage on the castle grounds. So she walked down to the auld henwife, the auld wife met her an tuik her in, an they had a sit an a talk. She told her the story I'm tellin you, said, 'Look, the king wants me tae get rid o my sons, not kill em or nothin, but banish them away from the land, send them on. They'll go somewhere, probably get killed an A'll never see them again. Not that I don't love my little girl too, but I would love them all to grow up together.'

The henwife said, 'I know what kind o man your husband is, what would ye like tae do?'

'Well,' she said, 'I don't want him tae send them out in the world, prob'ly some o them'll never come back. An if some comes back an tells me some o their brothers hes been killed in battle or been killed doin something, it'll jist break my heart.'

An the aul henwife said, 'What wad ye like tae do wi them?'

She says, 'I want them all with me, but the king won't allow hit.'

'Well,' says the auld henwife, 'it's a sad position ye're in, but what can I do fir ye?'

She says, 'You can work magic, I know you can work magic.'

The old henwife says, 'I only work *good* magic.'

'Well,' she says, 'this is the kin o magic I want – guid magic. You know that I have a large garden in the palace.'

The aul henwife says, 'Yes, I've visited it very often, you've tuik me flowers from hit an I walked with ye in it when you were jist a wee baby.'

She says, 'An you know in my garden is a large pool where I visit every day – wouldn't it be wonderful if my sons cuid be turned inta swans – white snowdriven swans that could float around the garden, unknown to the king? An I cuid feed them every day, A knew they were safe an nobody cuid touch em.'

'Oh,' the aul henwife says, 'yes, it's a wonderful thought.'

'Please,' said the queen, 'that's all I desire, jist give me a potion o some kind that I can turn these boys inta swans an put them in my pond in the garden. An I can visit them, feed them, I can be with them all my life till I die. And the king can have his daughter, I can have my sons – and I never want him tae know.'

'Well,' says the auld henwife, 'if that's what you want, if that's what you want – I'll give ye a potion, but you must never touch it yourself, the king or the princess – yir daughter princess must never touch it! You'll take yir twelve boys to the pool . . . I'll give ye a potion, you'll bake a special cake, an yir daughter the princess or yir husband must not know about this. You must talk to your sons secretly, take them down to the pool, an I'll give ye a potion in a special little flagon.' (It wis all wee stone flagons in these days.)

And the auld queen said, 'That wad jist be lovely if ye cuid do that fir me.'

So the auld henwife went away ben her little place bihind her bedroom. She wis gone fir about fifteen minutes, she cam back an the queen wis still sittin there. '*Now,*' she said to the queen, '*luik, ye see that little stone flagon: you'll take this, you'll bake a special cake yirself ind the castle kitchen an you'll empty the contents in the cake; you'll take yir twelve boys down to the little pond in the castle gardens an ye'll tell them tae "taste this", give em a piece o the cake each an tell them they mus eat hit all at wonst an enjoy it bicause their mother made it special fir them! An keep this between yirself an yir sons.*'

'Fair enough!' says the queen.

Now the boys were all away huntin, shootin, fishin, doin everything.

They cam home. An they loved their mother very well. They were young, there were some nineteen, some twenty, some fifteen, some seventeen, thirteen, twelve . . . you know, all these young men! So these boys were always fed by themselves, an the queen gev orders tae the cook an the maids that she wis gaunnae serve them herself that night in the kitchen. So the king went inta his chambers an he had his little daughter ond his knee; ye know, he was croonin tae her, tellin her stories an singin songs tae her. The queen walked in an all the boys wis gathered roond this great big long wooden table, they're all talkin about what they been doin an huntin an fishin an other things.

She says, 'You know, my sons, Mammy has got a special treat fir youse tomorrow!'

An the boys all said, 'Yes, Mother?'

She said, 'I have baked a special cake tae celebrate something at youse don't know about – it's my special birthday and I am a certain age tomorrow – an I want youse to come with me. Because I hed my first birthday by the pond, I want you to celebrate my birthday wonst more by the pond.'

'Oh, Mother, yes certainly!'

'Now,' she says, 'don't tell yir father or don't tell nobody.'

They swore to secrecy they wouldna tell their father the king, although they never spoke to him very much anyway.

So the next morning wis a beautiful May morning, all the boys gaithert at the pond in the castle garden. They waitit roond the pond an sure enough down comes their mother. She carried a cake, a small cake, 'Now,' she says, 'boys, I want youse to all have a piece o this to celebrate my birthday!' She gev them each a piece in turn, 'Now,' she said, 'I want youse all tae eat it together.' An lo an behold whan she divided it, there wis only enough fir the twelve o them and they all ett it together.

An they said, 'Mother, that was lovely, did ye bake it yirsel?' Then a wonderful thing happened – they all fell to the ground – lo an behold, one after the other became swans an they poppit into the pond, one efter the other an they swam round an round. An the queen sat down, she felt happy. An there they swam round this lovely pond inside the garden – now she wis happy an pleased.

She goes back home to the king fir her evening meal, she sat at the table an he said, 'Ye seem very quiet tonight, my dear. Where is the boys? Where is the young men, this sons of yirs? Are they not gaunna have any meal tonight?'

She said, 'Ir Majesty, King, you gave orders . . . yir sons hev gone.'

'Oh well,' he said, 'guid riddance, guid riddance, guid riddance! An where hev they gone?'

'They took off in all directions,' she said, 'they're off tae seek their fortune i the world.'

'Guid, guid-guid riddance,' he said, 'prob'ly they'll return wiser whan my little girl hes grown up.' An he tuik his little girl on his knee, he's pickin all the best bits that he cuid pick fir her an he's feedin her with it in his lap.

But to make a long story short, years passed by an the swans were still in the pond. An the queen fed them every day. The king got kin o worried an he said, 'How in the world, where did the beautiful swans come from?'

She says, 'Well, they were a gift from a great friend of mine.'

'Oh, they're quite tame,' he said tae the queen.

'Oh,' the queen says, 'yes, they're quite tame, an A love tae feed them.' But the king paid no attention to swans.

But his daughter grew up till she was about sixteen years old, an she used to go with her mother every day tae feed the swans, 'Mammy,' she says, 'they are lovely.'

'Yes, daughter, they are lovely swans,' she said, 'they're the most beautiful birds I've ever saw.'

Then one particular evening, when the daughter wis about seventeen years old and the father wis gettin auld bi this time, who was much older than the queen, hed retired an went to sleep, and the queen was sittin combin her hair, beautiful hair right down her back; the princess turned round an said, 'Mammy, hit's a funny thing . . .'

She says, 'What's so "funny", dear?'

She said, 'That I didn't have any brothers or any sisters.'

Then the queen said, 'You know, it's not very funny, but I'm gaunna let ye inta a secret – you must never tell a soul, not even yir father – ye're auld enough now to understand.' So she told her the story I'm tellin you, she said, 'Your brothers . . . you have twelve brothers.'

'Twelve brothers, Mother,' she said, 'would I love my twelve brothers! An where hev they been all these years? Why hevna I been told this before?'

She says, 'Yir daddy the king ordered them off the land.'

She said, 'If I knew my daddy ordered my brothers away off the land inta another world . . . when are they comin home, Mother?'

'Well,' she says, 'they're not comin home.'

She says, 'You mean tae tell me, my brothers are not comin home – I'll never see my brothers?'

She said, 'A'm guannae let ye inta a big secret, not to even tell yir father; your brothers are twelve white swans in the garden pond!'

The princess was flabbergastit, 'Mother,' she said, 'how could I have twelve white swans fir brothers?'

'Well,' she said, 'yir father wantit tae send them inta the world to disappear and get killed in battle, an wander inta other countries – we'd never see them again – so I got a magic spell from an auld friend of mine an got them made into swans, so's they wad always be there for you to see an me tae enjoy.'

'Mother,' she says, 'I want my brothers, I must have my brothers back!'

She says, 'Yir father'll be outrag –'

'I don't care,' she said, 'I'll never talk to my father again unless I get to see ma brothers!'

De very next mornin, true to her word the princess goes to her father, says, 'Father, Mammy told me I have brothers!'

'Ho-ha-ha, my dear,' said the king, 'yes, ye have brothers.'

'Well, Father, why aren't they here with me?'

'Dearie,' he said, 'you don't need brothers, you've got me!'

She says, 'Father, I know A have you, you're my father. But I need my brothers, I want tae grow up – I want to see ma brothers!'

So the king felt very sad about this, because the're nothing in the world he wadna do fir the princess, he'd give her anything in the world.

An she says, 'A'm very sad.'

'Well, you can't be sad,' he said. 'Luik, I'll tell ye what A'll do, tomorrow I'll send couriers all over the world an bring every brother you've got back tae you, if that's what you want.'

So next mornin true tae his word the king goes down to the court-room, he calls the queen an all the couriers to him, tells them, 'Look, I want youse to travel far an wide an bring back the princess's brothers wherever they be, you shall search for ever till you find them. Bicause if she is unhappy, then I am unhappy.' The couriers said they don't know where to start. But the queen never said a word, she kep it quiet, she knew they were never gaunna find them. But the princess wis happy, she knew now somethin wis bein done about her brothers.

So he sent couriers on horseback to go off in all directions. They were gone fir days, but they straggly returnt one efter the other – no news of the young men, no news of the princes o no kind. The princess got sadder an sadder every time a courier returned with no news of her brothers, ti the king was so upset he jist cuidna stand hit anymore.

And he went to the queen, said, 'There *must* be something ye can do, there must be *something* ye can do to find these lost brothers of hers! Because she's fadin away, I can see her fadin away, she can't go on like this!'

So the queen said, 'Husbant, Ir Majesty, I've got a guilty secret I've kept from you fir many years.'

'Tell me, wumman,' he said, 'tell me!'

She says, 'Your sons the princes have never left the palace.'

'Well, wumman, go find them! Why dae ye keep me in such suspense? Go find them, bring them back – so that my little girl can see them!'

She says, 'Husband, hit's not within my power tae bring them back.'

'Well, where are they, where are they – if you know so much – tell me!'

She says, 'They're in the pond in the palace garden, twelve white swans.'

The king said, 'Twelve white swans in the garden is my sons, that my little girl wants!'

'Yes, that's where they are,' she said. 'A went tae my aul friend the henwife who works in er magical powers, an I got a potion to turn them into swans because I didn't want to ... all these years I've enjoyed their company ... they were swans but they're still my sons!'

He says, 'Woman, you have deceived me!'

She says, 'I haven't deceived ye; wouldn't it be worse if you'd sent them all inta the world to be killed, off in the world an battle, fightin somewhere? I knew where they were all the time.'

'Well,' he said, 'tomorrow you must bring them back!'

Oh, the queen and the princess the next mornin true to their word, they made their way to the old henwife once more. The auld henwife bi this time wis gettin very old an frail because many years had passed. And when the queen cam in she barely recognized the old woman, but they came in an they sat down.

The old henwife says, 'What brings you now, my queen? What is it you really need this time?'

She says, 'I want my sons back.'

An the old henwife said, 'Hit's a hard task ye're givin me – the're nothing I can do.'

'There must be *something*,' she said, 'ye can do! There must be something that you can do!'

'The're nothing *I* can do,' de old woman said, 'the're nothing *you* can do, but there's something that the *princess* can do if she wants tae do it.'

'An what would that be?' says the queen.

'Well,' says the auld wumman, 'there's only one thing she can do, but it's a hard task she's got to perform: *she must go into the churchyard at the hour of ten o'clock, an within two hours she mus make twelve shirts from the stingy nettles that grow in the churchyard; an she's only got two hours to do it, she's tae use the stingy nettles, spin them with a spinnin wheel an make them inta twelve shirts before the clock strikes twelve, an throw them over the twelve white swans.'*

'I'll do it, Mammy,' says the princess, 'I'll do it – I'll do anything in the world!'

So the queen said, 'Tae help ye out, I'll get some o the men to gather the nettles for ye.'

'Now,' says the old henwife before they leave, 'she'll be disturbed durin her wurk makin these shirts, because this particular night that I give her de power tae bring her brothers back . . . also the power of the harpies!'

And the queen says, 'What, harpies?'

'Yes,' she says.

'What are harpies?'

'Well, harpies,' says the auld henwife, 'are birds with human faces. *An they'll come, they'll start diggin in the graveyard fir bodies, but if the princess . . . they won't come near her because she's alive, they only go after the dead . . . but if the princess gets one fright, the spell'll be broken for ever an she'll never see her brothers again!'*

Fair enough. So back they go to the palace. The queen sent some workers to gather all the nettles. It hed tae be the churchyard nettles, no other wad do, the nettles that grew in the auld churchyard where they buried everybody. All the nettles are gaithert an heapit in the corner of the yard. Ten o'clock the princess walks down with a spinnin wheel an she starts, she spins the nettles an starts makin shirts. She wurks hard, she never stops, but all she hears a flap o wings comin, flippety-flap o wings, an down they come in dozens – burds, with evil women's faces, long hair – they're scratchin the earth with their nails fir people that wis new-buried. An they're throwin bags o earth, they're huntin fir bodies an they're diggin an they're diggin an diggin! They're squawkin an they're screechin, they're screekin at er, lookin at er, an she's carryin on, spinnin away. She never paid no attention to them for nearly ae hour and a half. An she's wurkin hard, wurkin hard, an they're hoppin around with their evil faces, their evil grins, they're tearin up the bodies from the graves efter they dug em oot. They're eatin em, they're squawkin an fightin like a lot o vultures over the bodies, an they're sharin bones an tearin hair an everything. An de princess jist stood there an spun away, paid no attention. An she wurk'd hard and wurk'd hard! Then all in a moment – twelve o'clock – she had twelve shirts, but one sleeve that she hed never finished when the clock struck twelve. The harpies disappeared as fast as they came.

She gaithert up the shirts, she ran down to the palace inta the garden round to the little lake, she waded inta the pond tae her waist. An one by one she pit a shirt over every swan's head till she came to the last one. And as she put a shirt over ae head, ae young man walked oot, tall handsome young man walked out o the water an stood in the bankway: one, two, three, four, five, six, seven, eight, nine, ten, eleven – till she came tae the last one – but the last shirt had only one sleeve. When she placed hit over, he walkit out o the pond, off the little lake in the garden, lo an behold there stood the twelve young princes an one o them had a wing. One had a swan's wing, a white wing.

The princess was delighted. She cuddled em, kissed em, took em all up to the palace. An the king who had forgiven the queen now saw that his daughter wis happy, was overjoyed. He turnt to the queen, said, 'Woman, it's a wonderful thing you've done.' The boys was no older, they never got old the swans, they were just young – way they were fra the minute they were pit in there. 'It's a wonderful thing ye done,' he said to the queen, 'but what's gaunna happen to him?' He wis left wi a wing instead o a arm, an the problem was he wis the youngest.

An the princess loved him more than the rest, she loved him best because he wis next tae her, he wis the youngest o them. And he felt sad. They sat down an they discussed, she told the story. An the boys felt very bad about their father, but they loved their mother, they all cam an kissed their mother, they forgev their mother fir what she done. But they never forgev their father. An the princess said, 'We shall hev tae find a way to get my brother's wing away an bring back his arm.'

After many days of feastin and rejoicin at the palace the princess began tae enjoy the company of her brothers. They huntit an shootit an fisht an done everything together, an she really loved to be with her brothers. The king who saw that the princess wis happy was overjoyed. Now he had his sons back an he had his daughter, who was happy for ever an just the radiant beautiful little girl like she ever was.

But the queen felt sad and the king felt kin o guilty when he saw the youngest brother, who very rarely spoke an never did very much because he had a wing, and he always kep it hidden under a cloak. An the princess, who loved the youngest brother more than any o the rest o the family, always had any time to spare she spent it with him. But one day she said tae her mother, 'Mother, this jist can't go on, we'll hev to find a way tae get ma brother's arm back.'

'Well,' says the queen, 'we've asked so many favours off the auld henwife, an she's gettin an auld wumman now, but I jist hate going back tae her so many times.'

'Well, Mother,' she says, 'there's only one thing we can do – we must – for wir brother's sake!'

So the princess and the queen visits the aul henwife once more. They landed back an lo an behold the auld henwife was happy to see them. They sat down an talked fir a wee while an she said, 'What's yir trouble this time? I hear you've got yir sons back once more.'

'Yes,' she said, 'A hev my sons back an nobody's happier than me, tae hev my sons around me once more – but there's one thing missin.'

'I know,' says the henwife, 'it's a sad ending. But there's very little we can do about hit.'

She said, 'There must be something we can do!'

She says, 'I know one o yir sons hes got a wing, a swan's wing.'

An the princess says, 'That's what we cam to see you about. I'll give ye everything at you need in this world – '

An the old henwife says, 'Look, I don't need nothing, my dearie.'

She says, 'I want you to help me, I want you to help me to get rid of my brother's wing!'

'Well,' she says, 'hit's a terrible thing that he hes, but it's not within my power tae help him in any way; *you* are the only one that can help im!'

'Me,' says the princess, 'I'll do *anything*, I'll go anywhere, I'll do anything under the sun tae help my brother tae get rid of this wing an have his arm wonst more. Because he feels so sad tae see the rest o his brothers – he canna ride, he cannae fire a bow, he canna do nothing because he hes to keep it under a cloak.'

The auld henwife says, 'Luik, you don't know, but many many many leagues from here there is another land, another country. An ind that country lives a queen who doesn't have a king, has only had one son. This queen is the Queen of Knowledge, at *knows* everything. An I know where the queen is, I know that she has the knowledge to cure yir brother, but that's all I can tell ye – the rest is left tae yirself.'

'But how,' said the princess, 'how am I gaunnae go there an – '

'If you go there,' she said, 'ye'll never even get near her – not as a princess.'

'What must I do?' said the princess.

She said, '*Ye'll hev tae go as a beggar girl, find employment in the palace an seek the knowledge from the queen herself.* But I hev a better idea, why don't you be a goose girl?' (In these bygone days girls did walk with geese, they swappit them an tradit em around.) 'An,' the auld wumman said, 'for yir safety's sake, get yir father tae send some huntsmen along with ye fir half o the journey, then go the other half by yirself. Take some geese an a ragged dress, dress yirsel as a goose girl an make yir way to the palace. Then it's up to yirself what you do from there because that's all the help I can tell ye; that's the only way you're gaunnae find the problem of your brother's wing.'

De girl, princess was overjoyed, she says, 'Yes, I'll do it, I'll go!'

The queen was very upset about this, she didna want to lose her wee daughter. When she went back an told the king, the king went out o his mind – 'no way' – he wouldna have hit no way. The queen got him finally talked around tae hit.

So the next day the king said, 'Well, if that's to be, what's to be shall be. But she's gaunna be well protectit if I can help it.' So he ordered fir ten soldiers, his best soldiers an ten horses. He even got panniers on the horses' backs to carry the geese, so's their feet wouldna be sore travellin too far. He ordered that the geese should be in baskets, an travel fir many leagues till they came to the land of the Queen of Knowledge, an then let the geese out; an promised the soldiers to wait for her return – suppose they hed tae wait fir a lifetime – not to return without her! So everything was planned an arranged fir the next day: ten soldiers were to look after the princess, guide her on her way till they came to the land of the Queen of Knowledge, and then they were to let her out an stay in one particular place till she came back. If she didn't come back, 'They were never to return,' said the king, 'fir the peril o their life – return without my daughter an yese'll be dead when youse come back!'

So the next day true to their word the king and queen bade the princess 'goodbye' – a ragged dress, bare feet – an ten soldiers, the horses an five geese, they set on their journey. They travelled far an they travellt wide an they're askin along the way how far it is to the next kingdom. They travelled for many many miles an many many days. At last they came into a green valley inta a land that was so flat there werena a hill fir miles, an beautiful forests an runnin streams. The soldiers 's amazed.

An the princess said, 'Look, A think this is far enough, I can make my way from here.' So she donned her ragged dress, took her geese and the soldiers said they would stay in the one spot till she returned. True enough we'll leave the soldiers there camped i the one spot an go wi the princess, the goose girl.

So the goose girl travelled on fir many days, traded the geese along the way, sold some, got some strange ones an traivellt on ti she came tae a town. When she landit i the town she made inquiries, 'Where was the palace of the queen?'

An they pointit to a large castle on the hill, 'That's the palace of the queen, but nobody goes there.' They were warned not to go there. The queen had one son who rides through the forest many many times but never comes near the town. And they askit her 'what she wantit'.

She said she jist wantit to see the queen. The goose girl made up her mind that she wad go to the palace. So the next mornin she left the village an took her geese, drove them on er way. She hed traivellt many miles, and the palace luikit as far away as ever when she came to a forest. She walked through, she came to a clearin, it was grass beautiful high. The geese wis hungry, began to pick the grass, she sat doon tae rest. When all in a minute who should come ridin through the forest but this young man, most beautiful young man she ever saw in her life! When he saw the young goose girl in the forest he stopped! And he sat there, he watched this beautiful young girl dressed in rags, long golden plaits doon her back an her bare feet, an the geese. He jumped off his horse, he walked over.

An he said, 'Hello, goose girl.'

She said, 'Hello, sir.'

He said, 'Where have you come from?'

She says, 'I cam from the village.'

'Where are you journeying to?'

She says, 'I'm journeying to seek the Queen of Knowledge.'

'Ha-ha,' he said, 'you're journeying to seek the Queen of Knowledge, are ye?'

'Yes,' she said, 'I am.'

'Well, why should you seek the Queen of Knowledge,' he said – 'just a goose girl?'

'Well,' she said, 'I may be a goose girl, but I have a problem.'

'Look,' he said, 'ye're no gettin near my mother. My mother knows all the problems of everything that goes on over the world, but hit's gettin er tae tell ye them is another thing.'

She said, 'Is the queen yir mother?'

'Yes,' he said, 'the queen's my mother, I'm the prince an the queen's my mother.' But he took a likin to the goose girl an he felt sorry fir her. He said, 'Luik, I couldn't take ye to the palace in any way, but me an my mother gets on very well together. If ye tell me yir problem I'll try an find it out fir ye.'

So de princess sat down an she told him the story I'm tellin you. An when he realized that she was a king's daughter he fell in love with her right away, he wouldna let her out o his sight.

'Now,' he says, 'I can't take ye, I can't take ye back to the palace with me because ye never know what my mother may do or may think. But, you wait here – nobody'll touch ye in this place because nobody's allowed here, ye'll be quite safe – you stay here an I'll be back!' Away rides the prince back to the palace, he'd no problem gettin to the palace. Jumps off his horse an his mother meets him at the door, he walks up.

She said, 'Where hev you been, my son?'

'Oh, Mother,' he said, 'I been ridin all over an the day was so warm.'

'Come and have somethin tae eat,' so he sat with his mother, an they talked fir a long while.

'You know, Mother,' he said . . . when she sat in the chair, she loved this boy so much – he always used to come by her side an place his head on her knee – she would run her hands through his hair, that's all she loved tae do, it was her only son. He said, 'Mother, when I was out ridin – '

She said, 'Tell me what ye been doin all day!'

'Whan I wis out ridin today, Mother,' he said, 'I fell asleep an A had a wonderful dream.'

'Oh, please tell me,' she said, 'what was it about?'

'Well,' he said, 'it's a funny dream, Mother; I dreamt that in a faraway land in a faraway place, a land I never seen, a land of hills an mountains and seas, there lived a king an queen and they had twelve sons.'

'Oh,' says the queen, "they had twelve sons".'

'An the king hatit the sons so much, an the queen loved the sons . . .' he told er the story I'm tellin you.

'Oh,' says the queen, 'that's a wonderful dream!'

'And,' he said, 'one o the sons – after everything came back – was left with a wing on his arm, an there I wakent up. But, Mother, I'm worried, I'm worried about my dream, Mother.' An she's still gropin his hair, ye see, he said, 'Mother, I wonder why that I should hev wakent up, I wanted my dream to finish!'

She said, 'I'll finish yir dream for ye, I'll finish yir dream for you, son, if it'll make ye happy.'

He said, 'I wonder why the prince in my dream had never got his arm back.'

'Oh, dear,' she said, 'he cuid get his arm back in your dream; if you'd hae dreamt a little more, you'd hev seen the end o yir dream: if he'd only went an found a swan's nest, that was where they would find a unhatched egg, an get someone to get the unhatcht egg that hed never came to be a young swan – an break it over his wing – the wing would disappear and he'd have his arm back wonst more. That's the bit o yir dream that ye misst.'

'Oh, Mother,' he said, 'thank you very much. Now A'm happy!' He couldna hardly wait ti the next day, now he had the secret that he wantit. So he's up and early as possible rode down the valley. An sure enough he came to the clearin, there was the princess wi her geese. He rode over.

He spoke tae her, said, 'I talked to my mother.'

She says, 'Did you find the solution to my brother's problem?'

He said, 'Yes, I found the solution to your brother's problem.'

She says, 'Tell me, tell me, please!'

He says, 'I'll tell ye on one condition.'

She says, 'Well, what is the condition?'

He said, 'On one condition I'll tell ye, if you marry me! An be my wife!'

An she really likit him, ye know, an he likit her. So she promised to marry him. He tuik er on the horse, he rode up to the palace. Nobody could stop him, rode right inta the palace, jumpit off, took the ragged goose girl inta the queen's chamber where she wis sittin. He says, 'Mother, I've brought you back the rest o my dream.'

And the queen said, 'What? You have deceived me!' she said tae her son.

'Yes, Mother,' he said, 'I knew that you would never hev told me, only in a dream. This is a princess, an it's her brother who has the wing! An I'm gaunna marry her, I'm gaunna take er to be my wife.'

'Well,' says the queen, 'hit's about time that ye're havin a wife!' An the queen liked this young woman right away, she ordered the rags to be taken off her, sent fir the beautiful dress. They had a great banquet an they had a great party, a great thing went on for days an the prince married the princess.

Now the soldiers are still waitan an waitan an waitan to see would she return, for the peril o their death they cuidna return. When they waitit fir over a month, when one day who should they see comin but a coach an five white horses. An the head man wi the soldiers went out, he stopped the coach an askit 'if they'd seen a goose girl'.

An the young man leaned out o the coach, says, 'No, I've never saw a goose girl, but I saw a princess – an she's here!' They told the soldiers all aboot it. The soldiers joint behind them, came behind the coach, an they all rode back, all the way they came, back to their own country to their own palace. An the king and queen was happy to see the return o them. An all the sons gathered there together . . . But still no egg.

Noo the princess had the secret, she was married, she had the secret but she still had no egg. She was still worried about her brother, so the next day she goes back to the auld henwife wonst more. She said, 'I've been there.'

An the auld henwife said, 'I know you've been, and now ye have a husband. An now you have the secret, but ye don't know were tae find an egg, a swan's egg.' (It hed tae be a swan's egg, no other wis any good, a buff.) 'But,' she says, 'ye're a lucky young woman tae have a beautiful husbant an twelve beautiful brothers.'

'But,' she says tae the aul henwife, 'I don't have an egg!'

'But,' she says, 'ye're luckier than ye thought, because yesterday jist below my house a swan hes walkit away with five young ones an left a buff egg in the nest.'

An the princess walked doon – sure enough – there wis the egg in the nest. She pickit it up, she walkit back. An when she walkit back there wis a great banquet in the palace, everybody wis dancin an singin an havin great fun – welcome back the princess – except fir the young brother who was sittin sad at the corner with a cloak round him wi one hand. The princess walks up, she whispers to him an both o them walks out the door.

An she said, 'Take back yir cloak!' He pulled back his cloak an she broke the rotten swan's egg on his wing. And lo an behold she no sooner broke . . . de rot, smelly stuff run down over his wing an droppit on the ground . . . an amazin thing happent – his fingers began tae appear, the feathers begin to disappear – an the wing was gone for ever!

And when he saw this he wis so happy, he threw his arms roond his sister's neck an kissed her, walked back into the banquet hall, held up his arms an said, 'Look at me, look at me!'

All her brothers walkit roon, said, 'What's so funny about ye, why ye wavin yir arms in the air?'

He said, 'I'm not wavin my arms in the air – I'm showin ye I don't have a wing anymore!' And they were *all* so happy, they all gaithért roon him. An he came tae his little sister the princess, said, 'Thank you, my little sister, fir what you've done fir me!'

She says, 'Don't thank me, thank your brother-in-law, *he's* the one that done it for ye, not me!' An everybody lived happy ever after, an that's the end o my story.

THE UGLY QUEEN

Jack stayed with his mother ind a little cottage in the forest. His father was a woodcutter an had died when Jack was very young. Jack's memory o his father wis very faint, but the one thing Jack always remembered – because Jack's father was a very good man – 'Ye remember, Jack,' he'd said, 'there's only one thing at's gaunnae stead ye in life, son, when I'm gone: be honest an kind and truthful!' Jack used tae go wi his father bi his hand to the wuid when he wis about three year old, an this is what the father told him, 'Be honest, be kind an be truthful!' That was the only memory Jack had of his father.

Now ind this land where Jack lived there lived a king an queen who ruled the kingdom. An the king had a accident, he fell off his horse an wis killed. The whole country mourned fir months an months about the king, because he wis only a young man an he left behind him a young daughter only one year old. An the queen adored this daughter. But the king had only one ambition in his life.

In his kingdom in the sea was a island, an ind this island was a giant fourteen feet high. He used tae come across the mainland an take cattle, sheep, anything that he wantit, an the're nothing that the king cuid do. The king's only ambition was tae get rid o this giant, but he hed never got a chance – he fell aff his horse an wis killed. Now this giant still remained ind the island. An there's no one cuid touch him or no one cuid do nothing to him, because he didna have any heart. The king had sent fir men, magicians of all description, an askit them 'how tae get rid o the giant'. And they told him, 'There's no way that ye can get rid o the giant,' because the giant didna have any heart, he was untouchable. No one knew where the giant's heart was. The only way tae get rid o the giant was to find out where the heart was, an no one knew. So there was the queen left to rule the kingdom with a young baby a year auld an this indestructible giant ind the island.

She called all her wisemen together an all her henwives, says, 'There's only one thing I want in my ambition, as of my late husband, is tae get rid of this giant.' An no way could she find a way to get rid o him because he was indestructible. Till one morning.

It was a nice summer's morning an she put her little baby daughter who wis coming up now near two years of age out in the front o the castle to play. She went back into the kitchen tae do something. (The queen wis just a wumman; it wis jist a matter o bein the head of the clan or the head of the race, respectit of course, but she had to do her part even in the kitchens.) She went back an left the child tae play, and who came across from his island at that very moment – the giant – takin ten-league steps at a time! An the first thing he saw passin by the castle was the wee child, he pickit it up in his oxters, in his bosom, an he set sail with the child through the sea back tae the island. Because he wantit this child!

An the queen came back – the child was gone – an she cried, she askit everybody around the place what happened, 'Where was the baby?' Nobody knew where the baby was, till somebody said, 'Oh, yes, Wir Majesty, the giant was here while you were gone. He took her an she's gone, the giant walkit across the sea with her in his arms back tae his island!'

An the queen was so upset, frantic, she didnae know what tae do. She knew there was no way she wis gaunnae get the baby back. So she gaithert all her couriers an all her holy people around her, all these magicians an people, how wis she tae get the child back? Nobody could tell her. Till one day she wis sittin i the front of the palace, when up comes an auld wumman with a basket on her arm, she's selling eggs.

She knocks at the door an one o the maids goes to the door, 'What do you want, auld wumman?'

She says, 'I'm selling eggs.'

'Eggs?'

'Yes,' she said, 'ask the good lady "would she buy some eggs?"'

So the maid being a good lassie jist walked up, said tae the queen, 'Her Majesty, there's an old lady at the door selling eggs.'

'Yes,' says the queen, 'bring the auld wumman in!' When the maid mentioned 'eggs', the queen knew the old wumman must be *a henwife*. 'Bring the auld wumman in,' says the queen.

So the maid says, 'Would you come in?'

An the aul granny with a basket laid full o eggs said, 'Would you buy some eggs, good lady?'

'Yes,' says the queen, 'I'll buy some eggs. Who are you?'

'Oh,' she said, 'I'm jist an auld henwife who is selling eggs.'

She says, 'Dae ye know who I am?'

'No,' says the auld wumman, 'ye're jist a natural wumman of a big castle I sell my eggs tae.'

She says, 'I am the queen of the country.'

'Oh!' the auld wumman went down on her knees, 'I am sorry,' she said, 'Ir Majesty. I have dreamed all my life o meetin the queen, but never in a million years hev ever I been here before!' An she went down on her knees an begged mercy frae the queen.

So the queen says, 'Well, it's all right, it's all right. We'll take yir eggs, we'll take the lot. But, eh, A wonder, could you help me?'

'Well,' says the auld lady, 'A prob'ly cuid, if ye tell me what's ailin ye – ye ill?'

'No,' says the queen, 'I'm not ill; I'm ill in a way, an I'm vexed an broken-heartit.'

'Oh,' says the auld wumman, 'why should you be broken-heartit if ye're de queen?'

'Well,' she said, 'prob'ly ye've heard – I jist newly lost Ir Majesty the King.'

'I heard,' says the auld wumman, 'an I'm very grieved about hit.'

'An,' she says, 'I have lost my baby.'

'Oh,' says the aul wumman, 'I'm very sorry that yir baby . . . is gone.'

'But,' the queen said, 'she's not dead.'

'I know,' says the auld wumman, 'she's not dead.'

'Then,' says the queen, '*you know* she's not dead!'

'Yes,' says the auld wumman, 'yir child is not dead.'

So the queen says tae the auld henwife, 'Look, would ye tell me something if ye know that much – ye're gaunna tell me a little more?'

'Oh yes,' says the auld wife, 'I can tell ye a little more . . . much more! Your child is in the hands of the Giant of the Island in the Sea.'

'Yes,' says the queen, 'that's true.'

'An,' she says, 'you would like tae get her back.'

'Yes,' says the queen, 'that's true, I would give my entire life to get her back!'

'But,' the auld woman said, 'hit's not as simple as that. I know of the giant – in fact he is a relation of mine. An he is indestructible, there's no way in the world at you cuid do him any harm, or there's no way in the worl ye're gaunna get yir child back.'

The queen said, 'There must be something A cuid do.'

'Yes,' said the auld woman, 'there's something ye can do: *you must go an find a man who is truthful an kind an gentle, who'll tell ye the honest truth from his heart.* But if you go as a queen, then you'll never find the truth. Luik, I'm gaunna do something for you, Our Majesty –'

An the queen says, 'You shall be repaid handsomely!'

An de old woman said, 'I want no payment. I'm going to do something for you, I'm gaunnae tell ye something, an if you do what I tell you you will get yir child!' She gropes in her basket an she takes out a little stone bottle, she says, '*Ir Majesty the Queen, I'll give you this: this is a potion an you must rub yirself wi this potion tonight at twelve o'clock. An by tomorrow morning you will be the ugliest person that ever walked on this earth. Now, to get your child, you must do this.* If you think that yir child is not worth hit, then don't do it.' An she takes another small bottle from the corner o er basket, she says, '*After everything is gone, remember – and ye have done yir task an received yir child – the only way in the world tae get yirsel back tae normal is use the second one. But don't use the second one first!*' So the auld wumman turned round to the queen an said, 'Remember, Ir Majesty, this is gaunnae make ye ugly, the most ugliest person in the world that ever walked, but through ugliness you're gaunna find *truth*! An you shall take with you a bag of gold, you shall give up yir entire reign as a queen an travel on through the country an find *truth*! You shall travel yirself as an ugly auld wumman with a bag of gold; sometimes along the way, for the greed, people will give you an tell ye "this" an tell ye "that". *But you must find truth before ye can find happiness.* You'll ask anyone and offer em yir bag o gold, tell them along the way that "you are beautiful", an if they agree with you then they are wrong – there is no truth in hit – because they are only doin hit fir the greed of the gold. But remember, I'll not be here with you when you return!'

And the queen turnt round an she was happy, 'But,' she says, 'will that bring me my daughter?'

'Yes,' she said, 'it'll bring ye yir daughter for evermore; an tae tell ye something else, it will end the entire life of the giant who yir husband long bifore ye wanted to destroy. You do my biddin!'

'Where can I get in touch with ye, auld wumman?' says the queen.

She says, 'You can never get in touch with me anymore. All I want of you is to buy my eggs.'

'I'll take yir eggs,' says the queen, 'but how in the world can I reward you?'

'You can never reward me, Our Majesty,' says the auld woman. 'You have rewarded me enough by buyin my eggs.' An like that the auld wumman left, she was gone.

Now the queen is left with these two bottles. 'Well,' says the queen, 'if I must get my daughter, I must!' an she knew what she must do. She took the last bottle, put it up in her bedroom an hid it. She took the first bottle, she went inta her bathroom an scattert hit around herself. She luikit at herself in the mirror – and lo an behold she was sick – what she saw. She saw the ugliest ol crone, warts on her face, nose as long as anything, chin hangin down, she wis the uglies' thing that ever walked on this earth! And the queen was happy, she knew, 'I must do this for my daughter's sake.' She walked down the stairs, met her servants an her servants turnt their heads. She walked into her bedroom, she packit a bag o gold an turnt round, tellt the servants, 'I'm on my way. I must find truth fir my daughter's sake.'

An the servants didna know who the queen was, 'Ugly auld wumman,' they said, 'what are ye doing here?'

She says, 'The queen is gone on a visit an I must follae her, but she'll be back.' So she lef the castle in charge of good hands. An then my story says the queen set off.

She traivellt round the country with a bag o gold – de ugliest auld wumman at ye ever saw in yir life – she walkit among the common people an she walkit among the down-an-outs. She walkit among woodcutters, farmers, an everywhere she cam along she had her bag o gold, everywhere she went she asked the same thing, 'Amint I the beautifules person you ever saw?' an she held the bag o gold, jingled the gold.

An they said, 'Lady, you are beautiful! You are a wonderful woman!' because they heard the tinkle of her gold.

An she said, 'No, I am ugly,' an she walkit on. She traivellt an she traivellt an she traivellt on, an . . . the same thing along the way. Till one night very late she came tae a forest, she luikit round and all the trees were cut an cleaned up. She walkit on, saw a little light. It became late at night an she says, 'I must have somewhere to stay fir the night.' She walkit to this little cottage, knocked at the door and out came this auld wumman. An the queen said, 'Excuse me, I am an auld woman on the road, would you give me shelter fir the night?'

'Yes,' says the auld woman, 'come in, there's only nobody here but my son an I. Ye're welcome tae share what we hev.'

'Oh,' she said, 'I've got gold tae pay fir hit.'

'Oh no,' says the old woman, 'we dinna want yir gold. Jist come in an make yirsel at home.'

And the queen was amazed because the auld wumman had never even luikit or paid any attention tae how she luikit. When the queen walked into the kitchen she luikit: sittin on a chair, an auld-fashioned chair by the peat fire, was the youngest, most handsomest an best-luikin man she hed ever saw in her life! Tall, blond, curly hair, blue eyes, the most best-luikin man she hed ever seen – it remembered her so much her husband – the queen was aghast to look at this young man sittin in the chair!

An the young man rose up, he took the old woman, said, 'Sit down, my lady, an have my chair. Heat yirsel by the fire an have something to eat.' And he never even looked or said 'ugly' or nothin, he never said nothing. So the queen sat down an she had something to eat, never givin a thought that she was in the mos humblest home that ever she cuid hev met, the home of a woodcutter's son and his mother. But the secret was, *he* had known the truth – told tae him by his father.

And after her meal the queen sat, she talked tae the auld wumman, says, 'I'm jist an auld wumman.' An she turned round to the son, says, 'Are you working?'

'No, my auld wumman, I'm not working,' he said, 'I'm idle, I can't find a job. My father was a woodcutter, but wood is gettin very scarce, we're not allowed to cut more wood around here.'

'Well,' she said, 'I've got money, I cuid give you money.'

'My lady, I cuidna accept yir money,' he says, 'no way.'

She says, 'I'll give ye my money, my two bags of gold . . .'

An this was Jack who stayed with his mother i a little cottage that she had wandered intae, an Jack said, 'Lady, I don't want yir gold. I have no need fir yir money or yir gold. I'm staying here with ma mother an we manage tae get by without yir gold. Poor old woman, you need it where you're goin.'

She says, 'Look, I'll give ye my full bag of gold if ye tell me one thing!'

'Yes,' he said, 'mother, I'll tell ye anything ye want – aye, there's only one thing A can tell ye – I hev tae tell ye the truth.'

She said, 'Am I not the most beautiful an handsomest woman ye hev ever saw in yir life – with my beautiful bags of gold? I can give you these bags o gold an make you rich fir evermore!'

An Jack turned roond, he said, 'Luik, no, my mother, auld woman, you are the most uglies' creature that ever walked through my mother's door! An you could never give me any gold because I would never accept it. I'm not gaun to deceive you, how you get by in this world by bein so ugly and so stupid – why people hes not tuik that from ye a long time ago – I don't know. But try an give that to me, and ask me to say that you are beautiful, an try to bribe me – I wouldna accept one single coin from you!'

She says, 'I am a beautiful woman!'

He says, 'You are the uglies' auld thing that ever walked through my mother's door!'

An de queen rose, she placed the two bags o gold in front o Jack. She put her arms round Jack's neck, 'John,' she said, 'dae ye know who I am?'

He says, 'You are still an ugly aul wumman!'

She says, 'I am Er Majesty the Queen!'

An John went down on his knees in front o her, he begged pardon fir what he said an asked forgiveness. An she sat an told him the story, but she never told him that she had become ugly through the aul henwife's bottle, she never mentioned that! But Jack accepted her tale and she told him that only him could save er daughter. She told Jack the story, 'In the island . . . I want you to do something fir me, Jack, my little daughter is a prisoner on the island.'

Jack said, 'Ir Majesty, why don't you send troops or men or something to re –'

She says, 'There's no way it can be done because the giant hesna got a heart, no way . . . hesna got a heart. Would ye do one thing fir me, would you rescue my daughter from the island an destroy that giant, take my daughter back, Jack? Because you survive on truth.'

'Well,' says Jack, 'it disna look like a big job to me.'

She said, 'I'll give ye everything under the sun. First you have got tae get to the island, an then you've got tae get to the home o the giant and rescue my daughter.'

So Jack's mother cam in, she sat down by the fire an the queen told her the whole tale. She says tae Jack, 'I think you'd be better tae do whit the queen asks ye fir tae do.'

'Well,' Jack said, 'hit's only a job fir me. In fact, I'm no doin very much at the moment, Mother. I'll do what the queen asks, I'll go and bring er daughter for her.'

So the queen turned round to Jack, 'You know what you've got to face!'

'Oh,' says Jack, 'I know what A've got to face, you told me, there's a giant that lives on the island an he has yir daughter a prisoner, it's very simple fir to take yir daughter from the giant, an bring her back to you is all you ask. Ir Majesty the Queen, I'll do that for you! But make me one promise.'

'What's that?' says the queen.

'That you'll be there – are ye tellin me the truth – that you'll be there whan I fetch yir daughter back!'

'Yes,' says the queen, 'I'll be there.'

So the next morning Jack bundled up a wee bag ond his back. His mother made him a bannock an fried him a wee collop, an Jack set sail tae do the job fir the queen. He wantit no money, he wantit nothin, an he left the auld queen wi his mother, bade his mother 'goodbye'. He set sail along his way an he walkit on, he walkit on an he walkit on and he made his way till he came tae the sea, the shoreside. He thought to hissel, said, 'I'll sit down here an rest fir a while.' An he tuik oot his wee piece o bannock that his mother hed gi'n him an his wee bit o ham, an what cam in beside him was a swan. And Jack naturally threw wee pieces of his meat to the swan. Though he wis hungry himsel he threw little pieces to the swan, and the swan came closer an closer an closer to him . . . an Jack threw pieces.

An the swan turned an spoke, 'Jack, you're good an truthful, an you fed me – A want to help you.'

Jack had never heard a swan speakin before an he wis mesmerized, he said, 'Swan, are you talkin to me?'

'Yes, Jack,' he said, 'I'm talkin to you. Well, I know what ye're gaunna do, but remember one thing, you are goin into the island of the indestructible giant who has the queen's daughter a prisoner. But, Jack, you'll never do it because the giant hes no heart.'

An Jack said, '"The giant has no heart", I never heard a thing in ma life – "the giant . . ." everybody's got a heart!' An Jack was young an strong, he thought hissel fit enough to face the giant.

An the swan says, 'You could never do nothing to the giant! *But remember, Jack, you fed me. You go inta the island, an ind the island is my nest. Ind my nest is an egg an ind at egg is the giant's heart. So you take that egg and squeeze it, take hit in yir hand an squeeze it. Then ye'll have the power over the giant.*' An like that the swan flew away!

Now Jack knows what he's got to do. Jack walks down an borrows a boat from an aul fisherman, he says to the fisherman, 'I would like to borrow a boat.'

An the ol fisherman said, 'Why do you want to borrow a boat?'

Jack says, 'I want to go out to the island.'

An the old fisherman said, 'Please, please, don't go out there. That is the home of the indestructible giant, you could never never . . .'

Jack said, 'I'm not asking you to take me, I jist want to borrow yir boat.'

The old fisherman said, 'Look, be it upon yir own head but you can have the boat, but I'll not go with ye.'

Jack said, 'Let me have the boat.' So de auld fisherman gev Jack the boat, Jack rowed an he rowed an he rowed out to sea, till he came to the island. He beacht the boat, walkit up an the first thing he saw when he landed in the island was a swan's nest. An inside de swan's nest was a large egg! Jack pickit up the egg and he held it in his hand. He walkit, he walkit up this path an the first thing he saw was a great castle! And when he walked up to the castle out cam the giant – fourteen feet tall.

'What are you doin here, what do ye want?'

Jack said, 'I have come tae take the queen's daughter that you hev a prisoner here.'

The giant said, 'I shall never part with er! Fir years the king hes destroyed * his wrath upon me – he hes tried tae destroy me fir years – an he hes never succeedit. And now, by sheer bad luck the king is gone an I have got his daughter, and I am gaunna keep her fir er entire life!'

An Jack said, 'You ain't gaunna keep her, I'm gaunna have her!' an he startit tae squ –

And the giant pit his hand on his heart, an Jack squeezt the egg. He says, 'You can never destroy me!'

Jack said, 'I am gaun tae destroy you – I have the egg – an I am gaun to destroy you!'

'Where,' said the giant, 'hev ever you discovered the power of my body?' An Jack squeezed the egg an the giant doubled in two, he said, 'Please, please don't do it!'

Jack said, 'I have you – hit – and you are gaunnae tell it in truth!'

An he squeezed the egg an the giant said, 'What is it you want? What is it you want!'

An Jack said, 'You shall return the baby to the queen!'

* destroyed – wasted

The giant said, '*Please* . . . hit, *please*, don't squeeze so hard, you're hurting me!'

Jack says, 'You shall take the baby in yir arms an you shall walk across the sea, and deliver the child back to the queen!'

And the giant said, 'Yes, I'll do that. But please don't squeeze it so hard, you're hurting my heart!'

The giant tuik the baby in his oxters an he walked across the sea, he delivert it to the queen. An the queen wis there at the door, he put the baby in the queen's arms and the queen wis as ugly as ever. She held the child and the child startit to cry when she looked at her mother!

Jack is still in the island by this time, he cuid see across the water an he's standing watching the giant comin through the water. An he waitit . . . till the giant was halfway in the sea, halfway through the water . . . he took the egg an he broke hit on the floor. Naturally, as he broke the egg, down went the giant into the sea an the waves covered him!

Jack tuik his boat an he walkit doon, he rowed across tae the land, an he walkit on. He came back to the castle where the queen was, an the first thing he saw was the ugly auld wumman with this baby in her oxters! He knew right away that she was the queen. There wis a great meetin an everyone wis carryin-on – the queen's baby hed come home an everybody wis excited.

The queen said, 'Make way, make way, make way fir the man who hes brung back my child!' An Jack was led up to the palace, they gev im the greatest reception in the world. An the queen said, 'We must have a great party, a great reception fir my child comin home. But we must give thanks to one person who hes made it possible fir hus to have wir child back, the princess; fir Jack – we must adore him an give him all that he asks for!'

An Jack was amazed, mesmerized, because he'd never been in this place before. Only one thing he wantit – wis tae get back tae his mother.

The queen said, 'We mus have a great feast an Jack is gaunna be with hus. Give him all the attention that we can give in this world because he hes brought back my daughter to the kingdom.' So the great feast wis held, the party wis held an dancin an singin went on and everybody cam, kissed the young princess because she hed come home. And the giant wis destroyed for ever an Jack was given a hero's welcome. But lo an behold Jack was so unhappy – he only wantit one thing – he wantit back tae his mother. An the queen cam in, ugly auld queen she says to Jack, 'Won't you stay, Jack? Why don't you stay with me, why don't you stay with me fir ever?'

He says, 'I cuid never stay with you, you are –'

She says, 'Jack, tell me the truth – am I not the nicest person you ever saw?'

He says, 'I have done for you – got yir daughter back – and you are Er Majesty the Queen of this country. But you are still to me the most ugliest auld person that ever I saw in my life! An tomorrow morning I would like tae be gone from this place because I have got tae go to my mother.'

The queen walkit up to her bedroom, she tuik the little bottle that the henwife gev her an she spread it around her face an her body, sprayed it around er. She looked i the mirror . . . an ye'll no believe hit, it breaks my heart to tell ye . . . it wis the most beautiful thing that ever walked ond earth she became after she'd put this ond her. She wis younger, handsomer and more beautiful than ever she'd been in her life before! An she walkit into her bedroom, she pickit up two bags o gold an she walkit doon the stairs. And there was Jack ready to take off tae see his mother.

She walkit doon to Jack, said, 'Jack, here's yir reward.'

He says, 'Reward fir what?'

She says, 'Fir bringin my –'

He said, '*Your* daughter? Who are you?'

She said, 'I am the queen.'

He said, 'You are no queen . . . you're the most beautiful person that ever walked in this earth!'

She says, 'Jack, I know.'

He says, 'Why do you know?'

'Because,' she said, 'you are tellin the truth.'

An Jack put his arms round the queen an kissed her; he says tae her, 'I don't want any gold, I want nothing.'

She says, 'What do you want, Jack?'

He says, 'I want *you* fir my wife!'

She says, 'I know, because you're telling the truth.' An Jack married the queen, an that is the end o my story!

A THORN IN THE KING'S FOOT

Many many years ago long before your time an mine, in a far-away country there wonst lived a king. He ruled his kingdom with a stern stern hand, he wis a very strong king, very powerful. An him and his wife lived in this large palace, they had many farms and many people in their land. He said to his queen, 'These people – my bees – they have to wurk fir me, they're jist my bees; bithout bees you wouldna hev any honey, an they'll work hard. Whatever they do an whatever they make is half mine, because I am their king.' He wis severe. The queen had to agree with him cause he was her husbant, but she knew that he had many faults in his life. An the one fault that she never forgave him for, they never hed any children.

So many many late evenings he wad go home when he would say to the queen, 'Isn't it wonderful we had a great harvest today! Tomorrow the horses'll come in, the donkeys'll come in, they'll bring hus all this harvest to my stores an we'll become richer an richer.'

An the queen turned round, she said, 'Husbant, all yir riches in the world you may fetch fir me'll never make me happy.'

An he said, 'Wumman, what is it you really want? What will make ye happy?'

She says, 'Husband, I know you enjoy riches. But the only riches that ever A'll enjoy is a baby, a baby son or a baby daughter fir me to love an cuddle an caress, an fir you – to follow after you an be the next king!'

'Oh,' he said, 'I am strong, a real man, I'll go on fir many many years!'

'Well,' she says, 'husband, you go on yir hunt, you shoot an you fight, you go among yir people. But what's about* me – I'm left all alone – husband, I want a baby.'

'Well,' he said, 'we've tried many times, but life hes been unkind to hus. But prob'ly something will turn up.'

An lo an behold something did happen, she had a baby. An he was born, a little boy with a hump on his back, not a humpit shoulder, but a hump right in the centre of his back! An he was beautiful but completely ugly, because his knees and his chin seemed to meet when he was born. The queen called fir the king to come an see the new baby. An when the king saw the baby he was so upset, because he wis a big strong powerful man himself.

She said, 'Look, husband, we have a baby, a beautiful boy – isn't he lovely!'

An the king took him, he stretched his legs oot, he luikit at him, saw this hump right in the middle of his back, an the king got so upset, said, 'A baby prince – a humpy prince – who in the world is ever wantin a humpy prince! Wumman, you longed fir something . . . in yir life you been curst with this baby!'

'Oh,' she says, 'husband, I love him!'

'Well,' he said, 'you might, but I don't; I'm disgraced! That can't walk before me, down through the courtroom an walk among the people . . . show off my son who's gaunna be the next king – with a hump on his back! It wouldn't be bad if it was jist his shoulder at was out o place, but it's right in the centre o his back, he is a born hunchback – he'll never be my son in no way!'

De queen loved him like nothing on this earth because he was a beautiful little boy – long golden hair – the only thing that wis wrong wi him was the hump on his back. An the queen used to pet it, try an shove it down wi her hand an . . . she was pleased that God had given her a baby, even suppose it was a hunchback! She didn't care, suppose it was like a gnome, suppose it was the ugliest thing in the world, she jist wantit something to cuddle an kiss an talk to while the king was off on his own. Someone to be with her, someone she cuid love, something from her own body.

But a year passed by an the boy grew up! He grew up a nice wee boy an he startit to walk, but he had a hump on his back. But other ways he was perfect – quite intelligent, quite happy, quite kind – and he loved his mother like nothing on the earth. But the king couldna luik at

* what's about – what would happen to

him. As far as the king 's concerned he didna exist, he wis no good to the king in any way. Truth was, the king was ashamed of him: he wouldna take him in his hand, wouldna walk him through the court-room, wouldna take him down tae a meetin or to anything. An everybody wantit to see the king's son. The king made many excuses, 'Oh, the queen is busy, an the queen's doing this, the queen's doin that, the queen's givin him a bath'; but he wad never show him to the court.

Till the people got fed up with this an they all said, 'Where is the prince? Where is the prince, we want to see the prince!'

An this upset the king greatly, he said to the queen, 'I can't stand it anymore. I can't stand hit, I can't go on like this. We hev tae tell em "the prince is dead"!'

'But,' she said, 'husbant, it's my baby, I love him! He's my child!'

He said, 'He hes tae die! Because it's either him or me – I can't stand to go fore all my couriers an all ma people, show off a hunchback son that will disgrace me in my kingdom.'

De queen was so upset, she cried, she cried an cried. But the king finally made up his mind that the baby had to go. She says, 'Husbant, what are you gaunna do with him?'

He says, 'Look, I'll not kill him an make you sad.' Noo he had the power to; he said, 'I'll take him into the forest, leave him fir the wild beats tae get him an you'll never know if he lives or dies.'

An the queen wis broken-hearted! She says, 'Please!' an she begged an she prayed, she begged fir the world to the king *not* to take her baby from her. But no, the king was stubborn.

He said, 'Ye're not gaun to shame me, I'm the king,' and he wis the head o the court, the head of the land – his word was law! 'He must go! There's no way in the world I'm gaunna have a hunchback son walk . . . if he wasna a hunchback,' he said, 'I'd be proud to show him t' the people. I would love him, I would carry him, show him t' the people, I'd be happy! But I'm not takin a hunchback in any way before my people an before my court; neither are you! He has to go.'

So very quietly, after he'd settled wi his wife, he talked to two of his finest huntsmen who were his dearest friends, told them, 'You must take this child to the forest an destroy it, but don't tell the queen! You must destroy hit immediately. Take hit to the forest as *far* away from the palace as possible, kill hit, don't ever bring hit back before me! An then I will tell the whole world, we'll have a funeral, we'll bury his remains in a cask in the castle gardens and everyone'll come, they'll feel sorry for me. An once more I'll be the king an A'll feel very happy.'

So true to his words the next evening very quietly he arranged with the queen who was very sad – they took the queen's baby who was only one year auld – wrappit him in a shawl. The huntsmen took him away an quietly slipped into the forest. And no one ever knew a thing.

Now these two huntsmen went fir many miles into the forest. They were family men of their own, an the baby was so beautiful a child, lovely little boy! Because he'd a hump on his back . . . an they talkit about it. One says, 'You kill him.'

The other says, 'No, I cuidna kill him, I've two babies o my own. If I killed him, I cuidna go home then to my wife tonight. You kill him!'

The other one said, 'No, I've two babies o ma own – I couldna!'

'Well,' he said, 'look, I can't do it.'

The other one said, 'Aye, neither can I.'

'Well,' he said, 'luik, the're many animals roamin in the forest tonight, wolfs an foxes an bears! Why don't we jist place him against a tree, quietly fade away an go back, tell the king that we destroyed him. An the king'll never know any better. Now we've rode many many miles from the palace, and a little infant of a year auld won't last very long in the forest.' So they finally made up their mind, they would leave the baby beside a tree. None o them had the heart to kill hit, it was so beautiful. An they took this little bundle, they placed it beside a tree an they blessed theirself. They walkit away, they left hit to the mercies of the earth. The baby lay beside the tree, an the owls called an the birds went to sleep, an he lay there all night . . . fell asleep.

But lo an behold, unknown to them in the forest lived an auld woman, a very very auld woman who was sufferin from a terrible disease known as 'King's Evil'. An her *face* was in a terrible mess, it's a cancer o skin disease. People believed in these olden days . . . it wis like *a leper* . . . it jist travelled in the skin an when one bit healed another bit startit over. An when the bit that healed – it left terrible holes, terrible places in their face. And she lived in the forest, she was ashamed to show her face before anybody. Always in the early morning when she knew no one was around she wad gae intae the forest, gather sticks for her fire. An she had this little house in the forest, she never cam in contact with a human soul. She was self-sufficient, she gathered berries, made her own food, kept a lot o hens an things, lived herself in the forest an took care of herself. She didn't want contact wi nobody because she was so deformt. Very very rarely she ever came to the town, an when she did come for any rations or any food she needed, she always kept her face covered with a veil.

So this particular mornin – she always rose early – she needed some sticks fir her fire an she walked into the forest. An she's pickin bits here, pickin bits there in her apron . . . when lo an behold she came to this large oak tree, an there sittin bilow the oak tree was the little bundle. She stoppit an she luikit, when she saw this, 'Upon my soul,' she says, 'a baby, a beautiful little baby!' An she pickit hit up, it smiled in her face, didn't even cry. An she carried it back to her little cottage in the forest, she cuddled it to her bosom, says, 'I wonder where you came from, little one?' Now she kept some goats in her little place in the forest, she milked the goats an fed the baby goats' milk. The baby laughed an giggled, never cried a minute. She says, 'I wonder where you cam from, little one; someone must hae left you here, they couldn't take care of ye. But *I'm* going to take care o ye and you'll never want fir nothing as long as you live!' Now the little child was with the auld woman, an he wis quite happy. She did *everything* fir him under the sun, she loved him dearly from her heart an he wis a gift tae her because she was a lonely auld person.

Now the queen back many many miles away in the large town in the palace was sad, an sadder an sadder. She lay in bed, wouldna eat, wouldna drink, she wad do nothing, an she pined away an she pined away. The king went up an tried tae coax her tae eat, but no, it was no use. She told the king . . .

He says, 'Please, have something to eat!'

She says, 'I don't want nothin to eat, I don't want nothing, I want my baby.'

'You know hit's impossible,' he said, 'you can't have yir baby.'

'Well,' she said, 'if I can't have ma baby, life is no good to me anymore.' An she pined away an pined away ti finally she died.

Now days before that the king hed had a funeral fir his baby son, he'd made a mock coffin an buried hit in the palace churchyard. They came from all over . . . the king's son hed died, the baby prince hed died. King made up his mind, he'd kid on he was being very sad, but in his own mind he wisna sat atall, it was jist a formality. But when the queen died, the king was really sad, he *knew* in his own heart that *he* wis the cause of his own wife's death – his queen died because he hed sent her little baby tae his death. An he thought, take second thought, 'If only, if I could overcome the thought of having a hunchback son my wife wad be alive today.' He really loved his queen, he really did. But the queen was dead an the're nothing he cuid do about hit. They had their funeral fir the queen, the queen was buried in a little churchyard within the palace. An the king was very upset, very very upset! Very sad – now he'd lost his baby and he'd lost his queen – all through his own fault. So he thought to his ownself, 'The best thing A can do is tae walk down to the village, walk among ma people an talk to them. It'll keep the worry off ma mind.'

He walked down to the town an walked among the people, an everyone said, 'Ir Majesty . . . sorry' here and 'sorry' there. When lo an behold who should he see come walkin up the street but an auld wumman – with a veil over her face an a hood on her head, carryin a basket. An she's hurryin on. She's walkin along the pathway an when she came to the king she stopped. She stepped off when she saw the king, aff the path leadin to the village.

An she said, *'On your way, Your Majesty, curse upon you!'*

The king said, 'What did you say, auld wumman?'

An the auld woman never said nothing, the auld woman hurried on.

But the king was walkin down towards the path an he thought it queer, he wondert to hissel, 'What did that auld woman say?' He thought he'd heard her sayin, 'Curse upon you', but he wasna sure he even heard a word atall. An he luikit back – an all in a minute something jagged his foot – *right* there in the path something jaggit his foot when he looked roond after the auld woman. He saw the auld woman disappear in the distance. (In these days they wore shoes made of skin, an between the foot an the skin wisna very much – like moccasins – an it wis easy for a thorn or anything that was sharp on the ground to jag yir foot!) An the king, it wis his toe, his big toe was *pierced* with some kind o thorn or something the king felt in his foot.

But he walkit on to the village, talked among the people an everyone said how they were sad, how they were so sorry for the king. In their own minds they werena really sorry, but they talked about this an talked about that. The king walked roond to try an find some comfort among his people, but he could find no comfort. Deep in his mind he had this worry about his queen and his little son whom he'd destroyed, all because of his own fault. But the more he walked, the sorer his toe begin to come. An it got sorer an sorer. Bi the time he'd walked through the little village where his pals was, bi the time he got home he cuid barely move his foot, hit was in such a sorry state.

Came inta his room, had his meal and went to his chamber tae lie down. An he ordered fir his people to come, to look at his foot. Now in these days they didn't have any doctors; they had court magicians, an they came, took off the king's boot (jist made of skin). They washed his foot an bathed his foot, they anoint't hit wi oil an did everything. But hit was 'throb-throb-throb-throb-throb-throb', an the king was annoyed, he wis in pain. He said, 'You must do something for this, it's terrible sore. Youse people who are learned people, I pay you so much money, youse must do something, I'm in terrible pain!'

But from that day on an days after an days after, the king's foot got worse an worse an worse. All round the country, they came from all places to try an cure the king's foot, but no way, he never got any better! An the king got a rest fir his foot, he got pillows under his foot, the pain was exas- . . . all they cuid do wis – he stuck it oot the window! Jist lay beside the window an he stuck his foot oot the windae. But all the time the days was passin an the months was passin, the king was gettin older, the thorn in his foot wis gettin bigger an bigger! An hit grew an it grew till a *branch* cam from hit! They sent fir couriers from all over, wisemen from all over the country to come an cure the king's foot, but there wis no way in the world – if they pulled the leaves off – the next mornin they were back again. An the king was in agony. The thorn in the king's foot grew an grew, an nobody seemed to help him, no way. The king offert rewards, he offert everything, he was in agony. People came from different countries, wisemen came an examint it, they cut the thorn off his foot, shaved hit, bathed hit, annoint't it with oil – next day it wis back as far as ever – there's no way in the world that the king cuid get any peace or any rest. He never slept, he never slept in any way.

Bi the first year the king was annoyed, by the second year the king was terrified, bi the third year the king hed made many promises an he'd suffered all this pain. An he promised *anything* tae anybody that wad come an rid him of this disease in his foot. But no way cuid the king get any peace, he had two-three catnaps, but always this naggin pain in his toe! An the more they cam an cut hit, every time they cut hit, it always cam again. The king said he was 'curst fir evermore', and he knew that his life was fadin away. An the only consolation the king had was to lie by the window, hold his foot out in the cold wind, and lo an behold the only time that the king got ony peace – when the wind was blowin from the forest – when the wind changed and was blowin from the forest, it blowed a cooler breeze o' the king's foot, the king wad go to sleep. But the minute the wind changed, the pain was so bad the king woke up once more!

Now, through the king's sufferin fir many many years, the little boy and the auld woman lived in the forest all together. An she taught him

everything, she learned him to hunt, learnt him to shoot, an she
schooled him, learned him everything under the sun till he became the
age o fifteen years auld. He never was away fae the forest in his life, an
he called her 'his mother'. An as she got aulder, she got uglier. When
one piece of her face healed, the other piece got broken out, ti her face
was jist a heap of marks like potwarts. But the young boy loved this
auld wumman like nothing on the earth. And he went on lovin her.
Always i the evening he used to love to come aside the auld wumman
because he had known nobody else. As far as he believed it was the
only mother and the only friend he had in his life. When the cold
winter winds wis howlin round the little house in the forest, he used to
come up beside his auld mother's knee, he wad put his head on her
knee, an he loved her. Because even though she wis the mos ugliest
bein that you an me would take to be ugly, to him she was just an
angel, she gev him everything he wantit. An it wisna all one-sided, he
work't hard, he cut sticks an dug the garden, he done everything in the
forest for her, tended the goats, tended the hens, whatever she needed –
an they had jist the greatest understanding between them. Till one
particular night, the wind was blowin strong an it was a terrible storm.

She sat down, said, 'Robin,' (she called him 'Robin' because he
looked like a wee robin beside a tree when she'd found him) 'Robin,
come beside me, son, I want tae tell you a wee story.'

He said, 'Mother, what is it you want to tell me? Are you gaun t' tell
me a story?'

She says, 'Yes, Robin, I'm gaunna tell you a story, a story about yir
father.'

He said, 'My father?'

'Yes,' she said, 'about yir father. Do you know, Robin, I'm not yir
mother.'

'But,' he said, 'you must be ma mother, I don't remember anyone
else but you!'

She said, 'I found you in the forest many years ago, I took you here
an brought ye up like ma own child.' This upset him a wee bit when he
heard this fir the first time.

'But,' he said, 'Mother, you're the only mother I've ever had.'

'But,' she said, 'I'm not yir real mother.'

'Well, where is ma real mother, who is my real mother?'

She said, 'Robin, it's a sad sad story I'm about to tell ye. Your
mother was the queen, the most loving an nices an gentle queen there
ever was in this land – our queen, *my* queen.'

Robin never said a word.

He listent and she said, 'Yir father is the king of the country many miles from here, an he was ashamed of you when you were a baby!'

An he said, 'Why was he ashamed?'

She says, 'Robin, because of the hump on yir back.' Now, he had grown this boy bi fifteen, but he still had the hump on his back right between his shoulder blades. He wis a little crooked, a little bent, but otherwise he was the most perfect boy in this world, fifteen years old, an all these years hed passed by. 'But,' she said, 'your father sent you into the forest to get killed, an the huntsmen who were family people wouldn't kill you, left you under a tree. I pickit you up fourteen years ago, I took you and I brought you up.'

'But, Mother,' he says, 'what hes that got to do with me? If they didn't want me as a hunchback then, they don't want me now.'

'But,' she says, 'look, this is something you must know, your father is still the king and he is sufferin terrible because of me.'

'But why, Mother,' he said, 'what did you do to hurt him?'

She said, 'I hurt him to pay him back for what he'd done to yir mother and what he'd done to you.'

'But,' he said, 'what has that got to do with me?'

'I think the time hes come,' she says, 'that you mus go an settle the problem between yir father, you an me. Look at my face – what do you see?'

An the boy looked at her face, he said, 'Mother, I don't see nothing.'

She says, 'Look at these scabs on my face. Luik at my face, hit's destroyed with "Evil"!'

He said, 'I don't see nothing out o the way in your face.'

She says, 'Luik, *this* is known as "King's Evil".'

'But,' he said, 'why did the king do this on you?'

She said, 'Robin, the king never done it on me. This 's a disease that comes to people, an it can only be cured by the touch of a king – *who must put his finger on this* – an make me better.'

'Well,' he said, 'if the king . . . I'll go and find the king an make him come to you, Mother!'

She says, 'Robin, before you go and find the king, you must hear the rest of the story. Your father the king he is sufferin from a terrible wound.'

'What kind o wound?' says Robin.

She said, 'He hes got a thorn in his foot at was put there by me fourteen years ago, an no one can ever cure hit – excepts you – you're the only one! He hes tried, he hes offered rewards, he hes sent people. He's had quacks an wise magicians come all over the world to try an cure his foot. An he's in agony, he hes little sleep except when the wind blows from the forest. But you must go an get his promise, *that if you cure him, he'll cure me.*'

'Mother,' he says, 'I'll do anything fir you, anything in the world. Tell me, please, what I must do!'

She said, 'Tomorrow morning, Robin, you mus make yir way to the palace an tell everyone who meets you along the way, if you're stoppit on the way, that you have come to cure the king's foot. But before you cure the king's foot, you must ask him fir two promises!'

'Yes, Mother,' he said, 'I'll do that, I'll do it, Mother, yes! What is the first promise?'

'The first promise is, *you must ask him to come back and touch my face!*'

'That's simple,' said the boy. 'If I get to the king an can cure his foot, I'm sure he'll be willin to do this fir me, if he's suffering as what you say.'

'But wait a minute,' said the auld woman, 'he mus make another promise: *he must leave you to be king while he goes an walks among his people as a tramp, an works an labours an toils in the fields fir two hunderd days. An you must become king, take his place while he is gone.*'

'But, Mother,' said the boy, 'there's no way in the world the king is gaunnae let *me*, a hunchback as I'm known to be, take his place an be king – *I'm* not qualified to be a king!'

She says, 'You're qualified to be a king – you are the king's *son* – an the sooner he knows it, the better. But don't ever tell him who you are, you must promise me, *you must never tell him who you are!* Just tell him you hev come to cure his foot, an before you took the thorn from his foot he must make these two promises to you!'

'Right,' says the boy, 'it shall be done!'

So, he sat and had his lovely evenin meal, an went to bed. But he lay an worried about this till morning. He hatit to part fae his aul mother in the forest, he hed never been away from her all his life. He hatit tae have a walk among strange people – oh, he hed seen many hunters an he'd seen people, he'd been i the village with her two-three times, but he jist hurried on – she'd done her little bit o shoppin an she'd hurried back to the forest wi the little boy, the hunchback by her side. Nobody paid very much attention, nobody ever knew they were seein the king's son, he wis jist another traveller goin about their business. So the next morning he had a little breakfast an said 'goodbye' to his mother, the auld wumman i the forest.

An she said, 'Don't worry, my son, everythin'll work out the way it shall be.'

He bade her 'goodbye' an said, 'Luik, I am not leavin you fir long, I'll be back.'

She said, 'I know you will, I know you will!'

'I'll be back,' he said, 'an when I come back I will fetch the king. If you're worried about that face of yours, I'm not worried; but if that makes ye happy, I'll bring back the king. An he pit his arms round her, cuddled her an walked away towards the village.

He travelled on fir a long distance, it wis mebbe fifteen miles to the village over paths, through forests, over hills, right down till he came to the town an the palace. An he made his way through the town, he knew the wey – but he'd never been back at the palace – he made his way to the palace. Everybody luikit at the ragged youth with the humpback walkin up towards the palace. When he came up he was stoppit bi the guards, they said, 'Whe're you goin, ragged youth?'

He said, 'I want to see the king.'

They said, 'You can't see the king, he's in terrible agony.'

He said, 'I have come to cure the king and let me pass!'

People said, 'He's come to cure the king!' Everybody'd give their life if the king wis cured of this terrible thing that happened to him, so word spread frae one to the other, 'He's come to cure the king! This is ae young man who's come to cure the king, mebbe he knows something, mebbe this is hit, mebbe *he's* come!'

Before the're anything else cuid happen, he wis rushed forward into the palace into the king's chamber. Walked into his great hall, his great bedroom, an there was the king lyin with his foot up on a cushion through the window. An the young man walkit up, he stude in front o the king – knowin he wis luikin at his father fir the first time. An the king turned round, he looked very sad an his beard wis long, his face was thin from many years o sufferin. But the boy felt no sorrow fir him.

The king looked round, said, 'Who are you? They tell me you've come to cure my foot.'

An the boy said, 'Yes, I hev come to cure yir foot, Ir Majesty, I've come to cure yir foot.'

The king said, 'It's not possible. Many have tried it, there's nothing fir me, I must go on sufferin fir many many years.'

The boy said, 'No, that is wrong! You shall not go on sufferin fir many years. *I* will cure yir foot.'

King said, 'How can a youth like you, especially a hunchback . . .'

But he ignored what the king said, he never said a word.

'A hunchback!' he said; 'have you any powers in medicine?'

'Oh,' the boy said, 'I've no powers in medicine.'

'Well, why do you come here an annoy me?' said the king.

He said, 'I have come to cure your foot.'

The king said, 'Well, please, I'm in terrible agony – don't torture me any longer – cure my foot!'

'Not,' said the boy, 'just a minute. First, you must gie me two promises!'

The king said, 'Luik, get on with hit, I'm in pain, in agony, I can't talk! I'm in pain an agony.'

'First, you must give me two promises,' said the boy.

'Yes,' said de king, 'yes, please, I'll give ye two promises. What is it you want – money, gold, jewels, anything – please, please get on with what you're gaunna do! Get my foot – take this pain from my foot!'

An the boy said, 'Just take yir time, you've suffert fir many years an a little time longer is not gaunna make any difference.' An the king was in agony.

'What is it you want?' said the king.

He said, 'I want *you*, bifore I cure yir foot, tae give me two promises!'

The king said, 'Luik, get on with hit; I'll make yir promises, what is it you want?'

He said, 'You'll come with me to the forest an see my auld mother, an touch her face!'

The king said, 'That's a . . . I'll go anywhere!'

'Next,' said the boy, 'you mus let me rule yir kingdom fir two hunderd days!'

The king said, '*You* rule my kingdom fir two hunderd days?'

'Yes,' said the boy, '"rule yir kingdom fir two hunderd days".'

'An what am I supposed to do,' he said, 'while you rule my kingdom?'

The boy said, 'You shall walk among the peasants in the village, among the peasants in the town, an you shall toil, you shall wurk, you shall help them an you shall see what like is to life * among the puir!'

The king said, 'Look, it's not very much to do, but if you will take this pain from my foot, I'll swear I'll give you my promise!'

An the boy walkit up, he walkit up an he walked round the window.

* what like is to life – what life is like

He lifted the king's foot up, he rubbed his hand around the king's foot an he done that – he catcht the thorn an he pulled it out – he threw it through the window. An he rubbed the king's foot with his hand like that, and lo an behold the king's foot . . . the pain was gone, the agony wis gone from the king's foot! 'Now,' he said, 'Ir Majesty, stand up!'

The king stood up – no more pain, no more nothing – no thorn, no nothing. King wis as *free* as it never happened! The king stood up, excited that the pain was gone, he felt like he never felt before for years, said, 'Where in the world do you come from?'

The boy said, 'I came from the forest tae help you. An you made yir promise.'

The king said, 'I am the king an I gev you ma promise, I won't break my word. A'll come with you right away, lead the way!' An the king walkit out – as free an fit an happy as ever he'd been in his life – he danced a wee jig wi his foot to see wis it really true! An there wis no more pain, no more nothing, there were no thorn in the king's foot anymore. The king was just like a lark, happy as cuid be, an he was so excited he said to the boy, 'This is magic!'

The boy said, 'No, it's no magic, no magic in any way.'

'Lead on!' says the king. The king called for horses immediately. Everyone wis happy, 'The king is better, the king is better, the king is better, the king's foot is healed! This magic youth hes worked wonders,' they made wey fir the king. The king ordered fir two horses – the young boy, one, the king got another – an they rode to the forest. They rode on an rode on ti they came to the little cottage in the forest.

An lo an behold the boy said, 'Stop!' there at the little house.

'Where have you brought me,' said the king, 'what place is this?'

The boy said, 'The're someone here I want you to see, someone who's been good to me an took care of me fir a long long time.'

The king felt very humble because the boy hed done so much fir him, an he wantit tae show his kindness towards the boy. He steppit off his horse, he said, 'Lead the way.' An the boy led the way inta the little house, an there sittin in an auld chair wis the auld wumman. The king said to the boy, 'What is it you want me to do, *who* do you want me to see?'

An the boy said, 'My mother.'

An the king luikit: her face hed got ten times worse since the boy left, an the king luikit, he said, 'What kind o person is that you have fir a mother?'

The boy said, 'That's my mother who's been guid to me.'

An the king said, 'What do you want me to do?'

He said, 'I want you to go over an touch her face with yir finger, because you are the king an she is sufferin from "King's Evil". De only thing that can cure her is the touch of the king.'

The king said, 'No!'

The boy said, 'Remember yir promise!'

An the king thought again, 'Well,' he said, 'you've done so much fir me, it's little that I cuid do fir you.' And he walked forward, he toucht one o the wicked scabs on the auld wumman's face with his finger. She stude there an looked straight into his eyes, and lo an behold after the king had toucht . . . amazin thing happened to the auld woman. Her skin became wrinkled but beautiful, all the marks an everything wis gone. And lo an behold, there wis a beautiful auld woman, old an wrinkled but beautiful, there wasn't a mark on her face or a mark on her skin. An the boy was happy, he ran forward, he pit his arms round her neck an kissed her. An the king was so happy an pleased that he hed done something worthwhile fir the first time in his life. They sat an they had a lunch together. An the king said, 'I mus be on ma way, A have tae go home to my people. I've done something . . .'

The boy said, 'Wait, you must fulfil yir second promise!'

An the king said, 'Yes.'

An the woman turned round to the king, she said, 'Ir Majesty, luik, I know it's a hard request to ask fir.'

He said, 'Woman, is this yir son?'

'Well,' she said, 'he's believed to be my son!'

'Well,' he said, 'he might be a hunchback, but he's a wonderful boy.'

The boy said, 'I'm gaun back with you because you made the promise to me.'

King said, 'Well, be it so.' They bade 'farewell' to the auld woman, they got ond their horses an they rode back to the palace. They rode back, the king ordered everything – meals, a room for the boy an everything in the palace.

'Now,' says the boy, 'tomorrow morning you make yir promise good to me an everything will be well!'

The king said, 'It is very hard for me, I've lived as a king fir so many years I don't know what to do.'

De boy said, 'Jist do it! Go on yir wey, meet the people, walk among them, work among them.'

'But,' the king said, 'I can't go as a king.'

The boy said, 'You're not goin as a king, you're gaun as a tramp.'
He called fir the most dirtiest old coat an the most worn shoes in the
palace that anyone cuid find, an told the king he must dress in the rags
an go among the people.

The king said, 'Well, so be it! You've cleared me frae all my pain an
I feel wonderful, I feel great.' An the king *wantit* to go among the
people. He felt he should, because he wantit to see this: he had taxed
them, he hed took half o their grain, he'd tuik half o their cattle, tuik
everything an he thought he'd want to go among the people, but he
felt kind o queer . . . that as if a great change wis comin over him. He
didn't *want* to tax them anymore, he didna want nothing from them,
he jist wantit to be among them an be *with* them, *talk* to them an *work*
in the fields. The great change cam over him, he felt so queer he
couldn't wait to be gone!

An the boy said, 'Look, *I'll* be here, I'll see that nothing goes wrong
in the palace ti you come back. You give orders that I've to take your
place while you go out among yir peasants an among your people as a
tramp. But on'y tell it tae the people in the castle, not to the peasants
in the land.'

So early next mornin true to his word the king put on his auld
scruffy shoes, ragged coat, the auld ragged hat, scarf round his neck an
walked away from the palace. An no one seemed to recognize him.
Before he had left he hed given orders that all orders in the palace were
to be passed through to the young hunchback who wad rule while he
wis gone for two hunderd days. Only the people in the palace knew the
difference, that the king wis gone. An the king walked away, just a
beggar.

An he travelled on fir many days, he viewed the land an saw the
crops o corn. He saw the people, he walked among the people antil he
got hungry. He hed no money, he hed no nothing, an he walked up to
this particular farm, he asked fir a job. An the man gave him a job to
work at the harvest, he worked at the harvest and lo and behold he
enjoyed hit. He carted the corn in, he stookit the corn, he helped
scythe the corn, he cut it, he dined with the old farmer and his wife an
he had such a lovely time ti the harvest wis stacked and put in the
sheds. Then they paid him a little wage an he said he must move on.
An the king carried on from place to place, from day tae day on his
way workin here, working there, diggin ditches, buildin dykes, cutting
trees, workin among the people, and he enjoyed every moment! An he
learnt more than he'd ever learned before in his life as a king, by

walkin an working among the poor people on the land – who his own kingdom depended upon!

Now the young hunchback Robin is in the palace, and all these people came in an they told him things, they took men before courts; he'd done orders, he gave orders an people realized that this young man who hed come over seemed to work things more wonderful than the king. The king is gone, the taxes were lowered, less grain was tuik in, people wis allowed to have more, people wis allowed more freedom, an this became wonderful. Where is the king? The king is gone, but everybody wad say, 'We don't worry if the king's gone or no; this young man who's tooken over the kingdom, who the king has left in charge, is a more wonderful person than the king. He's doin more wonderful things,' an the effects began to creep into the people – in the village, in the town.

An the same thing begint to happen to the king: he walkit among the people, he talkit to the people, he sat with them, he slept with them, he ate with them, and the days begint tae pass – till at last the two hunderd days were up. An the king felt sad and weary that he had to report once more back to the castle. He didna want to go! Now the hunchback in the palace had changed everything that the king stude for, an the people were so happy. When the king walkit inta the village ond his wey to the palace, he saw smilin faces, happy people in all the way. An he wondered about this because every time he went to the village and the town before, he never saw . . . people were always sad an wandered about with their heads droopit, nobody wis smilin, nobody wis happy, nobody 's singin. The king passed fires, ken, people 's singin, people is workin, happy at their work! The king wondered, 'What's gaun on here? A wonderful change hes come over the place.' An then he thought, 'Hit's all because of that boy – all because of him! But when I go back, I'm gaunna make sure that he's gaunna be paid well fir hit.' An the king was a different man, a changed man completely!

He walkit home to the palace, had a wonderful bath, had a wonderful wash, had a wonderful supper. And lo an behold, he couldna wait to call the young man before him, the young man wis called before him an he said, 'Luik, young man, I don't know what you've done to me – you made me well, you made me happy – I'm happier than ever I was before in my life, since I lost my queen!'

'Well,' the young man said, 'I'm happy too, because my mother his happy in the forest.'

The king said, 'Luik, I'm not fit to be a king; before, when I walkit across the land there were no smilin faces. You have taught me wonderful things, young man, an you're a hunchback. You're jist a common hunchback, an I'm a king. You have taught me more than I ever knew existed. Ma people are happy, I'm happy, I've never been happier before.'

'Well,' the young man said, 'I had come to cure your foot, because the only reason I wanted to cure yir foot – you cuid do somethin fir me.'

An the king said, 'Please, stay with me; *please, stay with me!* Be my prime minister, be *anything*, be anything you want! Be my second in command and run my country fir me, an be my friend!'

An the youth turned round, he said, 'Look, Father, you hev denied me wonst – and left me to perish in the forest.'

The king said, 'What?'

He said, 'Father, you have denied me wonst an left me to perish i the forest because I was a hunchback. But, a hunchback was no good to you as a son, why should a hunchback to you be good as a friend? I am your son, the person you abandont in the forest many years ago.'

An the king went down on his knees, he cried an he threw his arms around the hunchback, he said, 'Please, please, please, you've come back to me after all these years. An I'm sorry, please stay with me!'

An the hunchback said, 'No, Father. Now you're happy and free. An so am I. If ye ever want to find me, you can find me with ma mother in the forest, the only person that ever was good an kind to me.'

An the hunchback walkit away back to the forest tae his auld mother, and left the king to his own thoughts, his own ideas. An that is the last o my story!

JACK AN THE SINGIN LEAVES

Wonst upon a time a long long time ago, it was Jack and his two brothers an they steyed in this wee fairm. Oh, an they had a lovely wee fairm! But Jack he was lazy, he wadna dae very much aboot the place, but the other two brothers they were clever an did a bit o wurk. All Jack wad do he wad go away lie here an lie there in the woods, listen to the burds, an playin wi de wee rabbits an all the wee insects, he wis watchin the wee insects an watchin everything – he wis very kind-heartit, ken, he wadna touch nothin. If he got a wee animal wi a broken leg or a rabbit wi a broken leg or a burd wi a broken wing, he wad take hit hame, keep it in the hoose ti it was better an then he wad let it go. He used to fill the fairm-hoose full o wee animals. And his brothers didna like this. His brothers wis bad! They used to kill the wee rabbits, chase the deers oot o their corn, kill the wee rabbits fir eatin their hay an everything like this. But Jack wadna dae that, Jack wis very kind-heartit. But one day, wis jist aboot the end o summer, he wis away lyin alow this tree. His brothers wis wantin him to go an wurk wi them at the hay, but he wadna go.

'God bless hus,' they said, 'he is lazy! He'll no do nothing.'

But, he sees this thing comin hoppin in bilow the tree an hit's got a broken wing – hit was a cuckoo, a wee cuckoo! So he lifts hit up, pits it in his hand, takes it in his hand an back wi im tae the farm, tae his fairm-hoose. Now, his brothers they're back in fae their wurk an they're sittin at their tea. Jack he comes trailin into the hoose draggin his feet ahind him, takes aff his coat an sits doon t' the table. An he's this thing in his bosom, ye see!

De auldest brother Willie he says tae him, 'What hae ye got noo, Jack, in the name o creation, what hev ye got noo? Ye're ey bringin

230

somethin back, this hoose is like a pet shop wi ye, ye're ey bringin animals in here!'

He said, 'I got a cuckoo.'

'No a cuckoo,' he said, 'fir God's sake, ye cannae keep a cuckoo! A cuckoo when it comes a certain age ready to flee, it's got to fly away to another warm country – it canna stick the cauld winter.'

But Jack said, 'Luik, hoo can it . . . it's got a broken wing – it canna flee.'

'Well,' his brothers said, 'there's only one thing ye can dae is kill hit. Because all the other cuckoos are all away noo an hit's left its ainsel, it canna feed itself. The're nae insects wi the wintertime comin on, an that cuckoo'll dee wi ye.'

Jack says, 'It'll no dee wi me. I'll keep hit, an I'll look after hit an I'll feed it an I'll sort its wing. I'll make a pet oot o't.'

His brothers said, 'Luik, if ye make a pet out o a cuckoo – if it does live wi ye – when the summer comes, it'll only flee away an lea ye, it'll never come back to ye.'

'Ah, I'm no heedin,' he said, 'comes back to me or no.'

Anyway, Jack went up tae his bedroom up the stair an he got a wee box, filled it full o bonnie dry cotton wool. Got the cuckoo oot, sortit his wing, got wee sticks, made a wee splice, tied it up wi woollen thread; went down to the kitchen, got a lot of meat an he fed his wee cuckoo. And he fed hit wi a wee drink o water every day an every day an every day. Ti one day he went up the stair tae his bed, an the cuckoo floppit oot o the box an flied right roond the room – hits wing was better!

So it fleed up an it sat in the windowsill; it was sittin an Jack wis sittin in his chair in his room. His brothers 's away wurkin.

'Man,' he says, 'ye're a bonnie wee bird, a bonnie bird! But, ye're no sayin much. Of course, youse kind o birds canna speak – only yinst a year.'

An the cuckoo luiks at him, the cuckoo said, 'Jack, you're wrong!'

'What?' says Jack. Jack luikit all roond, thought it was his brothers, he says, 'Wha-wha's speakin?'

The cuckoo said, 'Hit's me, Jack, speakin.'

Jack says, 'A cuckoo canna speak – you're a bird.'

'Ah, but,' he said, 'I'm no the same kin o burd you think A am, *I'm a speakin cuckoo.*'

'But,' he said, 'hoo in creation can you speak? Come here, gie me a haud o you! Did somebody split yir tongue or something, mak you speak?'

231

'No,' he said, 'naebody split ma tongue, Jack. But I'll tell ye some-thin, you saved ma life, you mendit ma wing; I'd never go back to ma ain country, only fir you. I was changed inta a cuckoo an sent here with the rest o the cuckoos, I cam here wi the rest, but I'm no really a cuckoo.'

Jack said, 'If ye're no a cuckoo . . . you luik like a cuckoo to me, but A never heard ye shoutin like a cuckoo.'

'Anyway,' he says, 'you look after me, Jack, an feed me well. Ind the summertime when the end o summer comes, I'm goin away back to my ain country. An I'll no forget ye!'

So Jack luikit after the cuckoo, fed it, gien it water, tuik it wi him sittin on his shoulder. Down to the kitchen, an his brothers is luikin at this cuckoo, his two brothers Willie an Tom.

'Jack,' he said, 'that's a bonnie bird. It did live wi ye.'

'Oh, it lived wi me, all right,' he says. 'Boys, ye ken somethin I'm gaunna tell ye, at's no a cuckoo.'

'Tsst,' he said, '"no a cuckoo"! What is hit if it's no a cuckoo?'

He said, 'It's enchantit, it cam away from a foreign country, it cuid be a wumman or cuid be a man, an it cuid be a lassie or cuid be a laddie, but it can speak! An it spoke to me.'

The two brothers said, '"Speak tae ye"! Tell hit tae say somethin noo if it can speak tae ye, tell it to speak up noo!'

Jack says tae the cuckoo, 'Tell em what ye tellt me!'

Cuckoo sut, never said a word, never spoke.

Brothers made a fool o Jack, laughin an carryin on wi im.

So Jack said, 'All right, youse hae it yir way an I'll hae my way.' So he catcht the cuckoo, pits it on his shoulder, he gaes up to his ain room, shuts the door an he goes in, pits the cuckoo sittin on the table. Cuckoo hops on the table, see.

'Jack,' he said, 'A hed nae way tae tell ye, but I cannae speak tae naebody but *you*,' he said, 'you're the only body I'm allowed to speak to. Whenever any other strange body's aboot, I'm tongue-tied, I cannae say a word. In a year's time I'll be gaun away, flyin back tae a faraway country, to my ain country. But I'll no forget ye, I'll be back, when it comes the first day in May I'll come right back an see ye.'

'All right,' says Jack.

'But,' he says, 'dinna ask me to speak in front o yir brothers! I'll no speak in front o naebody, but I'll speak to you. Whan A come back I'll have a wee present fir ye!'

'All right,' said Jack.

But anyway, Jack workit away wi the cuckoo, luikit after the cuckoo, everywhere he went he tuik the cuckoo wi him, an it wadna lea im. He fed it, gien it plenty water. The spring cam in, de summer cam in, the summer passed by, an one day he went up tae his bed an the cuckoo's sittin.

He says, 'Jack, I'm sorry I hev tae go. Tomorrow all the cuckoos is gatherin an I'll have to go wi them.'

'Ah well,' Jack says, 'you been a good pet to me. I'll prob'ly never see ye again.'

'Oh,' he says, 'ye'll see me again, Jack. Next year I'll be back – I'll keep ma promise – I'll be back.'

Right, he opens the window the next morning as the sun wis gettin up an he lets de wee cuckoo oot. The wee cuckoo says, 'Cheerio, Jack, cheerio! I'm away, but I'll be back,' oot the cuckoo goes. Oh, Jack's awfa sad, he's near greetin fir his wee cuckoo. He pullt doon the window an went doon the stair. His two brothers 's sittin at breakfast, see.

'Well, Jack,' he says, 'where's yir cuckoo noo, your bonnie burd?'

'Ah,' he says, 'hit's away.'

He said, 'Didna we tell ye that it wadna stay wi ye! We tellt ye ye're only wastin yir time luikin after that cuckoo, cause ye get nae thanks fir hit.'

'Ah, but,' he said, 'I'll get thanks fir hit, some day hit'll come back!'

His brothers say, 'I bet ye a hunderd pound it'll never be back! You'll never see yir cuckoo again. Oh,' he said, 'there be cuckoos'll come back, ye'll hear them in the woods an the fields when we're at wurk. You dinna dae any wurk, but we do wurk. Oot in the woods cuttin wood an that, in the fields wurkin wi the hay an the harvest we hear the cuckoos, but no you – you're too busy lyin alow a tree sleepin half o the day awa!'

Jack says, 'My cuckoo'll come back to me!'

So the winter passed, an Jack wadna do nothin. Noo this wis aboot near away on about the end o April, they sut and crackit.

Willie says, 'Are ye ga'n to the toon the morn?' he says tae Jack.

Jack says, 'No, what am I gaun t' do i the toon?'

'Oh,' he says, 'the're a big do in the toon the morn, big day on. The morn's the princess's birthday. An,' he said, 'everybody in the district i the village hes got to go, as ye ken the rule – the king askit – everybody's got to go an bring the princess a present!'

233

Tom says, 'Luik, ye never workit this week an ye never workit the week afore, an we're no giein ye no pay.'

Jack said, 'I canna help hit. What are youse gettin?'

'Oh,' he said, 'we bought wir presents fir the princess lang ago; we're gaun away to the toon the morn. You bide, watch the fairm an keep everything ti we come back. An if onything's oot o place whan we come back, God help you – we'll kill ye deid when we come back!'

'All right,' says Jack, 'I'll stey at hame.'

But anyway, the two boys rises on the summer's mornin. Oh, de summer cam in nice – first day in May – they rise about six o'clock, washed theirsel, shaved theirsel, dressed theirsel in the best o their guid clothes, got their two presents an they're away oot, got their horses saddled up. They went away into the town tae give the princess her present. Everybody brought the princess a present fir her birthday, see!

But anyway, Jack he's sittin, had his breakfast. An he's away up to his room, he opened the windae, he's sittin thinkin on his wee cuckoo. It wis about ten o'clock in the day – after the boys were away a long while – an he hears 'flitter-flitter-flitter-flitter' right inta the windae!

'Cuck-oo!' In comes the cuckoo an lands o' the top of the table aside him, he says, 'I'm back, Jack.'

Jack catcht hit an he cuddlit hit to his bosom, he kisst hit. He luikit at it, he said, 'What's that you've got in yir neb, in yir mooth?'

The cuckoo said, 'I've got somethin fir you, Jack.'

Jack said, 'What is hit? Hit's a funny luikin thing you've got – it's mair like a leaf aff a tree, leaf – like a wee bush.'

He says, 'Jack, from a faraway country I brung ye the *Singin Leaves*! All ye need tae dae is take this leaves an pit them in a wee dish o water on a vase on the table. An soon as the wind starts to blow, these leaves'll sing ye any song that ye want – any kind o music ye want – you'll get hit off these leaves. Thes leaves cam away from a Singin Tree in a faraway country, an I brung this back fir a present to you!'

Jack says, 'You cuidna got a better thing!'

He says, 'Whaur's yir brothers?'

He said, 'Ma brothers are away tae the toon to the king's palace, an they're away wi a present tae the princess. But I've naethin,' he said, 'I hev naethin tae gie the princess, nothing o nae kind. I never workit through the weeks wi them an I've nae money tae buy her a present. It's too late i the day noo, everybody gies their present a' twelve o'clock an it's ten o'clock noo.'

'Luik,' says the cuckoo, 'I'll tell ye what tae dae, you tak at *Singin*

Leaves to the princess an gie them tae her. Give em to her as a present, an I bet ye it'll be the luckiest present ever you gien onybody in yir life!'

'Ye think so?' says Jack.

'Ay,' says the cuckoo, 'you do that. The're plenty mair whaur that cam fae, but I cannae get them to ye this year, no this year.'

But Jack says, 'Tell me one thing, where hae you been since I seen you last?'

'Oh,' he said, 'I been all over – I been in France, I been i Italy – A been all over an noo I'm back fir the summer. But I'll hev to go an leave ye, but I'll tell ye somethin, I'll come back an see ye before I gae awa!'

An Jack opened the window, the wee cuckoo fleed away, but it never went away back to its ain country, it went away roond this other country.

Jack went doon, shaved hissel, washed hissel, put on his best clothes, went doon to the stable an got his aul horse oot, saddled hit. Jumpit on his back, tuik the *Singin Leaves* in his hand an away he goes ridin, ridin into the toon. He lands in the toon. Oh, the great big fair in the toon an everybody's dressed in their best clothes, an the shows is goin, the're market stalls an everything, folk's sellin fruit an aa great big things – oh, town's all in a boil! Because everybody wis wantin the happiness o the princess's birthday, see! The princess wis t' come ridin down on her carriage very slowly through the town an everybody had tae go an hand her a present. Jack goes up an the folk's all standin two big rows, two big rows right doon, an the princess's coach an the king and her mother wad come drivin doon between all the people. She wad sit in an they wad hand her all their presents, she wad pack them in aside her, she'd take them home to the castle.

But Jack was kin o late an he had tae get to the end o the two big queues o folk, he wis the last body in. An he's standing wi de wee leaves in his hand, the wee bush that the cuckoo brung him. The wind startit tae blow an the leaves startit tae sing, an the people's all luikin roond. And the loveliest music's comin fae this leaves! Then the band starts tae play an drums starts to beat, an the music startit up. An they luikit up: comin drivin down between the two lines o people wis the coach; ind the coach wis the princess an the king an the queen, an two footmen stand at the back an the driver in the front. They're comin very slow, the horses wis walkin slowly. Everybody's handin t' the princess an wishin her 'happy birthday', everybody right doon the queue. An the're a man catchin all the presents an leein em down beside her. She cam down, right down, ti she cam tae Willie and Tommy, Jack's two brothers. They were standin each side o each other an they handed her their presents, said 'happy birthday' to the princess. The princess passed along – oh, she's a lovely bonnie lassie – she cam over right doon to the end o the queue an Jack's standin.

An he was ashamed o this wee thing he had in his hand, ye see, shamed o the leaves had in his hand. An he wisna carin if he gaunna gie them to her or no, ye see. 'Ach,' he said, 'the cuckoo tellt me "gie them",' an he held them up!

An the princess cam level wi im, she luikit at the leaves an she seen them. She shoutit to the driver, 'Stop, driver, at wonst! Stop,' she says, 'stop! I want to see this young man.' She roars Jack over, 'Well, young man, what hev you got fir me?'

Jack bowed down, he said, 'Her Highness, I wurk wi my brothers an they don't give me any pay, an I stoppit wurkin because I wurkit fir years wi them an they wadna give me any money. They make me wurk too hard an they'll not give me any pay, they only give me ma food. So, I'd no money but I brought ye the *Singin Leaves*!'

She says, 'What is *Singin Leaves*?'

'Well,' he says, 'Princess, when the wind blows, open yir window an that *Singin Leaves*'ll play ye any music under the sun!'

'Is that true?' she said.

'Yes,' he said, 'it's true.'

'Well,' she said, 'that is very nice. An I'll tell you something else, young man – what's yir name?'

He said, 'My name's Jack.'

'Where do you stay?'

'I stay wi ma two brothers,' he said, 'on a farm.'

'All right,' says the princess, 'Jack, I'll take yir *Singin Leaves* back to my father's palace to ma bedroom, an I'll put them in there. An if they're as guid as you say they are, ye'll prob'ly hear from me again.'

'Well,' says Jack, 'they come from a faraway country, they're the *Leaves of the Singin Tree*.'

'Well,' she said, 'how did you get them?'

He says, 'I got them from a cuckoo.'

She says, 'How could you get it from a cuckoo?'

'Well,' he says, 'I got hit frae the cuckoo . . .'

'Anyway,' she says, 'it won't matter where you got them, but they're very lovely – they're e' nicest things ever I saw in ma life – they're beautiful! Lovely,' an she thanked him very much.

He bade her a 'happy birthday', an away the coach goes drivin on.

But the princess still had these leaves in her hand, something in her leaves wadna let her let them go. She cuidna lea them doon, see, they were that beautiful! An they were begint tae quiver, ye ken, quiverin! She went home, tuik em up, put them in her bedroom into a lovely big vase, an she stuck them in filled full o water in her bedroom. An it was a lovely warm day, she opened the window i er bedroom, ye see! She went doon the stair an had her dinner wi her daddy an mammy in the palace. An she wis only half up the stair leadin up to her bedroom, when she hears . . . the wind startit up, heavy wind startit an she hears the loveliest music, see, that you cuid ever hear – comin fae her bedroom! She stops on the stair, said, 'There's someone in ma bedroom, someone in ma bedroom playin music!' (Noo, music in the aulden days, mebbe somebody played a fiddle or a lute, somethin like that, but that was all they played.) The *Singin Leaves* were singin in her room! She goes doon to her daddy an mammy, says tae the king an queen, 'Daddy, Mammy, come here!'

'What is hit?'

She says, 'Come here, I want ye tae hear something. Listen – up in ma bedroom!' An the wind was blowin an the leaves is singin away, the loveliest music you cuid hear!

De king says, 'Where is it comin from?'

'Well,' she said, 'I'll tell ye, we'll go up an see!'

So the king an the queen tiptoed up canny up the stair, an they opened the door canny. The wind wis blowin through de windae, an here are the leaves sittin in the jar – the leaves wis quiverin – the loveliest music in the world is comin from the *Singin Leaves*!

The king stood back, 'Well, upon my word,' he says, 'that is the greatest ever I heard in my life! Where did you get them?'

She says, 'I got them from a young man the day.'

He says, 'What man? Who is he? Is he a prince or is he a knight, is he a earl or is he a duke or something? Where did he get that? Wis he been in the foreign countries fightin away in the foreignt wars in the Holy Lands?'

'No,' she said, 'he's only a farmboy, an he gev –'

He says, 'Where did he get them?'

She says, 'He said he got them from a cuckoo.'

'Well,' he said, 'I must see this man, what's his name?'

She said, 'His name's Jack an he stays on a farm wi his two brothers.'

'Right,' says the king, 'I'll find him!'

King gaes doon, shouts four or five o his soldiers up, 'an I want ye,' he says to the soldiers, 't' go out tae such-an-such a farm, an bring in tae see me a young man known as Jack. He stays with his two brothers on the farm. Ye'll bring im back because I want to see him immediately! Tell him I want him!'

'Right!' says the soldiers. Ten soldiers an the guards with their horses jumped on their horses and away they go, ridin up to the fairm, see! Now, Willie an Tom an Jack were jist sittin after their breakfast, when up comes the soldiers. Right, stops at the door o the farm an the officer jumps off, he says, 'Anyone in?'

Willie comes oot, 'Yes,' he said, 'what is hit?'

He said, 'Have you a brother that stays in here wi ye called Jack?'

'Oh yes,' he said, 'I've got a brother called Jack.'

'Well,' he says, 'the king wants to see him.'

'Oh! Well, wait a minute,' he said. He gaes in, Jack's sittin a' the fire.

He says, 'What?'

'Jack,' he said, 'the soldiers fae the king's court's come fir ye. What were ye daein i the toon yesterday?'

He says, 'I wisna daein naethin in the toon yesterday.'

He said, 'Ye must hae been daein somethin, ye're wantit a' the palace.'

'But,' he says, 'I never dune nae hairm at the palace, I wisna even at the palace, I wis only —'

'What did ye gie the princess?' he says.

He said, 'I gien her 'e leaves.'

'That's hit,' he said, 'ye gien some kind a poisoned leaves to the princess, or some kind o jaggy thorns that you pickit up, ye silly stupid fool, mebbe jagged her hand or something an she's poisont! Ye're wantit! Ten chances tae one ye'll get a long time i the jail, ye'll be lockit up in the dungeons.'

'Oh well,' he says.

'You canna refuse,' he said, 'because they'll come an take ye by force if ye don't!'

Well, Jack comes oot to the guard o the soldiers – he said, 'You're wantit immediately, Ir Majesty requires ye to go to the palace, immediately ye're wantit!'

Jack says, 'All right, wait ti I get ma horse!'

Jack went in, washed his face, put on a clean coat on im, an got his horse an away he goes wi the soldiers, see, ridin up. Rode up to the palace, two soldiers jumpit off. One got on each side o Jack an marcht him up tae the palace steps, up the steps right into the palace, right into the king's room.

De king wis sittin, the queen wis sittin an the princess wis sittin. Oh, when the princess seen Jack she kent him right away, 'Yes, Daddy,' she says, 'that's the man. That's the man there brung me, that gev me the *Singin Leaves*.'

'Well, young man, right,' says the king, 'you were in the town yesterday at my daughter's birthday?'

'Yes,' he said, 'Our Majesty.' Jack went down on his knees in front o the king. (Ye had tae in them days or yet got yir heid choppit aff.)

'Rise, my young man,' he says, 'an stand straight in front o me! I want tae speak to ye. Don't be afraid, we're not gaunna touch ye. Ye'd never fir nae harm, we're not gaunna harm ye in the least.' Noo Jack was aa right when he heard this. He said, 'The queen and I wis wonderin – we fell in love with yir *Singin Leaves* – an so has the princess. We're *charmed* wi them an we wonder where you got them. Are there such a thing, if you could tell hus where there's any more?'

'Oh well,' says Jack, 'that's somethin I canna tell ye. I'll tell ye a story, but it's up tae yirsel, I tellt it to ma brothers but they'll no believe me.'

'Well,' he said to Jack, 'where did you get them?'

He said, 'I got them from a cuckoo.'

The king said, 'You mean to tell me that you got this leaves from a cuckoo?'

He says, 'Yes, Ir Majesty, I got them from a magic cuckoo!'

The king said, 'Luik, I'm king of all this country, A own all the country right roond here an I own all the cuckoos when they come here fae a faraway country. An *I've* never heard o a magic cuckoo, I never heard of a magic cuckoo!'

'Well,' said Jack, 'this is a magic cuckoo. An I'll tell ye something else, Ir Majesty, it can speak!'

'What?' says the king.

He says, 'This cuckoo can speak – it spoke to me.'

Noo, didn't the queen an the princess an the king think that Jack wis a wee bit on the *moich* side, kin o daft. 'Well, I'll tell ye what I'll dae,' he says, 'I'll make you a rich man if you can get me some more o them

Singin Leaves – some fir the queen and some for me tae gae into ma bedroom – we love these *Singin Leaves*. An I'll not be contentit till I get some more o them *Singin Leaves*! I'll tell ye somethin, Jack, you're the only man that can get them for me.'

'Well,' says Jack, 'if 'e cuckoo comes back, I can ask the cuckoo tae get me some, but hit'll be a while afore the cuckoo'll come back again – I might never see the cuckoo again!'

'All right,' says the king. 'So anyway, you told the princess that yir brothers disna give ye any pay fir wurkin.'

'No,' he said, 'they dinna give me any pay fir wurkin. I wurkit wi them fir years since I left the school, sin A was a wee toy boy. They dinnae give me nae money, they only give me ma food.'

'Well,' he said, 'luik, I'm sendin two guards back with ye tae order yir two brothers tae give you your pay. An you've to be wurkin fir me, ye'll do anything, go anywhere you want – search de whole country roon aboot – till ye get that cuckoo. An bring it to me! I'm no wantin ye tae get anything else – you get me the cuckoo – bring hit to me!'

'Right,' says Jack, 'I'll dae ma best. Well, he promist, the cuckoo promist to come back, so if I get it back, I'll bring hit to you.'

'You bring it to me,' says the king, 'an I'll make you a rich man!'

'Well!' says Jack.

Jack goes back wi his horse an two guards goes back wi him, right back to the wee fairm, back they come. Two guards jumps doon, he says, 'Jack, tell yir two brothers tae come oot here, we want tae speak to em!'

Right, Jack goes in. 'Luik,' he says tae his two brothers, 'Two o the king's guards is oot there an they want tae speak to ye.'

So one o them, Tommy, says, 'What hae you been daein? Ye're gettin yirself in awfa trouble. You got *hus* inta trouble next, noo you got yir ainsel inta trouble!'

'No me,' says Jack, 'I never got my ainsel in nae trouble, but *youse* is in trouble, no me!'

He said, 'Why hus – we never dune nae hairm?'

He said, 'The two guards is oot there, ye better go oot an speak to them!'

Oot goes Tommy an Willie tae the door. The two guards is standing at the door, he says, 'Thomas an Willie, your brother John's been tellin the king that he's been wurkin wi you fir years and you never gev him any pay.'

'No,' says Willie, 'that's true enough, he never does enough wurk.'

'But,' he says, 'what's about the time he wurkit years an years afore this an yese never paid him? Well, on the king's orders, you have to pay Jack all o the money that you owe him, all his back-lyin money you owe im! Ye've to pay im up an give him all the money at he needs, he hes to go an search fir this cuckoo – fir de king!'

'Whatten the cuckoo?' he says. 'Oh, his pet cuckoo – that cuckoo fleed away – Jack had it all winter an he kep hit here all winter, it had a broken wing. He fed it an looked after it an it fleed awa. He tellt us hit cuid speak, it wis a magic cuckoo, but we never listened tae that.'

'Well, never mind,' said the guards, 'you see that Jack gets everything he needs an everything he wants. An make sure that he gets enough money tae keep him goin, because now he's wurkin fir the king, he's got tae go an search fir the cuckoo.'

So next day Willie an Tom they got as much money as they cuid get rakit together, an they gien't tae Jack. Jack went away to the town, bought hissel some nice claes an bought hissel a guid horse an everything he needed. An he set sail roon the country. Every cuckoo he heard, 'cuck-oo' . . . wander fir miles here, wander fir miles there, luikin fir his cuckoo. But na, na, search as he did search – nothing – every cuckoo he heard roarin in the trees, he went up tae hit, shouted. Na, it wadna come near him, na. He searched fir aboot a month ti aa the summer wis nearly finisht, summer wis nearly gone.

Whan one day he goes back to the king, he says, 'Ir Majesty, I've searched noo fir nearly six weeks all over, I been all over de country an I cannae get the cuckoo.'

'But,' he says, 'my daughter's leaves is as lovely as ever, they're singin their heart away every night! She loves em an she'll no pairt wi them, an I'm pinin fir some fir me an ma queen.' (See, wonst ye seen these leaves ye fell in love with them, ye had tae get them!)

'Anyway,' says Jack, 'I cannae help hit. But I'll try ma best, if the cuckoo does come back, I'll tell him tae get ye some.'

'Right,' says the king.

So one day he goes hame. Ach, an he's knockin aboot the fairm here an there an that, comes late an he's away tae his bed, it wis the end o summer. And he opens the window, it was warm at night, an he hears 'flutter-flutter-flutter' – in comes the cuckoo. Jack goes over, shuts the windae, cuckoo jumps o' the table.

'Aye, Jack,' he said, 'how ye gettin on noo? Are ye better aff noo what you were whan I seen you last?'

'Ay,' says Jack, 'I been at the king, I've seen the princess –'

'Tellt you!' said the cuckoo.

An he said, 'The king made ma brothers give me aa my money, an the king tellt me –'

'I ken what the king tellt ye, the king wants me,' he said, 'the king wants me. An he wants mair o the *Singin Leaves*. But I'll tell ye, Jack, I'll tell ye a wee plan, luik, I be'n enchantit, I'm a prince an I been enchantit in my ain country. *An nothing but a princess's tear'll bring me back to my ain shape. A princess's tear, an that's 'e only one thing that'll ever bring me back to my ain shape!*'

'Well,' says Jack, 'I canna get ye a princess's tear.'

'No,' said the cuckoo, 'you cannae get me a princess's tear.'

'But,' he says, 'I made a promise to the king, an it's easy fir you, I can tak ye to the king an the first chance ye get, ye can flee awa again. But I made a promise to the king I bring ye.'

'But,' he says, 'Jack, I canna speak to the king, I'm no allowed to speak to kings, the enchantment says I cannae.'

'Well,' says Jack, 'I'll tak ye to the king onyway, an A'll tell him "this is the cuckoo".'

'You tak me to the king,' he said, 'an give me to the king an tell him "this is the cuckoo", an lea the rest to me!'

So next mornin, Jack gies the cuckoo some meat. Away he goes to the castle, tae the king's palace an the cuckoo wi him, cuckoo sits on his shoulder. Rides up to the palace, meets the guards. The guard says, 'Let him in, that's Jack – the king wants him in!' In he goes to the palace.

De queen wis sittin an de king wis sittin, an the princess is sittin in this big room, all sittin roond here. 'That's Jack comin, oh, Jack,' the king said, 'he's got a cuckoo – mebbe that's the cuckoo noo – the one that got the *Singin Leaves*!'

So in goes Jack tae the palace and he bows doon, the cuckoo sits on his shoulder. 'Ir Majesty,' he said, 'I've finally got the cuckoo, it cam in to me last night an it spoke to me.'

'Tsst,' king said, 'will it speak to me?'

'No,' he said, 'no speak to you.'

The queen said, 'Will it speak to me?'

'No,' he said, 'hit'll no speak to you.'

'Will it speak to me,' princess says, 'oh, isn't he a lovely burd!' And she catcht the wee cuckoo in her bosom, ken, she cuddlit hit. An it wis that bonnie, she said it was that bonnie an happy – she wis that glad to get hit – at she gret wi gladness! A tear fell aff her cheek an fell the top o the cuckoo's heid, an the minute the tear fell the top o the cuckoo's head there jumpit oot a bonnie young prince! Enchantit prince.

An he stude aside the princess, he tellt the king, 'I was enchantit back in ma ain country an the *Singin Leaves* is in my gairden i my castle.'

An the princess fell in love wi him, he steyed wi the king, he got married to the princess an he tuik the princess away home to his ain country. An he sent a hale tree back to the king, a hale tree wi *Singin Leaves*! The king plants hit in his garden, specially plants hit in a special place in his gairden. An every summer when hit wis in bloom, the queen and him went doon an they tuik a bush each, they pit hit inta their bedroom an they had plenty o music all the days of their life. An that's the last o the wee story!

JACK AND THE MONEYLENDER

Jack's mother died when he wis very young, an he never remembered much about his faither. But this rich merchant who hed known his faither, and his faither hed done two-three jobs fir im, hed nae family o his ain. He'd said tae Jack's mother, 'Dinna worry, I'll take care o Jack, I'll look after him. If ye give im tae me, I'll be guid tae him.' So, the rich merchant got Jack, and Jack wis very happy. An years passed by, the merchant was good to Jack – he had everything under the sun that he wantit – he 's jist like a son. Noo, Jack he grewed up tae be a young man, an one night he lay in his bed thinkin tae hissel.

He said, 'I faintly remember ma mother an I faintly remember ma faither. But there must be mair tae this worl than this place, jist here workin tae this merchant, no that he's no guid to me an A've got everything I want. I wad like tae see what goes on i the rest o the worl. There must be other places an other toons, ither people.' So Jack finally made up his mind that tomorrow mornin he wad tell his master the merchant that he wad like tae see a bit o the world. The next mornin when he cam doon tae hev his breakfast (cause he dined in the kitchen an wis jist treatit like a son wi the merchant), he was very quiet.

An the merchant said tae Jack, 'What's troublin ye this mornin, Jack?'

'Well,' he said, 'master, t' tell ye the truth, I had a funny dream last night.'

'Well, Jack,' he said, 'tell hus aboot hit!' Noo there were only the merchant and his wife in the hoose at the time.

He said, 'I dreamt that out there in the world there's roads goes on fir miles, an valleys, towns an cities an people fir as far as ye can see.'

'Oh-ho-ho,' the merchant said, 'Jack, that's true – fir as lang as you can walk – tae the end o yir life ye'll always find people.'

'Well,' he said, 'sir, I wad like tae see some o this.'

He said, 'Dinnae tell me, Jack, that ye're thinkin o leavin!'

'I'm no exactly thinkin o leavin,' he said, 'I wad like tae see what goes on the rest o the world. Ye know, master, I'm twenty-two years of age now an I've never been far away fae here. Not that ye're no good to me – both you an the mistress – an A've got everything I desire. But I've only got one ambition, tae see what goes on in the world.'

'Well,' says the merchant, 'Jack, it never done a young man any harm tae travel a bit an see a bit o the worl. But remember one thing, there's always a place here fir ye if ye ever think o comin back!'

Jack said, 'Thank ye very much!'

'When are ye thinkin o movin on?' the merchant said.

'Sir,' he said, 'I think tomorrow mornin, bein it the beginnin o summer, I wad like tae go on my way an see a bit o the worl.'

'Well, fair enough.'

So after supper he bade the merchant an his wife 'good night', an he went upstairs to bed. He went in his bed, but Jack cuidna sleep. He tosst an he turnt the whole fearin night thinkin what he wis gaunnae dae the morn. But anyway, he managed tae fall inta a bit troubled sleep, an de cock crowed in the mornin, wakened him at six o'clock. He cam downstairs an the merchant's wife hed his breakfast ready. An he sut, had his breakfast, but he wis in a happier cheerier mood bi this time, cause he knew fine he wis gaunnae go on his way an see a bit o the worl.

So after breakfast he done his chores; he wouldna go away an leave the merchant withoot daein a bit work that needed doin aroon' the place. And then he cam in, he kissed the merchant's wife, he shaked hands wi the merchant an he bade them 'goodbye'.

But 'e merchant said, 'Jack, wait, ye jist cannae go away like that!'

'Well, the're nothing else, sir,' he says. 'You been good to me an so his been the mistress, ye gev me everything I needit in the world, everything that any man cuid ask fir. It's jist my ambition tae see a bit o the world!'

'Well,' says the merchant, 'ye know what I told ye, "ye're always welcome tae come back anytime you fell like hit." The're always be a place fir you, Jack, an what's belongin tae me is yours, because we hev no family of wir own. If ye ever want tae return, ye can come back anytime you like, this place is always yir home. But wait a minute.' So in he goes an he comes oot; he has two bags, wee leather bags full o gold sovereigns, he says, 'Here, Jack, this is yir wages. You know ye been wi me fir nearly seventeen years, ye've never had a penny an I want tae give ye this – tae help ye on yir way.'

Jack says, 'Master, I'm no needin any money. I'm young, I'm strong, I'm fit, I can make ma way along the world, find another job an find employment, make mysel money – you keep hit!'

'No,' the master said, 'I've plenty money. Jack, you never know when ye'll need something tae help ye on yir way.' But anyway, the rich merchant coaxed Jack, an he finally tuik the money, he tied it tae his belt, two wee bags o gold pieces on his belt. He bade the master 'goodbye' an he walked on his way.

So it wis a fine summer's mornin, the birds wis whistlin an he wis happy as a lark. He traivellt on an traivellt on, not a care in the world, an he's singing a carefree song tae hissel. Jack traivelled on till it got dark, an he says tae himsel, 'A'll hev tae find a bit shelter fir the night before it gets too late,' because Jack hed never slept ootside at night. But the place he landed on, there wis a big forest on each side o the road an not a sight of a hoose fir miles an miles an miles. But he traivellt on an traivellt on, an at last he seen a wee light in the distance in the middle o the forest. 'Well,' he says, 'where there's light, there's bound to be life!' So he walkit up tae the wee light, he cam tae a auld-fashiont hoose away i the corner o this forest. Hit wis covered in ivy the hoose, an an aul-fashioned door wi an auld-fashioned brass knocker onta hit. The grass wis growin on the path.

So Jack walkit up, he knockit on the door two-three times, he waitit. Then he heard footsteps comin oot through the back o the hoose, an the door opens – 'creak' – the hinges wis rusty. And out comes an auld man wi a long white beard tae Jack. Jack stood an luikit at the aul man, but Jack cuid see that although he wis auld he hed the freshest complexion Jack hed ever seen in his life – as if he wis two people in one.

'Good evenin, my son,' says the auld man.

'Good evenin,' says Jack.

He says, 'What can I do fir ye?'

'Well,' says Jack, 'tae tell ye the truth, I'm a traveller on the road an I'm seekin lodgins fir the night. I wad wonder, if you'd pit me up fir the night, I wad pay you well.'

'Well,' de auld man says, 'I hevnae very much tae spare, but come in!' So he tuik Jack in, said, 'All I can give ye is some bread an some goats' milk.'

'Oh,' says Jack, 'that's fine fir me, that's very guid fir me!'

An he said, 'I can make ye a bed by the fire fir the evening, fir tae pass the cauld hoors o night.'

'Fine.' So him an the auld man sut an they talked fir a long long while, Jack discussed his troubles wi the auld man an the auld man wis quite happy tae talk to Jack. He gien him half a dozen o dried goat rugs an he made a bed by the fireside fir Jack. So Jack tuik the two bags o gold aff his waist an he pit them sittin on the table, an the auld man never even luikit at them. So that night Jack fell asleep, but the first thing at wakened him wis the auld man.

He shakit him up, 'Well, come on, young traiveller, get up! It's time fir breakfast. It's no much I can give ye, but whatever I've got, ye're welcome tae half hit.' So he gien Jack a bowl o porridge an goats' milk an some goats' cheese, an Jack had a good breakfast. So they sat an talked fir a wee while, then the aul man said, 'I know ye'll be wantin tae go on yir way. I want tae bid ye "goodbye" fore ye go.'

'Well,' Jack says, 'luik, auld man, you been very guid tae me tonight an ye gev me a guid supper, ye gev me a guid bed. Luik, these two bags o gold ats sittin there, you take em, they're no good to me. They're only a burden tae me; I'll find a job along ma way.'

The auld man said, 'Ye're very kind, my son, but I don't want yir money.'

Jack said, 'Take hit, you keep hit.'

'Well,' he said, 'if ye're gie'n me such a thing as a present, I wad like tae give ye a present before you go.'

Jack said, 'I hevna much time fir presents, but whatever hit is . . .'

'But,' the aul man says tae him, 'luik, this present I'm givin you – I want you tae give me a promise – you'll never part wi hit, you'll keep hit tae yirsel!'

'Oh,' Jack said, 'well, if it makes ye happy, I'll dae that.'

But the aul man climbed away up thes crickety stairs, up in the garret i the back o the wee hoose, hit wis covered wi cobwebs. An he cam doon, an in one hand he held an auld-fashioned blunderbuss gun, in the other hand an auld fiddle, auld-fashioned fiddle an a bow. He dustit them aff wi the front o his jersey. An he says tae Jack, 'These two things I want tae give ye as a present.'

Jack said, 'What is hit?'

He said, 'Hit's a fiddle an a gun.'

'But,' Jack said, 'aul man, I cannae play a fiddle an I've never shot a gun in my life!'

An the aul man smiled at him, ye see! 'Jack, ye'll no need tae worry about that!' he said. 'Luik, this is a gun – all ye need tae dae is point, point it an pull the trigger – whitever ye aim at is shot! An this fiddle, all ye need tae dae is put it under yir chin an jist drag the bow across – it'll play itsel – but the thing is, whoever hears the music can never stop fae dancin till you stop playin!'

'Oh, well,' Jack thanked the auld man very much! An there were a strap on the fiddle, he pit the fiddle on his back. An he stuck the gun in his belt, he bade the auld man 'farewell' an he walkit doon the path on to the driveway. An he traivelled on.

Noo, he hedna traivellt far, fir about five miles, an he got kin o tired, he sat doon tae rest. So he'd sat fir about five minutes, when he luikit. Comin over the hill was this auld man wi a long white beard, dressed in rags an the toes o his shoes wis stickin oot. His hair hed never been combed fir months an his beard wis in tatters, but his cheeks wis as red as a rosy apple. Whan the auld man cam up tae him he stopped, 'Good morning, young man,' he said.

'Good morning,' says Jack, 'auld man, good morning.'

He said, 'Ye're early o' the road this morning.'

'Well,' Jack said, 'early bird gets the early worm. I'm just restin before I go on ma way.'

The auld man says, 'Cuid I help ye?'

'Oh,' Jack says, 'I'm not needin any help.'

'Well,' the auld man said, 'look, I'm a moneylender, an I'll len ye as much money as ye want.'

'Hmmh,' Jack said, 'I'm no needin any money, I'm young an I'm strong an I'm able tae work, why shuid I need any money? I've heard aboot you back whaur I spent my young years, whaur I used tae wurk to a rich merchant – I heard aboot you – how you fleece people an ye give them so much money, an then you demand back twice as much ye lent. No, ye can do nothing fir me!'

'Well,' says the moneylender, 'seein that I cannae talk you inta helpin ye, wad ye help me?'

'Well,' says Jack, 'I can help ye if ye want any help. What is hit ye want?'

He says, 'I'm an auld man an I had no breakfast this mornin.'

Jack said, 'Ye've plenty money.'

'Ah, but,' he said, 'that's money fir lendin oot, that's no money fir buyin nothin wi. I see you got a fine gun in yir belt there, an my favourite breakfast is mavises.' An sittin ond a bramble bush, a big heap o bramble bush wis a mavis, an it wis singin away tae its heart's content, a big fat mavis. He said, 'That wad jist make a fine breakfast fir me, I cuid kinnel a fire an roast hit if you would shoot that mavis fir me!'

'Well,' Jack said, bein a kind-hearted young man, 'I don't like tae see any auld man hungry, even suppose he's got plenty money.' Jack pulls the gun from his belt, aims at the mavis, pulls the trigger. Down the mavis goes, inta the middle o the bramble bush – right in the centre o the bramble bush.

'Good enough, young man,' he said, 'that was a nice shot.' De moneylender goes down on his hands an knees an he crawls inta the middle o the jaggy bush, right into the centre the jaggy bush tae get the mavis, ye see!

Jack watcht him ti he seen his two feet disappear inta the middle o the bush tae get the mavis. An he took a thought tae hissel, said, 'How much people hes suffered o'er the heid o that aul man, how much people hes suffered, how he robbed an fleeced auld folk, an prob'ly pit some intae their grave fir the cause they cuidna pay their debts. I think I'll learn him a lesson!' So Jack takes aff his fiddle aff his neck, an he starts tae play an he starts tae play. An when *he* starts, the moneylender stude up in the middle o the bush, he starts tae dance. An the faster he danced the faster Jack played, an Jack fiddled an Jack fiddled, an Jack fiddled an Jack played, an Jack played an Jack played, an the moneylender dancit in the middle o the jaggy bush! Noo, you can imagine a person dancin in the middle o a jaggy bush – his beard wis torn, his face wis scratched, dher wur not a stitch o claes on him!

An he held up his two hands amang the thorns, he said tae Jack, 'Please, please stop, young man, stop! Please stop yir fiddlin!' an his tongue wis oot that length. He tuik his belt aff an he threw the belt tae Jack wi all the bags o money, he says, 'Take all ma money, please, but stop yir fiddlin!'

An Jack thought, 'He learned his lesson,' so Jack stopped his fiddlin. An the moneylender crawled oot. And you want tae see him when he crawled oot o that bush, you wadna recognize him! If he wis bad before, he wis worse, he was streamin blood an scratches, an if his clothes wis ragged before, there weren't a stitch left upon his body. An he'd lost both his sandals in the thorns. Jack picked up the money belt wi all the bags o gold, pit it roon his waist, pit his fiddle on his back an stuck his gun i his belt, walkit on an left the moneylender bithoot a 'goodbye'.

But the moneylender walkit oot on the main road, an he hadna gone a mile when the first thing he met on route was five o the king's soldiers an the captain o the king's guards. And they were on route because they were the polis in these days. An when he saw them comin he sat right in the middle o the road. An the captain o the guards stoppit, they all jumpit doon. They seen the auld man, they never seen an auld man in such a state in their life. One o them liftit him up an pit him on a horse, an he told them, 'A young man he robbed me, he beat me an he stole ma money, an he left me tae die in this state!'

Oh, the captain o the king's guards who wis a kindly man, said, 'Which wey did he go?'

He says, 'Ond the road to the next village, ma lord.'

They tuik the auld moneylender up in the saddle, an they werena long overtakin Jack. He wis marchin on. Jack was arrestit immediately, tooken inta the town an thrown i the dungeons. He lay in the dungeons ti the next day and all the next day – fir two days – without a bite or a drink. An then he wis tuik afore the king's court, an fir robbin a man on the king's highway he wis sentenced to be hung! An the last man who keekit in through de window wis the moneylender, 'I'll get my own back on, if it's the last thing . . . A'll be happy whan I see ye hung!' says the moneylender through the bars. De moneylender got his money back, Jack was tae be hung.

So all next day hammerin an hammerin wis gaun on right oot in the front o the coort – Jack cuid see hit through the windows. They were buildin a scaffol – Jack tae be hung. So next day dawnt, Jack wis led from the dungeons tae the scaffol an up the thirteen steps, an the rope 's put over his neck. Money wis tooken from im, gun wis tooken from im, fiddle was taken from him an everything. An hit wis a public hangin, they were gaithert in their hunderds right in the front o the court. So the captain o the king's guards an the lord mayor o the toon wis there, an the hangman was there standin biside Jack. Before they pit the black hood over Jack's head fir tae hang him, he asked Jack his last request.

An Jack said, 'Well, if ye're gaunnae hang me, I've only one request: all A want, sir, before I die – one shot o my fiddle!'

De moneylender who wis standin waitin tae see Jack hangit, held up his hands an screamed, 'No, please! Please,' he said tae the lord mayor, 'don't give him his fiddle!'

An the lord mayor said, 'Auld man, this man 's gaunnae be hung today. An do ye mean to tell me that ye grudge him one last request, "one shot of his fiddle"? Bring the young man his fiddle!'

They brung Jack his fiddle fae the dungeon an gev Jack his fiddle. Jack got the fiddle under his chin an he startit tae play. An as he startit tae play, they startit tae dance, everybody startit tae dance! The hangman he cuidna stand, hadna enough room tae dance aside Jack, so he got doon bi front o him; an the faster they danced the faster Jack fiddled. An he played an he fiddled, an he played an he fiddled, he played an he fiddled fir an hour – ti everybody was dancin ti dhey wur exhaustit – ti they cuidna dance another step! An still Jack fiddled on. The moneylender wis lyin gaspin at the fit o the steps, the lord mayor crawled up on his knees an he held up his hand, the dogs wis dancin an the cats was dancin, the pigeons – lyin on their back wi their feet up!

The lord mayor held up his hand, said, 'Please! Please, young man, I'll give you yir life if ye stop yir fiddlin!' At that, Jack tuik the bow an pulled it bilow his oxter, an tuik the rope off his neck, walkit doon the steps tae the moneylender.

'Now,' he says tae the moneylender, 'tell them how ye gev me yir gold – tell them before A start playin!'

'Please,' said the moneylender, 'please, please, I gev it tae him, I gev him every penny! He never robbit me, he shot me a bird an I crawled into a jaggy bush fir de burd, he played his fiddle an I promised him all ma money if he wad stop his fiddlin!'

So Jack stoppit fiddlin, the captain o the guards who wis a kindly man cam up, he says tae the lord mayor, 'Look, that auld man nearly sent a young handsome man tae his death because he wadna stop his fiddlin.'

The lord mayor says, 'Put him i the dungeons fir the rest o his days, an bring this man his gun an his fiddle an let him free!'

So Jack got his fiddle back and he got his gun back, he got the full bags o the moneylender's gold. He walkit over tae the lord mayor an he says, 'Luik, Lord Mayor, you spared me ma life. I have no need fir the moneylender's money. Take hit an give it tae the poor. All I want is ma fiddle an ma gun, tae be ond my way.'

An the lord mayor said, 'God bless ye, young man, God speed ye on yir journey!'

So Jack went on his way with his fiddle an his gun. But he hedna traivelled far before his fiddle an his gun wis tae get him inta mair trouble – but that is another story!

THOMAS THE RHYMER

People believes many different things about Thomas the Rhymer, or 'Thomas Rhymer' as he wis called, but in my story Thomas never remembered his mother an father because they hed died when he wis young. But he lived with his auld grandfather in Huntly in Aberdeenshire, an his grandfather was a clock maker. He had reared him up from a child, his grandfather hed gev him his own will to do anything he liked. Thomas never worked in his grandfather's shop, he done nothing, all Thomas ever done – he wis jist a lay-about. An the people i the village called him 'the village fool', the children used to make names about him when he grew up, he went with his old hat an his hose an jist walkit aboot the village. Only thing that Thomas really loved to do wis tae go oot an lie in the sunshine an enjoy hissel, hands bilow his head an lie back an think aboot things. Because he wis a great thinker, people thocht he wis a bit crazy and they called him 'Thomas the Fool'.

But Thomas knockit about the village fir many many years till he wis about twenty-two or twenty-three. Then one day Thomas was gone . . . he's never showed his face in the village for seven years. An people wondered an his grandfather wondered, his grandfather asked questions, he asked people, he searched among everybody. An everybody in the whole village knew that Thomas wis gone, but *nobody* had ever *knew* what happened tae him – not one single soul ever knew because he was *gone* fir seven long years. An this is what happened to Thomas, what really happened . . .

Note: This musical notation follows the narrator's verbal rhythms. And the metre is organized according to the poetic stress of the verse. Semi-bar lines and the indication of a general duple metre at the start, '2', are guidelines for realizing the complex rhythmic sub-divisions of each poetic foot. Beats, principally defined by groups of notes joined together with beans, are not of regular or consistent duration, but follow the actual rhythm of narration.

'Oh mount you up, oh Thomas,' she said, 'an you maun come along wi me;

For I am bound for Elfin Land, it is very far away!'

So they rode and they rode, and they merr'ly merr'ly rode and it's merrily they rode away,

Antil they came to a red river that lay across their way.

'What river is this?' oh Thomas he said, 'oh please to me do say!'

'Oh this is the River of Blood,' she said, 'that is spilled on this earth in one day!'

So they rode and they rode, and they merr'ly merrily rode an merrily they rode away,

Antil they came to a crystal river that lay across their way.

'What river is this?' oh Thomas he said, 'oh please to me do say!'

'Oh this is the River of Tears,' she said, 'that is spilled on this earth in one day!'

So they rode and they rode, and they merrily merrily rode an merr'ly they rode away,

Antil they came to a thorny road that lay across their way.

'What road is this?' oh Thomas he said, 'oh please to me do tell!'

'Oh this is the road you mus never lead, for that road it leads to Hell!'

Then they rode and they rode and they merrily merrily rode, they rode for a night and a day,

Antil they came to a great orchard that lay across their way.

'Light down, light down,' oh Thomas he said, 'oh it's hungry that I maun be!

Light down, light down,' oh Thomas he said, 'for some fine apples I do see!'

'Oh touch them not,' the Elfin Queen said, 'please touch them not I say!

For they are made from the curses that fall on this earth in one day!'

Then reachin up into a tree, into a tree so high,

She plucked an Apple from a tree as they went ridin by.

'Oh eat you this, oh Thomas,' she said, 'as we go riding by,

And it will give to you a tongue that shall never tell a lie!'

So they rode and they rode, and they merrily merrily rode and they rode fir a year and a day,

Antil they came to a great valley that lay across their way.

'What place is this?' oh Thomas he said, 'oh please to me do say!'

'Oh this is Elfin Land,' she said, 'and it's here that you maun stay!'

So Thomas got some shoes of lovely brown and a coat of Elfin green,

And for seven long years and a day ond earth he was never seen.

Then lo an behold one morning Thomas returned to the village of Huntly wonst more, dressed in his coat o elfin green an his brown shoes. An people were amazed when they saw Thomas comin home to his grandfather. Thomas walked the streets next morning an talked to all the people. They asked him questions an found that he was as different person who had left wi * the person who had returned. He took the people in the streets an he spoke to them, he lectured to them an he became a great seer. He told those people that the great wonderful things gaunna happen: he told them the two world wars; he told them that the North Sea an the Atlantic Ocean wad meet in the future, which people believed wis impossible. But then along came the Caledonian Canal tae prove Thomas's words were true in many later years.

Then about five years later, after Thomas hed preacht an foretold and forecast all these wonderful things, which people believe now had come true; that the people had seen a wonderful sight in the village of Huntly. An the first person they wantit to find out who cuid tell them the truth why it shuid happen, was *a white hind an a white hart* had came inta the village? Cause no one had ever saw such things before.

An they ran up to Thomas's house, said, 'Thomas, you must come an explain this to hus – there's a white hart an a white hind in the village!'

And Thomas said, '*Yes, I know, but they've come to visit me.*'

Thomas walked out into the street. An people watched, they seen *three white deers* disappearin inta the River Spey . . . Thomas wis gone fir evermore, he never returned. The elfs came back from Elfin Land an tuik Thomas away with them fir evermore; that is the legend o Thomas the Rhymer in one particular wey, but no one knows the truth!

* as different person who had left wi – a different person from

TAM LIN

In bygone times when lairds had large estates ind the West Country, if a boy wis born and a girl wis born, it made no matter the age of the child, they were betrothed to each other. So this laird had a small son, an whan he was a year auld the laird next to him tae the next estate had a daughter. They met together over a drinkin party and they said, 'Oh, it would be wonderful if my son cuid marry yir daughter,' an so they're betrothed to each other as childer. But then a queer thing happened. When the little boy whose name wis William was only a year old, he hed disappeared from his cradle, he jist disappeared from the world. People searched high and low, they accused his mother for doin away with im, they accused his father . . . but young William wis *gone*. He wis gone fir many many years.

But the little girl whose name was Margaret grew up to a handsome young woman. She hed never found another boyfriend, she never went nowhere, but she always been told by her mother that the person she wis to marry had disappeared as a child – gone firever. All the comfort she cuid get at evening time, she used to go walkin an leave her own estate, cross the fence an go inta the neighbourin estate – which was beautiful too – but hit wis covert with beautiful hazel trees. An she used to go an collect the hazelnuts. So she wis sittin late one evening in about October month, when the nuts were ready, an she wis sittin sewin her seams – maybe makin cushions or sewin a dress or something – when she took a notion that she wad like to have some hazelnuts. She left doon her sewin, she walked down an crossed the fence into the neighbourin estate. And there she had the greatest experience in her life, which was to change her life entirely. And now, this is how it happent.

Oh Lady Marg'ret she sat ind her high chamber, she was sewing her silken seams;

She luikit east an she luikit west, an she saw those woods grow green.

So picking up her petticoat beneath her harlin gown...

An when she came to the merry green wood, it was there that she let them down.

For she had not pulled one nut, one nut, one nut nor scarcely three,

When the highest lord in aa the countryside came a-riding through the trees.

He said, 'Why do you pull those nuts, those nuts; how dare you bend those trees!

How dare you come to this merry green woods without the leave of me!'

♪ = 100

She said, 'Wonst on time those woods were mine, without a leave of yours,

And I can pull those nuts, those nuts, and I sure can bend those trees, those trees,

I sure can bend those trees.'

So he took her gently by the hand and he gently laid her down;

An when he had his will of her, he rose her up again.

♩ = 54

She said, 'Now you've had your will of me, come tell to me your name!

And if a baby I do have, I will call it the same.'

He said, 'I'm an earl's son from Carlisle, and I own all those woods so green,

♩ = 46   rubato

But I was taken when I was young by an evil Fairy Queen.

But,' he said, 'tomorrow night is Halloween, and all those nobles you can see;

And if you will come to the five-mile gate, it is there you can set me free, oh free,

It is there you can set me free!

Oh first they will come some dark, some dark, and then they will come some brown;

But when there comes a milk-white steed, you must pull its rider down, down,

You must pull its rider down!

Oh first I'll turn to a wicked snake and then to a lion so wild,

Oh hold me fast an fear me not, I may be the father of your child!

And then I'll turn to a nakit man, oh an angry man I'll be!

Just throw your mantle over me, an then you will have me free, oh free,

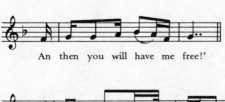

An then you will have me free!'

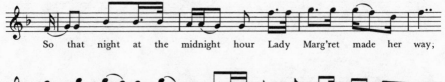

So that night at the midnight hour Lady Marg'ret made her way,

And when she came to the five-mile gate, she waitit patiently, oh lee,

She waited patiently!

Oh first there came some dark, some dark, and then there came some brown,

But when there came a milk-white steed, she pulled its rider down, down,

She pulled its rider down!

Oh first he turned to a wicked snake an then to a lion so wild;

She held him fast an feared him not — he could be the father of her child, her child,

Be the father of her child!

rubato

Then he changed to a nakit man, oh an angry man was he!

She threw her mantle over him, an then she had him free, oh free,

And then she had him free!

Then cried de voice of the Fairy Queen, oh an angry queen was she,

♩ = 58

Sayin, 'If I had hae known yesterday, oh what I know today

♩ = 48

I'd took out your very heart's blood an put in a heart of clay, of clay,

An put in a heart of clay!'

So Lady Marg'ret on the white-milk steed, Lord William on a dapple grey;

With the bugle an the horn hangin down by their sides, it's merrily they rode away, away,

It's merrily they rode away!

So after she had done all these things, she broke the spell fra the Fairy Queen who'd tuik him away as a child. Lady Margaret got her betrothed who wis stolen away with the fairies back wonst more, an they married, they lived happy ever after. And that is the end of the story!

LA MER LA MOOCHT

Many years ago in a faraway land there wonst lived a fisherman, an him and his wife didna have any family, he steyed bi the beach and all their life's wurk depended on what he cuid catch. Some days he caught very little an some days he caught a lot. When he caught a lot o fish his wife wis very happy, but when some days he caught very little his wife wis very upset. So it was very hard to please her because she was a very unpleasant woman. The puir fisherman loved her dearly and they didna have any children, so he tried his best every day to catch as much as possible.

One day he cast his nets an the sun was shining beautiful in a deep pool that he never fished before behind some rocks, wonderful rocks covered with seaweed. An he said, 'Today I must catch something!' An then he pulled the net out, an lo an behold he pulled . . . it seemed to be stuck in some way. He pulled it an he pulled it, but there was not one fish in the net. But he pulled it out – the' it cam up – a man's caught in his net, tangled and his arms wis through the net. An the fisherman pulled an he pulled an he pulled, and he wis upset – there ind his net stood the mos beautiful being he'd ever saw in his life – long golden hair, blue eyes, the most wonderful person he ever saw! The fisherman was aghast.

An he said, 'This is something that must be sent to me,' and he pulled the net in, took this person out of his net. An the person seemed so very friendly; he was a man younger than himself, not more than a boy, about fifteen or seventeen years of age. An his fingers wis beautiful, his nails and his hands were beautiful, his toes were beautiful, an he was dressed in a suit of seaweed. The fisherman who was way up in his thirties or forties was so amazed, he'd heard many wonderful stories

about mermaids, but never in his life hed he ever saw a merman – he
had took from the deep sea – the most beautiful person he'd ever saw
in his life. An the merman just stood and looked at him with the most
beautiful blue eyes he'd ever saw, the most wonderful person he'd ever
saw . . . An the fisherman was aghast.

He thought, 'What shall I do with this person?' who stood before
him, 'will I send him back in the sea or will I take him home with me?
If A go back to my wife and tell her about this wonderful person I've
caught in ma net, would she be pleased or angry? Would she say, "Why
didn't you bring him home an show him to me to prove to me that such
a person exists, or is this another story because you've prob'ly fell asleep
while you set yir net an brung me home no fish?"' An the fisherman
made up his mind he would take him home with him.

But the man he had tuik from his nets never said one single word, he
jist stood there as if he was carved of stone. An the fisherman took him
bi the hand and he led him. His hand was cold, as cold as if he was
handlin a fish, and he never said a word. The fisherman led him up
across the shoreway, an he walked on his feet – the fisherman looked
down – his feet were just like everybody else's, but his toenails was as
clean as clean could be. An the fisherman felt a wee bit ashamed, a bit
sad tae capture such a beautiful person, he thought, 'I can't take this
person back to ma wife. But if I don't, she'll never look at me again.'

The young man he'd tooken frae his nets hed never said a word.
When he'd rolled up his net he'd just stood there, he didna want to
escape in any way. He didna want to run away – as if he would hae
been sent to the fisherman. An the fisherman had said tae himself, 'I've
caught many's a fish before . . . I've heard of mermaids, but never in
my life have I seen a merman!' And now the sun came up, the sun was
shining and his hair begint to dry – an his hair was glitterin like gold!
And his seaweed dress begint to dry with the sun, an the fisherman fell
in love with him! He couldna let him go, in no way would he let him
go. So he had only one thing . . . tae bring him back to his wife. He
took him bi the hand, led him along the beach an took him intae his
little cottage by the shoreside.

When he led him in his wife was busy wurkin i the kitchen. She was
very poor, she says, 'Have you got me something today?'

'Oh yes,' he said, 'I've got you something today.'

And his wife turned round, she looked, and there before her stood
the most wonderful bein that she'd ever saw in her life! She says,
'Husband, what have you brought me?'

'Well,' he says, 'look, I've caught no fish today, but I've brought someone – I found im i my net.'

And the woman stood amazed before him, says, 'You mean to tell me you've – '

He said, 'Look, he . . . I found i ma net, he was caught in my net, an I didna want to let him go because you wouldna believe me. I didna want to let him go, because I know you would think I was wastin ma time an cast my nets fir nothing. But believe me, when I cast ma net this morning this 's what I found i my net – this man.'

She says, 'What is he?'

'Look,' he said, 'I don't know what he is, but he's never said a wurd since A tuik him.'

She said, 'Husbant, he's *a merman.*'

'A merman?' said her husband.

'Yes,' she said, 'husbant, he's a merman. But what are we gaunna do with him?'

'Well,' he said, 'you were always upset because I couldna catch enough fish to bring back to ye. But I brought this back I caught in ma net today, and I fought a battle with myself: either let him go or to bring him back; and come back to you who would scold me for catchin nothing, if A told you what I had caught and let him go, you would never believe me.'

'Well,' she said, 'I'm glad you've brought him back. Bring him in and sit him down by the fireside!' An bi this time the seaweed vest that was on him begint tae dry, an the more he dried the more beautiful he becam. He became so more beautiful that the wumman – the tears was runnin doon her cheeks to see this merman! She says, 'Husband, this is the most wonderful bein in the world!'

Tae his wife he said, 'Look, this is a merman. And what are we gaunna do with him, in the name of the world what are we gaunna do wi im?'

She says, 'We'll keep him to wirselfs.' She put on the kettle an she made some tea, she offered him some. His fingers wis as guid as yir an my fingers, his feet wis as good as yir feet and his hair was the most beautiful that anything* in the world! And she gev him a bowl of tea, he took it in his hand and he drank it up.

An then he spoke to them, he said, '*I am La Mer la Moocht.*'

---

* that anything – of any

An the husband an the wife sat back by the fireside; he said, 'You can speak!'

'Of course,' he said, 'I can speak. I am La Mer la Moocht, I am the King of the Mermen.'

'You are the King of the Mermen?' said the fisherman when he found his voice, he was so aghast. 'You are the King of the Mermen?'

He said, 'I am the King of the Mermen, an you hev caught me, I am your prisoner. An hit's up to you tae do what you like with me.'

The fisherman an his wife stood there aghast, an they *loved* him – anybody cuid love him. They were so amazed. They took im, they kep him and they taught him to say the words an they spoke tae him, an they loved him both. And they were afraid to show him to anybody in case they would take him away. He was just . . . out o this world. An he was only about seventeen or eighteen years of age, they had never hed any family and they jist loved him bi their heart.

Then one day things wis very bad with them, they had no more food lef an no fish to sell . . . They couldna even let him sleep, when he fell asleep they sat beside him an watched him. And when he fell sound asleep they sat beside him, and they were sufferin from sleep theirselves! But they were afraid tae let him go in case he wad disappear, they were so much in love with him. They loved him so much they jist couldna part with him . . . Till they got hungry and they got puir.

An then they turned roon to him, they said one day, 'La Mer, we're puir.'

'I know,' said La Mer, 'you're puir.'

He said, 'You want fish? I'll get you fish, come with me an I'll take you to fish.'

And the fisherman's wife said, 'If you're goin, I'm goin too!' She wouldna even let him out of her sight!

So the three o them walked to the beach. An he took the net, said, 'Give the net to me,' an La Mer cast, he threw hit oot like that. An he clappit his hands, the net sunk into the sea. 'Now,' he says, 'pull the net in!' An they pulled the net – it was loaded with fish of all descriptions! Fish that the fisherman hed never seen before in his life, there were more fish than they could ever use. An La Mer stude while they pulled the net in.

An the fisherman said, 'Look,' after they pulled, took all their fish, more an they ever needed, 'we mus sell some of these fish in the village.'

An La Mer he never spoke very much, but he said, 'If you want to go to the village, then let's sell some fish! An they pulled them in – hundreds o fish in the net! They kept some for theirself an the fisherman packed up a bag o fish, a large bag, an they walked to the village. An fish was in fair demand in these times. La Mer said, 'I'll go with you!'

An the fisherman's wife said, 'Please, please, please, take good care of him!' He was so beautiful she jist hatit tae see him go. 'But,' she says, 'please, please bring him back!' An they really loved him.

So the fisherman an La Mer walked into the village. And when he walked in the village he was tall an straight, so handsome that everybody luikit. The fisherman was carryin the fish ond his back, an everybody luikit, heads wis turnin ower direction tae see this so beautiful man who walkit with this fisherman. An they came to the market, they sold their fish. But lo an behold at that very moment, who should drive doon through the village but the princess and her father. She drove doon through the village in her carriage an she 's luikin, she's wavin to the people. The princess, the only daughter the king hed ever had, an she passed by through the market where people 's sellin fish. An the king's sittin, the footman's drivin the carriage, an when there she came – who was standing – La Mer. He's standing there beside the fisherman waitin to sell his fish, when lo an behold the princess espied him – she luikit – there before her stude the most wonderful bein she ever saw ind her life! She demanded the coach should be stoppit immediately, demandit that the coach be stoppit!

An the footman stoppit the coach, an the king said, 'What is hit, my daughter?'

She said, 'Look, Father, look what I see! Do you see what I see?'

'No, my daughter,' he says.

'Look, Father,' she says, 'luik, look! What do you see – who's standing there by the place selling the fish – have a look!'

An the king looked, he saw a person that he'd never saw before in his life, the most wonderful person in his life. An the daughter couldna wait, she jumped out, she ran down to La Mer an she stood before him, said, 'Who are ye?'

He says, 'I'm La Mer la Moocht.'

She said, 'Who owns ye? Who was yir father? Who are ye, where do you come from?'

He said, 'I cam from nowhere, I cam from the sea, an I'm here with my friend the fisherman.'

She says, 'Come with me!'

Bi this time the fisherman stood up an he said to the princess, 'Look,

Ir Majesty, this is my friend an we are fishermen. We are very poor. Can we please go home, we don't want tae interfere with you in any way.'

She says, 'I must have this man, I must have this man! Come to me, come up to my palace tonight, an I want to see you once more! A want to see ye wonst more, I *love* that person!'

An the fisherman said, 'So do all we, *so do we all!*'

'Please,' said the princess, 'I haven't much time to wait, ma father's anxious to get on! But give me your promise you'll bring him here tonight!'

An the fisherman said, 'A'll be there.' But he never said he would bring La Mer.

So the fisherman and La Mer walked home with all the money they got from the fish, he took him home. And his wife was very pleased, they bought many things on their way home fir his wife. La Mer never said a word. And he turned round, he says tae his wife, 'Look, we'll hev tae do something about La Mer. We cannae send him off to the princess, she's in love with him.'

And his wife said, 'I'm in love with – '

He said, '*I'm in love with him too!* I'm in love with him too! We can't send him off; if we send him to the princess we'll never see him again. What are we gaunna do?'

And his wife said, 'We love him, we don't want to hurt him.'

And La Mer said, 'I know yir problem. I don't want to go and leave youse, I don't want to go to marry a princess. Come with me back to the sea, come with me and set me free!'

An his wife said, 'Please, take him back and set him free.'

So La Mer and the fisherman walked back to the same rocks where he catcht him, he said, 'La Mer, you're free. Go, La Mer.'

And La Mer turned round, said, 'Won't you come with me, auld man? Come with me to the sea, I'll take ye to a place where you will never need to fish anymore, where there diamonds is an pearls, where the land – you will be free – where everything is a wonderful place.'

He said, 'I couldn't leave my auld wife.'

'Walk with me,' said La Mer, 'please, come with me! Just put your feet in the sea, an I'll take you with me.'

'I'll walk with ye,' said the fisherman, 'I'll see you off, because I don't want tae give you to anyone. Because we love you dearly.'

So 'e auld fisherman walked into the sea with La Mer behind the rocks, and then lo an behold La Mer turnt roond – he catcht the auld fisherman bi the hand – he held on to the fisherman's hand, 'Come with me,' said La Mer. 'Please, come with me – *you* been good to me an you treatit me so square and so wonderful – please, come and join me in my land, come, please . . .'

And the auld fisherman went in to his waist, then the auld fisherman went up tae his neck, then the auld fisherman went up tae his head and the water cam in tae his eyes. But La Mer jist was like a fish and the water didna seem to affect him any way. But the water 's gaun into the auld fisherman's neck and he begint tae feel that he wis drownin. He said, 'Please, La Mer, please, La Mer, let go your grip – ye're far too strong for me!'

'Come with me,' says La Mer, 'an I'll take you to the bottom o the sea, where you'll never need to worry, where everything is free!'

'Please, please,' said the fisherman, 'let go your grip, ye're far too strong for me!' And then La Mer let go his grip, the auld fisherman walked back to the shoreside and La Mer was gone.

He walkit home and he told his wife, she said, 'Where is La Mer?'

He said, 'La Mer is gone . . . fir evermore, but someday I'll gae back tae the sea.'

She says, 'Look, husband, if you go back to the sea, *will ye take me with you?*' And that is the end of my story.

NOTES ON THE NARRATIONS

Bartimeus, SA/1984/39/B2 and SA/1978/90/A3.

Five short stories about Bartimeus the blind beggar have been grouped together here as one narrative. But the stories were told separately on two different occasions; the first three were narrated to an American folklorist in 1984, the last two to a Scots non-traveller friend in 1978. In the earlier recordings Bartimeus was not blind: 'he is luikin at the brothers, and he seen this big cane' being placed by one in front of the other. But a discussion about Homer before the latter recordings prompted Duncan to recall then, Bartimeus 'had the gift of sight an he couldna see'.

The narrator's attitude towards his traveller versions of stories about the wise beggar was markedly different during the two sessions. In 1978 he was on the defensive to one of his countrymen: after telling 'Bartimeus and the Child', Duncan said,

Noo the traivellers tells that story their wey, ken in their ain language; now you've got stories told about Bartimeus that were mixed up wi stories told by other great men – that 's supposed tae be Great King Solomon or somebody who done that.

(78/90)

In 1984, when Duncan warmly embraced the interest of a foreign scholar, his perspective was much wider:

Bartimeus was to the traveller people what Homer was to you, an A hev fifty stories o Bartimeus; A don't know if he really existit, but he was a person that the travelling people loved; he was Bartimeus the patron saint of the travelling folk; this cuidhae been Jesus Christ as far as anybody else ... what the traivellin people understood!

(84/39)

When Duncan was asked where he learned these stories, he said, 'It's by travellin an listenin – I got my knowledge from everyone. But the sweetest story A ever had in ma life about Bartimeus [and the child] was one which my father used tae tell me a long time ago' (*ibid*).

The Giant with the Golden Hair of Knowledge, SA/1985/195–6/A.

'This is a well-known popular story i my time among the traivellin folk. Some had different versions from others. But this version is rather long, but it's one I likit most,' said Duncan introducing the narrative as it was recorded here for Penguin. At least three other recordings of this long international tale as Duncan tells it have been taped: in 1976, 1978 and 1980, and the first was published in *Tocher* 33 (spring 1980, pp. 165–83). In the 1940s and 50s this wonder tale was told at any number of travellers' campfires across Scotland: 'All the old travellers knew the story and liked to talk about it or tell it,' explained Duncan when he testified to having heard 'fifteen' different versions of the story. 'Differences' would be in minor events and details, e.g. in the narration of 1976: only one auld wumman helped the queen 'get a baby' – with a necklace of flowers she had to wear for four days – but she was warned, 'There's a bad thing'll go along wi it'; the baby's age when the king discovers him is three weeks; the miller divulges the young laddie's origin when he and the king get drunk together; the three golden hairs 'give eternal life' as well as knowledge; an auld wumman wi a staff tells the laddie ahead of time about the villages he will pass through, and about the boatman (her brother), in return for his goodness in helping her home; the Tree of Health grows golden pears; the giant's mother helps the laddie because 'him bein sae young and sae good-looking she took a likin tae him right away' (1976/66).

While the main events of the plot would remain constant throughout travellers' versions, styles of narration would vary according to the tellers' regional dialects. But in the course of ten years a narrator's approach to storytelling can also change, affecting the amount of detail expressed in a story, the degree of elaboration of episodes and the balancing of story parts – 'Every story has a beginning, middle and end,' says Duncan. Many of his early narrations from 1976–78 focus prominently on the 'middle' or central journey (re 'Jack and the Water fae the World's End', below), with notably less time and emphasis given to the home scenes at the beginnings and ends of tales. By comparison, recent narrations from 1984–86 feature a more evenly rounded three-part structure, with a more lengthy development of the conflict or problem in the first part, a more refined (less eventful) middle and a stronger, fuller 'return home' at the finish.

'The Giant with the Golden Hair of Knowledge' in 1985 was narrated in two sessions, defined by Duncan and separated in the recording time by an interval of five hours – represented in print by the story break after the son-in-law promised to bring the king the three golden hairs. Telling a long story with intermissions was a common practice among the older travellers:

He [Father, also Johnny MacDonald of Perthshire and others] wad tell us the one bit one night, an then mebbe he'd tell hus the next bit the next night an then mebbe another bit the next night. He wadna tell hus all at wonst. But we had tae work fir hit: we hed to get sticks, get water an run messages, dae everything before we got a bit o story . . . tell hus a bit story every night . . . mostly the winter time.

(1976/62/A2)

In my transcription I am primarily concerned with the pendular rhythm of Duncan's extended thoughts. While an oral performance loses nothing in the high frequency of main and subordinate clauses tied continually with 'an(d)', this is indeed monotonous in print, defeating the colourful and varied expression of ideas. While some transcribers deal with the problem of creating interesting phrasal movement with a heavy complicated use of punctuation, I prefer to keep it minimal – that the ebb and swell of phrases might be free, natural.

Mary Rashiecoats and the Wee Black Bull, SA/1985/189/A2 – 190/A.

Although this is 'a common story with a lot of travellers', says Duncan, it is not one he tells often; this is his only recorded narration. Very rarely does Duncan tell a story without paying tribute to the storyteller from whom he heard it, and 'Mary Rashiecoats' is no exception:

This story A'm about to tell you tonight is a wonderful auld story, it was told to me a long time ago by a old mother-in-law of mine, my first wife's mother. She was one of de MacDonald people an she had a large collection of stories.

This was one she really loved to tell which she was really good at . . . But I would like to tell it the way she told it as close as possible. An I like this story, it's a guid story. I've never saw any versions of the story wrote down in any book or any way. But I've heard it told in different ways fra many travellers along the way. Jist because she was my first mother-in-law, I would like you to hear her version.

(1985/189)

In the narration Duncan forgot, 'missed a bit', Mary's taking of the salt until after the hunchback awoke. Rather than disrupt the narrative thread, I have shown the story as Duncan corrected it. In the backtracking Duncan called the hunchback a 'dwarf' and an 'ogre'.

From the moment the bull spoke to Mary, the narrator began to make dynamic use of his voice. The bull speaks softly in whispering tones when he wants Mary to listen most attentively: when he speaks his first words to her, when he knows the hunchback is about to appear and when he is certain the hunchback has fallen asleep. The bull's supreme chivalry is polarized with the hunchback's hideous vulgarity – as a strong loud deep voice is used with heavy stresses on the ogre's gross wants and objects. The 'souking' of water and salt in the story is acted out, indicated by the onomatopoeia in the text; and the narrator did spit (into the fire) before saying 'spittin'.

Some of the scenes and motifs in 'Mary Rashiecoats' are arguably the most magical of any in our set of *barrie mooskins*, especially Mary with her bull on the moor cutting rashes, and the dropping of blood from the bull's ear. Listening to the story I have felt these acts and others as powerful incantations; these have dictated my liberal use of exact verbal repetition together with the run-on construction of thoughts, mirroring the oral narration. Highly formular language is the narrative's incense.

The Boy and the Blacksmith, SA/1982/192/A2.

Duncan tells this story on the average of twice a year, although he told it more often when he began recording traditional stories in 1976 and 1977. This performance for a close traveller friend, 'Big Willie' (McPhee) of Perth, was selected for a number of reasons: firstly, Willie praised the narrative as a 'bloody guid yin'. It is a good version of the story in which the ugly women, with twisted torsos as well as heads, are completely burnt to ashes and totally reformed into beautiful women; preferred by the travellers, says Duncan, to the other version he heard where the malady is only a head backside-foremost. The remedy, chopping a head to dust and leaving the body untouched, is less strong, 'nicer', says Duncan, than 'destroying' the whole woman; and that's why he records the version approximating a Phoenix theme only rarely.

Some variants of 'The Boy and the Blacksmith' Duncan tells are definitely 'dream stories', and without the implicit magic of the gold sovereigns remaining in the blacksmith's pocket after he wakens at the end; for example, in 1978 when Duncan told it to an audience of seven travellers in Montrose. But this performance was just as appealing as the 1982 variant with its pervasive traveller vocabulary and precious imagery: 'shan aul mort' = not a very good wife; 'aul crooked cratur' = 'old wife bended in two halfs' (1978/37/A1). The first half of the story told in 1978 elicited peals of laughter from listeners as Duncan described the decrepit features of the blacksmith's wife and his hopeless relationship with her. But in a recent performance of the story, 1985/180/A3, the opening scene in the smiddie was lacking humour all together – the wife was characterized as a 'naggin wumman' with 'never enough money', and the blacksmith's 'meagre earnings' were emphasized much more than his age or predicament.

The diachronic differences in atmosphere of a narrative scene depend partly on the different performing circumstances and the different natures of audiences – as the narrator sees fit to tailor the story for its greatest effect. The 1985 performance of this story for a young non-traveller lad of high intelligence and imagination ended on a note of optimism not present in other performances – 'I know now wir luck hes changed,' said the blacksmith to his wife after giving her two lots of seven gold sovereigns for work done since the boy's last appearance. Twice in this telling the boy was described as a 'beautiful young man dressed in green'; in the 1978 telling his suit was not mentioned once.

In the oral narration of 1982 Duncan omitted the king's warning to the blacksmith 'not to harm his daughter' – present in all other variants. It has been added to the written story, though not bracketed, because Duncan's own words have been used and he indicated that this is an essential part of the narrative.

Storytellers would note the anti-dramatic climax in performing: when the boy 'hut the blacksmith a welt . . . and knockit him scatterin' for not following his instructions, Duncan's voice was intense but very quiet – in contrast to the outburst of physical violence in the scene and branding the content of the lesson.

The Happy Man's Shirt, SA/1985/220/B3 – 221/A1.

In his commentary on the source and popularity of this short story about a sad king, Duncan spoke about styles of narration among his people:

That was the most popular story among all travellers at one time. That was one o ma Uncle Duncan's, my mother's brother, favourite stories. In later years [from the late 1940s to the late 1960s] aa the travellers that ye ever went tae would tell 'The Happy Man's Shirt'. I've heard it told in different ways, some people told it better than others. But that version was my Uncle Duncan's wey o tellin it an he was a good storyteller. Cause stories varied accordin tae the teller. Some people had a different wey o tellin hit – not actually the theme o the story – but a different wey of puttin it. When it came tae the king laughin, the beggarman laughin, they would really laugh, ye know. An they laught fir about ten minutes before ye heard the next o yir story. Ma Uncle Duncan wis the worst in the world fir that, he would jist burst out laughin, he cuid see it in his ain mind, ye ken.

(85/221)

Laughing was not a feature in Duncan's earlier narration, 1976/112/B2. There were no children listening on that occasion as there were in the 1985 session, which may be one reason for the different emotional climates of the two narrations. The earlier began with a more extroverted scene: the queen 'sent for court jesters from all over the world to come and sing and dance to the king, try and make him laugh'; and there was a more mystical aura about the Wiseman who knew the solution, 'an old tramp came to the queen fae a faraway land – only dressed as a tramp – tells the king *to leave the palace and dress in rags . . .*' (76/112). When the tramp the king met was asked why he was happy, his reply made no mention of money or possessions: 'A listen to the singin o the birds an I drink from a brook, and the noise of the wind an the sunshine and rain . . . why should I be sad?' (*ibid*).

Ten years ago Duncan was still leading a nomadic life, he had no responsibilities of family or employment, he was quite free in spirit and mind. This seems to be reflected in his narrations, for they admit of a higher degree of aggregation, a density of activity by characters in the stories that is not so much in evidence now. Psychological development of characters, motives for their behaviour and feelings play a bigger part in narrations of the present (see Notes to 'Jack and the Water fae the World's End' below).

George Buchanan the King's Fool, SA/1976/226/B2–227/A1.

'My faither used tae tell us this wee stories . . . not another soul ever tellt me about George Buchanan,' recalled Duncan before and after this narration in December 1976. The place of these robust pieces angled on puns in the Scots traveller tradition, as Duncan has experienced it, is rather specialized and limited. Only the folk of his father's generation and the related Argyllshire clans (Townsleys, Johnstones and Williamsons) told 'cracks' about the King's Fool. This ran counter to the wider pertinence of the lore, evident in Duncan's explanation of 'king' and his connection of the theme with other monarchs in search of common knowledge:

At's when like every county had a king o their ain; there werena jist yin king rulin aa the country i them days . . . Like Fife hed a king an Perthshire hed a king, ken. An this king would say tae his queen, 'I'm gaun on horseback today, I'll gae wanner roond ma country' – like King Arthur burnin the scones . . . Like 'on wee story I tellt ye aboot de king wi the thorn in his fit' [see story below].

(76/226, 227)

On another occasion when Duncan was telling about the various George Buchanan stories he could remember, he mentioned the 'second episode' following the fool's begging pardon for knocking the man's hat over the bridge: George is banisht – the king warns him 'never to show his face or stand before him on Scottish soil ever again'. So George goes to Ireland, fills his boots full of sand and stands with his back to the king on his return. Another missing part in the 1976 narration was the third question the king asked on his first meeting George, 'How old are ye?' George said 'he was born *before his granny*' because his mother couldn't afford a doctor, so his granny was the midwife. Yet another King's Fool story known by Duncan, but not yet recorded in full from him, is 'The Boiled Eggs': the king gives George twelve hard-boiled eggs and tells him he must hatch him twelve chickens; George gives the king twelve boiled beans telling him '*the chickens will be ready when the beans begin to sprout*'. This particular story was told by traveller Martha Johnstone (1901–80) during a Sunday ceilidh in 1977 after Duncan had told three of the same stories he'd recorded in 1976 (1977/145/A2–B1). On that occasion for his traveller audience, the cant term 'loodnie' was used for the 'auld hen' George took back to the king as his *piece of chicken*. And to the delight of the listeners, the king was told explicitly, 'Ye can wurk away with hit as much as ye want!' (77/145).

Some of the linguistic features of Duncan's early narrative style – the ellipses of verbs and prepositions e.g., (at) 'the end o' and the frequent use of the unemphatic 'I', 'A' – make this text more difficult to absorb by comparison with stories recorded in 1985–86, sixteen making up the core of this collection. Nevertheless, I hope readers will take pleasure in meeting the challenge of the rough-hewn lines and thoughts: where in the six narrations from 1976 and 1982 they tell most truly the folktale's personalism.

Jack and the Horse's Skin, SA/1982/129/B3–130/A1.

Every 'Jack tale' narrated by the travellers is a portrait of their hero. Here he is the clever trickster outwitting the miserly crofter, the pretentious minister and the greedy brother. Some of Jack's other attributes, celebrated in five other stories about him below, are physical strength, devotion to his mother, care for others in need, honesty, kind-heartedness and generosity. Travellers are taught to identify with Jack from an early age and interest in his exploits is still as strong as ever: dozens of stories about Jack are told by travellers to their children every month of the year. The great appeal and value of these stories stem from Jack's ability to survive adversity against all odds; for Jack's knowledge is innate, he follows his instincts.

Because 'the lad' is so very close to the heart and soul of travelling life, and because this particular trickster narrative is both popular and widespread among the travelling folk, it is fitting to include a narration of 'Jack and the Horse's Skin' in Duncan's richest colloquial style – when he told it to his good friend traveller Willie McPhee, saying, 'This 's the story that'll really interest you.' Willie was moved by it, for after hearing Duncan's narration in 1982, he responded intimately, 'That's a bloody guid story that, ged!'

Noteworthy in the narration was the male chauvinism, quite typical of traveller men, in the phrase 'my mother's fault', when the older brother rationalized Jack's innocence in their mother's death at childbirth. Dying was a 'mistake' the mother had made, Duncan later explained, 'a shortcoming' on the woman's part.

A wonderful imitation of gospel song occurred in the story when Jack was in the bag – just when the minister was within earshot – 'I'm gaun to heaven' and the lines thereafter were intoned as chant. 'My prayers hae been answered', and the balance of that passage, were delivered in a very shallow sweet voice – hooking the minister perfectly with *his* own bait.

Death in a Nut, SA/1985/221/A4–B1.

'Well, that wis aul Sandy Reid's version o Death an I think it wis a bloody guid one!' exclaimed Duncan at the finish of this narration on the first night of the New Year 1986. (The actual date of recording is not coincident with the tape registration number.) Before telling the story Duncan paid tribute to his informant:

An this one particular version [of 'Death in a Nut'] that I really like was told to me a long time ago by an auld uncle of mine who was married to my mother's sister, aul Sandy Reid, he's dead now, God rest his soul, and I think this wis one of his favourite stories because he wis really good at it. An I'll try my best to tell hit tae ye as close to the natural way he told it to me as possible.

(85/221)

Duncan heard many different versions of this didactic 'Jack tale' 'in the years when I used to travel among the travelling folk an was very interestit in telling stories an collectin stories roond the campfires; it is a very well-known story among the travelling folk' (*ibid*).

During an earlier recording session, with Barbara McDermit in 1979, Duncan narrated another version of 'Death in a Nut'. Its differences from this latest recording were not as much in plot details as in the portrayal of Jack; he was more argumentative and capable of stronger altercation in the earlier version: he argues with his mother about going to find Death to set him free, and his mother only convinces him by saying, 'Death is a friend, not an enemy; he didn't fight with you – *you* fought with *him*'; Jack decides before searching for the nut that 'Death has got to make me a bargain'; the search was not difficult or very long and when the nut is found, Death cries, 'Let me oot, let me oot!' but Jack says, 'No until Death promises not to touch my aul mother' and at the finish Jack's mother makes him promise, 'I swear that I'll never again, will A ever pit Daith back in the nut!' (1979/140). Duncan explained then, 'That wis the story my auld Uncle Duncan tellt me . . . This is the way he tellt hit to me.' ('Uncle Duncan' was also the teller of 'The Happy Man's Shirt' above.)

One reason for the more agreeable, more docile Jack featuring in the later 1986 narration was the younger audience for whom the story was told. It was narrated especially for Duncan's youngest son, aged six, and his less mature understanding of Death may certainly have prompted his father to play up the scene when Jack and his mother were trying to cook eggs, kill the cockerel and make soup. Readers may find the narrative long-winded here.

The Henwife an Aul Father Time, SA/1985/195/B1.

This 'wis one o my special stories because hit wis a story with a purpose, a meaning', said Duncan introducing the narration in the eleventh hour of the Old Year (twelfth December). I had requested the story, intending to use it in the Penguin collection because it tells of the most important event in the year to all Scotland's folk; Hogmanay festivities continue for several days as families celebrate by getting together visiting, forgetting old scores, drinking and eating, singing, playing pipes and fiddles and discussing cracks and stories. The symbol of an old life turning young again is deeply significant to the travellers, for 'everyone looks forward to the New Year comin in – it is a new beginning', says Duncan. And everyone in the country is fervid in the sun's repossession of the North.

Just how traditional this story of Father Time is among the travellers Duncan doesn't know, but he did learn it aurally:

That wis told tae me a long time ago by an auld man called Johnny Stewart. He wis a widower and he lost his wife when he wis very young, an he walkit roond Scotland. Johnny was one of the Highland Stewarts from Inverness; where he hed got hit I don't know.

(85/195)

This recording is one of Duncan's first narrations of the story, he can't recall ever telling it to a traveller. The opening scene, before the henwife saw the auld man standing by the door of her cottage, was oblique – with three images of the henwife as driftwood-gatherer, remote seaside dweller and egg-seller intermingled. I have taken the liberty of ordering the narrator's thoughts for a more coherent text, dispensing with some of the repetitions and inconsistencies.

The Coming of the Unicorn, SA/1985/195/B2.

Duncan chose this story for inclusion as a *barrie mooskin*, and it was narrated in the same session following the recording of 'The Henwife . . .' above. Neither is told with any frequency or regularity by Duncan, although he said the story of the Unicorn was 'well-known among the travelling people in my time when I used tae walk among my people, because everyone loved hit', and he heard it more often than 'The Henwife'. But there is an improvisatory air about the narration, as with the Hogmanay story told just before it, evident in the lack of plot development; rather, a main character is developed who learns something to make him or her happier or wiser, and their activities are limited to a very specific operation – designed to illustrate one particular theme or lesson. There is no doubt, however, that the 'monographic' type of story was as much appreciated in traditional storytelling circles as the longer (usually) more complex hero tales:

That's where the unicorn really began, because it was a made-up animal. There were no two species of the unicorn, it wis only one, an hit was made to please a king, tae make a king come back to his ownself again. Oh, I heard that a long time ago; hit was told roond the campfire as usual, same as the rest, an we were so interestit, ken what A mean. That was one o aul Hector's stories, aul Hector Kelby in Aberdeenshire, he wis a great storyteller and he told me many tales.

(85/195)

Compared to some other narrations in this collection, 'The Coming of the Unicorn' was a most exciting performance for the teller – Duncan was shouting as the king was chasing the unicorn – the thrill of the hunt taking him over. The narrator is himself an experienced hunter of game.

Friday and Saturday, SA/1985/179/B3–180/A1.

'It's a popular story among the traivellers; A've heard dozens o different folk tellin that story,' explained Duncan after his first narration of the twins' encounter with witchcraft (1976/86/A1). On another occasion Duncan summarized the version told him by auld Johnny MacDonald of Perthshire, in which twin boys were born after the mother became fertile eating crow's eggs, and the boys had two pet crows they'd tamed instead of hawks. A very interesting version, attributed to the narrator's father, was told by Duncan to his daughter and granddaughters in 1976: the first half was very much different from the 1985 narration, for a miller's wife gave birth to twins without any magic at all; as young men, Friday and Saturday fought for the king and became 'the greatest knights in the country' and the king presented them with his two best horses; when the lads returned home they acquired two dogs and two hawks which they trained so very well that the 'fame of Friday and Saturday an their horse, their hound an their hawk spread through the whole country'; four years later the king sent a message to them that his twin daughters had been 'a-missin for a month'; Friday set off to honour the king's request to help find them, but he first confessed to the king his love for the oldest; from the witch's 'crooked hoose', the 'farder the witch shoved de [hair] rope through the keyhole, the thicker it wis gettin'; the hair 'wad haud the bigges boat in the biggest storm the wund ever blew'; Friday's horse, hound and hawk were turned into toadstools; Saturday pledged his love for the king's other daughter, 'but I'm only a miller's son', he said; the witch was forced with 'her two hands twistit at er back' to turn the white chuckie-stanes back into the travellers she had waylaid; the witch was tied 'in her hoose wi some o her ain hair and burnt tae the grund, cat and aa' (76/85–86).

The adult travellers' version of 'Friday and Saturday' has the witch pulling a hair from her pubis. But the 1985 recording from Duncan, when his audience was two non-traveller adults, reverts to the less private source for the hair, the way traveller children always hear it. Introducing this narration Duncan said:

Now this story takes me back many many years to my childhood, hit was told tae me by an aul cousin o my father's. [Since then] I've heard it told many times around the campfires of the travelling people, but I cuid always go back to this one particular way hit wis told tae me by my father's cousin Willie Williamson in Argyllshire when I wis about ten year old.

(85/179)

'Friday and Saturday' is not one of Duncan's favourite stories, partly because of the negative connotations of 'witch' – 'Witches were *tabu* to the traivellin people'; their idea of a 'witch' is someone miserable and 'very evil', according to Duncan (re. Williamson 1983:19). Travellers prefer to tell stories in which the henwife, a generous 'bird-woman' who has supernatural powers and the gift of second sight, plays a significant role, e.g., in 'The Twelve White Swans' and 'The Ugly Queen' below.

Readers will note a heavier English element in this narration by comparison with the predominant Scots in others, cf. the three narrations from 1982 for traveller friend Willie McPhee ('The Boy and the Blacksmith', 'Jack and the Horse's Skin' and 'Jack and the Moneylender') and the two from 1976 for Duncan's young granddaughters ('Jack and the Water fae the World's End' and 'Jack an the

Singin Leaves') in this collection. There is a strong correlation between the narrator's use of English, preference for English, and the
presence of non-traveller non-Scots listeners. Duncan's main concern
in storytelling is that the narrative 'gets through to people'; he knows
that foreigners cannot have a proper understanding of traveller dialect,
thus there is no justification in a 'traveller-telling' to them. An approxi-
mate grasp of words and phrases by their context is simply not good
enough for taking in the living tale.

The Sheep of Thorns, SA/1986/1/A2–B1.

This West Highland devil story was 'mair told among the croftin
community than the travellers', surmises Duncan, although he claims
it's an 'auld auld story' among his travelling family. It was a favourite
of Sandy Williamson's, Duncan's oldest brother, and 'he said his grandfather aul Willie Williamson of Tarbert tellt it tae him when he ran
awa wi Betsy first' (eloped in 1933).

This narration for our children and me early in the New Year was
the first Duncan ever told the 'evil story' (86/1); but he heard it at least
a dozen times before he married in 1949, on the average of once a year
from his oldest brother. Stories appeal to tellers for different reasons –
some complex and perhaps subliminal. 'The Sheep of Thorns' was
described by Duncan as 'fantastic' in 1986 partly because of the extraordinary meaning it held for the man who planted it so firmly on his
younger brother's memory: 'Sandy liked the man who followed *the sheep*,
he would have loved the experience o chasin *the sheep of thorns*,' affirmed
Duncan. Entering the Other World was a powerful, overwhelming
theme to some members of the Williamson family . . . A correlation
may be seen in the suicides of two of its gifted storytellers.

The Tailor and the Skeleton, SA/1986/1/A1.

Of all the *mooskins* current among travelling folk, few can compare with
this ghost story in breadth of popularity. There is no doubt in the
minds of tellers and listeners that the story is true, and one can easily
collect in disparate regions of Scotland testimonies as adamant as
Duncan's about the origin of the broken gravestone:*

* See Alec Stewart's narration, 'The Cripple in the Churchyard', (MacColl and
Seeger 1986:69).

But I seen the stane; I'll take ye tae hit some day an show hit tae ye in 'Woe be tae Ye', the graveyard up Loch Aweside jist above Ford. The're lots o travellers tell that story i Argyllshire . . . Oh, of course, it's widespread in Aberdeenshire and aa, they're supposed tae have a place in Aberdeenshire where hit happened an the're supposed to be a place in Inverness-shire where hit happened, an supposed to be a place in Perthshire where it happened. But they canna get the proof, they hevna got the proof . . . My brother Jock tuik me up to the graveyard – ind through the gate an there's a wee corner, an auld tumbled doon dyke an a wee shed fir haudin spicks an spades . . . but they dinna bury naebody in hit any more, it's only a ruins o a shed. An there is the stone, a great big pillar o granite, halfed through an the *mark o five fingers on the stane*. An hit's broken frae the top. An that's the truth an I saw hit.

(86/1)

Given the strength of the travellers' beliefs in ghosts and the devil as manifested in their many 'evil spirit' stories (Duncan knows at least thirty); and given the religious premise in this story and 'The Sheep of Thorns', 'You cannae believe in God without believing in Evil'; there exists the concept of God as *divine goodness* among the travellers. Religious import, the moral value of stories, is the primary justification for transmitting them, according to Duncan (re. 'The Importance of Storytelling to the Traveller Children' in Williamson 1983:17–20). And before narrating 'The Tailor and the Skeleton' for the first time to his youngest child of six, on this third evening of 1986, Duncan said sternly, 'Sit doon and listen to the story – if you dinna listen to the story, how are you gaunnae be able tae tell hit to your son when *you* grow up?' (86/1).

Unlike televised story-presenting or broadcasts of ghost stories, the traditional traveller narrator lowers the volume of his voice for the climax of the story. As 'the grund cracks' and the skeleton emerges bit by bit, Duncan speaks in hushed tones with no *crescendo*. Only his heartbeat and pulse increase aurally, the breathing becomes louder – the listener can hear the narrator's inhaling and exhaling as the full-sized skeleton 'liftit hits hand an opened hits fingers' and spoke to the tailor. There was not a loud word spoken in the narration until near the end when the younger brother said, '*Thank God*'.

The Noddies, SA/1985/221/B3–4.

These two short burker stories were narrated on the first night of the New Year 1986 at my request for the Folklore Library. (The registration number is not in accord with the actual date of recording.) But Duncan instructed me after the second story, 'You cannae write and tell the country folk burker stories – it's impossible – because burkers' stories is travellers' stories.' In his opinion, non-travellers cannot appreciate the import of 'these kind o things' – without first-hand knowledge of body-snatchers. 'It wis jist short cracks tellt . . . the traivellers discussed wi each other when they got together like, and what happened in their ain experiences, what really happened to them wi burkers' (85/221).

According to Duncan, the point of this specialized lore was its deterrent to traveller children: to keep them from wandering away on their own and being too noisy at night (re. *Tocher* 1980: 144). And consequently, the majority of fireside stories travellers told about the body-snatchers are 'experiences o bein nearly burkit', e.g. 'The Boy and the Boots' (Williamson 1983:137–146).

Although Duncan has catalogued ten burker story summaries, only three have been fully narrated. He very rarely tells these stories, just on special request, because he feels strongly about the exclusivity of their meaning. Some common motifs in the summaries are farm and grave-yard scenes – where the burkers regularly find living specimens asleep in outbuildings or fresh corpses in newly-dug graves; would-be victims clinging to the back step of the noddies' coach – where burkers would never think to look for them; and specific camping places where burkers have made (or nearly made) catches – *tabu* to the travellers now – e.g. 'Murder us All', a forgotten inn on the banks of Loch Lomond, a stopping-over place for all types of travellers on the road, and where the landlord was a murderer and body-snatcher.

Boy an the Knight, SA/1985/193/A1.

Having been born on Loch Fyne and having spent the first fifteen years of life surviving in the forests, burns and mountains of Argyllshire, the narrator imparts to West Coast stories a magic all their own: in these narrations Land and Sea are havens for entities of a Highland Spirit (re. Duncan's collection *The Broonie, Silkies and Fairies*, 1985). And it is perhaps chiefly the insular feature of life in the Western Highlands, as in the Islands, behind her folk's clannish regard for lore:

Because the people of Argyll are very primitive people an they love tae keep their stories and all their things within their own country; and if you hear something, 'it always supposed to happen in Argyll' because – these people came from the West Coast of Scotland.

(85/193)

So when Duncan tells us there is a whole corpus of stories connected with 'the fine side of Loch Awe' (the easier-travelled east side) we are not surprised . . . 'Woe be tae Ye' graveyard, the location of the broken stane with the mark of the skeleton's five fingers from its strike at the crippled tailor (see note on 'The Tailor and the Skeleton' above), is very near 'Woe be tae Ye' castle (Ardchonnel Castle in the middle of the loch); somewhere between the camp halfway up the loch and Ford, a traveller mother Mrs Brown née McPhee was 'burkit' after hawking the houses (selling at doors) one day a hundred years ago; by one of the five camps along the twenty-four-mile stretch of road is the well cursed by the traveller who couldn't get clear water – and later found a witch's hair in his porridge; on a wee hill farm nearby is where the jealous shepherd murdered his wife and died fatefully himself when he tripped one foggy night after taking a bone from his dog's mouth and the 'bane went into his throat' – the shank bone of his dead wife's broken leg . . . What all the stories have in common is a 'dreich' content, says Duncan, likened to the doleful timbre of a piper's lament.

The low-key note of the 'Boy an the Knight' is most evident in the scene when the boy finds the knight. Duncan's tone of voice is very casual, as though the boy had not come across anything unnatural in the castle ruins. When the knight starts to rise, Duncan's voice is quiet but animated – with no rise in pitch or increase in volume. When the knight commands the boy he speaks quietly but intensely. The boy's reactions were very very faintly spoken, whispered when he 'cuidna go back doon'. As the knight 'fell back', the narrator, sitting on the edge of his chair, did as well – 'like that'.

Jack and the Water fae the World's End, SA/1976/210/A2–211/A1.

Of the sixty 'Jack tales' Duncan has narrated or summarized, this one has the strongest political overtones, manifested in puir Jack's sociality with a king, a queen, a nobleman and a giant landowner. The major theme of the narrative is Jack's humane responsibility, an unselfish desire to help friends, shirking their offers of rewards, when he might well have ignored their wants and returned from his travels sooner for his mother's sake. In the most recently recorded performance of the story, 1985/181/A2–B1, Jack had only thirty-one days to save his mother from death, and he was very much 'in a hurry' when he agreed to take along his four travel companions who would each 'work their way' and be his equal on the road.

One of the secondary themes, not given equal treatment in diachronic performances of the story, is the family bond. The sister of Jack's mother, a henwife in most narrations, had a major role at the start and finish of the 1976 narration; but in a later recording, 1981/5/A1–B1, she was absent when Jack returned. At the end of the 1985 telling, the mother's first thought when she heard Jack say he'd been away to the World's End, was that he should have 'brought back her auld sister'; to which Jack replied, 'Some day I'll take ye tae see her' (85/181). The family bond was a significant factor in the source of the curse on Jack's mother (not explained in 1976) related as family history in 'stories' told by Jack's mother herself as well as by the aunties: in the 1981 narration Jack's mother was a triplet and 'some day wad follow her sister', who went into a 'trance' as a young woman after receiving 'The Gift' of healing and knowledge from a 'wee man' on top of a hillock; in the 1985 narration the curse originated in the older sister, when she inherited 'supernatural powers' from her mother, Jack's grannie. Family bond was also important to the four unhappy souls who required the 'magic water that cures all ails' (81/5), for their needs were made known to Jack with references to their mothers and fathers or siblings, who had rejected or alienated them.

Slight variations in the ritual for obtaining the water and for putting its magic to work were evident in different narrations of the story. In 1981 Duncan made no mention of torches or candles, and when the 'dreep fell aff his finger gaun tae his auntie's tongue', it was because of the 'fricht Jack got when the cock startit tae whistle and the hen startit tae crow' (*ibid*). In 1985 no mention of a light in the tunnel was made, but Jack's auntie did light a candle at the start of Jack's task, putting the drops of water on each person in turn. Instructing the wee king before going into the tunnel the witch had said,

There are three steps to the well, but ye must gae down facewards to the steps, but ye must gang back backwards – but if ye ever turn yir face before ye come up the three steps – ye'll never return.

(85/181)

Jack put the drop of water on the head of each person rather than on their tongues in 1985, and there was no stipulation then about the persons *saying* what they wanted before receiving the water. In this narration 'the bloody cock startit tae whistle and the hen startit tae crow, the candle went oot an the drop fell aff Jack's finger', ending his auntie's chance of ever getting away from the World's End (*ibid*).

Dialogues and explanatory interjections in the latter narrations of 'Jack and the Water fae the World's End' are fuller and take up more of the narrative by comparison with the 1976 recording, the first of many performances given by Duncan over the past eleven years. In 1981 he had been telling the story to foreign students from France and Africa and he was intent on getting the best picture of Jack across to them as possible – the hero was exquisitely drawn at length in the scene with the wee king:

Jack was a beautiful man, he wis about six-foot-four high, an he had the beautifules curly hair an the bluest eyes ye ever saw. He wis the most hand-somes beautiful man ye ever saw – he wis always like that in traveller tales – he stude out among . . . *anywhere*, wherever ye saw Jack, ye couldna mistake him. Everybody wis fascinated by Jack – he luikit like that – 'Man, you are a specimen o manhood,' said the wee king.

(81/5)

But his typical laziness was uppermost at the end of the story when Jack's mother replied, after she'd been told of her cure, 'Aye, that'll be the day you'll gang fir water – ye'll hardly go an get me a drink frae the well!' (*ibid*). Listeners in 1985 were also foreigners and on that occasion Jack's journey was lacking in wonder, minus encounters with minor characters and without the dynamic adventures Jack had in 1976 meeting his four mates.

'Jack and the Water fae the World's End' was popular among the travelling folk from the 1930s to the 1950s, when Duncan heard it from several storytellers including his uncle Sandy Reid and auld Johnny MacDonald – 'but there were only two inta hit bi him, jist the wee king and the hunchback' (76/211). Duncan's first recorded narration was chosen as the best for inclusion here because of its language: he had been telling the story to his most natural audience of young family members inside the gelly camp at the fireside, and his everyday mode of speech was thoroughly in evidence. And because this 'Jack tale' has such a splendid array of characters and activities, a narration in the indigenous language is most suitable for our aims to communicate a good traditional story.

The Twelve White Swans, SA/1985/182/A1.

'I like that story very much, it was one o my favourites,' said Duncan after first recording this narrative eleven years ago (1976/112/A1). On that occasion he attributed the two-part story to aul Johnny Mac-Donald, the crippled traveller who was a professional storyteller or 'the storymannie', as he was called in Aberdeenshire. Johnny told Duncan the two halves of 'Twelve White Swans' in two nights. The story also had a break mid-way when Duncan narrated it in 1985, marked by the break in the story, though the intermission was only a few minutes. Some travellers, however, ended the story with the youngest brother having no hope of ever being normal; this was how Duncan's uncle Duncan Townsley told it. And there were other oral versions of the story: not every traveller who told it included the part about the harpies, and some elaborated the scene between the son and the Queen of Knowledge – he asked her many trivial questions before the all-important one about the cure – 'to put her off guard because she knew everything' (*ibid*).

Duncan has only recorded this fine international tale twice, and the more recent one was chosen because its prominent English is easy to comprehend. The narration is representative of the way Duncan tells traditional stories today, particularly with the more expansive scenes beginning and ending his long tales. Ternary design was not as strong a feature of early recordings, re. 'Jack and the Water fae the World's End' above. Comparable to that narration, the 1976 recording of 'The Twelve White Swans' was full of intrigue: e.g., with the henwife fore-seeing the birth of the queen's daughter two months ahead of time, and the two planning then, secretly, how to keep the sons from being banished; the prince falling in love with the goose girl, not knowing who she really is or that her story about the young man with a swan's-wing arm was true. The magic was vividly created in 1976: with the sister's cruel task requiring she pull the stingy nettles, beat them into threads and weave them into twelve shirts over a period of twelve nights, and every night beginning with the third she is visited by harpies – 'burd-like wummen that comes inta the graveyard huntin fir human beins newly buried and tearin up the flesh, and they'll offer her parts of the flesh – tryin their best tae keep her from gettin on with her wurk; she began on the first o the month, the first night o the full moon, and she must do it by herself'; on the last night she ran out of nettles and couldn't finish the twelfth shirt (76/112).

The cast of characters in the earlier narration was also fuller: one of the seven couriers staggered in to tell the king his companions 'were probably killed' and 'the're not one person in the whole kingdom knows where your sons is'; a 'lady in the forest', known by the prince, took care of the goose girl while he found the answer to her problem. Finally, the structure of the early narration (like others from this period) was noticeably cyclical, with the closing state of affairs returning to that of the story opening: the newly married heroine went away with her husband to stay with his mother, and her father 'the king was delighted to get his sons back' (*ibid*).

The Ugly Queen, SA/1979/146/B2–147/A.

Before recording this narration from Duncan in his gelly camp near Lochgilphead, folklore researcher Barbara McDermitt had been discussing the import of stories and storytelling with him:

And my aul grannie came to live with hus whan she wis very old an she had a grip over hus, because if she wanted something done we would do it fir her; but she had to pay for hit – no bi money, money didna mean nothin tae hus – she had tae tell hus a story. Sayin, 'C'mon, Grannie, tell hus a wee story an we'll go fir anything for ye,' go fir tobacco, get her a drink or sort her shoes . . . An aul Grannie would tell hus a story. If she hed never told me a story, A wouldna be sittin here wi you today – nearly forty-five year later – tellin you the same thing that wis told to me forty-five year ago, would A, at this present moment? So I hope in the future that *you* will be able, will tell your daughter a story that prob'ly *she* will tell *her* daughter, mebbe fifty or sixty year later.

(79/146)

Compared to other narratives and other narrations of this story, Duncan's performance in 1979 was serious to the point of being melodramatic. The narrator was keen to get the main theme across, the lesson, how the widowed queen attained truth and beauty in overcoming fraud and deception.

As far as Duncan can remember, Grannie MacDonald, who 'had a grip over him', did not tell 'The Ugly Queen'. But her immemorial storytelling infused the young travellers who listened with a sense of spiritual solidarity they might never forget. It was not so much the particular ideas and themes of 'the story' that moved Duncan, but its power to dispel barriers of death and time:

That was the travellers' idea, tae get children together and tell the story. They werena [just] tellin the story tae children . . . by telling a story tae hus they were bringin back their own parents, bringin back their own childhood and makin theirselves young again – and visualizin their own self a' their own campfire with their own daddy an their own mammy listenin tae a story that wis told tae them a long time ago – this is what the stories are all about. And this is the story he told to me.

(1985/180/B4)

Here Duncan was introducing 'The Ugly Queen' in his most recent narration of the story, paying tribute to his father's cousin Willie Williamson of Argyllshire.

On this occasion in 1985, when Duncan had been narrating the story especially for Ben Haggarty from London, the queen was more knowledgeable and more in command than in earlier narrations: she was 'good friends' with the henwife, who was godmother to her daughter, and she asked the henwife for 'something to make her the ugliest person in the world'; the queen already knew about the giant's heart in the egg, for word had 'leaked out', and she went in search of the 'man of truth' with soldiers and two coaches, then took Jack herself to the shore across from the giant's island; her will was so grand that 'Jack became king and ruled the land fir evermore' at the end of the tale (*ibid*).

'The Giant's Heart in the Egg' is the story's alternative title among the travellers, and it applies when the fiendish giant proves a most formidable opponent; for example, when the story was first recorded from Duncan in 1976. That narration featured a queen in need of instruction from henwives at numerous points in the story; she was vulnerable from the start – with her twin lassies kidnapped by the giant and her husband being killed while defending them. The henwife, who came and told her how to get rid of the indestructible giant, returned to her at the castle in the last part of the story, after Jack had succeeded in bringing her the swan's egg – she would deal with the giant herself – advised by the henwife. Yet another henwife, Jack's auntie, had assisted her in finding the 'man of truth' she sought; and at the finish the queen proposes, realizing her feelings for Jack; then, "'I'll marry ye," says Jack, and he's still there yet!' (1976/68–69).

A Thorn in the King's Foot, SA/1985/182/B2–183/A1.

After the early and only other narration of this story from Duncan, in 1976, he testified to having heard it 'fae ma father when A wis about five or six year auld' (1976/203/B1). He says he also heard it from his mother's brother Duncan Townsley, but apart from the West Coast travellers and after he'd left Argyllshire at the age of fifteen, he never heard it. Knowledge of the disease 'King's Evil' was widespread among the travelling people, but this particular narrative was not, according to Duncan's experience.

By comparison with Duncan's narrations today and typical of his stories when they were first recorded, the 1976 performance of 'A Thorn in the King's Foot' entailed more magic and more romance. The order of events starting the tale was reversed, with the wicked king stepping on a thorn – put in his path by a woodland fairy – before his son was born. His son was not a hunchback, but the king disowned him anyway, because he was ugly. When the lad returned to cure his father's foot, he set the king three well-defined tasks which had to be completed before the thorn was completely removed: the first task was to renounce the throne in front of everyone in the district; the second was to spend three nights alone with the auld wumman in the hut who had the leprosy-like disease, and 'every night at twelve o'clock ye'll come and touch er face'; the third task was to spend one week among the poor folk in his kingdom – and a barley farmer and peat cutter for whom he worked couldn't afford to give him any pay. At the end the son stays with his father and real mother (who hadn't died) and becomes king, while the old king 'potters aboot helping the villagers' (*ibid*).

Unlike the performance in 1976, the 1985 'Thorn' was told with two breaks in the narration: the second part of the story began when the hunchback learned from his foster mother who he really was; the third 'bit' began when the king set off to work with the poor. These parts were separated by intervals of a few minutes, a form of storytelling not related to splitting the longer tales over a period of two or more nights. The reason for telling a narrative with long intermission(s) is because the audience or narrator cannot continue the session, having to leave and take up other activities. But breaking a narrative into sections within one session is done for effect, as a means of building suspense. This practice is largely dependent on the quality of attention shown the teller by his listeners – the narrator will trust that interest in his story is high enough to withstand a momentary pause.

It wis whan all the children went to sleep and all the people who were fed up listenin tae this tales went away to bed, an some people who loved stories, mebbe two and three would sit round the fireside, they'd put on mair fire, make more tea and carry on with the story. And they all had to stop for a cup o tea or a crack and a smoke, an then carry on the next bit. Noo that's the wey it wis taught to me, that's the wey hit went on.

(85/183)

Different categories of stories have been defined by Duncan, relevant to levels of complexity and demands of concentration. About 'A Thorn in the King's Foot' he said, 'It's what you call "a story for a winter's evening"; as I told ye it's no a story fir tellin i schools, hit's a story fir when ye *want* tae sit round an listen tae a story' (*ibid*). Stories with involved psychological development of a character fall into the category of 'evening tales', in contrast to those stories where the protagonist goes through a varied sequence of events. Stories with a high density of changing scenes, like 'Jack and the Moneylender' below, are ones which Duncan tells regularly in schools and in public.

Three parts of 'A Thorn in the King's Foot' were delineated by different tones of voice. The first part, featuring the king's cruelty, was told in a deep stern voice; the middle of the story, centring on the son's journey to his father, was spoken at the narrator's normal pitch level; the third part was narrated at a higher tessitura with a wider range of vocal pitches, corresponding to the king's newly found compassion for his people.

Jack an the Singin Leaves, SA/1976/62/A2–B1.

In another version summarized by Duncan, the Singing Leaves are found by a king who goes on a journey and falls asleep under the Singing Tree; he thinks the leaves would be a good present for the princess on his return. But the version recorded here completely, with a Cinderella-like Jack as the protagonist, Duncan said he 'heard fae auld Johnny MacDonald [a traveller storyteller of Perthshire] about twenty-five years ago [1950]'. The narration in 1976 was among the first ten stories Duncan ever recorded; it was told to his most natural audience in those early years of recording, to his young granddaughters and other traveller children around the campfire on a berry farm in Fife. One five-year-old became very involved in the story and inter-rupted Duncan several times to ask questions and make her own comments about Jack. One comment was made just after the cuckoo left Jack for the first time, and here in the story occurred a hiatus in events: Duncan juxtaposed the crack about going 'tomorrow' to the princess's birthday with the boys' argument that Jack would never see his cuckoo again – dialogues separated by half a year in the story-time.

Upon hearing the transcription read aloud Duncan felt strongly that non-travellers should appreciate the context of this narration: 'The old travellers were illiterate and told stories in their ain wey; the language was understandable to them, and in "Jack an the Singin Leaves" this is the way it was done in bygone times.' This primitive style of story-telling, which Duncan says 'sounds better when told to travellers', I have altered very little for publication. It includes a free use of different verb tenses within single thoughts, and a pronounced 'spartan' grammar – ellipses of verbs, subjects in main clauses and prepositions – these have been inserted in the text as the abridged 'e, i, a', etc. Exact verbal repetitions of complete thoughts were threefold; these I have usually modified by omitting one or replacing the second utterance with the third. Musical word 'painting' occurred for 'cuck-oo', a descending M3 in *falsetto*. 'Loveliest' in the phrase, 'the loveliest music', was consistently articulated as three equally stressed syllables, preceded and followed by ascending and descending leaps of half an octave, more and less.

Jack and the Moneylender, SA/1981/97/B3– 1982/129/A1.

Told in May 1982 to the narrator's traveller friend Willie McPhee, who praised it as a 'very guid story', this 'Jack tale' was not widely known among the travelling people, at least from the 1940s to the 1970s when Duncan was nomadic. Like 'A Thorn in the King's Foot', it was apparently exclusive to the oral tradition of the West Coast travellers. In the main it is a story for children:

This wee story has been in wir family fir many's a long day an it wis a great favourite when everybody got together. Because the reason it wis a great favourite wis they had what you call 'a wee bit fun' in the tale fir the weans. Noo Jack tales wis their favourite . . .

(82/129)

Duncan tells it now more often than any other story he knows to children in Scotland's primary schools.

The most humorous narration of 'The Moneylender' on tape, when he told it to a group of non-traveller children near Christmas in 1978, featured a very carefree Jack, full of spirit: his wages, the bags of gold, 'is a burden tae me, A can't walk fast enough', said Jack to the auld man who then gave him the magic fiddle and gun; at the scaffold when Jack played, the moneylender was overcome with dancing, 'I' the nude the moneylender was an his tongue wis out that length – "sto-sto-stop yir fiddlin!"' (1978/128/B1). But the narrative can also be a serious ethical portrait of the travellers' hero, as in the latest recording when Jack was drawn in his most patriarchal setting: Jack lived with his father who was a miller and widower; at fifteen Jack's father died and he became caretaker of the mill for the rich merchant who owned it; at twenty Jack set off on his travels, and before leaving the merchant told him, 'Everything I own is yours'; the very old man with the 'kind o quaint, very very tired voice', who gave Jack the fiddle and gun, lived in a 'little cottage in the side of a hill, ivy-covered and cobwebs in the windows'; and when Jack left him 'he luikit back – the cottage wis gone – not one single thing 's in the hillside'; the moneylender who had broken up many families emerged in such a sorry state from the bush – 'crying for mercy' with his 'feet full o thorns' – he swore vengeance on Jack; at the end evil was utterly defeated when the narrator (Jack) diddled eight phrases of 'The Maid behind the Bar' *vivace*, because 'when Jack got them dancin he meant that they were gaun tae dance . . . till everyone was completely exhaustit – down!' (85/179). Everlasting life was not impossible for Jack from then on with his fiddle and gun!

In the narration for Willie McPhee, our 1981 text, Duncan omitted the old man's explanation of the fiddle's magic. And Duncan backtracked when Jack mistakenly encountered the moneylender before meeting the auld man in the forest. Magic was not the primary theme to the narrator on this occasion, but rather Jack's exemplary Christian heart – as he was told at the end, 'God bless ye, young man, God speed ye on yir journey!'

Thomas the Rhymer, SA/1986/4/A1.

The story of 'True Thomas' is not apparently well known among the travelling people. A few informants have testified to hearing the story and part of the song; but no one, apart from Duncan, has been recorded performing even part of the narrative. This version of the story in song, sung regularly by Duncan for audiences of travellers and non-travellers, took him about twelve months (from the summer of 1976) to formulate. The tune and twenty verses of the song in its early structural stages were printed in *Tocher* 1977:175–7. Although virtually complete, the ballad was not formally set in 1977 by comparison with later variants which stabilized, word-for-word, as in the 1986 performance: in 1977 verse four preceded verses two and three; the length of the Elfin Queen's command to 'come along' required an extra verse; the River of Tears was encountered before the River of Blood; and the Queen did not tell Thomas when they finally arrived in Elfin Land, 'It's here that you maun stay'. Duncan says, 'I heard the story and the song from an auld uncle o mine a long time ago when I wis stayin with him, and we had travelled intae Huntly wi a wee handcart tae camp in Huntly Green'; now Duncan never sings 'Thomas the Rhymer' without paying tribute to his mother's cousin Sandy Townsley, 'The way he told it to me is the way that I know it' (1986/4/A2).

In keeping with the aim of this collection, to represent a vivid aural sense of the narration – without interrupting the flow of the story visually in print – 'Thomas the Rhymer' is shown with its music transcribed fully above the words of the story. The rhythm of the music follows that of the poetry, with beams joined up within phrases according to the divisions of the iambic feet. The '2' in the time signature indicates basically two 'beats' per 'measure'; measures are delimited by semi-bar lines, allowing for the singer's fluidity of metre. Duncan's beats are often unequal, with the first one short and the second long, increasing the 'lilt' as the musical metre moves congruously with the verbal rhythm. In each strophe (terminated by the double bars), the internal phrases in the upper octave are sung *rubato*, the third phrase carrying the most dynamic idea of each verse.

Tam Lin, SA/1986/4/A3–B1.

Of the twenty-two ballads Duncan sings regularly, this narrative commands the most attention from every type of listener. Under the title 'Lady Margaret' it has always been very popular among the Scots travelling folk: 'Them that didna ken it aa, kent bits o it,' said Duncan. Lady Margaret's act, meeting the forces of the Other World hand to hand, took great courage – what the travellers 'respect' most in story and song – according to Duncan.

Until 1982 the verses of the song were not completely or properly formulated, certain lines and motifs were missing from the narrator's aural recall or experience; but in October, when his mother's cousin Rabbie Townsley came for an extended visit, Duncan learned verses eight, nine and ten, enabling him to sing the entire story. All earlier recordings were more or less fragmentary and improvised, although the story was virtually intact (see the collation of two performances in *Tocher* 1980:156–9). Most of the ballad was committed to memory in Duncan's childhood when he heard his paternal grandmother Bett MacColl sing it.

The exceptionally fluid melody in the first half of the song is not due to the singer's inability to settle on a fixed quadriphrasal strophe. Duncan, like many of the older traveller singers, knows several melodic *ideas*, composed of interrelated motives and phrases which may be realized in a number of different combinations. There is a very close melodic correspondence of phrases one, three and four (after verse eight) with the standard strophe of 'Thomas the Rhymer' above, as well as with other ballads and songs in Duncan's repertoire. Rhythmically, however, there is little to compare with 'Thomas the Rhymer', for the metre of 'Tam Lin' is strictly duple with well-defined beats, the dotted figures suggesting dance rhythms. The contrasting metrical movements of the two ballads stem from their different roles as testaments to the Other World: 'True Thomas' mirrors spiritual or religious instruction; 'Lady Margaret' relates physical or bodily communion.

A most expressive and most typical (of travellers' ballad singing) irregularity occurs in the penultimate verse eighteen, an extended strophe in the scene carrying the dénouement, when the Fairy Queen reveals that her power over William has indeed been vanquished. (On the significance of irregular strophes in traveller balladry see Williamson, L.J. 1985:156–99). Another salient feature of 'Tam Lin' is its optional refrain: in this performance it occurs consistently from verse nine, but not when William refers to his probable procreation. Refrain omission is not accidental, but is partly dependent upon the narrator's slackened rapport with his listener(s) (re. *ibid*: 184–9).

La Mer la Moocht, SA/1985/193/B2.

This is the only story Duncan 'ever heard about a merman', although he knows dozens of 'stories aboot water-men, kelpies an silkies, an stories about mermaids an sea witches' (85/193). Duncan was born and reared up on the side of a sea-loch, and it is not suprising to find his strongest feelings, the most sentient part of his spirit, expressed in narratives about sea-folk:

Ye see, the funny thing was that mermaids were s'posed to be beautiful, but the *men was more beautiful*. You see how they sung – that took the sailors away by their beauty – so this was the sirens, the mermaids. But this, to have come in contact with the most beautiful bein in the world, was a merman, La Mer la Moocht.
(*ibid*).

Bella MacDonald, Duncan's former mother-in-law from Fife, told him the story; but he also heard it in Aberdeenshire from Hector Kelby, who thought it originally came from Greece, re. 1976/269/A1.

The 1976 narration differed considerably from the most recent recording, our 1985 text. The earlier recorded version took place in

Greece; the 'merman boy' was 'about fourteen or fifteen' when he was caught, and twenty-five years old when the princess first saw him; he had a tail covering his legs which the fisherman pulled off and hid; the fisherman was named Karl Ramucht and he called the merman 'Marine Ramucht', his brother; Marine went back to the sea when Karl's wife found his tail; Marine soon after returned to the beach, hid his tail and tried to trick Karl to 'come and spend some time wi him'; the princess fell totally under his beautiful power and joined him as a mermaid at the end (*ibid*).

The greatest difference between the two recorded narrations in 1976 and 1985, however, was in the mode of speech. The earlier performance was told in the narrator's ordinary speaking voice, but the later performance was very close to song. The opening, how La Mer first impressed the fisherman, simulated a lullaby, narrated in subdued tones with a lilting effect – like waves lapping a shore. Describing La Mer when the fisherman had decided to take him home, the narrator adopted a 'glassy' vocal timbre, 'He jist stood there as if was jist carved of stone.' When La Mer finally spoke, it was a monotone, entrancing. The centre of the story was more animated, corresponding to La Mer's effect on the old man's fishing; the narrator's pitch range increased rapidly during the fabulous catch, and when the princess saw 'the most wonderful bein she ever saw ind her life', the narrator's tempo quickened. Towards the end of the story the tone became languid again, when the fisherman replied to the princess, 'So do we all,' admitting the universal love for La Mer. Agonizing over the threat posed by the princess, the old man and woman decided to put La Mer back: the narration reached a climax when the fisherman's poignant exhortation, '*I'm in love with him too*' was equated with the wife's, 'We don't want to hurt him'. La Mer responded softly, intently, in a high-pitched voice, 'Come back with me to the sea.' This was the heart of the unsung song which Duncan has recited,

> *La Mer la Moocht, let go yir grip,*
> *Ye're far too strong for me.*
>
> *Come with me, said La Mer la Moocht,*
> *And I'll take you to the bottom of the sea,*
> *Where everything is wonderful*
> *And everything is free.*
>
> *Let go yir grip, La Mer la Moocht,*
> *Ye're far too strong for me.*

(85/193/B2)

REFERENCES CITED

CON. SCOTS DICT.
>   1985 *The Concise Scots Dictionary*, ed. Mairi Robinson. Aberdeen: Aberdeen University Press.

GRANT, W. AND DIXON, J.
>   1921 *Manual of Modern Scots*. Cambridge: Cambridge University Press.

SA/1976/62 TO 1986/4
>   Original recordings in the main chronological series of tapes lodged in the Sound-recording Archives of the School of Scottish Studies, University of Edinburgh. (Citations of the archive registration numbers are often abbreviated with 'SA/19' omitted.)

THE SCOTTISH ARTS COUNCIL
>   1984 'The Traditional Arts of Scotland: Report of the Traditional and Folk Arts of Scotland Working Party'. Edinburgh.

TOCHER
>   1977–80 *Tocher: Tales, Songs, Tradition, Selected from the Archives of the School of Scottish Studies*; No. 27 (pp. 175–7), No. 33 (pp. 141–87). Edinburgh.

WILLIAMSON, D.
>   1983 *Fireside Tales of the Traveller Children*. Edinburgh: Canongate.
>   1985 *The Broonie, Silkies and Fairies*. Edinburgh: Canongate.

WILLIAMSON, L. J.
>   1985 'Narrative Singing among the Scots Travellers: A Study of Strophic Variation in Ballad Performance', unpublished PhD dissertation, University of Edinburgh.

GLOSSARY

A	I	*bild*	built
a'	at	*bing*	come; go; large number, lots (cant)
aa	all		
ae	one	*bithoot*	without
aer	there	*blether*	talk nonsensically, loquaciously
ainsel	himself		
airms	arms	*boil*	commotion
alow	below	*boilan*	boiling
amint	am I not	*brig*	bridge
an	and; than; although, if, when	*broo*	brow
		buff	unhatched egg
argiean	arguing	*burker; burkit*	body-snatcher; kidnapped and murdered for medical research
as, as of	so, as regards		
aside	beside		
at	that		
aul, auldes(t)	old, oldest	*burn*	stream
awfa(e)	awful, large amount of, much, terrible	*but*	and, if, besides, also; only
ay	yes		
aye	indeed	*cairriet*	carried
		camp	camping place; tent
		can	pot
baet	bet	*canny*	carefully
bankin	corrie, hillside hollow	*carry-on*	fuss
bannock	oatmeal cake	*chuckie-stane*	white pebble
bannt	banned	*claes*	clothes
bare than busy	all one can manage	*clap*	affectionate pat
barrie	good	*click*	fasten, seize
became	came	*clift*	cleft, cliff
becepts	except	*collop*	piece of meat
begint	began	*cotter*	cottager, tenant farmworker
ben	to the back of		
bene	fine (cant)	*country folk*	non-travellers
beraggled	ragged	*county*	country
bi	by	*cowp*	tip, dump (v)

GLOSSARY

crack	news, gossip (v); discussion	*fearin*	entire
cratur, wee	dear one, darling	*feart*	afraid
crickety	rickety and creaking	*fit*	satisfied; foot, feet
cripple	crippled	*fleece*	rob
croft	smallholding (Highland)	*flooer*	flour
crone	old body, friend	*follae, follaein*	follow, following
cry	call, name	*forbyes*	also, as well as
cuid, cuidna	could, couldn't	*foremost*	forward
		forrit	forward
d'	do	*fra(e)*	from
dae	do	*frichen*	frighten
danderin	sauntering	*fuil*	fool
de	the		
dee, dee'd	die, died	*gaen*	gone
deek	look, see	*gain*	by the time that
deid	dead	*gan*	going
dher wur	there were	*gang*	go
di'	did	*gaun, gaunna(e)*	going, going to
diddled	sang a dance tune with nonsense syllables	*ged*	dearest friend (male) (cant)
didna	didn't	*gelly camp*	enlarged traditional bow tent with inside fire in a home-made stove
dis	does		
div	did have		
dooduch	kettle pot (cant)	*gev*	give
dook	duck (v)	*gied*	gave
doot	doubt; fear, expect	*gien, gi'n*	gave
dotent	feeble-minded	*gie'n*	giving
down an out wummen	prostitutes	*go another bite*	taken another bite
draggling	straggling	*gran bene mort*	high-class woman
dreep	drop	*greet*	cry, weep
dreich	doleful	*grippit*	gripped
drop	small amount of	*gruf*	horse (cant)
du	do	*guid; guid thocht o*	good; well thought of
dune	did, done		
		haet, devil a	have (it) not even the smallest amount
'e	the	*hairm*	harm
een	eyes	*hale*	whole
efter	after	*hap*	cover (v)
eichty	eighty	*harlin*	trailing (cf. harl)
elton	thorn	*haud*	hold
empy	empty	*hed, hedna*	had, hadn't
er	her	*heid; heid yins*	head; head ones, top people
ett	ate		
event	indeed	*hes*	has, have
ey	always	*hese*	his
		hevna	haven't
faa	fall	*hing*	hang
fae	from	*hit*	it, her, him
fairm	farm	*Hogmanay*	New Year's Eve
fasselt	was busy	*hokin*	digging, unearthing

hold	held	mon	money
hoo	how	mooskin	story (cant)
hoose	house	mooth	mouth
hose	long stockings made of cotton, sewed up the front and up the back	mort	woman (cant)
		moss	bog
		muir	moor
hurl	ride; wheel (v)		
hus	us		
		naebody	anybody
		narkin	nagging
i	in	narra	narrow
im	him	neep	turnip
ind	in	noddies	burkers, body-snatchers (cant)
Ir	Yir (Your)		
ither	other	noo	now
		not	no
jist	just		
		o	of
		o'	on
keek	peep	of'	off
ken; kent	know, understand; knew	ond	on
killt	killed	on'y	only
kinnel	kindle	oot	out
kin o	kind of	outrageous	outraged
knewn	known	outwith	outside the boundaries of
knowe	knoll		
		ower	over; every
landit up	arrived at	oxter	arm; underarm, bosom
lane	lend		
langside	alongside	pad	footpath, track or way
lastten	last	pairt	part
lea	leave	park	enclosure, field
learn	teach	peats	peat blocks, used as fuel
leit sittin	left as it was	piece	bread (slice of)
len	lend	pit	put
loodnie	prostitute (cant)	ploo	plough
lowse	loosen	plook	pimple
luikit	looked	pou'd	pulled
lunch	snack	press	cupboard
		puckle	small amount
mair	more		
maist	most	quota	delivery
makit	made		
manse	minister's house		
marriet	married	raa	row (n)
maun; maun be	must; an unavoidable necessity	raisin hammer	raising hammer, for making dents in tin
mavis	thrush, songbird	rake	search
messages	groceries	rape	rope
middle the	middle of the	rash	rush (n)
mind	remember	reek	smoke

GLOSSARY

richt	right
roar	call, shout
rummle	shake vigorously
's	is; was
sae	as
scart't	scratched
screekin	screaming
set sail	set off, start a journey
shot	a brief loan, a turn
shui'	should
sin	since
snap	snatch, seize quickly
so	as
soukin	sucking
spick	pick
spirls	strings
sput	spat
square	farmyard
stack	haystack
stane, stanit	stone, stoned
steyed	lived
stottert	stumbled
strachlit	walked with difficulty
straggly	stragglingly
stude	stood
sut	sat
sway, swey	movable iron bar over the fire
t'	to
tackery	ragged
tae; tae me, tae ye	to, for; for me, for you
tae intend	by law
take	catch
taste	small amount of
tatters	rags
tatties	potatoes
teem	pour
tha'	that
thae	those
the'	there (cf. they)
the day	today
theirsels	themselves
the morn, morrow	tomorrow
the night	tonight
the're	there is, there are
they	there
this	these
thocht	thought
thon	those, that

thread	yarn
threuw	threw
ti	till
tightener	filling supper
tile hat	top hat
to	by, at
traivellt	travelled
trembly	shivering
tuik	took
two-three	a few
van man	grocer with a horse-drawn van
wad, wadna	would, wouldn't
wag-at-the-wa clock	old-fashioned pendulum clock
waiskit	waistcoat
walkan	walking
wanner	wander
wap	wrap (v)
waste	empty
wat	wet
waurse	worse
wean	child
weepan	weeping
weighs	pair of scales
well-on	intoxicated
welt	smack; slap (v)
whand	when
whaur	where
wheesht	be quiet!
whe're	where is, where are
whippit	whipped off
who	that, which
wi	with
windae	window
wir	our
withert	worn out, ragged
wonst	once
wrang	wrong
wuid	wood
wumman	woman
wur	were
wurkit	worked
yese	you
yin	one
yirsel	yourself
youse	you